Textbook written according to revised syllabus of S.Y.B.Com.
prescribed by University of Pune from 2014-2015.
Also useful for other Universities in Maharashtra.

I0632044

ELEMENTS OF COMPANY LAW

Prin. Dr. Kishor Jagtap

Prof. Suresh Bhirud

Diamond Publications

Elements of Company Law

Prin. Dr. Kishor Jagtap
Prof. Suresh Bhirud

First Edition : June 2014

ISBN : 978-81-8483-571-7

© Diamond Publications

Type Setting :
Diamond Publications

Cover Page :
Sham Bhalekar

Published by :
Diamond Publications
264/3 Shaniwar Peth, 302 Anugrah Apartment
Near Omkareshwar Temple, Pune - 411 030
☎ 020-24452387, 24466642

info@diamondbookspune.com
www.diamondbookspune.com

Sale Distributor :
Diamond Book Depot
661 Narayan Peth
Appa Balwant Chowk
Pune 411 030
Tel. - 24480677, 66020282

PREFACE

It is a matter of great pleasure for us to present this book to our esteemed readers and students. This book has been designed as standard text on 'Elements of Company Law' for Second Year B. Com.

This book comprehensively covers the entire syllabus of S. Y. B. Com. course of University of Pune w. e. f. June-2014. It has been written to meet the requirement of students. The special features of the book are :

- Full coverage of the revised syllabus.
- Chapter outline at the beginning of each chapter to give a bird's eye view of the topics covered in the chapter.
- Point wise explanation of each topic in the chapter.
- Topics are logically arranged in numbered paragraphs exactly according to the modified syllabus.
- Proposed questions at the end of each chapter.
- Extensive use of diagrams, tables and various forms to give visual view of key concepts and techniques.
- Conversional, lucid and simple language.

Every effort has been made to provide the readers with most up-to-date and authentic material on the subject.

We are also very grateful to our Publisher Mr. Dattatray Pashte of Diamond Publication, Pune who have rendered all possible assistance in bringing out this book. We wish to acknowledge our deep gratitude to staff who have assisted and helped us in preparing this book.

We will consider our efforts amply rewarded in case the book proves useful to the students and Faculty Members of the subject.

Suggestions of readers are welcome and shall be acknowledged with gratitude.

With best wishes.

Prin. Dr. Kishor N. Jagtap
Prof. Suresh Bhirud

CONTENTS

Term - I

1. Introduction to the New Act and Concept of Companies   1

2. Formation and Incorporation of a Company   37

3. Documents Relating to Incorporation and Raising of Capital   45

4. Capital of the Company   78

5. Forfeiture, Surrender and Transfer of Shares   110

Term - II

6. E-Governance and E-Filing   134

7. Management of Company   143

8. Key Managerial Personnel (KMP)   184

9. Company Meetings   201

10. Compromises, Arrangements, Reconstructions, Amalgamations and Winding Up of Company   266

References   308

<table>
<tr><td>

Chapter
1

</td><td>

INTRODUCTION TO THE NEW ACT AND CONCEPT OF COMPANIES

</td></tr>
</table>

CONTENTS

1.1 Background overview & Salient Features of the Act 2013
  1.1.1 Background
  1.1.2 Overview
  1.1.3 Salient Features

1.2 Definitions and Characteristics of a Company
  1.2.1 Introduction
  1.2.2 Meaning and Definition
  1.2.3 Characteristics of a Company
  1.2.4 Lifting the Corporate Veil
  1.2.5 Difference between a company and partnership

1.3 Kinds of Companies
  1.3.1 On the basis of incorporation
  1.3.2 On the basis of Liability
  1.3.3 On the basis of number of members
  1.3.4 On the basis of Control
  1.3.5 Other kinds of Companies
       i) Government Company
       ii) Foreign Company
       iii) Producer Company

1.4 Private and Public Company
  1.4.1 Distinction between private and public company
  1.4.2 Special Privileges and Exemptions available to private companies
  1.4.3 Conversion of a private company into a Public Company
  1.4.4 Conversion of Public Company into Private Comany

1.1 BACKGROUND, OVERVIEW AND SALIENT FEATURES OF COMPANY ACT-2013

1.1.1 Background

The 1956 Act has been in need of a substantial revamp for quite some time now, to make it more contemporary and relevant to corporates, regulators and other stakeholders in India.

While several unsuccessful attempts have been made in the past to revise the existing 1956 Act, there have been quite a few changes in the administrative portion of the 1956 Act. The most recent attempt to revise the 1956 Act was the Companies Bill, 2009 which was introduced in the Lok Sabha, one of the two Houses of Parliament of India, on 3 August 2009. This Companies Bill, 2009 was referred to the Parliamentary Standing Committee on Finance, which submitted its report on 31 August 2010 and was withdrawn after the introduction of the Companies Bill, .2011. The Companies Bill, 2011 was also considered by the Parliamentary Standing Committee on Finance which submitted its report on 26 June 2012. Subsequently, the Bill was considered and approved by the Lok Sabha on 18 December 2012 as the Companies Bill, 2012 (the Bill). The Bill was then considered and approved by the Rajya Sabha too on 8 August 2013. It received the President's assent on 29 August 2013 and has now become the Companies Act, 2013.

The changes in the 2013 Act have far-reaching implications that are set to significantly change the manner in which corporates operate in India. In this publication, we have encapsulated the major changes as compared to the 1956 Act and the potential implications of these changes. We have also included, where relevant, the provisions of the draft rules, which have been issued by the Ministry of Corporate Affairs (the MCA) till date for public comments. Such inclusions have been highlighted with an asterix at the end of the sentence. However, please note that these are only draft rules and will undergo changes before being notified.

1.1.2 Overview

The 2013 Act has introduced several new concepts and has also tried to streamline many of the requirements by introducing new definitions. This chapter covers some of these new concepts and definitions in brief.

1. Companies

1.1 One-person company: The 2013 Act introduces a new type of entity to the existing list i.e. apart from forming a public or private limited company, the 2013 Act enables the formation of a new entity a 'one-person company' (OPC). An OPC means a company with only one person as its member [sec. 3(1) of 2013 Act].

1.2. Private company: The 2013 Act introduces a change in the definition for a private company, inter-alia, the new requirement increases the limit of the number of members from 50 to 200. [sec. 2(68) of 2013 Act].

1.3. Small company: A small company has been defined as a company, other than a public company.

(i) Paid-up share capital of which does not exceed 50 lakh INR or such higher amount as may be prescribed which shall not be more than five crore INR

(ii) Turnover of which as per its last profit-and-loss account does not exceed two crore INR or such higher amount as may be prescribed which shall not be more than 20 crore INR:

As set out in the 2013 Act, this section will not be applicable to the following:

- A holding company or a subsidiary company
- A company registered under section 8
- A company or body corporate governed by any special Act [sec. 2(85) of 2013 Act]

1.4. Dormant company: The 2013 Act states that a company can be classified as dormant when it is formed and registered under this 2013 Act for a future project or to hold an asset or intellectual property and has no significant accounting transaction. Such a company or an inactive one may apply to the ROC in such manner as may be prescribed for obtaining the status of a dormant company. [sec. 455 of 2013 Act]

2. Roles and responsibilities

2.1 Officer: The definition of officer has been extended to include promoters and key managerial personnel [sec. 2(59) of 2013 Act].

2.2 Key managerial personnel: The term 'key managerial personnel' has been defined in the 2013 Act and has been used in several sections, thus expanding the scope of persons covered by such sections [sec. 2(51) of 2013 Act].

2.3. Promoter: The term 'promoter' has been defined in the following ways:· A person who has been named as such in a prospectus or is identified by the company in the annual return referred to in Sec. 92 of 2013 Act that deals with annual return; or

- Who has control over the affairs of the company, directly or indirectly whether as a shareholder, director or otherwise; or
- In accordance with whose advice, directions or instructions the Board of Directors of the company is accustomed to act.

The proviso to this section states that sub-section (c) would not apply to a person who is acting merely in a professional capacity. [sec. 2(69) of 2013 Act]

2.4: Independent Director: The term' Independent Director' has now been defined in the 2013 Act, along with several new requirements relating to their appointment, role and responsibilities. Further some of these requirements are not in line with the corresponding requirements under the equity listing agreement [sec. 2(47), 149(5) of 2013 Act].

3. Investments

3.1 Subsidiary: The definition of subsidiary as included in the 2013 Act states that certain class or classes of holding company (as may be prescribed) shall not have layers of subsidiaries beyond such numbers as may be prescribed. With such a restrictive section, it appears that a holding company will no longer be able to hold subsidiaries beyond a specified number [sec. 2(87) of 2013 Act].

4. Financial statements

4.1. Financial year: It has been defined as the period ending on the 31st day of March every year, and where it has been incorporated on or after the 1st day of January of a, the period ending on the 31 st day of March of the following year, in respect whereof financial statement of the company or body corporate is made up. [sec. 2(41) of 2013 Act]. While there are certain exceptions included, this section mandates a uniform accounting year for all companies and may create significant implementation issues.

4.2. Consolidated financial statements: The 2013 Act now mandates consolidated financial statements (CFS) for any company having a subsidiary or an associate or a joint venture, to prepare and present consolidated financial statements in addition to standalone financial statements.

4.3. Conflicting definitions: There are several definitions in the 2013 Act divergent from those used in the notified accounting standards, such as a joint venture or an associate" etc., which may lead to hardships in compliance.

5. Audit and auditors

5.1 Mandatory auditor rotation and joint auditors: The 2013 Act now mandates the rotation of auditors after the specified time period. The 2013 Act also includes an enabling provision for joint audits.

5.2 Non-audit services: The 2013 Act now states that any services to be rendered by the auditor should be approved by the board of directors or the audit committee. Additionally, the auditor is also restricted from providing certain specific services.

5.3. Auditing standards: The Standards on Auditing have been accorded legal sanctity in the 2013 Act and would be subject to notification by the NFRA. Auditors are now mandatorily bound by the 2013 Act to ensure compliance with Standards on Auditing.

5.4 Cognisance to Indian Accounting Standards (Ind AS): The 2013 Act, in several sections, has given cognisance to the Indian Accounting Standards, which are standards converged with International Financial Reporting Standards, in view of their becoming applicable in future. For example, the definition of a financial statement includes a 'statement of changes in equity', which would be required under Ind AS. [Sec. 2(40) of 2013 Act]

5.5. Secretarial audit for bigger companies: In respect of listed companies and other class of companies as may be prescribed, the 2013 Act provides for a mandatory requirement to have secretarial audit. The draft rules make it applicable to every public company with paid-up share capital > Rs. 100 crores. As specified in the 2013 Act, such companies would be required to annex a secretarial audit report given by a Company Secretary in practice with its Board's report. [Sec. 204 of 2013 Act]

5.6. Secretarial Standards: The 2013 Act requires every company to observe secretarial standards specified by the Institute of Company Secretaries of India with respect to general and board meetings [Sec. 118 (10) of 2013 Act], which were hitherto not given cognizance under the 1956 Act.

5.7. Internal Audit: The importance of internal audit has been well acknowledged in Companies (Auditor Report) Order, 2003 (the 'Order'), pursuant to which auditor of a company is required to comment on the fact that the internal audit system of the company is commensurate with the nature and size of the company's operations. However, the Order did not mandate that an internal audit should be conducted by the internal auditor of the company. The Order acknowledged that an internal audit can be conducted by an individual who is not in appointment by the company.

The 2013 Act now moves a step forward and mandates the appointment of an internal auditor who shall either be a chartered accountant or a cost accountant, or such other professional as may be decided by the Board to conduct internal audit of the functions and activities of the company.

The class or classes of companies which shall be required to mandatorily appoint an internal auditor as per the draft rules are as follows:

- Every listed company
- Every public company having paid-up share capital of more than 10 crore INR
- Every other public company which has any outstanding loans or borrowings from banks or public financial institutions more than 25 crore INR or which has accepted deposits of more than 25 crore INR at any point of time during the last financial year

5.8. Audit of items of cost: The central government may, by order, in respect of such class of companies engaged in the production of such goods or providing such services as may be prescribed, direct that particulars relating to the utilisation of material or labour or to other items of cost as may be prescribed shall also be included in the books of account kept by that class of companies. By virtue of this section of the 2013 Act, the cost audit would be mandated for certain companies. [sec. 148 of 2013 Act]. It is pertinent to note that similar requirements have recently been notified by the central government.

6. Regulators

6.1. ational Company Law Tribunal (Tribunal or NCLT): In accordance with the Supreme Court's (SC) judgement, on 11 May 2010, on the composition and constitution of the Tribunal, modifications relating to qualification and experience, etc. of the members of the Tribunal has been made. Appeals from the Tribunal shall lie with the NCLT. Chapter XXVII of the 2013 Act consisting of sec. 407 to 434 deals with NCLT and appellate Tribunal.

6.2. **ational Financial Reporting Authority (NFRA):** The 2013 Act requires the constitution of NFRA, which has been bestowed with significant powers not only in issuing the authoritative pronouncements, but also in regulating the audit profession.

6.3. **Serious Fraud Investigation Office (SFIO):** The 2013 Act has bestowed legal status to SFIO. Companies Act, 2013 9

7. Mergers and acquisitions

The 2013 Act has streamlined as well as introduced concepts such as reverse mergers (merger of foreign companies with Indian companies) and squeeze-out provisions, which are significant. The 2013 Act has also introduced the requirement for valuations in several cases, including mergers and acquisitions, by registered valuers .

8. Corporate social responsibility

The 2013 Act makes an effort to introduce the culture of corporate social responsibility (CSR) in Indian corporates by requiring companies to formulate a corporate social responsibility policy and at least incur a given minimum expenditure on social activities.

9. Class action suits

The 2013 Act introduces a new concept of class action suits which can be initiated by shareholders against the company and auditors.

10. Prohibition of association or partnership of persons exceeding certain number

The 2013 Act puts a restriction on the number of partners that can be admitted to a partnership at 100. To be specific, the 2013 Act states that no association or partnership consisting of more than the given number of persons as may be prescribed shall be formed for the purpose of carrying on any business that has for its object the acquisition of gain by the association or partnership or by the individual members thereof, unless it is registered as a company under this 1956 Act or is formed under any other law for the time being in force: As an exception, the aforesaid restriction would not apply to the following:

A Hindu undivided family carrying on any business

An association or partnership, if it is formed by professionals who are governed by. special acts like the Chartered Accountants Act, etc.[sec. 464 of2013 Act]

11. Power to remove difficulties

The central government will have the power to exempt or modify provisions of the 2013 Act for a class or classes of companies in public interest. Relevant notification shall be required to be laid in draft form in Parliament for a period of30 days. The 2013 Act further states no such order shall be made after the expiry of a period of five years from the date of commencement of sec. 1 of the 2013 Act [sec. 470 of2013 Act].

12. Insider trading and prohibition on forward dealings

The 2013 Act for the first time defines 'insider trading and price-sensitive information and prohibits any person including the director or key managerial person from entering into insider trading [sec. 195 of 2013 Act]. Further, the Act also prohibits directors and key managerial personnel from forward dealings in the company or its holding, subsidiary or associate company [sec. 194 of2013 Act].

The new Companies Act (hereinafter referred as CA2013) is replacing old Companies Act, 1956 (hereinafter referred as CAI956). The CA2013 makes comprehensive provisions to govern all listed and unlisted companies in the country. The CA2013 is partially made effective w.e.f. 12th September, 2013, by way of implementing 98 Sections and repealing the relevant sections corresponded with CA1956. Some of the Salient features of the CA2013 are as under:

1.1.3 Salient Features

1. **Democracy of Shareholders:** The CA2013 has introduced new concept of class action suits with a view of making shareholders and other stakeholders, more informed and knowledgeable about their rights.

2. **Supremacy of Shareholders:** The CA2013 focused and provide major aspect on approvals from shareholders on various significant transactions. The Government has rightly reduced the need for the companies to seek approvals to managerial remuneration and the shareholders have been vested with the power to sanction the limit.

3. **Strengthening Women Contributions through Board Room:** The CA2013 stipulates appointment of at least one woman Director on the Board of the prescribed class of Companies so as to widen the talent pool enabling big Corporates to benefit from diversified backgrounds with different viewpoints.

4. **Corporate Social Responsibility:** The CA2013 stipulates certain class of Companies to spend a certain amount of money every year on activities/initiatives reflecting Corporate Social Responsibility. There may be difficulties in implementing in the initial years but this measure would help in improving the Under-privileged & backward sections of Society and the Corporate would in fact gain in terms of their reputation and image in the Society.

5. **National Company Law Tribunal:** The CA2013 introduced National Company Law Tribunal and the National Company Law Appellate Tribunal to replace the Company Law Board and Board for Industrial and Financial Reconstruction. They would relieve the Courts of their burden while simultaneously providing specialized justice.

6. **Fast Track Mergers:** The CA2013 proposes a fast track and simplified procedure for mergers and amalgamations of certain class of companies such as holding and subsidiary, and small companies after obtaining approval of the Indian government.

7. **Cross Border Mergers:** The CA2013 permits cross border mergers, both ways; a foreign company merging with an India Company and vice versa but with prior permission of RBI.

8. **Prohibition on forward dealings and insider trading:** The CA2013 prohibits directors and key managerial personnel from purchasing call and put options of shares ofthe company, its holding company and its subsidiary and associate companies as if such person is reasonably expected to have access to price-sensitive information (being information which, if published, is likely to affect the price of the company's securities). Earlier these provisions were contained in regulations framed by SEBI, as the capital market regulator. Now, it has also been informed that SEBI is expected to discuss changes in certain norms for listed firms so as to make them in line with the rules in the new Act.

9. **Increase in number of Shareholders:** The CA 2013 increased the number of maximum shareholders in a private company from 50 to 200.

10. **Limit on Maximum Partners:** The maximum number of persons/partners in any association/partnership may be upto such number as may be prescribed but not exceeding one hundred. This restriction will not apply to an association or partnership, constituted by professionals like lawyer, chartered accountants, company secretaries, etc. who are governed by their special laws. Under the CA 1956, there was a limit of maximum 20 persons/partners and there was no exemption granted to the professionals.

11. **One Person Company:** The CA2013 provides new form of private company, i.e., one person company is introduced that may have only one director and one shareholder. The CA 1956 requires minimum two shareholders and two directors in case of a private company.

12. **Entrenchment in Articles of Association:** The CA2013 provides for entrenchment of articles of association have been introduced.

13. **Electronic Mode:** The CA2013 proposed E-Governance for various company processes like maintenance and inspection of documents in electronic form, option of keeping of books of accounts in electronic form, financial statements to be placed on company's web site, etc.

14. **Restriction on Composition:** Every company shall have at least one director who has stayed in India for a total period of not less than 182 (one hundred and eighty two) days in the previous calendar year.

15. **Independent Directors:** The CA2013 provides that all listed companies should have at least one-third of the Board as independent directors. Such other class or classes of public companies as may be prescribed by the Central Government shall also be required to appoint independent directors. No independent director shall hold office for more than two consecutive terms of five years.

16. **Serving Notice of Board Meeting:** The CA2013 requires at least seven days' notice to call a board meeting. The notice may be sent by electronic means to every director at his address registered with the company. The CA1956 did not prescribe any notice period to call the board meeting of a company.

17. **Duties of Director defined:** Under the CA 1956, a director had fiduciary duties towards a company. However, the CA2013 has NOW defined the duties of a director.

18. **Liability on Directors and Officers:** The CA2013 does not restrict an Indian company from indemnifying its directors and officers like the CA1956.

19. **Rotation of Auditors:** The CA2013 provides for rotation of auditors and audit firms in case of publicly traded companies.

20. **Auditors performing Non-Audit Services:** The CA2013 prohibits Auditors from performing non-audit services to the company where they are auditor to ensure independence and accountability of auditor.

21. **Financial Year:** Every company's financial year will be the period ending on 31 March every year

22. **Rehabilitation and Liquidation Process:** The entire rehabilitation and liquidation process of the companies in financial crisis has been made time bound under CA2013.

1.2 DEFINITIONS AND CHARACTERISTICS OF A COMPANY

1.2.1 Introduction

Rapid growth of business and industrialisation brought about significant changes in business and industrial organisations. Proprietory firms found it difficult to face the challenges of rapidly expanding business activities. Partnership organisations have observed that they had to face the limitations of limited capacities of partners.

In order to control the companies in public interest, Indian Government had to enact the first company legislation in India, on the pattern of English law in 1850 as Joint Stock Companies Act. This Act was revised several times to suit the changing conditions of business and industry. After independence in August 1947, an exhaustive legislation was passed under the title companies Act 1956 to achieve socio economic objectives of Independent India.

1.2.2 Meaning and Definition

The term company means an association of persons, formed for some common object. When such an organisation is registered under the Companies Act, it becomes a legal or artificial person with perpetual succession and a common seal.

According to Sec. 2(20) of the Companies Act 2013, a company means "A company formed and registered under this Act or an existing company." An existing company means a company formed and registered under any of the previous Companies Laws.

The definition given in the Companies Act is not exhaustive and it does not reveal the true characteristics of a company.

According to Lord Justice Lindley a British company is, "An association of many persons who contribute money or money's worth to a common stock and employed it in some trade or business and who share the profit or loss arising there from. The common stock so contributed is denoted in money and is capital of the company. The persons who contribute it or to whom it belongs are members. The proportion of capital to which each member is entitled to is his share. Shares are always transferable although the right to transfer them is often more or less restricted."

"A company may be defined as an incorporated association, which is an artificial person, having an independent legal entity, with a perpetual succession, a common seal, a common capital in the form of transferable shares and carrying a limited liability in relation to its members."

If an association is not incorporated under the Companies Act 2013, it cannot enjoy independent and distinct status and it does not become a body corporate. It is an "illegal association".

1.2.3 Characteristics of a Company

When a company is incorporated, it enjoys certain advantages over other associations. These advantages are termed as characteristics of a company. These features are discussed below.

1) Voluntary Association of Persons : A Joint Stock Company is basically a voluntary association of persons which aims at achieving some purpose in a legal manner.

2) Seperate Legal Entity/Corporate Personality : A Company formed and registered under the Companies Act is a distinct legal entity, separate from its shareholders or members. It is an artificial person created by law. It is invisible and intangible still it has existence. Although it is not a natural person, it enjoys certain attributes of a natural person. It has indivisibility and the power to sue and be sued in its own name. It has right to hold and dispose off its own property. It has right to enter into contracts with the third parties in its own name.

The principle that a company is a legal person seperate from its members is illustrated in a leading case of Salomon V A Salomon and Co. Ltd.

Example :

Salomon had a shoe business. He sold his business to a company named Salomon and Company Limited, and which was formed by him. There were seven members which included his wife, a daughter and four sons who took 1 share each and Salomon himself took 20,000 shares. The price paid by the company to Salomon was £ 30,000. The company gave him 20,000 fully paid shares of £1 each and £ 10,000 in debentures, instead of paying him cash. On account of strike in shoe trade, the company was closed down. The asset of the company were valued £6000 only and debts amounted to £ 10,000, due to Salomon and secured by debentures and a further £7000 due to unsecured creditors. The unsecured creditors claimed that, as Salomon and Co. Ltd. was really the same person as Salomon, he could not owe money to himself and that they should be paid their £7000 first.

It was held by the House of Lords that Salomon was entitled to £ 6000 as the compny was an independent and separate entity from Salomon. The unsecured creditors got nothing [(1897) A (22)]

Salomon's case established beyond doubt that, in law, a registered Company is an entity distinct from its members, even if one person holds all the shares of the company.

3) Perpetual Succession : A Company never dies like a human being. It is an entity with perpetual succession. Its existence is not affected by the death, lunacy or insolvency of its members. Members may come and go but the company survives and continues its operations unless it is closed down. The existence of the company is not affected by the death of all its members. In a case where all the members of a company were killed by a bomb or killed in any type of accident, the company is deemed to survive.

4) Limited Liability : Liability of a member, in case of a company, is limited to the face value of shares subscribed to by him. If the shares are fully paid up, then the liability is nil. In case of a partnership concern, the liability of each partner is unlimited but there is limited liability of members in case of a company. But the company itself being an artificial legal person is always fully liable and hence has unlimited liability.

5) Common Seal : A Company is an artificial person hence it cannot sign its name on a contract. So it uses a seal for this purpose. The common seal is used as a substitute for its signature. Every company has a seal with its name engraved on it. Any agreement between the company and the third party requires acceptance of the company in the form of an official seal.

6) Transferability of shares : The shares of a company are freely transferable and can be purchased and sold in the share market. Sec. 82 of the Companies Act recognises the right of transferability of shares and provides that, "the shares or other interest of any member shall be moveable property transferable in the manner provided for in the articles of the company."

7) Capacity to sue and be sued : On incorporation, a company acquires a separate and independent legal personality. As a legal person, it can sue and can be sued in its own name.

8) Not a Citizen : The company is a legal person having both nationality and domicile, but it is not a citizen. Hence, a company cannot claim advantages of those fundamental rights which are specifically guaranteed to citizens only, for example, the right of franchise.

9) Limited Actions : A Company has to carry out all its activities within the powers of its charter. i.e. the memorandum of association. Any other activity can only be carried out after making necessary amendments in the memorandum.

10) Separate Property : As a legal person, a company can own, enjoy and dispose off any property in its own name. No shareholder or member can claim himself to be the owner of the company's property. It is the property of a company only.

1.2.4 Lifting the Corporate Veil

The general rule is that a company is a legal person and is distinct from its members. A legal concept that seperates the personality of a corporaton from the personalities of ts shareholders, and protects them from being personally liable for the company's depts and other obligations. This protectin is not impenetrable. Where a court determines that a company's business was not conducted in accordance with the provisions of corporate legislation or it may sense that the activities are carried out for some illegal motive; it may hold the shareholders personally liable for the companies obligations under the legal concept of lifting or piercing the corporate veil. The principle is regarded as a curtain, a veil or shield between the company and its members, used to defeat public convenience, justify wrong, protect fraud or defend crime, the law will regard the company as an association of persons. These cases are exceptions to the principle in Salomon V A Salomon and Co. Ltd. Because in these exceptional cases, the law goes behind the corporate personality to the individual members or ignores the separate personality of the company in order to find out the economic reality constituted by a group of associated concerns. When this protection is taken away, the veil is said to have been lifted or pierced.

The veil is lifted in the following cases :

i) **Determination of Character :** In times of war, the court will lift the veil to see whether a company is controlled by enemy or aliens. Consequently, a company registered in England may be alien enemy if its agents or persons who infact control its affairs, are alien enemies. [Daimler Company Ltd. Vs Continental Tyre and Rubber Ltd. 1916]

ii) **Where company is Sham :** The court will lift the veil where the is a mere cloak or sham i.e. where the device of incorporation is used for some illegal or improper purpose [Jones V Lipman (1962)]

iii) **Where the company is acting as the agent of share holders :** Where the company is acting as an agent for its shareholders, they will be liable for its acts. Whether it is acting as an agent is a question of fact in each case.

iv) **Protection of revenue :** The court may disregard the corporate entity of a company where it is used for tax evasion or to circumvent tax obligation. Further, where it is desired to establish for tax purposes, the residential status or character of a company, the court will lift the veil and find out where its central management is and the place determines its residence.

v) Where a company has been formed by certain persons to avoid their own valid obligation.

vi) Where a company formed is against public interest or public policy.

vii) Where the holding company holds all the shares in a subsidiary company.

viii) Where a number of members falls below the statutory minimum.

ix) Where a cheque, promissory note or bills of exchange is signed by an officer of a company on behalf of company without mentioning the name of the company thereon, he is personally liable to the holder of the instrument.

x) Where holding and subsidiary companies are not treated as separate legal entities.

xi) Investigation into related companies under the same management.

xii) For investigation of ownership of the company.

xiii) Where the company is used for any fraudulant purpose.

xiv) Where breach of economic offence is involved.

xv) Where company is used as a medium to avoid welfare legislation.

xvi) To punish for contempt of court.

Statutory Exceptions

The Companies Act 2013, disregards the separate existence of the company in certain cases to check the misuse of the corporate personality by directors or members of the company. These are called as Statutory exceptions. These include the following :

i) **Number of members below statutory minimum :** If at any time the number of members of a company is reduced below two, in the case of a private company or below seven in the case of a public company and it carries the business for more than six months while the number is so reduced, every member who knows of this fact, will become liable to an unlimited extent for the payment of the whole debts of the company contracted during that time (sec. 45)

ii) Company name not mentioned on a bill of exchange etc. : Where an officer of the company or any person signs on behalf of the company, a bill of exchange, promissory note, cheque or order for money or goods, wherein the name of the company is not mentioned, he is personally liable unless the amount is paid by the company (Sec. 12)

iii) Group Accounts : The Principle of separate legal entity may be disregarded where a company has subsidiaries, and the group accounts must be laid before the company in general meeting when the company's own profit and loss account and Balance Sheet is so laid (Sec. 212).

iv) Fraudulent Trading : If in the course of the closing down of a company it appears that, any business of the company has been carried on with intent to defraud creditors, the court may declare that any person or persons who were knowingly parties to the carrying on of such business in the manner aforesaid shall be personally liable for the debts and other liabilities of the company (Sec. 339)

v) Investigation into related companies : An inspector appointed under sec. 219 by the Central Government may lift the veil of incorporation if he thinks it necessary for the purpose of investigation into the affairs of its subsidiary or holding company.

1.2.5 Difference between Partnership Firm and a Joint Stock Company

Sr. No.	Point of Distinction	Partnership Firm	Joint Stock Company
1.	Meaning	A partnership is a form of the business organisation in which two or more individuals carry on a business as co-owners for profits. It is formed by a contract among partners, to conduct a lawful business.	Joint stock Company is a voluntary association of individuals for profit having a capital divided into transferable shares.
2.	Membership	The number of members in a firm can be upto ten in banking business and twenty in other cases, but minimum two persons are required to form partnership.	Minimum seven persons are needed to form a joint stock company, but there is restriction prescribed by the companies act regarding any limit for maximum number of members. In the case of private limited company minimum two persons are needed for it's formation and maximum members can be fifty only.
3.	Registration	Registration of the partnership is not compulsory according to the Partnership Act.	A company, whether it is private or public cannot come in existence unless and until it is registered.

Introduction to the New Act and Concept of Companies : 15

4	Capital Raising Capacity	A firm can definitely raise more capital as compared to the proprietorship but it can not raise large capital like any company.	A company, especially a public company, can raise capital on huge scale as it has no upper limit for maximum number of members.
5.	Liability	The liability of the partners in firm is unlimited. It is joint and several. Their private property cannot remain safe in case of liquidation of the firm.	The liability of members of the company is limited to the face value of the shares and their private property can remain safe even in the situation of the liquidation of the company.
6.	Stability	An existence of the partnership firm depends on the life of the partners. A firm is not treated as a separate legal entity.	An existence of the company is perpetual. It remains unaffected despite death, insolvency, or lunacy of the member. A company is treated as a separate legal entity.
7.	Transferability of Interest	A partners interest in the firm is non transferable. It can be transferred only with the consent of all partners.	A share in joint stock company of any member is freely transferable as it is treated as a private property of the shareholder.

		Partnership Firm	Company
8.	Management	The activities of the firm are managed and controlled by the partners. Additional managerial services are sometimes hired by the firm by employing management consultants for special assignments.	The company follows democratic set up for its management. Members elect their representatives called 'directors' who looks after all managerial work. General body has right to take a review of the work done by the board.
9.	Statutory Control	There are no legal restrictions over the partnership. The firm need not observe legal bindings. The firm need not publish its accounts, submit reports etc.	There is strict statutory control of the companies act, state and central government over the companies. A company has to observe all legal formalities concerning accounts, audit directors etc.
10.	Dissolution	A firm need to be dissolved in the case of death, insolvency or insanity of any of the partners. It can also be dissolved at the desire of all partners.	Since company has a perpetual existence it remains unaffected even in the case of death, insanity, or insolvency of any of its members.

1.3 KINDS OF COMPANIES

According to the Companies Act 2013, the kinds of Companies are discussed below :

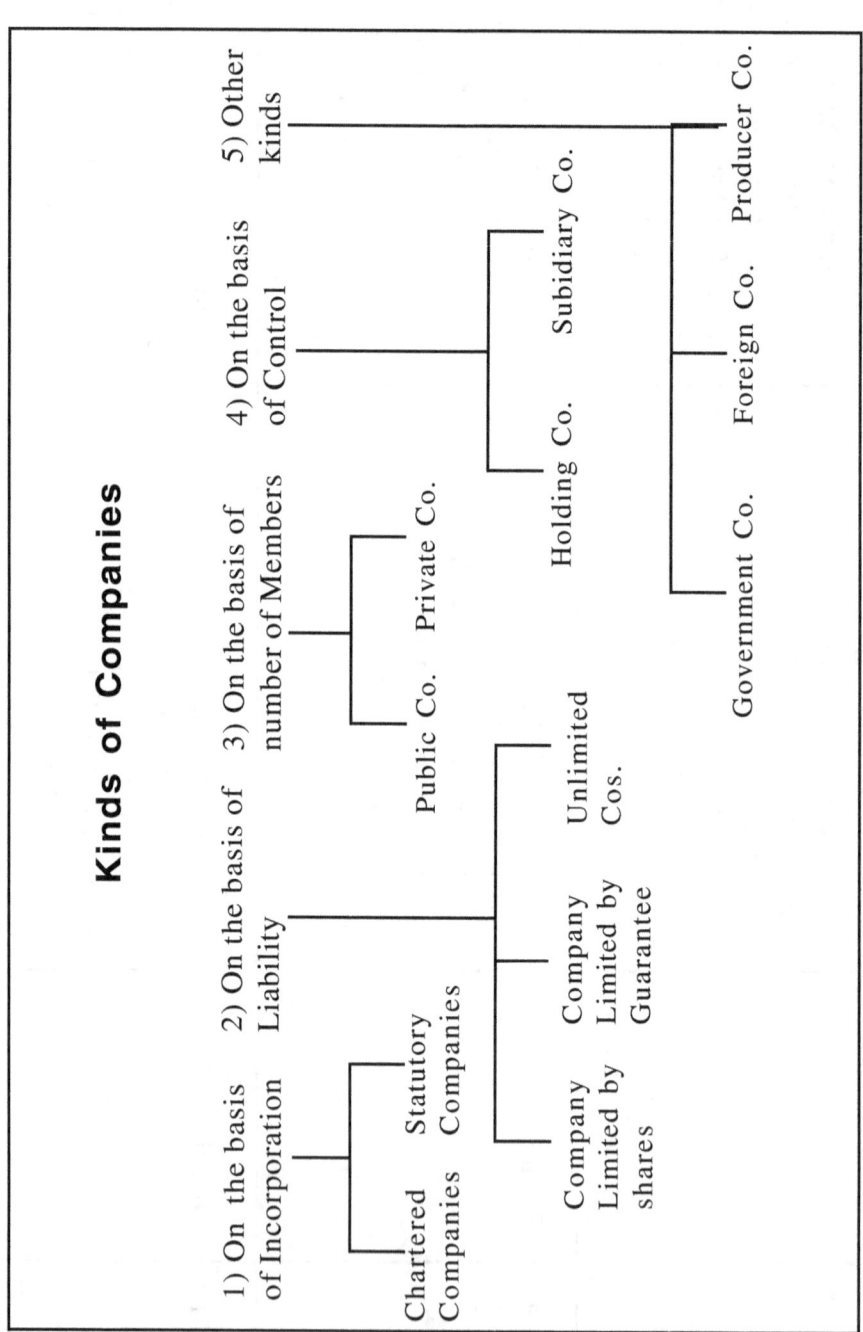

1.3.1. On the Basis of Incorporation

a) Chartered Companies :

The Crown (King), in the exercise of the royal prerogative has power to create a corporation by the grant of a charter to persons assenting to be incorporated. Such Companies or Corporations are knows as Chartered Companies. For example, Bank of England, East India Company. The powers and the nature of business of a chartered company are defined by the charter which incorporates it.

b) Statutory Companies :

A company may be incorporated by means of a Special Act of the Parliament or any State Legislature. Such companies are called Statutory Companies. They are generally formed to carry out some special public undertaking. For example, railways, water works, gas, electricity generation etc. In India there are many such companies or corporations such as Reserve Bank of India, The Life Insurance Corporation of India, Unit Trust of India, State Trading Corporation etc.

Statutory Companies are governed by the Acts creating them. They are not required to have any memorandum or articles of association. Their structure can be changed only by the amendments in the original Acts creating them. The annual reports of the working of these statutory companies are required to be placed before the Parliament or the State Legislature, as the case may be. A Statutory Company, although owned by the Government, has a separate legal entity and it cannot be regarded as a department of the Government.

The provisions of the Companies Act 2013 are applicable to the Statutory Companies except where the said provisions are inconsistent with the provisions of the Act creating them.

1.3.2 On the Basis of Liabilities

a) Registered Companies :

Companies registered under the Companies Act 2013 or the earlier Acts are called registered Companies. These companies come into existence when they are registered under the Companies Act and a Certificate of incorporation is granted to them by the Registrar. A company registered under the Act may be a) a company limited by shares, (b) a Company limited by guarantee and c) an unlimited company.

b) Companies Limited By Shares - Sec. 2(22):

Companies limited by shares are the most common type of Companies. This is a company where the liability of its members is limited by the memorandum to the amount, if any, unpaid on the Shares respectively held by them. The liabliity can be enforced during the existence of the Company as well as during the winding up. Where the Shares are fully paid up, no further liability rests on them.

c) Companies Limited by Guarantee - Sec. 2(21) :

This is a company where the liability of its members is limited to such amounts, as they may respectively undertake by the memorandum to contribute to the assets of the company in the event of its winding up. In the case of such companies the liability of its members is limited to the amount of guarantee undertaken by them.

A Company limited by guarantee may or may not have a share capital. If it has a share capital then the liability of the members is twofold, i) liability to pay the share amount ii) the amount guaranteed.

A guarantee company may not be suitable for ordinary business purposes. Clubs, trade associations, research associations and societies for promoting various objects are the examples of guarantee companies. Many such companies obtain permission of the Central Government to dispense with the word "limited".

d) Unlimited Companies :

It is a company where the liability of its members is not limited at all. In such a company, the liability of each member extends to the whole amount of the company's debts and liabilities, but he will be entitled to claim contribution from other members. The articles shall state the number of members with which the company is to be registered and if the company has a share capital, the amount of share capital with which the company is to be registered. An unlimited company may be converted into a limited company either limited by shares or limited by guarantee. Unlimited company must not incorporate 'limited' as the last word. It need not have a share capital, but it must file the articles and the memorandum.

There are two types of each of these kind of companies. A company may be either a public company or a private company.

1.3.3. On the Basis of Number of Members

a) Public Limited Companies [Sec. 2(71)]

A Public Company means a company which is not a private company. Any seven or more persons may come together to form a public company. There is no limit for maximum membership.

By Companies (Amendment) Act 2012, a public company shall mean a Company which

a) is not a private company.

b) has minimum paid up capital of Rs. five lakhs or such higher paid up capital, as may be prescribed.

c) is a private company which is a subsidiary of a company which is not a private company.

It was also stipulated that, every public company existing on 13/12/2012 with a paid up capital of less than five lakh rupees, shall within a period of two years from 13/12/2012 increase its paid up capital to Rs. Five lakhs. If it fails to do so, such a company shall be deemed to be a defunct company and its name shall be struck off from the register of the Registrar.

A Company registered under Section 8 shall not be required to have minimum paid up Capital as specified above.

Public Companies are further classified as :
   i) Companies limited by shares.
   ii) Companies limited by guarantee.
   iii) Unlimited Companies.

b) Private Limited Companies - Sec. 2(68) :

Private Company means a Company which has a minimum paid up capital of Rs. One lakh or more as may be prescribed by its articles –

   i) it restricts the right to transfer its shares, if any

   ii) limits the number of its members to 50 not including

      a) persons who are in the employment of the company and

      b) persons who, having been formally in the employment of the company, were members of the company while in that employment and have continued to be members after the employment ceased and

   iii) prohibits any invitation to the public to subscribe for any share in, or debentures of the company.

   iv) prohibits any invitation or acceptance of deposits from persons other than its members, directors or their relatives.

Every private company existing on 13/12/2012 with paid up capital of less than one lakh rupees shall within a period of two years, from 13/12/2012 enhance its paid up capital to one lakh rupees.

Where a Private company fails to enhance its paid up capital to one lakh rupees within a period of two years, such company shall be deemed to be a defunct company and its name shall be struck off from the register by the Registrar.

A Company registered under section 8 shall not be required to have minimum paid up capital as specified above.

Any two or more persons can come together to register a private limited company. The maximum membership should not exceed 50. The words "private limited" should be used at the end of the company's name. A Private Ltd. Company must have its own Articles of Association.

Private Companies are classified as :

a) Companies limited by shares.

b) Companies limited by guarantee (if it has share capital)

c) Unlimited Companies (if it has share capital)

1.3.4 On the Basis of Control

Holding Company and Subsidiary Company (Sec. 46 and Sec. 87)

A company which controls the other company is known as holding company and the company controlled by holding company is called Subsidiary Company.

For the purpose of this Act, a company shall, subject to the provisions of sub-section (3), be deemed to be a subsidiary of another if, but only if,..

a) that other controls the composition of its Board of directors; or

b) that other-

i) exercises or controls more than half of the total voting power of such company.

ii) where the first -mentioned company is any other company, holds more than half in nominal value of its equity share capital; or

c) the first mentioned company is a subsidiery of any other company which is that other's subsidiery.

Illustration : Company B is subsidiary of company A and company C is subsidiary of the company B. Then company C is, therefore, subsidiary of company A. It may be noted that, holding company and subsidiary are basically separate companies and have separate legal existence.

The Subsidiary company cannot hold shares or acquire membership or make investments in holding company and also it cannot be treated as an asset of holding company.

1.3.5. Other Kinds of Companies

a) Government companies Sec. 2 (45)

Under Sec. 2(45) of the Companies Act, a government company is defined as a company in which not less than 51% of the paid up share capital is held by the Central Government, or any State Government or more State Governments or partly by the Central Government and partly by one or more State Governments.

A subsidiary Company of a Government Company is also a Government Company.

The Act also provides certain special provisions for a Government Company as stated below.

i) The auditor of Government Company shall be appointed and re-appointed by the Central Government on the advice of the Comptroller and Auditor General (CAG) of India.

ii) The auditor will submit a copy of the audit report to the CAG of India, who may comment upon or supplement the audit report in such a manner as he thinks fit, such comments or supplementary report shall be placed before the annual general meeting along with the audit report. (Sec. 137)

iii) Where the Central Government is a member of the Government Company, it shall cause an annual report on the working and affairs of the Company to be prepared and laid before both House of Parliament, along with the audit report and the comments if any, of the CAG of India. The report shall be prepared within 3 months of the company's annual general meeting. Where the state Government is also a member, the report shall also be laid before the State Legislature.

If a Government Company is incorporated and registered outside India, such a Government company comes within the definition of an unregistered company and for the purposes of jurisdiction, the company shall be deemed to be registered in the state where its principal place of business is situated.

The Central Government empowered to declare by notification in the Official Gazette, that any of the provisions of the Act shall not apply to any Government Company or what provisions shall apply to any such Company.

The concept of Government Company is expanded alongwith state and central Governments, State Government companies and Central Government Companies or Corporations and their combinations are included under the concept of Government company.

b) Foreign companies - Sec. 2(42)

Foreign Company is a company incorporated outside India and having a place of business in India. If not less than 51% of the paid up capital of a company incorporated outside India and having established place of business in India, is held by one or more citizens of India or by one or more bodies corporate incorporated in India, such companies shall comply with such provisions of the Act as may be prescribed, with regard to the business carried on by it in India, as if it were a company incorporated in India. (Sec. 379)

The Foreign Company has to comply the following regulations.

1) Documents - Within 30 days of the establishment of the place of business in India, the foreign company shall deliver to the Registrar of the state where the principal place of business is situated and to the Registrar at New Delhi, following documents.

    i) A certified copy of the Charter, Statutes or Memorandum and Articles of the company.

    ii) The full address of the registered and principal office of the company.

    iii) A list of directors and secretary of the company.

    iv) Names and addresses of a person / persons in India, authorised to accept on behalf of the company services of process and any notices or other documents required to be served on the company.

    v) The full address of the office of the company in India which is deemed to be its principal place of business in India. (Sec. 380)

2) Alterations - If any alteration is made in the above documents, the company shall, within prescribed time, deliver to the Registrar for registration, the detailed particulars of the alterations. (Sec. 380)

3) Accounts - Every foreign company shall, in every calendar year deliver three copies of Balance Sheet and Profit and Loss Account to the Registrar and also three copies of a list, in the prescribed form, of all places of business established by the company in India. (Sec. 381)

4) Name and Country of Incorporation - Every foreign company shall exhibit on the outside of every office or place of business, its name and the country of incorporation in English and in one of the local languages. It shall also have the name of the company and country of incorporation stated in English on prospectus, business letters, bill heads and letter papers and on all notices and other official publications of the company.

5) Other Provisions - Provisions regarding registration charges, books of accounts, annual returns, inspection of books of accounts, special audit, audit of cost accounts, investigation and calling for information shall apply to a foreign company having place of business in India. (Sec. 26)

6) Prospectus of Foreign Company - The Prospectus of foreign company shall be dated and contain particulars regarding

   i) the instrument defining the constitution of the company.

   ii) name of the company.

   iii) date and country in which it is incorporated.

   iv) Address of its principal office in India

   v) provisions of law under which the company was incorporated

   vi) general matters required to be included in prospectus issued by the company incorporated in India, It must be registered before it is issued. (Sec. 389)

7) Winding up - Where a foreign company ceases to carry on business in India, it may be wound up as an unregistered company.

c) Producer companies

Companies (Amendment) Act 2002 introduced producer companies, which provides for corporate governance of members joining together to achieve specified objectives. The registration of a Produce Company helps co-operative organisations as companies and also conversion of existing co-operatives into companies on optional basis.

Producer company means a body corporate registered under the Companies Act 2013 as a Producer company having following objects.

a) Production, harvesting, procurement, grading, pooling, handling, marketing, selling, export of primary produce of the members or import of goods or services for their benefit.

b) Processing, including preserving, drying, distilling, brewing, vinting, canning and packaging of produce of its members.

c) Manufacture, sale or supply of machinery, equipment or consumables mainly to its members.

d) Providing education on the mutual assistance principles to its members and others.

e) Rendering technical services, consultancy services, training, research and development and all other activities for the promotion of the interests of its members.

f) Generation, transmission and distribution of power, revitalisation of land and water resources, their use, conservation and communications relating to primary produce.

g) Insurance of producers or their primary produce.

h) Promoting techniques of mutuality and mutual assistance.

i) Welfare measures or facility for the benefit of members, as may be decided by the Board.

j) Any other activity, ancillary or incidental to any of the above activities or other activities which may promote the principles of mutuality and mutual assistance amongst the members in any other manner.

k) Financing of procurement, marketing or other above specified activities which include extending of credit facilities or any other financial services to its members.

Every Produce company has to deal with the produce of its active members for carrying out any of the objects stated above. Active member is a member who fulfills the quantum and period of patronage of the producer company according to the articles of the company. Producer is any person engaged in any activity connected with any primary produce. A member means a person or producer institution, admitted a member of a producer company and who retains the qualification necessary for continuing as a member.

Producer Institution means a producer company or any other institution having only producers or producer companies as its members, whether corporated or not, having any of the above objects and which agrees to make use of the services of the producer companies as provided in its articles.

Patronage means the use of services offered by the producer company to its members by participation in its business activities. Patronage bonus is the payment made by a producer company out of its surplus income to the members in proportion to their patronage.

Primary Produce [Sec. 581 A (j)]

i) Produce of farmers arising from agriculture and related activities such as animal husbandry, horticulture, pissiculture, viticulture, forestry and forest produce, bee raising, re-vegetation and farming plantation products.

ii) Produce of persons engaged in handloom, handicraft and other cottage industries.

iii) any product resulting from any of the above activities, including by- products of such products.

iv) any product resulting from ancillary activity that would assist or promote any of the aforesaid activity or anything ancillary to it.

v) Any other activity which is intended to increase the production of any of the above products or improve quality thereof.

Formation of a Producer Company and its Registration

Any ten or more individuals, each of them being a producer or any two or more producer institutions or a combination of ten or more individuals and producer institutions having objects, stated above, may form an incorporated company as a Producer Company.

If the Registrar is satisfied, that all the requirements have been complied with in respect of registration and matters precedent and incidental thereto, within 30 days of the receipt of the documents required for registration, register the memorandum, the articles and other documents, if any, and issue a certificate of incorporation.

The producer company shall be a company limited by shares. On registration, the producer company shall become a body corporate, as if it is a private company, without having any limit to its membership. The producer company under any circumstances cannot become or deemed to be a public company.

Option to Inter-State Co-operative Societies to become Producer Companies.

Inter State Co-operative society means a multi- state co-operative society. It includes any co-operative society registered under law and which has after its formation extended any of its objects to more than one state, by listing the participation of persons or by extending any of its activities outside the state, directly or indirectly or through an institution of which it is a constituent.

An Inter State co-operative society, with objects not confined to one state, may make an application to the Registrar for registration as producer company. On compliance with the requirements for registration, the Registrar shall within a period of 30 days from the receipt of the application, register such a society as a producer company. Once the society is registered as producer company the words "Producer Company Limited" shall form the part of its name. After registration, the inter state co-operative society shall be transformed into a producer company. All the assets, properties, privileges, obligations and all contracts entered into and belonging to inter state co-operative society on the date of transformation, shall vest in the producer company and shall be deemed to have been incurred, engaged to be done by or entered into, for the producer company. All the fiscal and other concessions, license, benefits and exemptions granted to inter state co-operative society shall be deemed to have been granted to the producer company. All the directors of inter state co-operative society shall continue in office for a period of one year from the date of transformation. Every officer shall continue to hold his office with the same tenure and privileges.

A producer company may make an application to the High Court for re-conversion to the inter-state co-operative society.

1.4. PRIVATE AND PUBLIC COMPANIES

1.4.1 Distinction between Private and Public Companies

There was no distinction between a private and public company till The Companies Act 1913. It was only under the Companies Act 1956 that Private and Public Companies are distinguished.

Point of Difference	Private Co.	Public Co.
1) Membership	Minimum two and maximum fifty (excluding present and past employees)	Minimum seven - No limit to maximum number of members.
2) Formation	(a) Only one certificate that of incorporation is enough. No need of Trading Certificate. (b) No need of filing a prospectus or statement in lieu of prospectus. c) No need to file documents relating to Directors.	(a) Both the certificates i.e. the certificate of incorporation and the trading certificate should be obtained. (b) Prospectus or statement in lieu of prospectus must be filed before allotment of shares. c) Written consent of director to act as directors and their contracts to buy qualification shares must be filed.
3. Allotment of Shares	Share can be alloted without restriction of minimum subscription.	There are a number of legal restrictions on allotment of shares. It can allot shares to the public only after minimum subscription is collected.
4. Memorandum of Associations and Articles of Association	Only two members have to sign Memorandum and Articles.	Seven members have to sign Memorandum and Articles.
5. Monetary support from public	It is not authorised to sell shares to general public or in the open market.	It has to make proper announcement to general public to get monetary support from the public regarding issue of shares. The shares are sold through brokers, bankers or in stock exchange.

6. Transfer of Shares.	Transferability of shares is restricted by Articles. Its shares are not quoted on stock exchange. They have no open market.	Shares are freely transferable and are generally quoted on stock exchange and they have an open market.
7. Board of Directors and Managing Directors	a) There is no legal restriction regarding the number of directors. b) It must have atleast two directors. c) The directors are not subject to retirement by rotation. d) No limit on Directorship of private companies. e) No restrictions on Managing Directorship. f) No legal restrictions on remuneration of Directors. g) Directors can borrow from their company. h) A Director can occupy any office of proift. i) The interested Directors can vote in the Board Meetings.	a) The directors cannot together draw remuneration more than 11% of the net profit made by the company. b) It must have at least three directors. c) The directors are subject to retirement by rotation. d) Limit on Directorship of public companies (20). e) There are restrictions on appointment, remuneration etc. of the Managing Directors. f) There are legal restrictions on remuneration of Directors. g) No loans to Directors without Central Govt.'s Approval. h) For an office of profit by Director requires special resolution. i) The interested Directors cannot vote in the Board Meeting.
8. Statutory Meeting and Report	It need not hold a statutory meeting nor file a statutory report with Registrar.	It must hold a statutory meeting and must file the statutory report with the Registrar.
9. End Words of the Name.	A private limited company must have the words "Private Limitcd" in its name.	A Public limited company must have only the word "Limited" in its name.

10. Types of Shares	It can issue deferred shares even with disproportionate voting rights.	It can issue only equity and preference shares. (since 1956 no public company can have deferred shares.)
11. Quorum	The quorum in case of meeting of a private company is two members who must be personally present.	The quorum in case of a meeting of public company is five members who must be present, unless the Articles provide otherwise.
12. Special Privileges	The Companies Act has conferred some special privileges on a private company.	No such privileges are offered to a public company.
13. Index of Member	A memership is limited. There is no need of separate Index of Members.	If membership exceeds so it must have separate Index of Members.
14. Share Warrant	It cannot issue share warrant per bearer.	It can issue share warrants per bearer.
15. Provisions regarding General Meetings (Sec. 171 to 186)	Articles may provide otherwise, these provisions are not compulsory e.g.Notice of General Meeting may be shorter than 21 days.	These provisions are compulsory for all public companies, e.g. Notice of General Meetings must be of 21 days.
16. Issue of Right Shares (Sec. 81)	No first preference to members in further issue of shares.	Right of pre-emption to members in further issues of shares.
17. Appeal against refusal to transfer of shares.	Shareholders have no right of appeal against the Board's refusal to register a transfer of shares.	Shareholder has a right of appeal to the Central Govt. against Board's refusal to register a transfer of shares.

1.4.2 Special Privileges and Exemptions available to Private Companies

The provisions of the Companies Act 2013 are applicable to both, private and public companies. But certain provisions of the Act do not apply to a private company. Following are the special privileges which a private company can enjoy over the public company :

i) A Private Company may consist of two members only as compared to seven for a public company.

ii) Provisions regarding minimum subscription before allotment of shares do not apply to private company.

iii) A private company need not file a prospectus or a statement in lieu of prospectus with the Registrar.

iv) Further issue of shares need not be offered to the existing members.

v) A private company can commence its business immediately after incorporation.

vi) Private Company may issue share capital of such kinds in such forms and with such voting rights as it may think suitable.

vii) Private Company need not keep an index of members.

viii) Private Company need not hold statutory meeting or file a statutory report.

ix) Minimum number of directors is only two in a Private Company.

x) Provisions relating to overall maximum managerial remuneration and remuneration to directors do not apply to a Private Company

xi) Directors consent to act as directors is not required.

xii) Provisions regarding proportion of directors liable to retire by rotation do not apply to a Private Company.

xiii) Government's approval to appointment or amendment of provisions relating to managing or wholetime or rotational directors is not required.

xiv) Restrictions on appointment of directors regarding their consent and holding qualification of shares do not apply to a private company.

xv) Provisions regarding loans to directors are not applicable.

xvi) Director's contract to take up qualification shares need not be filed with the Registrar of Companies.

xvii) Provisions regarding interested directors not to participate or vote in Boards proceedings do not apply to a private company.

xviii) Provisions requiring Government approval for increasing remuneration of a director or managing director do not apply.

xix) Provisions regarding appointment of a managing director for more than five years at a time is not applicable to private company.

xx) Restrictions on advancing loans to other companies do not apply to a private company.

xxi) A private company can give financial assistance for purchase of shares or its holding company's shares.

xxii) Copies of Balance Sheet or Profit and Loss Account filed with the Registrar cannot be inspected by the public.

These privileges are not available to a private company which is a subsidiary of public company. They are applicable to a private company which becomes a public company by virtue.

A private company ceases to be entitled to the privileges mentioned above if, having made provisions required of a private company in its articles, the company makes default in complying with any one of these provisions.

1.4.3 Procedire For Converting a private company into a public limited company

The Companies Act prescribes the following procedure for converting a Private Limited Company into a Public Limited Company.

i) Alter the articles of the Company by a special resolution to eliminate restrictions of a Private Company

ii) Raise the number of members at least to seven if it is less than seven.

iii) Raise the number of directors at least to three if it is less than three.

A Private Company shall cease to exist on the date of such alterations and it shall become a public company. It has to file with the Registrar either a prospectus or a statement in lieu of prospectus and the resolution altering the articles, within thirty days.

In one case, it was held that, on such conversion no new company comes into existence. There is only change in the name. The constitution and the entity of the company is not affected in any manner and the legal proceedings instituted in its former name can be continued by its new name. ("Hindustan Lever Ltd. V/s Bombay Soda Factory." AIR 1964)

When a private company becomes a public company

A Private Company shall become a Public Company in following cases :

i) Conversion by Choice : A private company may decide to become a public company when a private company so decides. It will have to comply with all the provisions of the companies Act, which are applicable to public company. It must pass a special resolution and delete from its articles the requirements of Sec. 3 (i) (iii) by alteration of articles. Within 30 days of its becoming a public company, it shall file with the Registrar a prospectus or a statement in lieu of prospectus.

ii) Conversion by Default : A private company enjoys certain privileges and exemptions. It can enjoy these privileges so long as it complies with the requirements of its definitions as given in Sec. 3 (i) (iii). When any default is made in complying with these requirements, the company loses all the privileges and exemptions of the Act and it becomes a non private company. However, if the company makes application to the court and if the court is satisfied that the failure to comply with the conditions is not intentional or that it is just and equitable to grant relief, then the company may be relieved of the consequences of non-compliance of certain conditions.

iii) By Provisions of Law.
a) Where not less than 25 percent of the paid up capital of private company is held by one or more bodies corporate, such a private company shall become a public company from the date on which such 25 percent is held by a body corporate.

b) Where average annual turnover of a private company is not less than Rs. ten crores during the relevant period, such a private company shall become a public company after the expiry of period of three months from the last day of the relevant period, when the accounts show the said average annual turnover.

c) When a private company holds not less than 25% of the paid up share capital of a public company, the private company shall become a public company from the date on which the private company holds such 25 percent.

d) Where a private company accepts, after an invitation is made by an advertisement or renews deposits from the public other than its members, directors or their relatives, such private company shall become a public company.

1.4.4 Procedure for Converting a public company into a private company

A Public Company can get itself converted into a private company by following the procedure given below.

i) Pass a special resolution authorising conversion of the company.

ii) Alter the Articles so as to contain the restrictions under the Act.

iii) Change the name of the company by passing a special resolution.

iv) Obtain approval of the central government.

v) File the altered articles with the Registrar within 30 days of the receipt of the approval from the Central Government.

QUESTIONS

A) Explain the following concepts in 20 words.

1) What do you mean by 'Company?'
2) Explain the concept of 'Limited Liability.'
3) What is the meaning of 'Separate legal Entity?'
4) Explain the term 'Perpetual Succession.'
5) Give the meaning of 'Common Seal.'
6) Define 'Private Company.'
7) Define 'Public Company.'
8) Define 'Government Company.'
9) What do you mean by 'Registered Company?'
10) What is 'Holding Company.'
11) Explain the concept of 'One Man Company.'
12) Explain how the principle of Limited Liability is beneficial to the company.
13) Define 'Foreign Company.'
14) Explain the term 'Producer Company.'

B) Explain in brief the following (in 50 words)

1) Give some definitions of the term 'Company'.
2) Explain in brief the concept of 'Separate legal entity.'
3) Explain the concept of 'Limited liability' with some examples.
4) Explain in brief why 'Company' developed as a form of organisation.
5) When company gets 'Legal entity'? Explain.
6) State the different kinds of Companies.
7) What are the effects of registration?
8) State the features of 'Govt. Company.'

9) Explain the concept of 'Private Limited Company.'
10) Explain the statutory provisions relating to foreign companies.
11) Explain the features of 'Producer Companies.'
12) Explain the ways of becoming a Holding Company.
13) What are the statutory provisions relating to Public company.
14) What is 'Illegal Association?'
15) Explain the type of company which is created by passing a Special Act in Parliament or state legistature.
16) Explain overview of the changes introduced by the Act 2013?

C) Write in short (about 150 words)

1) Define 'Company.' Give any four characteristics of the company.
2) Give different definitions of the term 'Company' explaining its meaning and state any two features of them.
3) What do you mean by 'Lifting the corporate Veil?' Explain the circumstances of lifting the corporate veil under Judicial interpretations.
4) Lifting the corporate Veil is an exception to the rule 'Salomon V/s Salomon and Co. Ltd.' case.
5) Explain the court case 'Salomon V/s Salomon Co. Ltd.'
6) State the difference between a Company and a Partnership.
7) Explain the different types of companies on the basis of registration.
8) Distinguish between Private Ltd. Co. and Public Ltd. Co.
9) Explain the special privileges granted by an Act to the Private Ltd. company.
10) Explain how Private Ltd. Co. is converted into Public Ltd. Co.
11) Explain the procedure of conversion of Public co. into Private Co.
12) Define 'Private Ltd. Co.'. What are the statutory provisions in respect of Private Ltd. Co.?
13) What are the different types of companies according to the principle of liability.
14) What is 'Producer Company'? Explain its features.
15) State the other types of companies besides registered companies.
16) What is 'Foreign Company?' What are the statutory provisions regarding foreign company?

D) Explain in detail the following (about 300/500 words)

1) What is 'Company'? Explain its characteristics.
2) Give different definitions of company explaining its meaning and features.
3) Why 'Company' becomes popular as a form of organisation?
4) Explain the concept of 'Lifting the corporate veil' by giving circumstances under statutory provisions and Judicial interpretation.

5) Explain the term 'Lifting of corporate veil'. Explain circumstances in these respects.
6) State the difference between partnership firm and Joint Stock Company.
7) Explain the different types of company.
8) State the types of companies on the basis of registration.
9) Define 'Private Limited Company'. What are the statutory Provisions regarding Private Ltd. Co? State special privileges obtained by Private co.
10) Define 'Public Limited Company'. Explain how it differs from public co.
11) Define 'Public Limited Company'. State the different statutory provisions in this respect and explain how it is converted into private Ltd. Co.
12) What is 'Private Limited Company?' What are the steps of converting it into Public Ltd. co?
13) Define 'Foreign Company'. State its features and statutory provisions.
14) What do you mean by 'Government Company?' What are the provisions in companies Act, 1917 relating to it?
15) What do you mean by 'Producer Company?' State its features.
16) Define 'Producer Company.' How it is formed and registered?
17) Explain the sailent features of the Act 2013.

<table>
<tr><td>**Chapter
2**</td><td>**FORMATION AND INCORPORATION OF
A COMPANY**</td></tr>
</table>

CONTENTS

2.1 Steps involved in Formation and Incorporation

    2.1.1. Promotion

    2.1.2. Registration / Incorporation of a company

    2.1.3. Floatation / Raising of Capital

    2.1.4. Commencement of business

2.1 STEPS INVOLVED IN FORMATION AND INCORPORATION

A person or group of persons come together and decide to form a company to achieve certain objectives. The person who takes initiative is called as promoter. The term promoter is not defined in the Companies Act. Section 34 and 35 refers to the liabilities of a promoter. "The term promoter is a term not of law but of business, usefully summing up in a single word a number of business operations familiar to the commercial world by which a company is generally brought into existence". Thus, the term promater refers to those persons who mobilise the resources and form an association so that the Act helps them to create an incorporated company.

2.1.1 Promotion

Promotion is an important term. It indicates the preliminary steps taken for the purpose of registration and commencement of the company. The persons who undertake the task of promotion are called promoters. The Promoter may be an individual, partnership or a company.

A Promoter is one, "who undertakes to form a company with reference to a given object and to set it going and who takes necessary steps to accomplish that purpose". The promoters of a company decide the scope of business activities. They negotiate, if necessary, for the purpose of existing business. They instruct solicitors to prepare necessary documents and secure services of directors. They provide the registration fees and carry out all the activities required for the formation of a company. They also make necessary arrangements for advertising and circulating prospectus. A person acting in a professional capacity on behalf of promoter, such as solicitor, engineer etc. is not a promoter in the eyes of law. Whether a person is promoter or not is a question of fact in each case. It depends upon the role played by a person in the promotion of business.

A promoter is not an agent for the company, which he is going to form, hence a company cannot have an agent before its formation. Similarly, he is not a trustee of the company for the same reason. As soon as he acts in mind with the company and brings company in existence, he becomes a promoter and stands in a fiduciary position towards the company. The promoter is in the situation similar to that of a trustee of the company, hence his dealings with the company must be open and fair.

A promoter cannot make, directly or indirectly, profit at the expense of the company he promotes. If he does so, the company can compel him to account for it.

A promoter is not allowed to earn profit by selling his own property to the company unless all material facts are disclosed.

A) Liability of Promoters : A promoter is subject to the following liabilities under the Companies Act. (Sec. 34 and 35)

i) The above section lays down matters to be stated and reports to be set out in the prospectus. He may be held liable for the non-compliance of the provisions of this section.

ii) A promoter is liable for any untrue statement in the prospectus to a person who has subscribed for any shares or debentures on the faith of prospectus. Such a person can sue the promoter for compensation for any loss or damage sustained by him.

iii) There is a provision for imposing severe penalty on promoters who make untrue and deceptive statements in a prospectus with a view of gathering capital.

iv) A promoter may be liable to Public examination like any other director or officer of the company if the court so directs on a liquidator's report alleging fraud in the promotion or formation of the company.

v) A Company may proceed against a promoter on action for deceit or breach of duty, where the promoter has misapplied or retained any property of the company or is guilty of misfeasance or breach of trust in relation to the company.

B) Duties of Promoter : A promoter has certain duties in the context of the prospectus, issued or the statement in Lieu of prospectus. These duties include –

a) To see that the documents contain the details required under schedule II to the Act.

b) To see that the documents do not contain any untrue statement.

If he fails to perform these duties, then the promoter

i) is liable to pay compensation to any person who buys shares on the basis of erroneous prospectus or statement in lieu of prospectus and has to suffer damage, and

ii) he may be prosecuted in the criminal court according to provisions of the Companies Act.

iii) The promoters remain personally liable to a contract made on behalf of the company not yet in existence. Such a contract is deemed to have been entered into personally by the promoters.

iv) The company cannot offer incorporation to enforce the contract made before its incorporation.

C) Remuneration of Promoters : The formation of a company is a job which requires considerable skill, so promoter needs to be remunerated properly. A promoter has no right against the company for his remuneration unless there is provision to that effect. In the absence of such provision he cannot even recover from the company, payments he has made in connection with the formation of the company.

Remuneration may be paid to a promoter in any of the following ways. :

i) The promoter may purchase the business or other property and sell the same of the company at a higher price or he may sell his own business to the company at a profit.

ii) Commission may be paid to the promoter on the purchase price of the business or property acquired by the company through him.

iii) He may be paid a certain lump sum amount by the company as remuneration for the services.

iv) He may be given a commission on the shares sold.

v) Promoters may be given an option to subscribe within a fixed period for a certain portion of the company's unissued shares at par.

The nature of remuneration must be disclosed in the prospectus if paid within the preceding two years or intended to be paid at any time.

2.1.2 Incorporation of a Company (Sec.7)

A company comes into existence when a number of persons come together with a view to exploit some business opportunity. These persons are called Promoters.

Under section 7 of the Companies Act 2013, any seven or more persons, in case of public company may form an incorporated company for a lawful purpose by subscribing their names to the Memorandum of Association and complying with other requirements essential for registration.

The application for registration of a company should be presented to the respective Registrar of the State in which the business office of the company is established. The application shall be accompanied with the following documents.

i) The Memorandum of Association.

ii) The Articles of Association, if any, signed by the subscribers to the Memorandum of Association.

iii) The Agreement, if any, which the company proposes to enter into with any individual for appointment as its managing or full time director or manager.

iv) A statement of the nominal or authorised capital.

v) A list of directors and their consent to act as director, signed by each of them.

vi) An undertaking in writing signed by each director to take and pay for their qualification shares.

vii) A notice of address of the registered office of the company. This may be done within 30 days of registration if it cannot be filed at the time of registration.

viii) A declaration that all the requirements or provisions of the Companies Act have been complied with. This declaration may be signed by an advocate of the Supreme Court or High Court, an attorney or pleader entitled to appear before a High Court or a Chartered Accountant practicing in India, who is engaged in the formation of the company or by a person named in the articles as director, manager or secretary of the company.

Points V and VI stated above are not required to be filed in case of a private company.

If the Registrar is satisfied that all the required documents delivered to him are in order, he shall register the Memorandum and the Articles.

Certificate of Incorporation

When the required documents are filed with the Registrar and necessary fees paid, the Registrar, if he is fully satisfied, enters the name of the company on the Register of companies maintained by him and then will issue a Certificate of Incorporation, under his signature, in token of registration of the company on the date noted on it.

"On registration the company comes into existence as legal person distinct from its members who constitute it from the earliest moment of the day of incorporation stated in the certificate of incorporation, with rights and liabilities similar to a natural person, competent to enter into contracts"

The certificate of incorporation is conclusive evidence that all the requirements of the Companies Act in respect of registration and all the matter precedent and incidental to it have been complied with. Once the certificate is issued and later on if some irregularities are noticed in memorandum or any other limitation, it does not affect the status and existence of the company as a legal person. On account of this provision reopening of matter prior and during the registration is totally prevented and the existence of a company as an independent legal person continues unaffected. But if any company is incorporated with illegal objects, the illegal objects would not become legal by the issue of the certificate.

According to the Section 68, on registration, the Memorandum and Articles of the company bind the company and its members, as if all the members have signed it and all the covenants or conditions are applicable to them as well as to the company.

2.1.3 Minimum Subscription

When the public company for the first time invites the public to subscribe for its shares, it cannot allot those shares until total minimum amount stated in the prospectus subscribed. This amount which is stated in the prospectus is known as minimum subscription. In the prospectus, the total minimum subscription has to be mentioned.

The total minimum subscription is the amount, as stated in the prospectus which in the opinion of the Board of Directors must be raised by the issue of share capital before the allotment is made to the public. This total minimum amount which in the opinion of the directors must be raised, in order to provide for

i) The purchase price of any property purchased or to be purchased.

ii) The preliminary expenses and any underwriting commission payable by the company.

iii) repayment of money borrowed by the company in respect of any of the foregoing matters.

iv) working capital and

v) any other expenditure stating the nature and purpose of it and the estimated amount in each case.

Sufficient applications must be received to cover the total minimum subscription amount. The sum payable on application for the amount so stated has been paid to and received by the company, whether in cash or cheque. The amount payable on application of each share shall not be less than 5% of the nominal amount of shares. In respect of subsequent allotments this condition is not applicable. All money received by applications for shares shall be deposited in a Scheduled Bank.

  i) Until the certificate of commencement of business is obtained, and

 ii) Until the entire amount payable on applications for shares in respect of the minimum subscription has been received by the company.

The Object of the Minimum Subscription

According to Grover, "the object of the 'minimum subscription' provision is to prevent the company getting underway until it has raised the capital needed to carry out the objects in which it has invited the public to participate. This also affords protection to the creditors by ensuring that a limited company is not able to incur commitments if it is grossly under capitalised."

An allotment made in contravention of the restriction of the minimum subscription is not void but is voidable and the applicant may avoid the allotment within the time.

If the minimum subscription is not received by the company within 120 days from the first issue of the prospective, all moneys received from applicants for shares shall be returned to them without interest. If such money is not repaid within 130 days after the issue of the prospectus, the directors of the company shall be jointly or severally liable to repay that money with interest of 6% per annum from the expiry of 130th day.

In the event of any contravention, every promoter, director or other person who is knowingly responsible for such contravention shall be punishable with fine which may extend upto Rs. 50,000/-

2.1.4 Certificate of Commencement of Business (Sec.11)

A private company can commence its business immediately on incorporation, but a public company cannot commence its business immediately after incorporation, unless it has obtained a certificate of commencement of business or Trading Certificate, from the Registrar.

If the company has share capital and has issued a prospectus inviting the public to subscribe for its shares or debentures, it cannot commence business unless –

  a) Shares payable in cash have been allotted to the extent of the minimum subscription.

  b) Every director has paid in cash the application and allotment money on shares taken by him.

  c) No money is liable to be repaid to the applicants for failure to apply or obtain permission for the shares or debentures to be dealt in on any recognised stock exchange.

d) A statutory declaration duly verified by one of the directors or the secretary in the prescribed form that the above conditions have been complied with has been filed with the Registrar.

When all the above requirements are fulfilled, the Registrar shall certify that the company is entitled to commence business.

If any public company having share capital commences business or exercises borrowing power without obtaining the certificate to commence business, then every person at fault is liable to fine upto Rs. 500/- every day of default.

QUESTIONS

A) **Answer in 20 words.**
1) Explain the term 'Promoter.'
2) What is 'Minimum Capital?'
3) State the names of different stages of company formation.
4) State the different stages required for formation of private Ltd. Co.
5) When Public Ltd. Co. is allowed to start its business?

B) **Answer in 50 words.**
1) Explain the functions of Promoter.
2) Explain the Liabilities of Promoter.
3) How Promoter discovers new opportunities?
4) State the documents required to be collected for registration of the company.
5) How remuneration of the promoter may be given?
6) Write short note on 'Certificate of Incorporation.'
7) State the factors to be considered while determining the amount of minimum capital.
8) Name the documents necessary for registration of company.
9) What are the conditions to be fulfilled for obtaining 'Certificate to Commencement of Business.'

C) **Answer in 150 words.**
1) What do you mean by the term 'Promoter'? State the functions of the promoter.
2) What is "Promotion"? State the Liabilities of the promoter.
3) Define 'Promoter'. Explain the functions of the Promoter and State how remuneration to promoter may be given?
4) What are the essential documents required to be prepared by the Promoter?

5) What are the points to be verified by Registrar before issuing Incorporation Certificate?
6) How capital is raised?
7) Explain the importance of 'Certificate to Commencement of Business.'

D) Answer in 300/500 words.
1) Explain the procedure in detail of the formation of Joint Stock Company.
2) Explain in detail the promotion stage and incorporation stage of the formation of Joint Stock Company.
3) What are the additional steps required to be completed by public company for its formation?
4) Explain the concept of Promoter. State the duties & liabilities of the promoter.
5) What are the steps involved in the Promotion stage? Explain the duties of company secretary in respect of Promotion stage.
6) Explain the procedure of registration. What are the duties of company secretary in respect of registration?
7) Explain the stages to be completed by Private Ltd. Company for its formation.
8) Explain in detail the stages to be completed by Public Company for its formation.
9) What is 'Registration'? Explain its importance and secretarial duties in this respect.
10) As a promoter, which functions to be done since promotion to obtain commencement of Business Certificate.

<table>
<tr><td>Chapter
3</td><td>DOCUMENTS RELATING TO
INCORPORATION AND RAISING OF
CAPITAL</td></tr>
</table>

CONTENTS

3.1 Memorandum of Association

3.1.1 Introduction.

3.1.2 Meaning of Memorandum of Association.

3.1.3 Form and Contents of Memorandum.

3.1.4 Alteration of Memorandum.

3.1.5 Doctrine of Ultra Vires.

3.1.6 Doctrine of Constructive Notice.

3.1.7 Doctrine of Indoor Management.

3.2 Articles of Association

3.2.1 Introduction

3.2.2 Meaning of Articles of Association.

3.2.3 Registration of Articles.

3.2.4 Contents of Articles.

3.2.5 Alteration of Articles.

3.2.6 Relationship between Memorandum of Association and Articles of Association.

3.2.7 Distinction between Memorandum of Association and Articles of Association

3.3 Prospectus

3.3.1 Meaning and Definition

3.3.2 Contents of Prospects

3.3.3 Abridged Prospectus

3.3.4 Prospects by Implication

3.3.5 Shelf Prospectus and Information Memorandum

3.3.6 Statement is Lieu of Prospectus

3.3.7 Liability for Mis-statements in Prospectus

3.1 MEMORANDUM OF ASSOCIATION

3.1.1 Introduction

Memorandum of Association is a very important document pertaining to the affairs of the company. It provides the constitution of the company, and lays down basic conditions on the basis of the company which is incorporated. The company can pursue the only objects and use the only powers that are stated in the Memorandum. A company cannot execute any thing which is not according to the provisions of the Memorandum. If it does then it would be ultra vires the company and therefore completely void. Memorandum not only deals with the scope of the company activities but also defines its relation with the outside world.

3.1.2 Meaning of Memorandum of Association

Defination : "According to Sec. 2(56) Memorandun means the memorondum of association of a company as originaly framed or as altered from time to time in pursuance of any previous company law or of this act."

Meaning : The Memorandum of Association of a company is a fundamental document of the company. It contains "the fundamental conditions upon which alone the company is allowed to be incorporated" It is a document which deals with the constitution of the company. It defines its reason of existence and the area of operation of the company. It also regulates the external affairs of the company in relation to outsiders. A company may pursue only those objects and exercise only such powers as are expressly stated in the Memorandum. Its purpose is to enable the shareholders and outsiders dealing with the company to know about its permitted range of activities. Thus, it not only states the object of the formation of the company but also the scope of its activities. It defines powers of the company. If anything is done beyond these powers, that will be ultra vires (beyond power of) the company and hence void.

3.1.3 Form & Contents of Memorandum

The memorandum of a company shall be in such one of the Forms in Tables. B, C, D and E in Schedule I to the Companies Act 2013 as may be applicable in the case of the company, or in Forms as nearer thereto as circumstances admit.

The Memorandum to be printed, divided into paragraphs, numbered consecutively and signed at least by seven persons in case of public company and two persons in case of private company, in the presence of at least one witness, who will attest the signatures. Each of the members should take at least one share and write opposite his name the number of shares taken by him.

The Memorandum of a limited company should contain-

i) The name of the company with 'limited' as the last word of the name in the case of a Public company and 'Private Limited' as the last word in the case of a private company.

ii) The name of the state in which the registered office of the company is to be situated.

iii) Objects of the company – stating seperately main objects to be pursued by the company and other objects that are essential to achieve main objects.

iv) The declaration that the liability of members is limited and

v) The amount of the authorised share capital divided into shares of fixed amounts.

These clauses are briefly discussed below :

1) The Name Clause : A company may be registered with any name according to the choice of its founder members or promoters. But no company shall be registered by a name which in the opinion of the Central Government is undesirable or which is identical or too nearly resembles the name of the existing company. Every public company must write word 'limited' after its name and every private company must write 'private limited' after its name.

Every company is required to display its name outside its registered office and outside every place where its business is carried out. It has to engrave its name on a seal and have the name on all business letters, bill heads, notices and other official publications of the company.

2) The Object Clause : The object clause defines objects of the company and indicates scope of its activities. A company cannot do anything beyond its objectives and if it does it will be ultra vires and void. But a company can do anything which is incidental to the objects if a Trading Company has implied power to borrow funds.

Under Sec. 13 the company has to divide its objects into two categories. The main objects and other objects.

a) Main Objects : Which are to be pursued by the company on its incorporation and objects incidental or ancillary to the attainment of the main objects.

b) Other Objects : These are the objects not included under main objects. A company after receiving a Certificate of Commencement of Business, has to pursue only that business given in the main objects. The Objects mentioned under other objects cannot be pursued unless there is prior approval of Sharehlders through special resolution passed in general meeting or the Central, Government may on an application made by the Board of Directors allow a company to commence business in the other objects, provided the votes cast in favour of the resolution exceed the votes cast against the resolution.

The objects should not be against the policy of the Constitution, or public policy; illegal and against provisions of the companies act. For example, authorising the company to purchase its own shares.

3) Liability Clause : This clause states that the liability of the members of the company is limited. In case of a company limited by shares, the member is liable only to the amount unpaid on the shares taken by him. In case of a company limited by guarantee, the members are liable to the amount agreed to be contributed by them to the assets of the company in the event of its winding up. In case of unlimited companies this clause need not be included in the memorandum. This implies that the liability of members is unlimited.

Any alteration in the memorandum compelling a member to take up more shares or which increases his liability would be null and void.

If a company carries on business for more than six months, while the number of members is less than 7 in case of public company, and less than 2 in case of private company, each member being aware of this fact, is liable for all the debts contracted by the company after the period of six months has elapsed. (Sec. 45)

4) The Capital Clause : The memorandum of a company limited by shares must state the authorised or nominal share capital, the different kinds of shares and the nominal value of each share. If there are both equity and preference shares, then the division of the capital is to be shown under these two heads.

5) Association or Subscription Clause : Under this clause, those who have agreed to subscribe to the memorandum must signify their willingness to associate and form a company. According to Sec. 12 of the Companies Act, at least seven persons are required to sign the memorandum in case of a public company and at least two persons in the case of Private Company.

The Memorandum has to be signed by each subscriber in the presence of at least one witness, who has to attest the signatures. Each subscriber must write opposite his name the number of shares he shall take. No subscriber of the Memorandum shall take less than one share. This clause need not be numbered.

3.1.4 Alteration of Memorandum (Sec. 13)

According to Sec. 16, the company cannot alter the conditions contained in the memorandum, except in the cases, in the manner and to the extent provided by the Act. These provisions are as follows.

1) Change of Name : Provides that the name of company can be changed at any time by passing a special resolution in a general meeting of the company and with the written approval of the Central Government. However, no such approval of the

Government is necessary for merely including or deleting the word 'private' when public company is converted into a private company and vice versa.

If through invertence or otherwise, a company has been registered with a name which is identical with or too closely resembles with the name of the existing company, the company may change its name by passing an ordinary resolution and by obtaining approval of the Central Government in writing.

The change of name must be communicated to the Registrar within 30 days. The Registrar shall enter the new name on the register in place of the 'former name and shall issue a fresh certificate of incorporation, with necessary alterations. The change of the name becomes effective on the issue of fresh certificate of incorporation. The Registrar will also make necessary alteration in the memorandum of association of the company.

However, the change of name shall not affect any rights or obligations of the company or render defective legal proceedings which might have been continued by or against the company by its former name may be continued by or against the company by its new name.

2) Change of Registered Office : Such a change includes :

a) Change of Registered Office from premises to the other in the same city, town or village.

A company may shift its registered office from one place to another at any time i) by passing a resolution by the Board of directors and ii) giving a notice of the change, within 30 days after the date of change, to the Registrar, who shall record it.

b) Change of Registered Office from one town or city to another town or city in the same state.

The following procedure is to be followed for this purpose.

i) A special resolution is required to be passed at a general meeting of the shareholders.

ii) A copy of it is to be filed with the Registrar within 30 days.

iii) A notice of new location has to be given, within 30 days of the removal of the registered office, to the Registrar who shall record the same.

Both the changes do not involve alteration in memorandum.

c) Change of Registered Office from one State to another state.

The change of registered office of the company from one state to another involves the following procedure.

i) A printed or type written copy of the special resolution should be sent to the Registrar of companies within 30 days of its passing.

ii) The special resolution is required to be confirmed by the Company Law Board (CLB), which, before confirming the resolution, will satisfy itself that sufficient notice has been given to every creditor and all other persons whose interests are likely to be affected by the alteration, including the Registrar of Companies and the Government of the State in which the registered office is located. The CLB also will give opportunity to members and creditors of the company, the Registrar and other person interested in the company, to be heard.

The CLB may confirm the resolution on such terms and conditions as it thinks fit. A certified copy of the CLB's order should be filed within three months thereof, with the Registrar of companies of the old and the new state. If it is not filed within the prescribed time, then the alteration shall, at the expiry of such period, become void and inoperative.

A company can shift its registered office from one state to another for certain purposes only. These purposes are discussed under the heading 'Alteration of objects.'

3) Alteration of Objects Clause : A company by a special resolution duly confirmed by the Company Law Board to alter the objects or to change the place of its registered office from one state to another only if the alteration is sought on any of the following grounds.

i) To carry on its business more economically and efficiently.
ii) To attain its main purpose by new and improved means.
iii) To enlarge or change the local area of its operation.
iv) To carry on some business which under existing circumstances may be conveniently or advantageously combined with the business of the company.
v) To restrict or abandon any of the objects specified in the memorandum.
vi) To sell or dispose off the whole or any part of the undertaking.
vii) To amalgamate with any other company or body of persons.

4) Alteration of Liability Clause (Sec. 13) : The liability clause cannot be altered so as to make the liability of members unlimited, unless the member agrees in writing. The consent of the member may be given either before or after the alteration. Such an increase in liability may be by subscribing for more shares than the number held by him at the date on which the alteration is made or in any other manner.

In case of unlimited liability company, the liability may be made limited by passing a special resolution and obtaining the Court's approval. A copy of the special resolution and that of the Court's confirmation must be filed with the Registrar within specified time. The alteration will not affect any debts, liabilities, obligations or contracts entered into by or with the company before the registration.

5) Alteration of Capital Clause : A limited company having a share capital may change its capital clause subject to the provisions of its articles by a resolution in the general meeting. The confirmation of the Court is not required in case of the alterations for the following purposes.

i) to increase its share capital.

ii) to consolidate and divide its capital into shares of larger amount.

iii) to convert its fully paid shares into stock and to reconvert stock into fully paid up shares.

iv) to subdivide its shares into shares of smaller amount.

v) to cancel its shares.

But for reduction of share capital, special resolution and confirmation by the court is required.

3.1.5 Doctrine of Ultra Vires

The company's activities must be confined strictly to the objects mentioned in its Memorandum. If they go beyond these objects, then such acts will be ultra vires. "Ultra" means beyond, "Vires" means powers. An action outside the memorandum is ultra vires the company. A company may do any act which is a) necessary for or b) incidental to the attainment of its objects or c) which is authorised by the Act.

The object of declaring certain acts as ultra vires is to protect the interests of shareholders and all other parties who deal with the company.

A company exists only for the objects which are expressly stated in its objects clause or which are incidental to or consequential upon those specified objects. Any act done outside the express or implied objects is ultra vires. The ultra vires acts are null and void ab initio. The company is not bound by these acts, and neither the company nor the other contracting party can sue upon it.

The ultra vires doctrine confines corporate action within fixed limits. It handicaps the ambitious manager and it lays a trap for the unwary creditor. Hence, there has been a revolt against it since its inception.

Consequences of Ultra Vires Transactions

When a company gets involved in an Ultra Vires transactions. It has following effects :

1) Injunction : Wherever an ultra vires act has been or is about to be undertaken, any member of the company can get an injunction to restrain it from proceeding with it.

2) Personal liability of directors : It is the duty of directors to see that the corporate capital is utilised only for the legitimate business of the company. If any part of it is diverted for purposes other than those in memorandum, the directors will be personally liable to replace it.

3) Breach of warranty of authority. : It is the duty of agent to act within the scope of his authority. The directors of a company are its agents, hence it is their duty to keep within the limits of the company's powers. If they induce an outsider to contract with the company in a matter in which the company does not have the power to act, they will be personally liable to him for his loss.

4) Ultra Vires Contracts : A contract by a company outside its objects is wholly null and void . Neither side is capable of enforcing the contract against the other. The knowledge of third party is immaterial. Persons who deal with the company are deemed to have knowledge of the memorandum. So, if they make a contract which is to their knowledge actual or constructive, ultra vires the company, they cannot enforce it. An ultra vires contract cannot become intra vires by reason of estoppels, lapse of time, ratification or delay. No performance on either side can give the unlawful contract any validity or be the foundation of any right of action upon it.

5) Ultra Vires Acquired property : A company, however, can protect its property acquired by an ultra vires expenditure. If a company's money has been spent ultra vires in purchasing some property, the company's right over the property is held secured, because that asset, though wrongly acquired, represents the corporate capital.

6) Ultra Vires Borrowing : When a person lends money to a company and the company either has no borrowing power or has already exceeded them or the borrowing is for the purpose of which is ultra vires, then the contract of loan is void and no action can be brought under it to recover the money lent. Ultra vires borrowing does not create the relationship of creditor and debtor and the only possible remedy is in *rem* and not *personam*. But nothing prevents the company from repaying the money, though it cannot recover the money repaid.

The lender may be able to recover his money by the following methods.

i) He may be able to assert a claim to subrogation. Where the company has used the loan to pay the intra vires debts, the lender is subrogated to the rights of the creditors so paid. If 'A' lends Rs. 15,000 to B Co. Ltd., the loan being ultra vires, A will not be able to recover it. But if the company has used the money to pay off Rs. 10,000 worth of enforceable debts, A may stand in the shoes of the creditor paid off and sue the company as the creditors have done. A will have an action for Rs. 10,000.

ii) The lender may be able to trace his money into an asset which the company has purchased with it, or into the funds of the company. In equity, the lender of money can obtain redress by means of a tracing order, provided the lender can identify his money or any property purchased with it. The company in such a case is regarded as holding the money lent to it on trust for the lender.

7) Ultra Vires Torts : A company will be liable for torts or crimes committed in the pursuit of its stated objects. But a tort or crime committed in the course of activity which is ultra vires the company, the company would not be liable in respect of it. However, the officer, agent or servant of the company who commits the act would be personally liable in such a case.

3.1.6 Doctrine of Constructive Notice

Notice of memorandum and articles

The memorandum and articles of association of every company are registered with the Registrar of companies. The office of the Registrar is a public office and hence the memorandum and articles become public documents. They are open and accessible to all. (Sec. 399). It is therefore the duty of every person dealing with a company to inspect its public documents and make sure that his contract is in conformity with their provisions. Whether a person actually reads it or not, he is to be in the same position as if he had read them. It will be assumed that he knows the contents of those documents. This kind of presumed notice is called Constructive notice.

Another effect of the doctrine is that a person dealing with the company is taken not only to have read these documents but to have understood them according to their proper meaning. He is presumed to have understood not only company's powers but also those of its officers. There is constructive notice not only of memorandum and articles but also, of all the documents, such as special resolutions and particulars of changes which are required by the Act to be registered with the Registrar. But there is no notice of documents which are filed only for the sake of record of returns and accounts. The Principle applies only to documents which affect powers of the company. All the documents which are open to public inspection may be regarded as public documents. Thus Memorandum and Articles of Association of a company are presumed to be notice to the public. Such notice is called 'Constructive Notice'.

3.1.7 Doctorine of Indoor Management

The Doctorine of Indoor Management is an exception to the rule of constructive notice. The rule of constructive notice seeks to protect the company against the outsider, where as the doctorine of Indoor Management operates to protect outsiders against the company.

Articles of the company allots powers to the directors of the company, so that they can lay down rules, regulations, procedure. Hence, outsiders have a right to assume that, the rules and procedures have been strictly followed by the company in carrying out their internal proceedings of the company and that the directors are dealing within their authority and within the rules laid down.

Although it is the duty of every person to read the Memorandum and Articles of the company, he is not bound to inquire into the internal affairs of the company, whether they are being carried out according to the provisions of the Articles of the company. He has right to assume that all the internal proceedings and affairs of the company are being carried out within the framework of the rules and regulations. This exception to the doctorine of constructive notice is called as 'indoor management'. The doctorine had its origin in the famous case of Royal British Bank V Turquand (1856)

3.2 ARTICLES OF ASSOCIATION (Sec. 5)

3.2.1 Introduction

For any type of organisation a system of rules and regulations is necessary for conducting various activities of the organisation smoothly and efficiently. It also helps in maintaining order and discipline in the organisation. The Companies Act provides regulations in Table A in Schedule I to the Act.

The articles of association contains rules and regulations framed or accepted by the company for internal management of its affairs and explaining right of the members of the company with each other. The articles helps organisation in carrying out the aims and objectives of the Memorandum of Association. Hence, the Articles of a company are subordinate to and controlled by the Memorandum. Articles do not contain anything which may alter a condition in the Memorandum. In case of conflict between the Memorandum and Articles, Memorandum prevails.

3.2.2 Meaning of Articles of Association

Sec. 2 (5) of the Companies Act defines Articles. "Article means Articles of Association of a company as originally framed or as altered from time to time in pursuance of any previous companies Law or of the Act". The Articles of Association are the rules and regulations of a company framed for the purpose of internal management of its affairs and for the conduct of its business. They define the duties, rights, powers and authority of shareholders and the directors. The Articles are framed for carrying out aims and objectives of the Memorandum of Association. Thus, the articles of association of a company are subordinate to and are controlled by the Memorandum of Association. The Articles of association of a company have a contractual force between company and its members as also between the members inter se in relation to their rights as such members.

The Memorandum lays down the scope and powers of the company, whereas the articles govern the ways in which the objects of the company are to be carried out. Articles must not be inconsistent with the Memorandum and should not contain anything which is against or repugnant to the provisions of the Companies Act.

3.2.3 Registration of Articles

According to sec. 9, a public company limited by shares may register articles of association signed by the subscribers to the memorandum. If it does not register its own articles, then the articles given in Table A of Schedule I automatically become applicable.

A company limited by guarantee and unlimited liability company and a private company limited by shares, have to register their articles compulsorily.

The articles of a company must be

i) printed ii) divided into paragraphs, and numbered consecutively iii) signed by subscribers to the memorandum in the presence of at least one witness who shall attest the signatures. The articles are to be stamped with requisite court / revenue stamp and filed along with the Memorandum.

3.2.4 Contents of Articles

The Articles of a company usually deal with the following matters.

1) The business of the company.
2) The amount of capital issued, and classes of shares into which the capital is divided and the changes of share capital.
3) The rights of each class of shareholders and procedure for variation of their rights.
4) The execution or adoption of a preliminary agreement, if any.
5) Allotment of shares and payment, calls, transfer, lien, transmission, forfeiture etc. of shares.
6) Share certificates and warrants.
7) Exercise of borrowing powers.
8) General meetings, notices, quorum, proxy, poll voting, resolution, minutes.
9) Appointment, remunerations, qualifications, powers etc. of Board of Directors.
10) Dividends – interim and final and general reserves.
11) Accounts and audit.
12) Indemnity.
13) Winding up.
14) Keeping of books – both statutory and others.

Inspection of copies of Articles

A company on the requests of a member sends him a copy of the articles within seven days on payment of one rupee. If a company makes default, the company and every officer of the company, who is in default, shall be punishable with fine upto Rs. 50

3.2.5 Alteration of Articles (Sec. 14)

According to sec. 14, subject to the provisions of the Act and to the conditions mentioned in its Memorandum, a company by special resolution can alter or add to its articles. A printed or typewritten copy of every special resolution altering the articles must be filed with the Registrar within 30 days of the passing of the special resolution.

Limitations of Power to Alter Articles.

These limitations are as follows.

i) The alteration should be within the powers given by the memorandum and it should not conflict with other provisions of the memorandum.

ii) The alterations must not be inconsistent with any provision of the Companies Act or any other Statute. For example, no company can purchase its own shares and if the articles of a company are altered for having power to purchase its own shares, then such power will be void.

iii) The altered articles must not include anything which is illegal or unlawful or opposed to public policy.

iv) The alterations must be bonafide for the benefit of the company as a whole.

v) Alteration must not constitute a fraud on the minority by the majority.

vi) Alteration must not compel the existing members to take or subscribe for more shares or in any way to contribute to the share capital, unless they give their consent in writing.

vii) An alteration of articles for converting a public company into a private company cannot be made without the approval of the Central Government.

viii) Alteration of articles should not be for breach of contract with third parties or avoid contractual liability.

ix) The amended regulation of the Articles of Association cannot operate retrospectively, but only from the date of amendment.

Thus it is seen that regulations provided in the articles do not exceed the power of the company as laid down by its memorandum [Asbury Vs. Wastson (1885).] Articles going beyond the memorandum are ultra-vires (Shyamchand Vs. Calcuttta Stock Exchange).

Hence it is safe to read memorandum and articles together to remove an ambiguity or uncertainty. The relationship between memorandum and articles has been aptly summed up by Lord Cairns, L.C. in Asbury Railway Carriage & Iran Co. Ltd. Vs. Riche as follows,

"The articles play a part subsidiary to a memorandum of association. They accept the memorandum of assciation as a charter of incorporation of the company, and so accepting it, the articles proceed to define the duties, right and powers of governing body as between themselves and the company at large, and the node and form in which business of the companys to be carried on, and the mode and form in which changes ..... internal regullations of the company may from time to time be made..... The memorandum is as it were..... the area beyond which the actions of the company cannot go, inside that area the shareholders may make such regulations for their own government as they think fit."

3.2.6 Relationship between Memorandum of Association and Articles of Association

	Memorandum of Association	Articles of Association
1)	The Memorandum defines the companies objects and various powers it possesses.	The Articles regulate the manner in which the company's affairs will be managed.
2)	The Memorandum is fundamental and can be altered only under certain circumstances provided by the Act.	The Articles of a company are subordinate and controlled by the memorandum of association which is the dominant instrument and contains the general Constitution of the company.
3)	Memorandum contains general Constitution of the company.	The Articles are only internal regulations and members have full control over them.

3.2.7 Distinction between Memorandum of Association and Articles of Association

Basis	Memorandum of Association	Articles of Association
1) Nature	The Memorandum defines the companies objects and various powers it possesses.	The Articles regulate the manner in which the company's affairs will be managed.
2) Objects	The Memorandum is fundamental and can be altered only under certain circumstances provided by the Act.	The Articles of a company are subordinate and controlled by the memorandum of association which is the dominant instrument and contains the general Constitution of the company.
3) Role	Memorandum contains general Constitution of the company.	The Articles are only internal regulations and members have full control over them.
4) Filing with the Registrar	It is compulsory for all the companies to file their duly signed memorandum to the Registrar for obtaining certificate of incorporation.	Companies adopting Articles given in Table A need not file seperate set of Articles.
5) Observance of Provisions	The clauses of memorandum of Association are subject to the Provisions of the companies Act. These clauses have to be strictly followed.	The Articles cannot voilate provisions of the Act and Memorandum of Association.
6) Alterability	Alterations of a Memorandum of Association is complex task. They can be altered only under exceptional circumstances as laid down in the Act. It needs passing of special resolution, permission of the court or Central Government.	Articles are alterable easily by passing a special resolution.

7) **Legal Status**	Memorandum has higher legal status than Articles. An agreement which is not permitted by the Memorandum cannot be enforced by law.	If violation of Articles takes place, it is not void unless other party is aware of this violation.
8) **Ratification of violation**	Any violation of memorandum by doing something beyond the scope of memorandum is absolutely void. It cannot be ratified even by full consent of all shareholders.	Anything done beyond the scope of Articles but within the power of the company is not void and be ratified by a special resolution subsequently.
9) **Determination of Relationship**	Memorandum determines relationship between the company and other outside parties.	It determines relationship between the company and internal members.
10) **Mutual Relationship**	Memorandum is not dependent on Articles. On Statutory matters it is unchallanged but on non-statutory matters, Articles may amplify memorandum.	Articles are dependent on memorandum. They are interpreted in the light of memorandum. They compliment and supplement the memorandum.
11) **Importance**	Memorandum is an important document of the company like the Constitution of a country.	It is a document subsidiary to memorandum. It is like laws and regulations in a country which cannot violate the Constitution.

Floatation / Commencement

When a company is registered and it has received the certificate of incorporation, then it is ready for floatation which means that it can go ahead with raising capital required for conducting business activities smoothly. When a private company is formed, it can collect funds from friends and relatives by private arrangment.

It is obligatory for every public company to take one of the following steps.

a) If the public is to be invited to subscribe to its capital, a prospectus has to be issued or

b) If the capital has been arranged privately, then it has to submit a 'Statement in lieu of Prospectus' at least three days before allotment.

3.3 PROSPECTUS

3.3.1 Meaning and Defination

A Public company requires huge amount of capital, so it can raise the capital by issuing shares and debentures. The company may invite the public to subscribe for its shares and debentures. The invitation contains offer which states the prospects of the company and also the purposes for which the capital is required. The document inviting the public to purchase shares and debentures of the company is called a prospectus.

According to Sec. 2(70), "A prospectus means any document described or issued as prospectus and includes any notice, circular, advertisement or other document inviting deposits from the public or inviting offers from the public for the subscription or purchase of any shares or debentures of a body corporate." Thus, prospectus is an invitation issued to the public to purchase shares or debentures of the company or to deposit money with the company.

The 'public' need not include the public at a large but may include any section of the society whether selected as members or debentureholders or as clients of the person issuing the prospectus or any other manner.

Application Forms with Prospectus

Any advertisement offering to the public shares or debentures of the company for sale is prospectus. Hence application forms for shares or debentures cannot be issued without prospectus. Taking into consideration high cost of printing of prospectus, the 1988 amendment introduced the concept of abridged prospectus. It is a memorandum containing salient features of a prospectus as may be prescribed. Abridged prospectus has to be prepared according to Form 2 A of Annexure A to the Companies (Central Government's) General Rules and Forms 1956. It should not contain anything which is not included in the main prospectus. It has to be a brief version of the salient features of the prospectus. One abridged prospectus can have two application forms.

Exceptions

In the following cases, although shares are offered and application forms are issued, a prospectus containing all the details is not necessary.

i) Where the offer is made in connection with a bonafide invitation to a person to enter into an underwriting agreement with respect to the shares and debentures.

ii) Where shares and debentures are not offered to the public.

iii) Where the offer is made only to the existing members or debenture holders of the company.

iv) Where the shares or debentures offered are in all respects uniform with shares and debentures already issued and quoted on a recognised stock exchange.

v) Where prospectus is issued as a newspaper advertisement ; it is not necessary to specify contents of memorandum or the names etc. of the signatories to the memorandum or the number of shares subscribed by them.

vi) A private company is not required to issue prospectus.

Characteristics of a Prospectus

A document issued by a company can become a prospectus when it has the following features.

i) It should be a proposal or an invitation for the general public.

ii) It should invite the public to purchase shares or debentures.

Aims and Objectives of a Prospectus

i) To inform the public about the company that it is an incorporated public company.

ii) To communicate with the public that the company is providing golden opportunity for profitable investment as the directors of the company are most efficient and honest.

iii) To attract the public by providing true and certified record and motivate people to purchase shares and debentures.

iv) To declare that the information given in the prospectus is true and the responsibility about the matters mentioned in the prospectus is on the directors of the company.

3.3.2 Contents of Prospectus (Sec. 26)

As investors prefer a sound concern, prospectus provides means for informing investors about the soundness of the company's venture. But this opportunity may be exploited by the directors and promoters to impose fraud on the public. So the Companies Act provided detailed regulation for protecting the investing public from such frauds, by providing full disclosure of all material and essential details. The relevant rules and regulations may be stated as follows.

Formalities in Issuing Prospectus

1) Every Prospectus must be dated

The date of issue is very important, hence every prospectus must be dated, and unless contrary is proved, the date shall be regarded as the date of its publication.

2) Every Prospectus to be Registered

The copy of the Prospectus must be registered with the Registrar of Companies, on or before the publication of prospectus. The copy sent for registration must be signed by all the directors or proposed directors of the company.

The copy of the prospectus sent for registration must be sent along with the following documents.

i) A copy of every contract relating to appointment and remuneration of managerial personnel.

ii) If the report of the expert is to be published, then consent of the expert.

iii) A copy of every material contract, unless it is entered into in the ordinary course of business or two years before the date of the prospectus.

iv) A written statement about adjustments if any in the figures of assets and liabilities, profits or losses in the reports included in the prospectus. The statement should also give reasons for adjustments and be signed by an expert.

v) The consent in writing of the person, if any, named in the prospectus as the auditor, legal advisor, attorney, solicitor, banker or broker of the company to act in that capacity.

The prospectus must be issued within 90 days of the registration.

The company or every person who knowingly issues a prospectus without registration is punishable with a fine upto 50,000 rupees. On the face of the prospectus, it must be stated that, it has been registered and that the required documents have been filed.

3) Expert's Consent

If the prospectus includes a statement made by the expert, then his consent in writing must be obtained and it should be stated in the prospectus. The expert should not be interested in the formation or management of the company.

4) Disclosure to be made

Every prospectus is required to disclose the matters stated in Schedule II of the Act, which contains three parts.

PART I

This part covers disclosure of the following information.

1) General Information

i) Name and address of registered office of the company.
ii) Names of stock exchanges where application for listing is made.
iii) Declaration about refund of the issue if minimum subscription of 90 percent is not received within 90 days from closure of the issue.
iv) Declaration about the issue of allotment letters / refunds within a period of ten weeks and interest in case of any delay in refund at the prescribed rate.
v) Date of opening and closing of the issue.
vi) Name and address of auditors and lead managers.
vii) Whether rating from CRISIL or any other agency has been obtained for proposed debentures or preference share issue. If not, mention as 'No'
viii) Names and addresses of the underwriters and the amount underwritten by them.

2) Capital Structure

i) Authorised, issued, subscribed and paid up capital.

ii) Size of the present issue, mentioning seperately reservation for preferential allotment to promoters and others.

3) Terms of Present Issue
i) Terms of payment
ii) How to apply
iii) Any special Tax benefits.

4) Particulars of Issue
i) Objects ii) Project Cost iii) Means of financing including contribution of promoters.

5) Company Management and Project
i) History, main objects and present business of the company.
ii) Promoters and their background.
iii) Location of the Project.
iv) Nature of products, export potential
v) Future prospects
vi) Collaborations, if any
vii) Stock market date

f) Prescribed particulars about the company and other listed companies under the same management which made capital issue during last three years.

g) Outstanding litigations about financial matters or criminal proceedings against the company or directors under schedule XIII.

h) Management perception of risk factors like sensitivity to foreign exchange rate fluctuations, difficulty in availability of raw materials or in marketing of products, cost, time over run etc.

PART II Schedule II

Under this part a company has to give detailed information about General information, Financial information, Statutory and Other information.

General Information – It includes

a) Consent of directors, auditors, solicitors, managers to the issue, Registrars to the issue, Bankers of the company, Bankers to the issue and experts.

ii) Change, if any, in directors and auditors during the last three years and reasons for it,

iii) Procedure and time schedule for allotment and issue of certificate.

iv) Names and addresses of Company Secretary, Legal advisor, Lead Managers, Co Managers, Auditors, Bankers to the issue and Brokers to the issue.

b) Financial Information

i) Reports of auditors of the company regarding profits and losses, assets and liabilities, dividends paid during the five financial years immediately preceding the issue of prospectus.

ii) Report by accountants on profits or losses for the preceding five financial years and on the assets and liabilities on a date, 120 days before the date of the issue of prospectus.

c) Statutory and Other Information

It includes information about the following
  i) Minimum subscription
  ii) Expenses of the issue.
  iii) Undertaking commission and brokerage.
  iv) Previous public or rights issue along with date of allotment, refunds, premium, discount etc.
  v) Issue of shares otherwise than cash.
  vi) Details about purchase of property, if any.
  vii) Revaluation of assets, if any.
  viii) Material contracts and time and place where such documents may be inspected.

PART III of Schedule II

Part III of Schedule II contains provisions applying to the Part I and II of the Schedule II. It includes interpretation of expressions used. These are as follows. :

i) In the case of a company which is carrying on business for a period of less than five financial years, reference to five financial years means reference to that number of financial years for which business has been carried out.

ii) Any report required under Part II of the schedule shall be made only by the accountant who is qualified for appointment as an auditor of the company under the Act and who is not an officer or servant, or a partner or in the employment of an officer or servant of the company, or of the company's subsidiary or the company's holding company.

For the purpose of this clause the expression officer shall include a proposed director but not an auditor.

iii) Reasonable time and place at which the copies of all balance sheets and profit and loss accounts, if any, on which the report of the auditor is based, and material contracts and other documents may be inspected.

Declaration that all the relevant provisions of the Companies Act and the guidelines issued by the government have been complied with and no statement made in the prospectus is contrary to the provisions of the Companies Act 2013 and the rules thereunder.

These provisions are important because they have to be strictly followed by the applicant for the shares. Even if he has been pursuaded to waive the compliance of the provisions of the act, the waiver would be void.

3.3.3 Abridged Prospectus

The Central Government has prescribed the salient features of prospectus. It lays down that, no one shall issue any form of application for shares or debentures of a company unless the form is accompanied by a memorandum containing such salient features of a prospectus as may be prescribed. The rule 4CC has been inserted for this purpose, in the Companies (Central Government's) General Rules and Forms 1956. According to the rule 4CC, the salient features required to be included in the abridged prospectus shall be in Form 2A

FORM 2 A

Memorandum containing Salient features of prospectus

I) General Information.
   a) Name and address of registered office of the Company.
   b) Issue listed at : [Name(s) of the stock exchanges]
   c) Opening, Closing and earliest closing date of the issue.
   d) Name and address of lead managers.
   e) Name and address of trustees under debenture trust deeds (in case of debenture issue)
   f) Rating for the debenture/preference Shares, if any, obtained from CRISIL or any recognised agency.

II) Capital structure of the Company
   a) Issued, subscribed and paid up capital.
   b) Size of present issue, giving seperately reservation for preferential allotment to promoters and others.
   c) Paid up capital i) after the present issue and ii) after conversion of debentures (if applicable)

III) Terms of the present issue.
   a) Authority for the issue, terms of payments and procedure and time schedule for allotment and issue of certificates.
   b) How to apply – availability of forms, prospectus and mode of payment.
   c) Special tax benefits to company and shareholders under the Income Tax Act, if any

IV) Particulars of the Issue
   a) Objects of the issue
   b) Project Cost
      Means of financing (including contribution of promoters)

V) Company Management and Project
   a) History, main objects and present business of the company.
   b) Background of promoters, managing director / whole time director and names of nominees of institutions, if any, on the board of directors.

c) Location of the project.

d) Plant and machinery, technology, process etc.

e) Collaboration, performance guarantee, if any, or assistance in marketing by the collaborators.

f) Infrastructure facilities for raw materials and utilities like water, electricity etc.

g) Schedule of implementation of the project and progress made so far, giving details of land acquisition, execution of civil works, installation of plant and machinery, trial production, date of commercial production, if any.

h) The Products

    i) nature of product(s) – consumer / industrial and end users.

    ii) Existing, licensed and installed capacity of the product, demand of the product,- existing and estimated by a government authority or by any other reliable institution, giving source of the information.

    iii) Approach to marketing and proposed marketing setup.

In case of company providing services, relevant information regarding nature / extent of service etc. to be furnished.

VI) Financial performance of the company for the last five years.
(Figures to be taken from the audited annual accounts in tabular form)

a) Balance Sheet data ; Equity Capital, Reserves (State revaluation reserve, the year of revaluation and its monetary effect on assets) and Borrowings.

b) Profit and Loss data – Sales, gross profit, dividend paid, if any.

c) Any change in accounting policies during the last three years and their effect on the profits and the reserves of the company.

d) Stock market quotation of shares / debentures of the company, if any, (high / low price in each of the last three years and monthly high / low price during the last six months.)

VII) Whether all payments / refunds, debentures, fixed deposits, interest on fixed deposits, debenture interest, institutional dues have been paid upto date. If not, details of the arrears to be stated.

VIII) Following particulars in regard to the listed companies under the same management within the meaning of the sec. 370 (1B) which made any capital issue in the last three years.

a) Name of the company.

b) Year of issue.

c) Type of issue (public/rights/composite)

d) Amount of issue.

e) Date of closure of issue.

f) Date of dispatch of share / debenture certificate completed.

g) Date of completion of the project, where object of the issue was financing of a project.

h) Rate of dividend paid.

IX) Management perceptions of risk factors (e.g. sensitivity to foreign exchange rate fluctuation, difficulty in availability of raw materials or in marketing of products, cost / time overrun)

NOTE – The term year, wherever used, here in before, means Financial Year.

If the company does not receive application money for at least 90 percent of the issued amount, the entire subscription will be returned to the applicants, within 90 days from the date of closure of issue. If there is delay in the refund of application money by more than eight days after the company becomes liable to pay the excess amount, the company will pay interest for the delayed period, at prescribed rates in the act. No statement made in this form shall contravene any of the provisions of the Companies Act, and the rules made there under.

Signature of Directors

Place
Date

Voluntary Statement to Prospectus

In addition to compulsory particulars as required under the Act, any other information may be given in the prospectus relating to the terms of the issue or, application to deal with shares of the company on the stock exchange and only the true nature of company's venture should be disclosed.

3.3.4 Prospectus by Implication

Under Sec. 29, certain information is required to be disclosed and certain reports have to be included in the Prospectus. But certain companies may by-pass the provisions of Sec. 29 by making an offer of sale of shares and debentures through the Issue Houses. The shares are allotted to an Issue House who in turn issues advertisement offering shares for sale. As the advertisement is not issued by the company, it does not amount to a prospectus. Thus, companies avoid the liability of compliance.

In order to check such a malpractice, the act provides that, all documents containing offer of shares and debentures for sale shall be included within the definition of prospectus and all such documents shall be deemed as prospectus by implication, of law. All the enactments, rules and regulations of law relating to the contents of prospectuses and the liability in respect of statements and omissions from prospectuses shall apply to all such documents.

Unless the contrary is proved, an allotment or an agreement to allot shares or debentures shall be deemed to have been made with a view to the shares and debentures being offered for sale to the public, if it is shown-

a) that the offer of the shares or debentures or any of them for sale to the public was made within six months after the allotment or agreement to allot or

b) that the date when the offer was made, the whole consideration to be received by the company in respect of the shares or debentures had not been received by it.

In case of a document that is deemed as prospectus, under section, it is required that it must contain certain information in addition to the information required to be stated in a prospectus.

Thus, it should also state that -

a) the net amount of consideration received or to be received by the company in respect of the shares or debentures to which the offer relates and

b) the place and time at which the contract under which the said shares or debentures have been or are to be allotted may be inspected.

The purpose of registration of a prospectus, the persons making the offer of sale to the public are to be deemed as directors of the company.

3.3.5 Shelf Propectus and Information Memorandum (Sec. 31)

Sometimes, securities are issued in stages spread over a period of time, particularly in respect of infrastrucure projects where issue size is large as huge funds have to be collected. In such case, filing of prospectus each time will be very expensive. In such cases a provision of 'Shelf Prospectus' has been made. The advantage is that, at each stage of offer of securities during validity of shelf prospectus, filing of prospectus is not required.

'Shelf Prospectus' means a prospectus issued by financial institution or bank for one or more issues of the securities or class of securitieis specified in the propsectus. Once such shelf prospectus is filed, it is not required to file prospectus at every stage of its offer of securities, during the period of validity of shelf prospectus. At subsequent stages, only 'information memorandum' is required to be filed.

Applicability of provision : The provision for issue of shelf prospectus is applicable only to issue of securities by public financial institutions, public sector banks or scheduled banks whose main object is financing. As per explanation (a) to sec. 60A (4) 'Financing' means making loans to or subscribing in the capital of, a private enterprise engaged in infrastructure financing or to such other company as may be notified by Central Government. Thus, at present, the provision is available only to institutions and banks engaged in insfrastructure finance as its main object. Such companies can file a 'Shelf Prospectus.'

Information memorandum : At the second and subsequent stages of issue of securities, the company will have to file a 'Information Memorandum' on (a) all material facts relating to new charges created and (b) changes in financial position as have occurred between the first offer of securities, previous offer of securities and the succeeding offer of securities. Such 'information memorandum' is required to be filed prior to making of second or subsequent offer of securities under the shelf prospectus. The memorandum is required to be filed within such time as may be prescribed by Central Government. [sec. 60A (3)]. The prescribed time limit for filing information memorandum between the first offer of securities, previous offer of securities and the succeeding offer of securities shall be three months, as per rule 4CCCA of Companies General Rules, 1956.

The information memorandum along with the shelf propectus shall constitute the 'prospectus' and such 'prospectus' will have to be issued to public at each subsequent stage of offer.

Validity period of information memmorandum : The 'information memorandum along with 'shelf prospectus' is valid for one year from date of opening of first issue of securities under that prospectus. [sec. 60A (4)]. [Note that drafting of the sub-section is very clumsy and it is not very clear whether the shelf prospectus itself is valid for one year or whether the information memorandum is valid for one year. It appears that shelf prospectus can be valid for a longer period, but 'information memorandum' will be valid for one year.]

3.3.6 Statement in lieu of Prospectus (Sec. 28)

Sometimes, public company is able to raise original capital without inviting the public to subscribe. Hence, it need not issue a prospectus, but it has to prepare a document named 'A statement in lieu of prospectus' and file it with the Registrar. It cannot allot any shares without first filing this document. The statement has to be prepared according to the form given in Schedule III and must contain the same information as is required for the prospectus.

The document has to be delivered to the Registrar at least three days before the first allotment of shares. The statement must be signed by all or proposed directors or their agents.

If a company fails to deliver a Statement in Lieu of Prospectus it cannot allot any shares or debentures. If an allotment is made, it is voidable if the allottee notifies the company within two months after the statutory meeting or if there is no such meeting then within two months after allotment.

If a company fails to fulfill above conditions, the company and every director who has been knowingly a party of this contravention shall be liable for fine upto Rs. 1000/-.

If a statement in lieu of prospectus, delivered to the Registrar contains an untrue or misleading statement, every person who authorised the delivery of the statement shall be liable to imprisonment for two years or fine upto Rs. 5,000 or both. He can avoid the liability if he proves either that the statement was immaterial or that he had reasonable ground to believe that the statement was true.

These provisions are not applicable to a Private Company.

3.3.7 Liability for Mis-Statements in the Prospectus (Sec. 34)

A Prospectus is the basis of the contract between the company and the person who purchase shares or debentures. The persons forming the company have all the knowledge or means of knowledge regarding present position and future prospects of the enterprise while investing public has no knowledge about it. Hence, the promoters should not only disclose all the matters known to them about the company which might affect the investing public but should state them honestly, accurately, correctly and unambiguously.

Golden Rule of framing prospectus

Promotors having full knowledge about the activities of the company should prepare prospectus very carefully. A prospectus must tell the truth, the whole truth and nothing but the truth. It must not conceal any fact which is necessary to be disclosed. This is known as the 'Golden rule' of framing of the prospectus. This rule was laid down by Kindersley in New Brunswick Co. V/s Muggeridge.

Some company promoters may make mis-statements or false statements in the prospectus to practice fraud on the public. In order to prevent such practices, the law imposes certain duties and responsibilities on all the persons who are responsible for the issue of prospectus.

Mis-Statement or Untrue Statement

Whether a statement is untrue or not is to be judged in the context in which it appears and the totality of impression it would create. "A statement included in a prospectus shall be deemed to be untrue, if the statement is misleading in the form and context in which it is included." A statement may be false, not only because of what it states, but also because of what it omits or conceals. Where a certain matter which is material enough if omitted from the prospectus, then it will be deemed to be an untrue statement. Taking into consideration the prospectus as a whole, if there is really a misrepresentation of fact, then the contract may be set aside, though each statement by itself is literally true.

A person subscribes for shares on the basis of prospectus is not bound to verify the accuracy of the statements in it and is entitled to avoid the contract if they turn out to be untrue, even though he had means to discover inaccuracy. The prospectus is called as misleading only when there is misrepresentation of facts and not of law.

Liability for untrue statements in Prospectus

Where a person has bought shares on the faith of a prospectus which is misleading on account of mis-statement in or omission from the prospectus, he may have legal remedy against all or any one of the following.

i) The company ii) every director iii) every person whose name is given in the prospectus as a proposed director iv) every promoter v) every person who has authorised the issue of prospectus.

An allottee must prove that –

i) The misrepresentation was of fact.
ii) It was in respect of material fact.
iii) He acted on the misrepresentation
iv) He has suffered damages in consequence.

Regarding liabilities for untrue statements, the Companies Act imposed twofold liability on those who are responsible for untrue statements in prospectus.

1) Civil liability
2) Criminal liability

Civil liabilities (Sec. 35) –

A person who has subscribed for shares on the faith of the misleading prospectus has remedies against a) The company and b) the directors, promoters and experts.

1) Remedies against the company

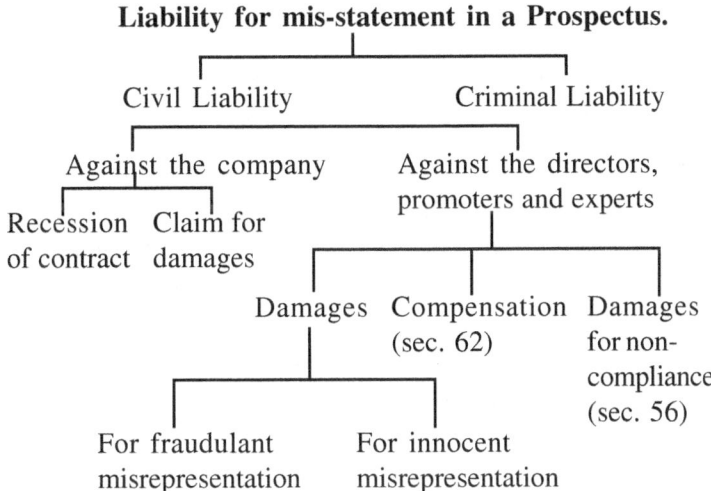

Liability for mis-statement in a Prospectus.

If a mis-statement of a material information in a prospectus has induced any shareholder to purchase shares then he may i) rescind the contract to take the shares or ii) claim damages from the company.

A) Recession of the contract

A person who purchases shares on the faith of statements of fact contained in the prospectus can apply to the court for the recession of the contract, if those statements are false or fraudulent or some material information is omitted. He must apply for the recession within a reasonable time and before the company goes for liquidation.

The contract can be rescinded if the following conditions are satisfied.

i) Prospectus was issued by or on behalf of the company.
ii) The statement must be material misrepresentation of fact.
iii) The misrepresentation must have induced the shareholder to take the shares.
iv) It must be untrue or misleading in the form and context in which it is included.
v) The shareholder must have relied on the statement in the prospectus.
vi) That he has taken action promptly to rescind the contract.

Loss of right to rescind the contract

The shareholder loses his right to rescind the contract if (i) There is unnecessary delay after knowing the misrepresentation in the prospectus or ii) he affirms the contract inspite of misrepresentation or iii) winding up procedure of the company has started.

B) Right of action for damages for deceit

If a person has been induced by a fraudulent statement in a prospectus to take shares is entitled to sue the company for damages. While claiming for damages he has to prove-

2) Remedies against the directors, promoters and experts

Any person who has purchased shares or debentures on the faith of the prospectus containing the untrue statements are as follows

i) every director at the time of issue of the prospectus.

ii) every person whose name is given in the prospectus as a proposed director.

iii) every promoter and

iv) every person who authorised the issue of prospectus

A) Liability for damages for mis-statements in prospectus

Under sec. 62, directors, promoters and all other persons who authorised the issue of the prospectus are liable to compensate persons who purchase shares having faith in the prospectus for loss suffered by the reason of untrue statement in it. The principle of estimating compensation for damages is stated in sec. 73 of the Indian contract Act 1872. The compensation payable is the difference between the price paid for the shares or debentures and their actual value at the date they were allotted to the subscriber.

Defences of directors, promoters etc.

The person sued for damages can escape liability of damages by successfully pleading any of the following defences.

i) Withdrawal of consent

A director or promoter etc. may escape liability if he proves that he withdrew his consent to act as a director, promoter etc. before the prospectus was issued and it was issued without his consent and authority.

ii) Issue without knowledge

A director will not be liable if he proves that the prospectus was issued without his knowledge or consent and as soon as he came to know about it he had given reasonable public notice to that effect.

iii) Igorance of Untrue Statement

A director can defend himself by proving that, after the issue of prospectus and before allotment, as he became aware of the untrue statement in it, withdrew his consent and gave reasonable public notice of the withdrawal along with reasons for it.

iv) Reasonable ground for belief

A director may prove that he had reasonable grounds to believe and did believe upto the time of allotment of shares or debentures, that the statement, was true.

v) Statement of expert

If a director proves that the statement was the correct copy or a correct and fair extract from the report of the expert who was competent to make it and he had given the consent and had not withdrawn it.

vi) Correct copy of an extract of official document

A director is also protected if he proves that the statement was a correct and fair representation or extract or copy of an official document or was based on the authority of an official person.

B) Damages for non-compliance

The omission from a prospectus of a matter required to be included by act, may give a rise to an action for damages at the instance of a shareholder who has suffered the loss thereby, even if the omission does not make the prospectus false or misleading.

The person would not be liable if he proves that,

i) He had no knowledge of the matter not disclosed in the prospectus.

ii) The non-compliance was the result of an honest mistake of fact on his part or

iii) The non compliance was not material and the court thinks that he may be excused.

C) Damages under General Law -

Under the General Law, a shareholder can hold all or any of the persons responsible for the issue of a prospectus liable for any mis-statement or fraud on his or their part, if he was actually deceived by having acted on the faith of the mis-statement or fraud in the prospectus.

The remedy under general law is available,

i) where the right of recession as against the company is lost through negligence and

ii) where the company goes into liquidation.

Criminal Liability of Directors (Sec. 34)

Where a prospectus contains any untrue statement, every person who authorised the issue of the prospectus is punishable with imprisonment which may extend to two years or with fine which may extend to Rs. 5000/- or both.

The accused person may not be liable if he proves that,

i) the statement was immaterial or

ii) that he had reasonable ground to believe upto the time of the issue of prospectus that the statement was true.

Penalty for fraudulently inducing persons to invest money (Sec. 36)

A person who makes an untrue, deceptive or misleading statement in a prospectus for inducing people to invest money, shall be liable for imprisonment for a term which may extend to five years or fine upto Rs. 10,000/- or both.

Issue and allotment of shares in fictitious names (Sec. 36A)

A makes it an offence to make applications for shares in the name of or to induce the allotment or transfer of shares to fictitious persons. The punishment for such offence is imprisonment which may be upto five years.

Example

The directors of the bank issued a bond to Mr. Turquand. The articles provided that the directors had power to issue bond if they are authorised by a proper resolution of the company. No such resolution was passed. It was held that Turquand could sue on the bond as he was entitled to assume that the resolution must have been passed. The persons dealing with the company are bound to read the registered documents and to see that the proposed dealing is not inconsistent. But, they are not bound to inquire into the reqularity of internal proceedings. The company was bound by the bond.

So the doctorine is also known as the Turquand Rule.

The Doctorine is subject to the following exceptions.

I) Knowledge of Irregularity

A person dealing with the company has the knowledge of irregularity in its internal management in connection with the subject matter of his dealings, cannot claim benefit of the Turquand's Rule.

II) Negligence

A person cannot claim the benefit of the rule in Turquand's case in circumstances under which he would have discovered the irregularity if he had made proper inquiries. In addition, where the circumstances relating to transaction are suspicious and therefore invite inquiry, the outsider cannot claim the benefit of this rule.

III) Forgery

The Turquand rule will not apply where a document on which the person seeks to rely is a forgery. The doctorine of indoor management applies to irregularities but not to forgery.

IV) Acts outside the Apparent Authority

If person acting on behalf of the company exceeds any actual or ostensible authority given to him, the rule of Tarquand is not applicable.

V) No Knowledge of the contents of the Articles

A person who has not actually read the memorandum or articles of a company and person while entering into contract was not aware of the contents of the articles or memorandum, cannot seek to rely on statement contained therein. The doctorine of indoor management is based on the principle of estoppel. Therefore, it cannot be invoked in favour of a person who has not consulted company's Memorandum and Articles of Association.

VI) Question is about the very existence of Agency

The doctorine of Indoor Management cannot apply where the question is not about the scope of the power exercised by apparent agent of the company, but is in regard to the very existence of the agency.

VII) Fulfilment of Pre-conditions

The doctorine is also not applicable where a pre-condition is to be fulfilled before company itself can exercise a particular power.

Underwriting Commission & Brokerage

Even if the share issue is not to public, companies act permits payment of underwriting commission and brokerage. Maximum total commission payable (excluding brokerage) cannot exceed 5% of the price of shares or 2.5% in case of debentures or lower rate if prescibed by Articles of Asscociation. Payment of brokerage or underwriting commission must be authorised by Articles of Association. The amount of commission payable must be disclosed in statement in lieu of prospectus. Copy of contract for payment of commission has to be filed with Registrar of Companies at the time of delivery of statement in lieu of prospectus.

Brokerage Permissible : In addition to commission, brokerage is permissible. Such brokerage should be 'as permissible here to before.' Thus, only brokerage can be paid only to those who deal in shares and whose business includes the procuring of subscribers for shares. Thus brokerage can be paid only to those who are registered with SEBI as brokers.

Except the underwriting commission or brokrage, no other commission, discount or allowance can be paid, either directly or indirectly, for subscribing of agreeing to subscribe for any shares or debentures of the company. In case of private office, direct commission to invertors is not permissible. Default can involve penalty upto Rs. 500/-

Underwriting of shares

When a public company offers shares to the public, it would like to ensure success of the issue. A company, therefore, may make an agreement with financ ial institutions, who, in consideration of the commission, agrees to subscribe for the shares "to the extent to which they are not taken up by the public." The agreement may be limited to a "certain number of shares if and so far as not applied for by the public."

An underwriter does not guarantee the success of the prospectus. He only agrees to take those shares which would not be taken by the public.

Underwriting is now compulsory for all issuesand minimum requirement of 90 percent subscription of the portion offered to the public is also mandatory for each issue of capital to public.

An underwriting agreement does not merely guarantee but also an application of shares which are not taken up by the public. Hence, the company can allot shares in terms of the contract without further application.

The prospectus should also indicate the number of shares or debentures which have been underwritten.

_____

QUESTIONS

A) Answer in 20 words.
1) What is 'Memorandum of Association'?
2) What do you mean by 'Ultra-Vires'?
3) What is the meaning of Constructive Notice?
4) What do you mean by 'Ultra-Vires contracts?
5) How many clauses are mentioned in Memorandum of Association? State them.
6) What is prospectus?
7) What do you mean by 'abridged prospectus'?
8) What is 'Statement in lieu of prospectus'?
9) What do you mean by 'deemed prospectus'?
10) What is the meaning of 'Mis-statement'?
11) What are the aims and objectives of a prospectus?
12) Explain the Prospectus by Implication.
13) What is the liability for mis-statement in a prospectus?
14) What is civil liability regarding prospectus?
15) What is the penalty for fraudulently inducing persons to invest money?

B) Answer in 50 words.
1) Explain the secretarial duties regarding formation of Joint Stock company.
2) Explain the contents of 'Name Clause.'
3) Explain the Liabilities clause of Memorandum of Association.
4) How name of the company can be altered?
5) What is the criteria of deciding the name of the company?
6) How change in registered office from one state to another is effected?
7) What are the aims and objectives of a prospectus ?
8) Explain the Prospectus by Implication.
9) What is the liability for mis-statement in a prospectus?
10) What is civil liability regarding prospectus ?
11) What is the penalty for fraudulently inducing persons to invest money ?

C) Answer in 150 words.

1) State the duties of company secretary relating to company formation.
2) Why 'Minimum Capital' is required for public company? How it is determined?
3) Explain the promotion and incorporation stage of company formation.
4) What is the procedure of alteration in Name Clause?
5) Explain the procedure of alteration of Registered office in different situations.
6) What is Memorandum of Association? Explain its importance.
7) Define Memorandum of Association. What are its contents?
8) What do you mean by Ultra Vires transaction? Explain its effects.
9) Define 'Prospectus', state its contents
10) What is Prospectus? What are aims and objectives of a prospectus?
11) What do you mean by prospectus by Implication? What are its provisions?
12) What do you mean by 'Mis-statement' in a prospectus? What are its effects?
13) Explain the liability of directors regarding mis-statement in a prospectus.

D) Answer in 300/500 words.

1) 'Memorandum is an unalterable charter of the company' Discuss.
2) Define Memorandum of Association. Explain its different clauses.
3) What is the procedure of alteration in Memorandum of Association.
4) Explain in detail the doctrine of Ultra-Vires and doctrine of Constructive Notice.
5) What is 'Memorandum of Association'? Explain the form and contents of Memorandum of Association.
6) Define 'Prospectus.' What are the statutory requirements regarding issue of prospectus?
7) Explain the importance of prospectus. What are the contents of prospectus?
8) What do you mean by 'mis-statement' in a prospectus? What are its consequences?
9) Explain the civil and criminal liability of directors regarding mis-statement in a prospectus.
10) Define 'Prospectus'. What are the statutory provisions regarding issue of a prospectus?

Chapter 4

CAPITAL OF THE COMPANY

CONTENTS

4.1   Raising of Share Capital
4.2   E SOP, Sweat Equity Share, Buy-Back of Shares
4.3   Application and Allotment of Shares
4.4   Calls on Shares
4.5   Share Certificates
4.6   Share Capital

A) Introduction

The capital of a company consists of certain indivisible units of a fixed amount. These units are called shares. A share is the interest of a shareholder in a definite portion of the capital. It indicates a proprietory relationship between the company and the shareholder. A shareholder is the proportionate owner of the company although he is not the owner of the company's assets which belong to a company as a separate legal entity.

B) Definitions

i) Under Section 2 (84) share is defined as , "A share in the share capital of a company and includes stock except where a distinction between stock and shares is expressed or implied ".

ii) Justice Farwell has stated, "A share is the interest of a shareholder in the company, measured by a sum of money, for the purpose of liability in the first place and of interest in the second, but also consisting of a series of mutual covenants entered into by all the shareholders interse in accordance with the Companies Act.

iii) "A share carries with it certain rights and liabilities while company is going concern or while the company is being wound up.Thus, a share may be defined a bundle of rights and obligations ".

iv) "A share in a company is meant not only sum of money but an interest measured by a sum of money and made up of diverse rights conferred on its holder by the articles of the company which constitute a contract between him and the company".

v)"A share is a personal estate capable of being transferred in the manner laid down in the articles of association. It is a movable property which can be mortgaged or pledged "

A Share Certificate is issued by a company under its Common Seal which shows that the shares are held by a member and it is a prima facie evidence of the title of the member to the shares.

Each share issued by a company must be numbered so that one share may be distinguished from another share.

C) Stock and Shares

When shares are fully paid up, they may be converted into stock. Stock is the aggregate of fully paid up shares, consolidated and divided for the purpose of holding into different parts.

The term stock indicates that a company has recognised the fact of complete payment of shares and whenever required these shares may be assigned in fragments which could not be done before.

A company limited by shares may, if authorised by its Articles, by a resolution passed in a general meeting, convert all or any of its fully paid up shares into stock and reconvert stock into fully paid up shares of any denomination. When the shares are converted into stock, notice has to be given to the registrar within 30 days of the conversion. The register of members shall show the amount of stock held by each member instead of the amount of shares.

SHARE	STOCK
1) A share is one of the number of units in which the capital of a company is divided i.e. shares are units	Stock is the capital in the form of fund which may be divided into any amount as required. Thus, stock is lump holding.
2) Shares may be partly or fully paid up.	Stock is always fully paid up.
3) A share has a nominal value	Stock has no nominal value.
4) Shares can only be transferred in round numbers.	Stock may be transferred in small fraction also.
5) All share are of equal denomination.	Stock may be of unequal nomination.
6) Shares always bear distinctive numbers.	Parts or fractions of stock do not bear any distinctive numbers.
7) Shares can be directly issued to the public.	Stock cannot be of issued directly. Only fully paid up shares can be converted into stock.

D) Types of Shares

A company limited by shares can issue two types of shares, namely preference shares and equity shares.

I) Preference Shares

Preference shares of any company limited by shares, have the following characteristics.

i) They have a preferential right as to the payment of dividend at a fixed rate during the life time of the company.

ii) They have a preferential right to the return of capital when the company goes into liquidation

Kinds of preference shares

1) Cumulative and Non Cumulative Preference Shares : On the basis of payment of dividends, the preference shares can be classified into cumulative and non cumulative preference shares.

The cumulative preference shares are those which are entitled to receive dividend even if there are no profits in a particular year and the dividend has not been declared. Thus , the unpaid dividend goes on accumulating every year and when the company earns profit in any year the arrears of dividend on preference shares have to be paid first before paying dividend on other types of shares.

In case of non cumulative preference shares the dividend is only payable out of the net profits of each year. If there are no profits in any year, then the arrears of dividend cannot be claimed in the subsequent year.

The preference shares are presumed to be cumulative unless expressly, described as non cumulative.

2) Convertible and Non-Convertible Preference Shares : Convertible preference shares are those shares which can be converted into equity shares within a specified period of time.

Non-convertible preference shares are those shares which do not have the right of conversion into equity shares.

3) Redeemable and Irredemable Shares : Under Section 80, a company limited by shares, if so authorised by its articles, may issue redeemable preference shares. Such share may be redeemed after a fixed period or earlier at the option of the company, only subject to the following conditions.

i. The shares to be redeemed must be fully paid up.

ii. These shares shall be redeemed out of distributable profits or out of the proceeds of a fresh issue made for the purpose of redemption .

iii. Any premium payable on redemption must be paid out of the profits or out of the company's share premium account.

iv. Where redemption is made out of profits, a sum equivalent to the nominal value of shares redeemed must be transferred to the Capital Redemption Reserve account. This amount shall be treated as capital of the company and the provisions of reduction of capital shall apply. The amount credited to the account may be used to pay up unissued shares to be issued as fully paid bonus shares.

The redemption of redeemable preference shares must be notified to the registrar within 30 days of the redemption.

Irredeemable preference shares are those shares, where the capital is to be returned on the winding up of the company. After the commencement of the companies (Amendment) Act 1988, companies limited by shares are prohibited to issue any irredeemable preference shares or shares redeemable after the expiry of a period of ten years from the date of issue.

4) Participating and Non-participating preference shares - Participating preference shares are those shares which are not only entitled to a fixed rate of dividend but also to a share of surplus profits which remain after the claims of equity shareholders. These shares may also have right to share in the surplus assets of the company on its winding up, if such a right is expressly provided in the memorandum or articles of association of the company.

Non-participating preference shares are entitled only to a fixed rate of dividend and do not share in the surplus profits.The preference shares are presumed to be non-participative unless expressly provided in the memorandum or the articles or in the terms of issue.

II) Equity Shares

All shares which are not preference shares are equity shares. Equity shareholders have the residual right of the company. If the company is prosperous they may get higher dividend than preference share holders, or may get nothing if the company incurs losses. At the time of winding up, the equity share holders are entitled to the entire surplus assets remaining after the payment of liabilities and the capital of the company, unless articles confer right on the preference shares a right to participate in the distribution of surplus assets.

E) Distinction between Preference Shares and Equity Shares

Preference shares	Equity shares
1) Preference shares are entitled to a fixed rate of dividend	The rate of dividend on equity shares depends on the profit earned by the company
2) Dividend on preference shares is paid in priority over the equity shares	Dividends on equity shares is paid only after the payment of preference shares dividend.
3) The preference shares have preference over capital for repayment of capital on winding up of the company	Equity shares are residual claimants, after preference shares for repayment of capital on winding up.
4) If preference shares are cumulative then the dividends are allowed to accumulate until they are paid.	Equity divideds are not cumulative. Either they are paid or not paid every year.
5) Redeemable preference shares may be paid back by the company.	Equity shareholders cannot be paid back except under a scheme involving reduction of capital.
6) Voting rights of preference shareholders are restricted and vote only when their special rights are varied or their dividend is in arrear.	Equity shareholders can vote on all the matters affecting the company.
7) Preference shareholders do not get bonus shares nor new shares.	Equity shareholders are offered bonus shares or new issues at lower prices than outsiders.

F) Issue of Shares (Sec. 62)

Under Section 62 of the Act, where at anytime after the expiry of two years of the formation of a company or at any time after the expiry of one year from the allotment of shares in that company made for the first time after its formation, whichever is earlier, it is proposed to increase the subscribed capital of the company by allotment of further shares then -

i) Such shares shall be offered to the persons who at the date of offer, are holders of the equity shares of the company, in proportion to the capital paid up on those shares at that date.

ii) Such offer shall be made by notice specifying the number of shares offered and limiting the time not being less than 15 days from the date of offer within which the offer, if not accepted, will be deemed to have been declined.

iii) After the expiry at the time specified in the notice or on receipt of earlier limitation from the person to whom such notice is given that he declines to accept the shares offered, the Board of Directors may dispose then in a manner as they think most beneficial to the company.

Section 81 recognises preemptive right of the existing share holders of the public company to the issue of new shares. Shares thus issued are called right shares as the existing equity holders have first right to be allotted the new issue of shares.

However, the preemptive right can be taken away and the new shares may be offered to any person or outsiders, after passing a special resolution to that effect by the company in general meeting. If special resolution is not passed and the votes cast in favour of proposal exceed the votes cast against the proposal, then the Central Government should be satisfied, on an application made to it, that the proposal is most beneficial to the company.

According to Sec. 62 The general rule is that existing shareholders have a first right to be allotted the new issue of shares, except by a special resolution the company may decide that the directors need not offer the shares in the further issue to the existing equity shareholders and they may dispose off all the shares in any manner whatsoever.

The above provisions do not apply to -

(a) a private company or

(b) to the increase of the subscribed capital of a public company caused by the exercise of an option attached to debentures issued or loans raised by the company.

(i) to convert such debentures or loans into shares in any company or

(ii) to subscribe for shares in the company.

The terms of issue of such debentures should be approved by the Central Government and also by a special resolution passed by the company in general meeting before the issue of debentures on raising of the loans.

I) Issue of shares at premium (Sec. 52)

Issue of shares at premium means issue of shares at price more than its 'face value.' Where a company issues shares at a premium, whether for cash or otherwise, a sum equal to the aggregate amount or value of the premium on those shares shall be transferred to an account to be called the 'Securities Premium Account'

The securities premium account may be applied by the company.

i) For, paying up unissued shares of the company to be issued to members of the company as fully paid bonus shares.

ii) In writing off the preliminary expenses of the company.

iii) In writing off the expenses on the commission paid or discount allowed on any issue of securities or debentures of the company or

iv) in providing for the premium payable on the redemption of any redeemable preference shares or of debentures of the company.

Where the shares are issued at premium on consideration other than cash, a sum equal to the amount on value of the premium must be transferred to the Securities Premium Account.

II) Issue of shares at a discount (Sec. 53)

Issue of shares at a discount means issue of shares below its 'Par or face Value.' A company shall not issue shares at a discount except under the following conditions.

i) The issue of the shares at a discount is authorised by a resolution passed by the company in general meeting and sanctioned by the Central Government.

ii) The resolution specifies the maximum rate of discount at which the shares are to be issued. No such resolution shall be sanctioned by the Central Government, if the maximum rate of discount specified in the resolution exceeds 10 percent, unless the Central Government is of the opinion that a higher percentage of discount may be allowed in the special circumstances of the case.

iii) Not less than one year has at the date of the issue elapsed since the date on which the company was entitled to commence business and

iv) The shares to be issued at a discounted rate are issued within two months after the date on which the issue is sanctioned by the Central Government or within such extended time as the Central Government may allow.

Where a company has passed a resolution authorising the issue of shares at a discount, it may apply to the Central Government, if having regard to all the circumstances of the case, it thinks proper so to do, may make an order sanctioning the issue on such terms and conditions as it thinks fit.

Every prospectus relating to the issue of the shares shall contain particulars of the discount allowed on the issue of the shares.

If default is made in complying with these conditions, the company and every officer of the company who is in default shall be punishable with fine which may extend to five hundred rupees.

III) Issue of shares for consideration other than cash (Sec. 39)

Generally, a company issues its shares for cash, but a company may sometimes issue shares for consideration other than cash. Consideration may be property, goods or services received by the company for which the company issues shares.

The shares may be issued for consideration as partly or fully paid up shares.

Whenever a company having a share capital makes any allotment of its shares for consideration other than cash, then it must within 30 days of allotment be produced for inspection and examination of the Registrar a contract in writing constituting the title of the allottee to the allotment together with any contract of sale, or a contract for services or other consideration in respect of which that allotment was made, such contracts being duly stamped, and filed with the Registrar, copies are verified in the prescribed manner, of all such contracts and a return stating the number and nominal amount of shares so allotted, the extent to which they are to be treated as paid up, and the consideration for which they have been allotted.

4.1 PROCEDURE FOR ISSUE OF SHARES / WAYS FOR RAISING CAPITAL (Sec. 42)

Companies limited by shares have to issue shares to raise the necessary capital for their operations. Issue of shares may be made in three ways :
  i) By Private placement of shares
  ii) By an offer for sale
  iii) By inviting the public to subscribe for shares in the company through a prospectus.

i) By Privte placement of Shares : A private company limited by shares is prohibited by the Act and Articles from inviting the public for subscription of shares / debentures. It also need not file a statement in lieu of prospectus. Its shares are issued privately to a small number of persons known to the promoters or related to them by family connections.

Public company can also raise the capital by placing the shares privately and without inviting the public for subscription of its shares or debentures. In such a case, an underwriter or a broker finds persons, nomrally his clients who wish to buy the shares. He acts merely as an agent and his function is simply to procure buyer for the shares i.e. to place them. Since no public offter is made for shares there is no need to issue any prospectus. As per guidelines by SEBI, subscription of shares by friends, relatives and associations is allowed and not by any unrelated investors through brokers, merchant bankers etc.

2) By an offer for sale : Under their arrangement, the company allots or agrees to allot shares or debentures at a price to a financial institution or an Issue House for sale to the public. The issue house publishes a document called an offer for sale. An application form is attached with a document. On receipt of application from the public the Issue House announces the allotment of the number of shares mentioned in the application in favour of the applicant purchaser who becomes a direct allottee of the shares.

3) By inviting public through prospectus : In this case, the company invites offer from public to subscribed for the shares or debentures through prospectus. An investor is expected to study the prospectus and if convinced, may apply for shares.

4) Issue of shares to existing shareholders (right shares): In this case, the shares are allotted to the existing equity shareholders in proportion of their holdings.

5) Bonus Shares - (Sec. 63) : When existing shareholders are allotted additional shares without collecting any additional money from them it is called as Bonus Share. When a substantial amount stands to the credit of company's 'Reserves & Surplus Accounts', directors may decide to declare bonus issue by capitalising this amount.

Procedure for Issue of Bonus Shares:

The First and the most important requirement as to bonus issue is SEBI guidelines. These guidelines are mandatory on the part of every company. After having complied with SEBI guidelines the following steps have to be taken in regard to Bonus Issue:

1) The Articles must permit the issue of bonus shares. Otherwise the Articles must be suitably amended.

2) To ensure that the enhanced paid up share capital after the bonus issue does not exceed the authorised capital. Otherwise, the Memorandum and Articles have to be altered.

3) A Board Meeting has to be convened to consider the proposal of bonus issue.

4) An Extra Ordinary General Meeting must be convened to obtain approval.

5) Obtain the approval of Reserve Bank of India Under FERA, 1973, in case allotment of bonus shares is to be made to non-resident members.

6) To Convened Board Meeting to pass a resolution for allotment. In this meeting, a detailed list of existing members, showing their present holding and the proportion in which bonus shares are allotted, with be placed before the Board.

7) Allotment letters are issued to members.

8) A 'Return of allotment' must be filed with the Registrar within 30 days of such allotment.

9) New share certificates in respect of bonus shares are prepared and exchanged for the allotment letter.

10) The necessary entries are made in the Register of Members.

In case of listed company following additional formalities are required to be performed.

11) To intimate to stock exchange about the proposed issue and also about the final decision.

12) To arrange for closure of Register of Members and transfer book and intimate the stock exchange about the same atleast 42 days in advance.

13) To obtain approval of stock exchange for the procedure followed for allotment of bonus shares.

14) To obtain permission from stock exchange to list the bonus share also.

15) A certificate duly signed by issuer and counter signed by Statutory Auditor or by a Company Secretary in practice to the effect that the SEBI guidelines have been complied which should be forwarded to SEBI.

Advantage of Bonus Issue :

A) To the Shareholders:

1) Increases in Future Dividends:

When bonus shares are issued the number of shares held by a shareholder increases. Thus, the paid up value of his investment in the company also increases. So, in future he receives more dividend.

2) Indication of Higher Profit in Future:

A bonus issue signifies that the company is financially sound and stable and is likely to earn more profits in future. This results in capital appreciation of investment of the shareholders.

B) To the Company:

1) Good Reputation:

Companies making bonus issues have better standing and good reputation.

2) More Attraction Share Price :

The price of shares quoted at a stock exchange increases substantially when bonus issue is expected by the investors.

3) Ease in Collecting Capital in Future :

A company making a bonus issue enjoys stability, profitability and good reputation. As a result, it can collect capital easily in future whenever required at terms to itself.

4.2 E SOP, SWEAT EQUITY SHARE, BUY-BACK OF SHARES

4.2.1 Buy Back of Shares (Sec.67)

A) Introduction

No Company limited by shares and no company limited by guarantee and having a share capital, shall have power to buy its own shares, unless the consequent reduction of capital is effected and sanctioned by the court. Even financial assistance, by public companies and private companies which are their subsidiaries, for purchasing their shares is also prohibited.

But a holding company can purchase the shares of its subsidiary.

The act has prohibited purchase by company of its own shares because it amounts to the reduction of capital. However, the following transactions are not prohibited.

i) The lending of money by a banking company in the ordinary course or

ii) The provision of money by a company for the purchase of subscription for fully paid shares in the company or its holding by trustees or for the benefit of employees of the company, in accordance with any scheme for the time being in force.

iii) Making of loans by a company to persons, other than directors or managers, bonafide in the employment of the company with a view to enabling those persons to purchase or subscribe for fully paid shares in the company or its holding company to be held by themselves by way of beneficial ownership.

Recent Amendments in the Companies Act allow the companies to buy back their own shares or other specified securities, notwith standing anything contained in the Companies Act.

A company may purchase its own shares or other specified securities out of -
i) its free reserves or
ii) the securities premium account or
iii) The proceeds of any shares or other sepcified securities.

Provided that no buy back of any kind of shares or other specified securities shall be made out of the proceeds of the earlier issue of the same kind of shares or same kind of other specified securities.

The company shall purchase its own shares or other specified securities on compliance of the following conditions.

i) The buy back is authorised by its articles.

ii) A special resolution has been passed in general meeting of the company authorising the buy back.

iii) The buy back is or less than ten percent of the total paid up equity capital and free reserves of the company, and such buy back has been authorised by the Board by means of a resolution passed in its meeting.

iv) No offer of buyback shall be made within a period of 365 days reckoned from the date of the proceeding offer of buyback, if any

v) The buy back is less than 25 percent of the total paid up capital and free reserves of the company.

vi) The buy back of equity shares in any financial year shall not exceed 25 percent of its total paid up equity capital in that financial year.

vii) The ratio of the debt owned by the company is not more than twice the capital and its free reserves after such buyback. The Central Government may prescribe a higher ratio of the debt than that specified under this clause for a class or classes or companies. Debt includes all amounts of unsecured and secured debts.

viii) all the shares or other specified securities for buy back are fully paid up.

ix) The buy back of the shares or other specified securities listed on any recognised stock exchange is in accordance with the regulations made by the securities and Exchange Board of India in this behalf.

x) the buy back of shares or other securities not listed in any stock exchange is in accordance with the guidlines as may be prescribed.

The notice of meeting at which special resolution is proposed to be passed shall be accompanied by an explanatory statement stating,

a) a full and complete disclosure of all material facts

b) the necessity for the buy back

c) the class of security intended to be purchased under the buy back.

d) the amount to be invested under the buy back, and

e) time limit for completion of buy back

Every buy back shall be completed within twelve months from the date of passing the special resolution or a resolution passed by the board.

The buy back may be -

(a) from the existing security holders on a proportionate basis or

(b) from the open market or

(c) from odd lots, that is to say where the lot of securities in a listed public company is smaller than such marketable lot, as may be specified by the stock exchange or

(d) by purchasing securities issued to employees of the company pursuant to a scheme of stock option or sweat equity.

After passing special resolution or the Board has passed the resolution to buy back its own shares or other securities, the company before making such buyback file with the Registrar and the Securities and Exchange Board of India a declaration of solvency in the form as may be prescribed and verified by an affidavit to the effect that the Board has made a full inquiry into the affairs of the company, as a result of which they have formed an opinion that, it is capable of meeting its liabilities and will not be rendered insolvant within a period of one year of the date of declaration adopted by the Board, and signed at least by two directors of the company, one of whom shall be the Managing Director, if any. No declaration of solvency shall be filed with the Securities and Exchange Board of India by a company whose shares are not listed on any recognised stock exchange.

Where a company buy back its own securities, it shall extinguish and physically destroy the securities so bought back within seven days of the last date of completion of buyback.

The company once completes a buyback of its shares and other securities, then it shall not make further issue of the same kind of shares or other specified securities within a period of six months, except by way of bonus issue in the discharge of subsisting obligations such as, conversion of warrants, stock option schemes, sweat equity or conversion of preference shares or debentures into equity shares.

The company shall, after the completion of the buy back, file with the Registrar and the Securities and Exchange Board of India, a return containing such particulars relating to the buy back within thirty days of such completion, as may be prescribed. However, no return shall be filed with the Securities and Exchange Board of India by a company, whose shares are not listed on any recognised stock exchange.

If a company makes default in completing with these provisions, the company or any officer of the company who is in default shall be punishable with imprisonment for a term which may extend to two years or with fine which may extend to fifty thousand rupees or with both.

B) Prohibition for buy back in certain circumstances.

No company shall, directly or indirectly purchase its own shares or other specified securities -

a) through any subsidiary company including its own subsidiary companies ; or

b) through any investment company or group of investment companies or

c) if a default, by the company, in repayment of deposit or interest payable thereon, redemption of debentures, or preference shares or payment of dividend to any shareholder or repayment of any term loan or interest payable thereon, to any financial institution or bank, is subsisting.

No company shall directly or indirectly purchase its own shares or other specified securities, in case such company has not complied with the provisions of the act -

i) failed to prepare and file annual return with the Registrar

ii) failed to distribute dividend within 30 days

iii) failed to secure compliance by the company in respect of any account laid before the company in general meeting.

Transfer of certain sums to capital redemption reserve account.

Where a company purchases its own shares out of free reserves, then a sum equal to the nominal value of the share so purchased shall be transferred to the capital redemption reserve account and the details of such transfer shall be disclosed in the balance sheet.

Secretarial Practice for buy-back : A company should follow the following procedure for buy-back.

1) Check provision in Articles if buy-back is allowed. If not Articles have to be amended by a special resolution.

2) Decide policy of buy-back and get the same approved by BOD.

3) Inform stock exchange if company is listed.

4) Arrange general meeting or EOGM of members. Notice should contain proposed resolution and explanatory statement as prescribed u/s 77A (3) and also as per SEBI a declaration of solvency in the form and verified by an affidavit that Board has made full enquiry into affairs of the company and have formed an opinion that it is capable of meeting its liabilities and will not be rendered insolvent within a period of one year of the date of declaration.

5) The declaration should be adopted by Board of Directors and should be signed by two directors, out of which one should be Managing Director, if any. If company is not listed, such declaration should be filed only with ROC and filing with SEBI is not required.

6) The declaration of solvency should be in form 4A.

7) The securities bought back must be physically destroyed.

8) Company should maintain a register showing. 'Securities bought back', consideration paid for securities for buying back, Date of cancellation of securities, Date of extinguishing and physcially destroying the security, Other details as may be prescribed. The register shall be in form 4B.

9) After completion of buy-back, a return has to filed with ROC and SEBI within 30 days giving details as prescribed. If the company is not listed, filing details with SEBI is not required. The return should be in form 4C.

10) If company is unable to complete buy back within the specified period, reasons for the failure should be given in the report of Board of Directors to the members.

11) Listed companies should follow procedure prescribed by SEBI, which is in addition to above procedures. An unlisted company or private company has to follow procedures prescribed in Private Limited Company and Unlised Public Limited Company (buy back of Securities) Rules, 1999.

C) Accounting entry after buy-back shares : The security can be bought back from free reserves, securities premium account or proceeds of any shares or other specified securities. If the buy-back is from free reserves, a sum equal to nominal value of shares purchased will be transferred to capital redemption reserve account. After such transfer, nominal share capital will be reduced and capital redemption reserve account will be increased to the extent of nominal value of shares purchased under buy-back. Details of such transfer will be discloed in the balance sheet of the company. This entry is mandatory only if purchase is from free reserves. In other words, if purchase is from securities premium account or proceeds of any shares or other specified security, such an entry is not mandatory. [Really, such entry is required in all instances, as issued share capital gets reduced to the extent of shares bought back.]

The capital redemption reserve account is treated as paid up share capital of the company for purpose of reduction in share capital. However, fully paid bonus shares can be issued out of capital redemption reserve account.

Actual payment to shareholder will be more than nominal value of share. The nominal value will be debited to share capital account and thus share capital will be reduced to that extent. The amount paid above the nominal value will be debited to free reserves / security premium account/ proceeds from security from which the payment is made. Expenses incurred on buy-back should be allowed as business expenditure.

4.2.2 Issue of Sweat Equity Shares (Sec. 54)

A) Meaning : Sec. 2(88) "SES means such equity shares as are issued by a company to its directors or employees at a discount or for consideration, other than cash for porviding their know-how or making available rights in the nature of intellectual of properly rights or value additions, by whatever name called."

Sweat Equity to directors and employees - An employee or director works best when he has 'sense of belonging.' He will put in his best if he is amply rewarded. One way of rewarding him is by offering him shares of the company where he is working. This will give him more incentive to work as he will be indirectly participatng in the profits made due to efforts of himself and his colleagues. He develops keen interest in growth of company, as company grows and prospers, his stock value also goes up. This increases his interest and commitment to work. They develop feeling of 'participation' in management.

The offer of equity in company also encourages employees to join a new and relatively unknown company give his know-how. In absences of such incentive, a person may not be willing to leave job in a big and reputed company and join a relatively new and unknown company.

With this idea, the modern trend is to offer equity at low prices to employees and directors, inserted w.e.f. 31st Octorber, 1998, makes provision of issue of such' 'sweat equity' to directors of employees. It is termed as 'sweat equity' as it is earned by 'sweat' by employees (i.e. by hard work). Though it is terned as 'sweat equity' the employees become happy and hence it is 'sweat equity' for them.

B) Provisions

The provisions are as follows :

1) 'Sweat Equity Shares' means equity shares issued by company to its employees or directors at a discount or for consideration other than cash.

2) The 'consideration other than cash' may be for providing know-how or making available rights in the nature of intellectual property rights or value additions, by whatever name called. Thus, the right may be 'Patent' or 'Copyright' or it may be similar to patent or copyright.

3) Shares of a class which have already been issued only can be issued as 'Sweat Equity Shares.'

4) Issue of 'sweat equity shares' should be authorised by a special resolution by the company in general meeting. The resolution should specify number of shares, current market price, consideration, if any and class or classes of directors or employees to whom the 'sweat equity shares' may be issued.

5) The sweat equity shares can be issued only one year after the company was entitled to commence business.

6) If the company is listed on stock exchange 'sweat equtiy' shares can be issued as

per regulations made by SEBI. If company is not listed on stock exchange, sweat equity shares will be issued is accordance with guidelines of Central Government.

7) A subsidary of an Indian company can issue sweat equity to Indian employees, even if the subsidiary is incorporated out of India.

8) The 'sweat equity shares' have same limitations, restrictions and rights as are applicable to other equity shares.

Income Tax Aspects - As per explanation to section 17(2)(iii) of Income Tax Act, value of benefit provided by a company free of cost or at concessional rate to its employee by way of allotment of shares, debentures or warrants directly or indirectly under the Employee's Stock option Plan or Scheme approved by Central Government will not be treated as perquisite. However, if the person sales the security, he will have to pay capital gains.

As per section 47(iii) of Income Tax Act, transfer of shares obtained under ESOP as per scheme approved by Central Government, by a will or gift will be liable to capital gains. The amendment will apply w.e.f. 1-4-2001, i.e. for AY 2001-2002 and subsequent years. [This provision was made to plug loophole where shares received under ESOP were transferred by gift or will to avoid capital gains.]

C) SEBI Guidelines with respect to Sweat Equity

SEBI Guidelines dated 24.9.2002, *inter alia,* provide for the following :

1. Issue of Sweat Equity Shares to Promoters

  (i) In case of issue of sweat equity shares to promoters, the same must also be approved by simple majority of the shareholders in general meeting. Voting for the purpose should be through postal ballot and the allottee promoters should not participate in voting for such resolution.

 (ii) Each transaction of issue of sweat equity shall be voted by a separate resolution.

(iii) Resolution for issue of sweat equity shares shall be valid for not more than 12 months from the date of its passing.

(iv) The explanatory statement shall contain details specified in the Schedule.

2. Pricing of Sweat Equity Shares

The pricing of sweat equity shares has been brought at par with pricing in respect of allotment on preferential basis. viz, the price shall not be less than the higher of the following :

 (a) The average of the weekly high and low of the closing prices of the related equity shares during last 6 months preceding the relevant date; or

 (b) The average of the weekly high and low of the closing prices of the related equity shares during the two weeks preceding the relevant date.

'Relevant date' for this purpose means the date which is 30 days prior to the date on which the meeting of the general body of the shareholders is convened in terms of provision in the act.

If the shares are listed on more than one stock exchange, but quoted only on one stock exchange on the given date, the price on that stock exchange shall be considered. But, if the share price is quoted on more than one stock exchange, then the stock exchange where there is highest trading volume during that date shall be considered.

If shares are not quoted on the given date, then the share price on the next trading day shall be considered.

3. Valuation of Intellectual Property

The valuation of the intellectual property rights or of the know-how provided or other value addition shall be carried out by a merchant banker. The merchant banker may consult such experts and valuers, as he may deem fit having regard to the nature of the industry and the nature of the property or other value addition.

The merchant banker shall obtain a certificate from an independent chartered accountant that the valuation of the intellectual property or other value addition is in accordance with the relevant accounting standards.

4. Accounting Treatment

Where the sweat equity shares are issued for a non-cash consideration, such non-cash consideration shall be treated in the following manner in the books of account of the company,

(a) Where the non-cash consideration takes the form of a depreciable or amortizable asset, it shall be carried to the balance-sheet of the company as per the relevant accounting standards; or

(b) Where clause (a) is not applicable, it shall be expensed as per the relevent accounting standards.

5. Placing of Auditor's Certificate before AGM

In the AGM subsequent to the issue of sweat equity shares, the Board of Directors shall place before the shareholders, a certificate from the auditors of the company that the issue of sweat equity shares has been made in accordance with the regulations and in accordance with the resolution passed by the company authorising the issue of such sweat equity shares.

6. Ceiling on Managerial Remuneration

The amount of sweat equity shares issued shall be treated as part of managerial remuneration for the purposes of provision in the act if the following conditions are satisfied.

(i) the sweat equity shares are issued to any director or manager; and (ii) they are issued for non-cash consideration, which does not take the form of an asset which can be carried to the balance sheet of the company in accordance with the relevant accounting standards.

7. Lock-in of Sweat Equity Shares

(i) The sweat equity shares shall be locked in for a period of 3 years from the date of allotment.

(ii) SEBI (Disclosure and Investor Protection) Guidelines, 2000 on public issue in terms of lock-in and computation of promoters' contribution shall apply, if a company makes a public issue after it has issued sweat equity sahres.

8. Listing

The sweat equity shares issued by a listed company shall be eligible for listing only if such issue is in accordance with these regulations.

9. Applicability of Takeover Code

Any acquisitoion of sweat equity shares shall be subject to the provisions of SEBI (Substantial Acquisition of Shares and Takeover) Regulations, 1997.

10. Obligations of the Company

The company shall ensure that -

(a) Explanatory statement to the notice of the general meeting shall contain specified details.

(b) Auditor's certificate, as stated above, shall be placed in the general meeting,

(c) Within 7 days of the issue of sweat equity shares, a statement is sent to the recognized stock exchange disclosing;

- (i) number of sweat equity shares;
- (ii) price at which shares are issued
- (iii) total amount invested;
- (iv) details of persons to whom shares are issued; and
- (v) consequent changes in the capital structure and the shareholding pattern after and before the issue of sweat equity shares.

11. Action against Intermediaries

SEBI may, on failure of the merchant banker to comply with the obligations under these regulations or failing to observe due diligence in respect of valuation of intelletual property or value addition, initiate action against the merchant banker as per SEBI (Merchant Bankers) Regulations, 1992.

4.2.3 Employee Stock Option Scheme (ESOP)

A) Meaning

The expression has been defined in Section 2 (37) as follows

'Employees Stock Option' means the option given to the wholetime directors, officers, or employees of a company, which gives such directors, officers or employees the benefit or right to purchase or subscribe at a future date, the securities offered by the company at a pre-determined price.

'Option in Securities' has been given the same meaning as in Section 2 (d) of the Securities Contract (Regulation) Act 1956,

B) Employees Stock Option Scheme (ESOS) As amended by Notification dated 30.6.2003

1. No ESOS shall be offered unless the disclosures, as specified in Schedule IV, are made by the company to the prospective option grantees and the company constitutes a Compensation Committee for administration and superintendence of the ESOC.

1A. Issue of stock options at a discount to the market price would be regarded as another form of employee compensation and would be treated as such in the financial statements of the company, regardless of the quantum of discount on the exercise price of the options.

2. Subject to the aforesaid financial treatement ESOS would not be covered by the pricing provisions of SEBI's preferential allotment guidelines.

3. The issue of ESOS would be subject to approval by shareholders through a special resolution.

4. There would be no restriction on the maximum number of shares to be issued to a single employee. However, separate resolution in general meeting shall be obtained in case of: (a) employees being offered equal to or more than 1% shares during any one year, (b) grant of option to employees of subsidiary or holding company.

5. A minimum period of one year between grant of options and its vesting has been prescribed. After one year, the period during which the option can be exercised would be determined by the company. Company may specify a lock-in-period.

6. The operation of the ESOS scheme would have to be under the superintendence and directions of a Compensation Committee of the Board of Directors in which there would be a majority of independent directors.

7. ESOS would be open to all permanent employees (whether working in India or abroad) and to the directors (whole-time or part-time) of the company but not to (i) employer who in a promoter or belongs to the promoter group, (ii) a director who either by himself or through his relatives or through any body corporate holds more than 10% of the outstanding equity shares of the company. With the specific approval of the shareholders, the Scheme would be allowed to cover the employees of a subsidiary or a holding company.

8. Directors report shall contain the following disclosures.

(i) the total number of shares covered by the ESOS as approved by the shareholders;

(ii) the pricing formula;

(iii) options granted, options vested, options exercised , options forfeited, extinguishment or modification of options, money realised by exercise of options, total number of options in force, employee-wise details of options granted to senior managerial personnel and to any other employee who receives a grant in any one year of options amounting to 5% or more of options granted during that year.

(iv) Fully diluted earning per share (EPS) computed in accordance with international accounting standards.

9. Company may very the terms of ESOS by passing a special resolution provided variation :

(i) relates to options not yet exercised.

(ii) is not prejudicial to the interests of option holders.

Again, a company may reprice the options which are exercised if ESOSs were rendered unattractive due to fall in the price of the shares in the market. However, the company must ensure that such repricing shall not be detrimental to the interest of employees and approval of shareholders in General Meeting has been obtained for such repricing.

10. Option granted to an employee shall not be transferable to any person.

11. Options granted cannot be pledged, hypothecated, mortgaged or otherwise alienated in any other manner.

12. In the event of death, options granted to an employee shall vest in the legal successor / nominee.

13. In case of permanent incapacity, all options granted shall vest in him as on the date of incapacitation.

14. Auditor to certify that the scheme has been implemented as per guidelines. Certificate of the auditor to be placed at AGM.

4.3. APPLICATION AND ALLOTMENT OF SHARES (Sec.39)

When a company issues prospectus for inviting the public to subscribe to the shares of a company, it is an invitation. An application for shares is an offer by a prospective share holder to take shares when an application is accepted by the company, it is an allotment. Allotment creates a binding contract between the two parties.

Statutory Provisions

Under the Companies Act, private companies have no restrictions for allotment of shares and debentures. The act has prescribed certain restrictions regarding allotment of shares and debentures of public companies. These restrictions may be discussed as follows.

(A) When public offer is not made : A public company having a share capital which has not issued a prospectus or has issued a prospectus but has not proceeded to allot the shares, shall not make the first allotment of shares unless they delivered a statement in lieu of prospectus to the Registrar at least three days before the allotment.

If a company acts in contravention to this section, then every director of the company shall be punishable with fine which may extend to ten thousand rupees. The allotment shall be irregular and viodable at the option of the allottee.

(B) When public offer is made : The provisions relating to the allotment of shares and debentures in respect of a public company, is discussed as follows.

(i) Registration of Prospectus : The company must deliver a copy of the prospectus to the Registrar on or before the date of its publication. The prospectus must be signed by every person who is named therein as a director or proposed director of the company.

(ii) Minimum Subscription : No allotment shall be made of any share capital of a company, offered to the public for suscription, unless the amount stated in the prospectus as the minimum amount has been subscribed and the sum payable on the application has been paid and received by the company, in cash or by a cheque or other instrument.

The amount stated in the prospectus shall be reckoned exclusive of any amount payable otherwise than in money.

A company making any rights or public issue of shares or debentures must receive at least 90 percent subscription of the entire issue before making the allotment of shares or debentures to the public. If the minimum amount of 90 percent is not received, the entire amount collected shall be refunded to the applicants at the end of 120 days from the subscription list. If there is delay in refund of such amount by more than ten days, the company will pay interest at a rate of 15 percent per annum for the delayed period.

An allotment of shares made without the application money being paid is invalid and the directors are guilty of misfeasance.

(iii) Application Money : The amount payable on application on each share shall not be less than five percent of the nominal amount of the shares.

All money received from applicants for shares shall be deposited and kept in the Schedule Bank.

1) until certificate to commence the business is obtained.

2) where such certificate has already been obtained, until the entire amount payable on applications for shares in respect of the minimum subscription has been received by the company.

Any condition requiring any applicant for shares to wave compliance with any of these requirements shall be void.

If the minimum subscription is not subscribed within 120 days after the first issue of the prospectus, all moneys received from applicants for shares, shall be repaid without interest. If such money is not repaid within 130 days after the issue of the prospectus the directors of the company are jointly and severally liable to repay that amount with interest at the rate of six percent per annum from the expiry of 130 days. However, a director shall not be so liable if he proves that, the default in the repayment of the money was not due to any misconduct or negligence on his part.

iv) Statement in lieu of Prospectus : A company having a share capital, which does not issue a prospectus on its formation or which has issued a prospectus but has not proceeded to allot any of the shares offered to the public for subscription, shall not allot any of its shares or debentures unless at least three days before the first allotment of shares or debentures, there has been delivered to the Registrar a Statement in lieu of prospectus signed by all the directors or proposed director.

v) Opening and Closing of Subscription List : Where shares are offered by a prospectus, no allotment shall be made of shares and debentures until the beginning of the fifth day after the day on which the prospectus is issued allotment shall be made until the beginning of the fifth day after that on which such public notice is first given.

The prospectus shall be construed to have been issued on the day on which it is first issued as newspaper advertisement or if it is not so issued, from the date on which it is first issued in any other manner.

A company may proceed to allot shares soon after opening of the subscription list. According to the rules of stock exchanges, in case listed shares, the subscription list must be kept open at least for three days. However, the prospectus generally give the time when the subscription list will be closed.

The allotment of shares in contravention of these provisions stands as valid, but the company and every officer of the company who is in default shall be punishable with fine which may extend to fifty thousand rupees.

The application for shares or debentures of a company shall not be revocable until after the expiration of the fifth day after the time of the opening of the subscription lists.

vi) Allotment of shares and debentures to be dealt in Stock Exchange : Every company intending to offer shares or debentures to the public by the issue of a prospectus shall, before such issue, make an application to one or more stock exchanges for permission for the shares or debentures to be dealt with in the stock exchange.

Where a prospectus states that an application has been made for permission for the shares and debentures offered to be dealt with in stock exchanges such prospectus shall state the name of the stock exchange.

Any allotment made on an application in pursuance of such prospectus shall be void if the permission has not been granted by the stock exchange before the expiry of ten weeks from the date of closing of the subscription lists. Where an appeal against the decision of any recognised stock exchange refusing permission for the shares and debentures to be dealt with on that stock exchange has been deferred under section 22 of the Securities Contracts (Regulation) Act 1956, such allotment shall not be void until dismissal of the appeal.

If the application for permission made is not disposed off within the time specified in act then it shall be deemed that permission has not been granted.

Where the permission has not been applied under the act or such permission having been applied for, has not been granted, the company shall repay without interest all money received from applicants and if any such money is not repaid within eight days after the company became liable to repay it, the company and every director of the company shall, on the expiry of the eighth day, be jointly and severally liable to repay that money with interest from 4 to 15 percent as may be prescribed, having regard to the length of period of delay in making repayment of money.

Return of Excess Money where permission is granted.

Where permission has been granted by the recognised stock exchange for dealing in any shares or debentures in such stock exchange or each such stock exchange and the moneys received from applicants for shares and debentures are in excess of the aggregate of the application moneys relating to the shares and debentures for which allotment have been made, the company shall repay the moneys to the extent of such excess without interest, and if such money is not repaid within eight days from the day the company becomes liable to pay.

The company and every officer of the company who is in default shall be punishable with fine upto Rs.50,000/-, and where repayment is not made within six months from the expiry of the eighth day, also with imprisonment for a term which may exceed to one year.

All money to be kept in a Schedule Bank

All moneys received by application shall be kept in a separate bank account maintained with a Scheduled Bank -

1) Until the permission has been granted or

2) Where an appeal has been preferred against the refusal to grant such permission, until the disposal of the appeal. Where the permission has not been applied for as foresaid or has not been granted, the money standing in the separate account shall be repaid within time.

Utilisation of Money kept in Separate Account.

Money standing to the credit of the separate bank account, shall not be utilised for any purpose other than the following.

a) Adjustment against allotment of shares.

b) for repayment of money received from applicants, when the company is unable to make the allotment either because stock exchange permission could not be obtained or for any other reason.

Any agreement or condition that the applicant for shares or debentures will wave any non compliance with the provisions of act will be void.

vii) Return as to allotments : Whenever a company having a share capital makes any allotment of its shares, the company, shall within thirty days, file with the Registrar a Statement known as 'Return as to allotment.'

The return shall contain -

a) the number and nominal amount of the shares allotted for cash, the names addresses and occupations of allottees and the amount paid on each share.

b) particulars about the shares (not being bonus shares) allotted as fully or partly paid - up, for any consideration other than cash.

c) Particulars about the number and nominal amount of bonus shares and their allottees

d) A copy of the resolution passed by the company authorizing issue of the shares at a discount and a copy of the Tribunal sanctioning the issue.

Where the maximum rate of discount exceeds ten percent, a copy of the order of the Central Government permitting issue at the higher percentage.

4.4 CALLS ON SHARES

When shares are issued the full amount of each share is not paid at once. A part of it is paid at the time of application and a part on allotment and the remaining amount whenever called for. A call may be defined as a demand by the company on its shareholders to pay the part or balance remaining unpaid on the shares. The call may be made at any time to the company whenever the company calls for it or by the liquidator during the course of winding up of the company.

The Companies Act provides the following provisions in respect of calls on shares.

i) Resolution of the Board : The call must be made under a resolution of the Board of Directors passed at a meeting of the board.

ii) Amount, Place and Time of Payment : The resolution passed for making call must specify the amount of the call, the time and place of payment and to whom the call is to be paid.

iii) Bonafide and for the Benefit of the Company : The power to make calls is in the nature of trust to be exercised for the benefit of the company. If it is exercised for the benefit of directors, then it is malafied and it can be prevented by an injunction or the directors may be compelled to handover the benefit or advantage gained by them.

iv) Uniform Basis : The call must be made on uniform basis. A call cannot be made on some of the members only. A call must be made on a uniform basis on all shares falling in the same class.

v) Calls in Advance : If a company is authorised by its Articles, can accept advance payment from any shareholder in respect of the shares held by him. But for such payments the company has to pay interest as the shareholder becomes creditor of the company. On account of such payments, shareholders cannot claim extra voting rights. The power of directors to accept calls in advance must be exercised bonafide. Call may not be made until the company becomes entitled to commence business. Call must be paid in cash. If a person fails to pay money on calls for six months, he will be disqualified from holding the office of a director.

4.5 SHARE CERTIFICATES (Sec. 46)

1) every person whose name is entered as a member in the register of members shall be entitled to receive within three months after allotment or within two months after the application for the registration of transfer,

a) One certificate for all his shares without payment or

b) Several Certificates, each for one or more of his shares, upon payment of one rupee for every certificate after the first.

2) Every certificate shall be under the seal and shall specify the shares to which it relates and the amount paid up thereon.

3) In respect of any share on shares held jointly by several persons, the company shall not be bound to issue more than one certificate and delivery of a certificate for a share to one of several joint holders shall be sufficient delivery to all such holders.

Every company shall deliver within three months after the allotment of the shares and within two months to the transferee of making of the application for the registration of transfer of shares, debentures or debenture stock, subject to any proceedings pending before the court, tribunal or other authority.

If the company applies to the central government then the time period may be extended up to nine months. to deliver certificates.

A certificate under the common seal of the company, specifying any shares held by any member, shall be prima facie evidence of the title of the member to such shares.

A certificate may be renewed or a duplicate of a certificate may be issued if such certificate -

a) is proved to have been lost or destroyed or

b) having been defaced or mutilated or torn is surrendered to the company .

A small fee is charged on renewal of a Share Certificate or on issue of a duplicate certificate.

Where a company with intent to defraud renews a certificate or issues a duplicate thereof, the company would be punishable with fine which may extend to ten thousand rupees and every officer of the company who is in default shall be punishable with imprisonment for a term which may extend to six months on with fine which may extend to one lakh rupees or with both.

A share certificate of a company creates two kinds of estoppel against the company.

I) Estoppel as to the title and II) Estoppel as to payment. Hence, the company cannot dispute about the title of the registered holder and also in respect of payment for shares.

Share Warrant

A share warrant is a document issued under the common seal of the company stating that the bearer is entitled to the shares specified therein. A share warrant is a bearer document and is transferable by mere delivery. The share warrants are negotiable instruments.

A public company limited by shares, if so authorised by its articles, may, with the previous approval of the Central Government, where shares are fully paid, may issue share warrants. Such warrants should contain the number of shares for which they are issued. A warrant must state that the bearer is entitled to shares specified in it. The company may provide coupons or otherwise, for the payment of future dividends on the shares specified in the warrant.

When the share warrant is issued, the name of the member is struck out of the register of members and the following details are entered in it.

a) the fact of issue of warrant

b) a statement of the shares specified in the warrant, distinguishing each share by its number and

c) the date of the issue of the warrant

The bearer of a share warrant shall, subject to the articles of the company, be entitled, on surrendering the warrant for cancellation and paying such fee to the company as the Board of Directors may from time to time determine, to have his name entered as a member in the register of members. The bearer of a share warrant may, if the articles of the company so provide, be deemed to be a member of the company, though he is not strictly a member as his name is not entered in the register.

The bearer of a Share Warrant may deposit the warrant at the office of the company and so long his warrant is deposited with the company, can enjoy his rights.

A bearer of share warrant is not entitled to sign a requisition for calling a meeting of the company or attend or vote or exercise any other privilege of a member at a meeting of the company or be entitled to receive any notice from the company. However, the bearer of a share warrant shall be entitled to in all other respects to the same privilege and advantages as if he were named in register of members as the holder of the shares included in the warrant and he shall be a member of the company.

If default is made in complying with any of the requirements, the company who is in default shall be punishable with fine which may extend to five hundred rupees for every day during which the default continues.

Reconversion of warrants into shares

A share warrant may, at any time, be surrendered by the holder to the company for cancellation, and his name can again be entered in the register of members, subject to the provisions in the articles and on payment of the fee prescribed by the Board of Directors for this purpose is paid.

In the event of such conversion, if the company enters the name of a bearer of share warrant in respect of the shares therein specified, without the warrant being surrendered and cancelled, the company shall be responsible for any loss that may be occasioned to any person in this regard.

On surrender of the share warrant, the date of the surrender shall be entered in the register of members.

The bearer of a share warrant is not a member of the company. However, if company's Articles of association so provide, he may be treated as a member of the company for any purpose defined in the Articles. Thus, the Articles may provide that the bearer of a share warrant shall be allowed to exercise the rights of a member, such as attending meetings, approving annual accounts, appointing directors, etc. But, having regard to the express provisions of the artciles of a company cannot provide that the shares specified in a share warrant may be considered as qualification share for the office of a director.

Distinction between share warrant and share certificate

SHARE WARRANT	SHARE CERTIFICATE
1) A Share warrant can be issued only by public companies.	A share certificate can be issued by both public and private companies.
2) It can be issued by a public company only if it is empowered to do so by its Articles and has obtained prior approval of the Central Government.	There is statutory obligation on every company issuing shares to issue share certificate. No need to obtain such power from Articles or the Central Govt.
3) It can be issued only when shares are fully paid up.	A share certificate can be issued at any stage without the shares being fully paid up.
4) A holder of share warrant is not a member of the company unless the articles provide otherwise.	A holder of share certificate is a member company.
5) A share warrant is by mercantile usage a negotiable instrument.	A share certificate is not a negotiable instrument.
6) A share warrant can be transferred by mere delivery and no registration of transfer with the company is required	The shares can be transferred by execution of transfer deed and its delivery along with the share certificate. The transfer is complete only when it is registered by the company.
7) There is no stamp duty to be paid on transfer of share warrant.	Stamp duty is payable on transfer of shares, as specified in share certificate.
8) A share warrant does not need holding of qualification shares by a director.	A director is required to hold certain qualification shares.

9) A share warrant is the security of share itself transformed for the purpose of negotiation into a different character.	A share certificate is a document showing prima facie title to the shares repre sented by it.
10) The holder of share warrant cannot present a petition for winding up of the company.	The holder of share certificate can present a petition for the winding up of the company.
11) Dividend due on share warrant is advertised in news papers and is payable to the holder of dividend warrant on presentation of relevant coupon attached to the share warrant.	Dividend is paid to the holder of share certificate by the issue of dividend warrant in his favour.

4.6 SHARE CAPITAL (Sec. 43)

Meaning of Capital and share capital :

The term capital is used in a variety of meanings. In case of companies the term share capital is used to mean the capital raised by the issue of shares.

Various classes of capital of a Joint Stock Company

Share capital is the capital raised by a company through issue of shares. It is regarded as a own source of finance. Only companies limited by shares and registered with a share capital have the authority of raising capital through issue of shares.

Share capital can be received either at the time of the formation of the company for commencing the business or subsequently for the expansion of business.

Capital structure refers to the division and sub-division of capital into different kinds of shares through which the company is authorised to raise its capital.

Form/Classification of Capital is given below:

1) Authorised Capital - Sec. 2(8)

This is also known as Nominal or Registered Capital. This is the capital with which the company is registered and this is the limit beyond which the company cannot raise capital unless the capital clause of the Memorandum of Association is not altered.

The stamp to be affixed on Memorandum of Association before filing the same with Register of Company is calculated on the basis of this capital. This is a nominal capital and hence not a liability of the company.

2) Issued Capital - Sec. 2(50)

The capital which is issued by the company for subscription by the public is known as Issued Capital. If a company is registered with 10,000 Equity shares of Rs. 10 each and decides to issue 5,000 Equity shares, then its Authorised capital is Rs. 1,00,000 and issued capital is Rs. 50,000. This too is not a liability of the company.

3) Subscribed Capital - Sec. 2(86)

The Capital for the subscription of which applications have been received by the company is known as Subscribed Capital. If the applications are received in excess of issued capital the issue is applications are received in excess of issued capital the issue is said to be over subscribed and if applications received are less than the shares issued, such situation is called under subscription.

4) Called-up Capital - Sec. 2(15)

The capital which company calls from the applicants is known as Called-up Capital. Generally, capital is collected stage wise such as Application stage, Allotment Stage, First/ Second call, etc.

5) Uncalled Capital

The Company may not require the full amount of the subscribed capital and therefore, it may call up only a part of the capital subscribed and the part which has not been called up is called 'Uncalled Capital'. It may be agreed by the shareholders by a special resolution that full or part amount of uncalled capital shall be called up only on liquidation. In such a case the uncalled capital becomes Reserved Capital.

6) Paid-up Capital - Sec. 2(64)

The capital which actually has been paid by the shareholders is knowon as Paid-up Capital and is certainly the liability of the company as the company owes this capital to the shareholders and at the time of winding up the shareholders have a right to claim back the amount.

The terms 'Calls in Arrears' and 'Calls in advance' are related to the concept of 'Paid-up Capital'. **'Calls in Arrears'** are those calls which the shareholders have not paid in spite of making calls on them. **'Calls in Advance'** refers to those payment received from shareholders even if call is not made on them.

7) Reserved Capital - Sec. 65)

It is that part of the uncalled capital of the company which the company has decided by special resolution not to call except in the event of the company being wound up. The company cannot demand the payment of money on the shares to that extent during its life-time. Reserve capital may be created by means of a special resolution passed in its general meeting.

When once the reserve capital has been so created, it cannot be charged or mortgaged as security for any loan raised by the company and it cannot be called up. The reserve capital should not be confused with capital reserve which is created out of profits.

SHARE CERTIFICATE

CABLE AND WIRELESS LIMITED

Regd. Office :

Naulakha, Maksi Road, Dist. Ujjain (M.P.)

This is to certify that the person(s) named in this certificate is/are the Registered Holder(s) of the within mentioned Share(s) bearing the distinctive number(s) herein specified in the above Company subject to the Memorandum and Articles of Association of the Company and that the amount endorsed hereon has been paid up on each such share.

Equity Share, Each of................................	Rs. 10
Amount Paid up Per Share...........................	Rs. 5

(Authorised

Signatory)   Calls paid : 1st Call (Date)..... Rs. 2.50

2nd Call (Date).............. Rs.2.50

Regd. Follo No. SKGO 34   Certificte No. 41732

Name(s) of Holder(s)........... Mr. Sivkumar Ghosh

No. of Shares held................ Twenty-five (25)

Distinctive No.(s)................. 146601 to 146625

Given under the Common Seal of the Company this 25th Day of September, 2009

Company's
Seal

```
Revenue
Stamp
```

G. C. Bangar   A.K. Sen
Director   Director

For Cable and Wireless Limited

R. C. Sharma

Secretary

(Counterfoil)

No......................

Name ....

Address ....

Description ....

For .... Shares

Number .... to ....

Date of Certificate ....

Date on which delivered ....

Entered in the Register of Members

Folio ....

Capital of the Company :107

SHARE WARRANT

SHARE WARRANT TO BEARER

The......... Company Limited

(Incorporated under the Companies Act, 1956)

Stamp

Share Warrant No.........

This is to certify that the Bearer of this warrant is the proprietor of......... fully paidup Shares of Rs......... each. numbered......... to......... inclusive, in the......... Co. Ltd., subject to the Articles of Assciation of the Company and other conditions endorsed hereon.

Given under the Common Seal of the Company this......... day of.........2009.

.... Director

.... Director

Seal

.... Secretary

(Counterfoil)

No.........

The............ Co. Ltd.

For......... Shares

Numbered......... to......... inclusive.

No. of Certificate.........

Issued to.........

of.........

Date 2009

Register of Member Folio.........

Warrant No.........

Dividend Coupon No. 2

On......... shares included in

the Share Warrant numbered as above, payable according to advertsement to be issued by the Company.

Rs......... Secretary

Warrant No.........

Dividend Coupon No. 1

On......... shares included in

the Share Warrant numbered as above, payable according to advertsement to be issued by the Company.

Rs......... Secretary

QUESTIONS

A) Answer in 20 words

1) What is mean by 'Buy-back of Shares?
2) What do you mean by 'Sweat Equity Shares'?
3) Define 'Employee stock option.'
4) What do you mean by 'Consideration other than Cash ?
5) State the sources for Buy-back of shares.

B) Answer in 50 words

1) From which sources a company can purchase its own shares/debentures.
2) State any two conditions of Buy-back of shares.
3) State the options allowed for Buy-back of share.
4) How 'Sweat Equity Shares' be given to Promoters
5) State lock - in of sweat equity shares.

C) Answer in 150 words

1) State the conditions for Buy-back of shares.
2) State the circumstances in which Buy-back is not allowed.
3) How accounting entry is made after Buy-back of share?
4) State the provisions in respect of issue of Sweat Equity Shares.
5) What is the provision regarding pricing of Sweat Equity Shares?

D) Answer in 300 words

1) Define 'Buy-back of share' , State the conditions of Buy-back of shares.
2) What is the secretarial procedure regarding Buy-back of shares
3) What is the meaing of 'Sweat Equity Shares? State its provision.
4) State SEBI Guidelines with respect of Sweat Equity Share.
5) Define 'ESOP', what are the amendments made by notification dated 30-06-2003.

Chapter 5

FORFEITURE SURRENDER AND TRANSFER OF SHARES

CONTENTS

5.1 Forfeiture of shares
5.2 Surrender of Shares
5.3 Transfer and Transmission of Shares
5.4 Nomination of Shares

5.1 FORFEITURE OF SHARES

If a shareholder having been called upon to pay any call on his share, fails to pay then the company may sue him to recover the amount of the call or if the articles of the company so provide, the company may forfeit the shares of the shareholder, who has made the default.

Forfeited shares becomes the property of the company and to that extent it involves a reduction of the company's capital.

The right to forefit shares should be pursued with great exactness by proper parties i.e.directors properly appointed, in proper manner and for proper cause. The right must be exercised bonafide for the purpose for which it is conferred, and in the interest of the company. The power of expulsion is a trust and it should be exercised carefully and honestly.

Provisions (Rules) Regarding Forfeiture

A company cannot forfeit shares for non-payment of calls unless it has taken that power by provisions in its Articles of Association. Regulations 29-35 of Table A of Schedule 1 of the Companies Act, which are usually incorporated in the Articles of most companies, make the following provisions for the forfeiture of shares :

(1) If a member fails to pay any call or installment of a call within the stipulated date, the Board of directors may serve a notice on him requiring payment together with interest. The shares can be forfeited only for non-payment of calls and not for any other debt due from the shareholder,

(2) The notice must specify a date, not earlier than 14 days from the date of service of the notice, on or before which the payment is to be made and must also state that failure to pay within that date will make the shares liable to forfeiture.

(3) If the requirements of the notice are not complied with, the shares in respect of which the notice was issued may be forfeited by a resolution of the Board.

(4) The forfeited shares may be sold or otherwise disposed off on such terms that the Board may think fit. At any time before such sale or disposal of the forfeited shares, the Board may cancel the forfeiture on such terms as it may think fit.

(5) A member whose shares have been forfeited shall cease to be a member of the company. But he will still remain liable to the company for the payment of the unpaid calls on those shares. His liability will cease if and when the company receives full payment of the moneys in respect of those shares.

(6) A company may receive the consideration given for the shares sold or disposed off after forfeiture and shall have the power to execute a transfer in favour of the person to whom the shares are sold. The transferee shall thereupon be registered as the holder of these shares.

(7) Any irregularities in the proceedings in respect of the forfeiture, sale or disposal of the forfeited shares will not affect the title of the transferee.

(8) The provisions of these regulations shall be applicable in case of non-payment of any amount, whether on account of nominal value or premium payable by virtue of a call duly made.

Procedure Regarding Forfeiture

The provisions of the above regulations laid down in the Articles must be followed rigidly while adopting the procedure regarding forfeiture. Otherwise, the forfeiture may be set aside as invalid. The list of defaulters prepared by the Secretary's office is placed before a board meeting. The Board then authorises the Secretary, by a resolution, to send call reminders to the defaulters, asking them to pay the call dues within a further period, with interest at a specified rate. The Board resolution also authorises the secretary to send a Warning Notice (final reminder), as laid down in the Articles, to the defaulters if the first reminder proves ineffective. In the Warning Notice, the defaulting members are asked to make payment within a period of 14 days from the date of the notice and they are warned that failure to pay within that period will make the shares liable to forfeiture. Extracts of the relevant portions of the Articles are enclosed with the notice for information.

If this notice also fails to produce any result, the company may, if it thinks fit, send another notice. Otherwise, on the expiry of the 14 days' time limit, the Board adopts the following resolution forfeiting the shares :

"Resolved that.....shares of Rs....each and numbered........ to ....inclusive, whereon Rs....per share have been paid, and which at the date of the resolution were standing in the name of...,....,.of......be, and they are hereby, forfeited for

non-paymentof call made on the............. day ....2009 and for non-payment of interest thereon, and that the said shares be disposed off as the directors think fit."

By adopting another resolution (given below) at the same meeting, the Board authorises the secretary to send the notice of forfeiture to the defaulting member, to give a public notice of the forfeiture in the newspapers and also to intimate the Stock Exchange(s) concerned of the fact :

"Resolved that a notice of forfeiture be sent by the Secretary by registered post (as per specimen approved at this meeting) to each shareholder in respect of his shares forfeited with a request to surrender the relevant share certificates to the company and that a public notice of the forfeiture be also published in the leading newspapers.

"Resolved further that the.......Stock Exchange be intimated the names of the defaulting shareholders along with the distinctive numbers of shares forfeited against each name."

After the above resolutions are adopted, a formal notice of forfeiture incorporating the resolution is sent by registered post to the defaulting member, asking him to surrender the forfeited shares to the company. A public notice of the forfeiture is also given in leading newspapers before these shares are reissued. Finally, the name of the defaulter is removed from the Register of Members and this completes the forfeiture procedure.

Effects of Valid Forfeiture

A forfeiture of shares will be valid only when the company is expressly empowered by its Articles to forfeit shares and the procedure laid down in the Articles for forfeiture of shares is properly followed. Any irregularity in the procedure will make the forfeiture invalid. Therefore, in order to be a valid forfeiture :

(a) the forfeiture must be against a proper cause, i.e, non-payment of amount due on calls;

(b) the forfeiture must be passed by a proper resolution adopted in a duly constituted Board meeting; and

(c) the forfeiture must be effected after giving proper notice to the defaulting shareholder, i.e., a warning notice or final reminder to the defaulter before the forfeiture resolution is passed and a notice of forfeiture is issued after passing the Board resolution.

When shares have been validly forfeited, it will have the following effects :

(1) The defaulting shareholder ceases to be a member of the company and his name is removed from the Register of Members.

(2) The defaulting shareholder loses all rights and interest in the forfeited shares. He loses his claim to the paid-up amount on his shares and cannot recover it. He is not entitled to future dividends on those shares, nor can he exercise any rights of membership.

(3) If the Articles so provide, he will still remain liable for the payment of the unpaid calls outstanding against his name at the time of forfeiture, for a period of three years from the date of forfeiture. But the company cannot recover from him more than the difference be-

tween the amount payable on the shares at the time of forfeiture and the amount received, if any, from the person to whom the shares have been re-issued.

(4) The event of winding up of the company the defaulting shareholder shall remain liable, as a past member, to contribute in respect of any debt or liability of the company contracted before he ceased to be a member. However, he will be so liable as a past member only when the winding up commences within one year of the cessation of his membership and the present members are unable to satisfy the contributions required to be made.

(5) After forfeiture, the forfeited shares will be transferred to a new account in the share ledger, known as 'Forfeited Shares Account', These will remain in this account till these are re-issued to a new shareholder.

Duties of the Secretary regarding Forfeiture of Shares

The steps to be taken by the secretary in connection with forfeiture of shares are given below :

(i) To consult the provisions of the Articles regarding forfeiture and follow them strictly, otherwise the forfeiture may become invalid.

(ii) To prepare a list of defaulters and place it before the Board meeting convened to consider it.

(iii) On being authorised by a Board resolution, to send Call Reminders to the defaulters asking them to pay the call dues within a specified period with interest.

(iv) If the first reminder fails to issue a Warning Notice under authority of the Board resolution and the Articles, asking the defaulters to pay the dues within 14 days from the date of the notice and warning them that failure to pay within that date will make the shares liable to forfeiture.

(v) If the warning notice also fails and on the expiry of 14 days, to see that a Board meeting is held to pass a resolution forfeiting the shares. To send a formal notice to the defaulting shareholder informing him of the forfeiture and asking him to surrender the forfeited shares. Also to arrange for public notification of the forfeiture, if necessary.

(vi) To strike off the name of the defaulter from the Register of Members.

Re-issue of Forfeited Shares

Shares forfeited by a company may be cancelled or re-issued to another person at the discretion of the Board of Directors. Usually such shares are re-sold or re-issued. As these shares are issued in small lots, the company usually issues them at a discount. But the discount should not exceed the amount already paid by the defaulted member on those shares.

To sanction the re-issue, the Board of Directors passes a resolution in the following terms:

"Resolved.....shares of Rs.....each, Rs...per share paid-up numbered....to........ having been duly forfeited by a resolution of the Board dated. ....2009 be re-issued as fully paid-up to....of.. ..on his paying Rs.....per share and that the said shares be, and they are hereby, passed for registration, and that a certificate for the shares in the name of.........be duly signed and sealed."

After the new allottee has paid the required amount, the company will have to execute a transfer and issue a share certificate to him. If the previous holder surrenders the share certificate, it is duly transferred to the new holder. But if the previous holder does not surrender the share certificate, the company gives a public notice in the newspaper that the respective shares have been forfeited for non-payment of calls. Thereafter, a new share certificate is issued to the new holder. To confirm the legal claim of the new member on these shares, the company not only gives him a receipt for the amount paid but also a declaration to that effect, signed by a director or the secretary. The declaration states the circumstances under which the shares were forfeited, the steps taken for the realisation of the unpaid calls prior to forfeiture and affirms that the unpaid calls were never received from the previous holder and that the said shares have been duly sold to the new holder. The secretary then enters the name of the new member in the Register of Members and he becomes a member of the company.

Annulment of Forfeiture

Sometimes, the defaulting shareholder approaches the company after the forfeiture of shares with the request to cancel the forfeiture. On receipt of such a request, the Board of Directors first fixes the terms under which the forfeiture may be cancelled. Usually, the defaulted member is asked to pay all the unpaid calls together with interest if he agrees to these terms, the Board passes a resolution sanctioning the cancellation of forfeiture and restoration of his name in the Register of Members. When the person concerned pays the dues, his name is re-entered in the Register of Members.

5.2 SURRENDER OF SHARES

Voluntarily return of shares to the company by the shareholder is called 'Surrender of Shares'. In this case shareholder himself returning the shares to the company because he is not in a position to pay the call money in time.

Surrender of shares can be accepted only when forfeiture is justified, it means non-payments of call money. In any other situation, no surrender of shares can be accepted as it leads to reduction of share capital without permission of court, which is illegal and hence invalid. It is a involuntarily transfer of shares. When a shareholder is unable to pay call money, he himself approaches the company to cancel his membership. When the forfeiture is justified then only surrender is accepted. Board of Directors can accept it.

A surrender of shares, when the forfeiture is justified and the shares are liable for such a forfeiture on account of non-payment of call, may be accepted by the board and is regarded as a valid surrender in the eyes of Law and under this special circumstance the formality of forfeiture may be set aside if the member voluntarily, surrender his shares. Such a surrender may be regarded as a short - cut to the forfeiture and the company may accept it to avoid the complicated procedure of the forfeiture of shares.

Acceptance of surrender of fully paid up shares is not possible, as it leads to reduction of share capital.

Even though, it is possible to accept surrender of fully paid-up shares if -

(i) the permission from the court is obtained, or

(ii) it is in exchange of another category of shares of equal face value, or

(iii) in case of redeemable preference shares.

Provisions (Conditions) of Valid Surrender

(1) Indian Companies Act does not have any provision for this. Therefore, the directors derive their power to accept the surrender from the expressed provisions in Articles.

(2) The effect of surrender of shares is reduction in share capital. The directors are therefore, not allowed to accept it unless sanction from the court is obtained and a special resolution to the effect is passed in the General Meeting of the Shareholders.

(3) The directors, however, can accept the surrender of only partly paid up shares provided the Articles so authorise. Acceptance of surrender of fully paid up shares is prohibited by the Indian Companies Act.

(4) Surrender of partly paid up shares is, at times, accepted as the directors may desire to avoid complicated and lengthy procedure of forfeiture in case of non-payment of calls on such shares. Thus surrender may be accepted as the short cut to forfeiture.

From the above discussion it is clear that forfeiture is completely different than surrender.

Secretarial Procedure Relating to Surrender of Shares

(i) **Verification of Provision in the Articles of Association :** the Articles of the company for the acceptance of surrender of shares. Acceptance of surrendered shares is not possible without such provision.

(ii) **Scrutiny of Application for Surrender :** The secretary has to study carefully the application for surrender of shares by the shareholder. He has to confirm that the shares are partly paid up shares and are liable for forfeiture.

(iii) **Board Meeting for Consideration and Approval of Surrender:** The secretary has to place the application for surrender of shares before the Board for consideration and approval. The Board usually approves the application as per the provisions in the Articles and makes suitable resolution to that effect.

(iv) **Intimation to Concerned Shareholder :** As per the resolution of the Board, the company secretary has to inform the shareholder that the Board has accepted the surrender of shares. He has to ask for shares certificate from the shareholder.

(v) **Removal/Concellation of Name from the Register of Members :** The secretary has to remove the name of the shareholder from the Register of members. This amounts to cancellation of membership of concerned member.

Forfeiture of Shares and Surrender of Shares: Difference

Sr. Point	Forfeiture of Shares	Surrender of Shares
(1) **Meaning :**	Forfeiture means the compulsory termination of membership and the taking away of the shares of such members by way of penalty for the non-payment of a fixed instalment call or premium.	Surrender of shares means voluntary return of shares by a member to the company for cancellation.
(2) **Reason :**	Due to non-payment of call money.	If a share holder may find it difficult to pay the calls on the shares, he may surrender the shares to the company. It takes place due to inability of the share-holders to pay the call money.
(3) **Initiative :**	The procedure of this is initiated by the company.	The procedure of this is initiated by the share-holders.
(4) **Time limit :**	The procedure of forfeiting the shares is time-consuming.	The procedure for surrender of shares requires comparatively less time
(5) **Compensation :**	The Company does not pay any Compensation on the shares forfeited.	The Company may allow refund of a part of the amount already paid on the surrendered shares.
(6) **Type of Shares :**	Forfeiture is possible only in the case of partly paid up shares.	Surrender is possible in the case of partly as well as fully paid up shares.
(7) **Procedure :**	Lengthy procedural formalities required.	Limited procedural formalities required.

Company's Right of Lien on Shares

Lien means the right to retain something belonging to another until the claims of the person in possession of the thing are satisfied. Under the provisions of their Articles of Association, most companies are entitled to exercise a right of lien on the shares which are in the possession of the company. Companies are also empowered by the Articles to sell such shares if the outstanding dues are not paid. For this purpose, 14 days' notice is required to be given to members. The sale proceeds are to be applied towards the payment of debts outstanding and the balance returned to the member concerned. The right of lien on shares can also be exercised in respect of dividends due on the shares. Thus, a company may withhold delivery of share certificates as well as withhold payment of dividend to members until outstanding calls due on the shares have been paid. Though the right of lien should apply also to fully paid shares for any kind of debt due from members, stock exchange regulations generally prohibit the exercise of the right of lien on fully paid listed shares. Hence, for all practical purposes, the right can be exercised only in respect of partly paid-up shares which are listed on any stock exchange.

Difference between Lien and Forfeiture

The main points of difference between lien and forfeiture are enumerated below :

1. A company can exercise its right of lien on shares in respect of debts due for unpaid calls or debts due on other accounts. But forfeiture of shares can be effected for debts due on the shares only.

2. Lien is a kind of security for a debt; the right to retain the shares until the debt in respect of which the lien is exercised is paid off. Forfeiture is a kind of penal measure for default of the member to make payment of the calls in time.

3. A lien is usually enforced by sale of the share. The Articles of most companies empower them to sell the shares under lien to recover the outstanding dues, if the debts are not paid. Forfeiture is the act of depriving the member of his right to the shares forfeited.

4. In the case of lien, the debt due from the member is deducted from the sale proceeds of the shares and the balance returned to the former owner of the shares. In the case of forfeiture, the member concerned (former owner of the shares) forfeits the amount already paid on the shares and cannot claim refund of the same.

5. Lien does not result in reduction of capital as the shares held under lien are sold to recover the amount of the debt. But forfeiture may result in reduction of capital, if the forfeited shares are not re-issued.

5.3 TRANSFER AND TRANSMISSION OF SHARES : (Sec. 56)

5.3.1 Transfer of Shares

Shares of a public company are transferable from one person to another. The procedure for transfer of shares is laid down in the articles of Association of each public company.

Transfer may take place for various reasons. eg. when the shares are sold or gifted by another person or legally by death, insolvency or insanity of the member. A share is a movable and personal property. The shareholder has a right to sell or give away his shares as a gift.

The person who transfers his shares is known as transferrer and the one who receives the shares is known as transferee. The transfer of shares must be registered with the company. The shares of a private company are not transferable. The transferability of shares of a private company is restricted by its Articles.

Due to transfer, the name of the transferrer will be removed from the register of members and the name of transferee will be added in his place.

The Directors are empowered to reject the transfer on the following grounds :
(1) Transfer to Minor.
(2) Transfer to person of unsound mind.
(3) Where there is calls in arrears.
(4) If the instrument of transfer is not being duly signed.
(5) Any other reason which the directors think fit.

Provisions regarding Transfer of Shares

(1) A Company Shall not register a transfer unless a proper Instrument of Transfer, duly stamped and executed by the transferrer as well as the transferee has been delivered to the company. It must be accompanied by the relevant share certificate or letter of allotment.

(2) The application for transfer of shares should be made in the prescribed form by the transferrer or the transferee.

(3) If the transferrer makes an application for transfer of partly paid shares, the company gives a notice to the transferee regarding this transfer. If the transferee makes no objection on this within two weeks from the date and receipt of notice, then the company registers the transfer. This is so because the transferee will be liable to pay calls to be made by the Company to give notice to the transferee.

(4) If the board has decided to accept the transfer, the relevant share certificate should be completed for delivery and delivery should be made within 2 months of receipt of application for transfer.

(5) The Directors have the power to refuse the registration of transfer in the interest of the company. In such a case, the company must send the Notice of refusal to the transferrer and the transferee within 2 months of date of receipt of instrument of Transfer. Failure by the company in this case will make the company and its officers liable to penalty. The transferrer or transferee can make an appeal to the Central Government against the decisions of the Board. The appeal must be made within 2 months and must be accompanied with requisite fee not exceeding Rs. 50/-.

(6) The Central Government gives notice to the company, the transferrer and the transferee. After hearing their contentions, it issues orders directing the company to register the transfer or otherwise.

(7) If the Government directs and registers the transfer it must be given effect to by the company within 10 days of receipt of order. Otherwise the company and every officer of the company who is in default is liable to penalty.

Steps for Transfer of Shares

The following are the steps of transfer of share.

(1) The shareholder gets the prescribed transfer form and gets the date stamped by the Registrar of companies.

(2) Then he completes it by executing it, making entries into, it signing it before a witness who attests the former's signature.

(3) After the receipt of the instrument of transfer by or on behalf of the transferee, the particulars in respect of the transfree are entered into it. Then the same is signed by the transferee or on his behalf under the attestation of a witness.

(4) The instrument is then duly executed and stamped on the basis of the market price of shares.

(5) Then it is submitted to the company, enclosed with the relevant share certificates.

(6) The prescribed registration fee, stamp duly are paid generally by the transferee while delivering the instrument to the company.

(7) The company secretary has to scrutinise closely and to see whether the instrument is duly executed and properly stamped and whether registration fee has been paid as per requirements.

(8) The secretary, after being satisfied on these articles and the documents, issue to the transferee, the formal transfer receipt (in exchange of the Receipt) which acknowledges the receipt of the instrument of transfer for registration subject to the approval of the board of directors. It also states that the new share certificates will be ready for delivery against the presentation of the transfer receipt in a month from the date thereof.

(9) Then secretary proceeds to despatch Notice of lodgement of transfer to the transferrer and transferee which states that the instrument for the transfer has been lodged with the company and that objection to the proposed transfer should be conveyed to the company within a period of two weeks from the receipt of the notice. If no objection is received from either of them, the details of the documents are checked once again. If the secretary is satisfied, as endorsement in favour of the transferee is made on the reverse side of the share certificate. Hereafter, necessary entries are made in the transfer register.

(10) Then the secretary makes an arrangement for convening a board meeting. This meeting considers, decides and approves or rejects the transfer of shares in respect of instrument of transfer placed before it.

Procedure for Transfer of Shares (In physical form)

The procedure for transfer of shares can be divided into two broad categories, viz;
(i) Procedure for Transfer of All Shares included in the Share Certificate (Total Transfer of

Shares) and (ii) Procedure for Transfer of Part of the Shareholdings (Partial Transfer of Shares)

(i) Procedure for Transfer of All Shares included in the Share Certificate (Total Transfer of Shares)

    (a) The Shareholder has to obtain prescribed application form of transfer from the company duly stamped with the date of issue from the Registrar of the company.

    (b) The Shareholder after writing the detailed information in the columns of the form, get the instrument executed, stamped and withnessed properly.

    (c) The instrument of transfer is, then, sent to the transferee, along with share certificate. The transferee completes the instrument with necessary details and also signs the same. He has to get it witnessed. The instrument, then, needs to be deposited with the company.

    (d) On receipt of the instrument of transfer, the secretary after making thorough scrutiny of all the documents, issues a receipt of the instrument of transfer called 'Transfer Receipt' to the transferrer of shares.

    (e) Thereafter, a notice will be issued to both the transferrer and transferee about the receipt of the instrument and also asking them to communicate their objections (if any) to the proposed transfer within two weeks. This notice is called 'Notice of Lodgement of Transfer'.

    (f) If objections are not received from both the parties within a period of two weeks, it will be assumed that both are willing for the proposed transfer.

    (g) The Secretary than, goes ahead with the registration of transfer by com pleting all the necessary formalities, such as, entering the details of transfer in the 'Transfer Register', placing the necessary documents before the Board of Directors for approval etc.

    (h) The Board will study all the documents, and if satisfied, passes a resolution approving the transfer and authorising the secretary to issue new certificate in place of the old or cancelled certificate.

(ii) Procedure for Transfer of Part of the Shareholdings (Partial Transfer of Shares):

(A) Certification Stage :

    (a) The transferrer obtains the prescribed transfer form and gets the endorsement of date of presentation on it from the Registrar of Companies.

    (b) It is then executed by the transferrer mentioning the total number of shares and the distinctive number of shares to be transferred.

    (c) The instrument of transfer and the share certificate are sent to the company with request to certify the transfer.

    (d) The Secretary after scrutiny of the documents puts a certification stamp and his signature.

    (e) The share certificate is then stamped with the word 'cancelled'.

(f) All the details are then, entered on the back side of the share certificate. The company may maintain a separate register of certified transfers.

(g) The secretary then prepares a Balance Ticket in the name of the transferrer for shares to be retained in his name and is issued to the transferrer to be exchanged for the share certificate.

(B) Registration Stage :

(a) The secretary then enters all the particulars and issues a Transfer Receipt to the transferee to be exchanged for a share certificate.

(b) The instrument of transfer is stamped with registration stamp and the share certificate is cancelled after making entries in Register of Transfer.

(c) The Secretary then issues lodgement notice to the transferrer and transferee and undertakes the work of preparing two share certificates, one in the name of the transferrer for the number of shares retained which is exchanged for the Balance Ticket. Another for the number of shares transferred in the name of the transferee which is exchanged for the transfer-receipt.

Transfer of shares under depository system

Meaning of Depository System

Under depository system, otherwise known as Book Entry Transfer System, transfer of ownership of securities in exchange for payment takes place by means of book entry without the physical movement of scrips, It is a new clearing and settlement system. Under this system, the current practice of holding and moving scrips of quoted shares is replaced by a safe and dependable computerised book-entry system. In other words, there is no more need for delivery and receipt of scrips.

Dematerialisation and Immobilisation of Securities

There are two basic types of depository models 'dematerialisation' and ' immobilisa-tion'. In case of dematerialisation, there is no physical scrip in existence. The depository only maintains the electronic ledger of shares and debentures. All new issues are posted directly to the depository records by the issuer. It is economical in implementation and simple and efficient in operation. In case of immobilisation, physical scrips are held in depository vaults sup-ported by book entry records kept on the computer. Under this system, it is possible to take physical possession of the scrips. But the depository system provides for transfer of ownership of securities in exchange on payment by book entry on its ledgers without any physical movement of scrips. Accounts of new as well as existing securities are maintained on computers.

Shares in the Depository Mode shall Cease to have Distinctive Numbers

An investor, who opts for a depository mode, may, at any time, opt to choose out of it and claim Share Certificate from the company by substituting his name as the registered owner in the place of the depository.

Under the Depository System, the ownership changes will be a regular, mandatory flow of information about the details of ownership in the depository's record to the company concerned. An important right has been preserved for the company by making a provision in the Act that, if a company has any reservations about the admissibility of share acquisition by any person on the ground that transfer of security conflicts with the provisions pertaining to substantial acquisition of shares and take-overs, or conflicts with the Sick Industrial Companies (Special Provisions) Act, the company will be entitled to make an application to the CLB, for rectification of the ownership records with the depository. It has also been provided that during the pendency of the company's application with the CLB, the transferee would be entitled to all the rights and benefits of the shares except voting rights which will be subject to the orders of the CLB. The depository system is proposed to be implemented in a phased manner to provide orderly switch-over from existing system.

Free Transferability of Securities

The securities of all public companies have been made freely transferable. The depositories legislation has taken away the companies' right to use discretion in effecting transfer of securities by deleting Section 22-A from the Securities Contracts (Regulations) Act. 1956.

The insertion of Section in the Companies Act and Section 7 of the Depositories Act provide for free transfer of securities in any company (other than a private company and a deemed public company). For instance, once the agreed consideration is paid and the purchase transaction is settled, the transfer of a security is effected forthwith and the transferee enjoys all the rights and obligations associated with the security. If the securities are in the depository mode, depository would effect the transfer on the basis of intimation from the participants. If the securities are outside the depository mode, the company would effect the transfer on receipt of the transfer deed.

A new Section 56 has been added to the Companies Act, 2013 so as to provide for the following :

The securities of a Company other than a private company or deemed public company have been made freely transferable. The Board of Directors of such a company or the concerned depository does not have any discretion to refuse or withhold a transfer of such security. In respect of a public limited company, the transfer is effected by the depository or company immediately.

Whether Transfer of Securities can be Refused ?

Normally, in respect of a public limited company, the transfer of securities cannot be refused under any circumstances. However, if it is felt that the transfer has contravened any of the provisions of the SEBI Act. 1992 or the Sick Industrial Companies (Special Provisions) Act, 1985, the concerned company depository participants investor or SEBI can within 2 months from the date of transfer, move an application to the CLB to decide as to whether the alleged contravention has really taken place.

Direction of CLB after Inquiry

After inquiry, if the Company Law Board is satisfied of the contravention, it can direct the company or depository to rectify ownership records of securities. However, the CLB is empowered to suspend voting rights in respect of securities so transferred, before the enquiry is completed. The transferee has a right to further transfer securities during the pendency of application with the Company Law Board. During the pendency of the application with the CLB, the transferee is entitled to transfer the security and such transfer entitles the transferee to the voting rights also. However, the transferee would be deprived of such voting rights when the CLB suspends such rights by its order. According to new Section 111A(6) of the Companies Act, 1956 any further transfer, during the pendency of the application with the CLB of shares or debentures shall entitle the transferee to voting rights unless the voting rights in respect of such transferee have also been suspended.

According to the Depositories Related Laws (Amendment) Act. 1997, a new clause (a) to Section 111A(2) has been added. Accordingly, if a company without sufficient cause refuses to register transfer of shares within 2 months from the date on which the instrument of transfer or the intimation of transfer, as the case may be, is delivered to the company to register the transfer of shares.

Director's Power to Refuse Registration

The Companies Act confers the right of transferability of shares subject to restrictions laid down in the Articles. This right of transferability is absolute and cannot be taken away by the Articles. However, the Articles may impose reasonable restrictions and prescribe the manner in which the transfer will be effected. In fact, the Articles of most companies provide certain restrictions on the transfer of shares and empower the Board of Directors to refuse registration of transfers at their discretion on reasonable and bonafide grounds.

The Articles usually empower the Board to refuse registration of transfer on the following grounds :

(1) When partly paid-up shares are to be transferred to a buyer (transferee) who, in the opinion of the directors, is financially incapable of paying calls if made in the near future.

(2) When partly paid-up shares are to be transferred to a transferee who is a minor and is legally incapable of entering into a contract and hence may repudiate the transfer at any time making it impossible for the company to recover outstanding calls from him through legal action.

(3) When a call is unpaid against the shares which are to be transferred and the call money is due from the transferrer, the Board may refuse to register the transfer until the overdue call is paid.

(4) When the transferrer is a debtor of the company and the company has a lien on the shares to be transferred for the said debt, the board may refuse to register the transfer unless the transferrer pays off the debt.

(5) The Board may refuse to register a transfer if the instrument of transfer is incomplete, irregular or defective or is not properly stamped.

(6) The Board may also refuse registration of transfer for any other reason which is just and equitable and which, in the opinion of the directors, is in the general interest of the company.

However, if the Board refuses to register transfer of any shares on any of the above grounds, it must send a notice of the refusal to both the transferrer and transferee within two months of the date on which the instrument of transfer was deposited with the company. Failure to comply with this provision will make the company and its officers liable to penalty. On receipt of the notice, the transferrer or transferee has the right to appeal to the Company Law Board against the refusal by the Board to register the transfer.

The Articles of a company may give the Board of directors discretionary powers to register or refuse to register transfer of shares on some reasonable and bonafide grounds. But in exercising this power the Board must act bonafide in the best interest of the company and the general interest of the shareholders and in good faith. Otherwise, the Company Law Board can intervene on the appeal of the aggrieved party (Bajaj Auto Co. Ltd. vs. N. K. Firodia, A.I.R. 1971, S.C, 321).

Restriction on Transfer of Shares

(a) Every body corporate under the same management holding, singly or in aggregate, 10 per cent of the nominal value of the subscribed equity share capital of any other company shall, before transferring such shares, give intimation to the Central Government of their proposal with detailed particulars of the proposed transferee, and get the same approved by the Central Government within 60 days.

(b) No body or bodies corporate under the same management, holding in the aggregate 10 per cent or more of the nominal value of the equity shares of a foreign company having an established place of business in India, can transfer any of such shares to any citizen of India or to any body or bodies corporate in India, without the previous approval of the Central Government.

(c) Where the Central Government is satisfied that such a transfer of any share/shares of a company may result in a change in the controlling interest of the company and is likely to be prejudicial to the interest of the company, or to public interest, it may direct the company not to give effect to transfer of such shares.

Efferts of Transfer of Shares : The following are the effects of the transfer of shares :

(1) Change in the Register of Members : On the transfer of shares, the transferrer i.e. shareholder ceases to remain the member of the company and the transferee becomes the new member of the company. Thus, the name of the transferrer will be removed from the Register of Members and transferee's name will be entered on it.

(2) Position of transferrer and transferee before registration of tranfer of shares : Before the registration of transfer of shares, the transferrer will act as the trustee of the transferee, he will have to vote and act as per the directions of the transferee. He is supposed to hand over the dividend on shares to the transferee.

(3) Rights regarding dividends : When the shares are transferred, the transferrer transfers the right to future dividends and not the right to the dividends already received.

(4) Transferrer's liability in the case of liquidation : In case the company goes into liquidation within one year of transfer of partly paid-up shares, the transferrer is held liable even after the transfer of shares.

Forged Transfer

Where the signature of the transferrer on any instrument is forged, transfer made on the basis of such instrument in called forged transfer. When forged instrument of transfer is presented to the company for registration , then the company has to inquire into its validity.

Hence, it has become usual now that whenever a transfer is lodged the company writes to the shareholder to inform him about the fact that such a transfer has been lodged and if no objection is made before a day specified, it would be registered. In spite of such precaution, forged transfers may take place, which has the following consequences.

i) A forged transfer is a nullity and hence the original owner of shares continues to be the shareholder and the company is bound to restore his name to the register of members.

ii) If the company has issued a share certificate to the transferee and he has sold the shares to an innocent buyer, the company is liable to compensate such buyer if it refuses him to register as a shareholder.

iii) If the company has been put to loss by reason of the forged transfer, it may recover loss from the person who procured registration even though he might have acted in good faith.

Blank Transfer

A transfer signed by the transferrer without writing the name of transferee is called a blank transfer. In a blank transfer even the date of sale is not filled up, hence the process of purchase and sale can taken place many times with the blank deed and finally one who wants to retain the shares, can enter his name and date and get it registered in the company's books. Until the transferee is so registered as a shareholder, the transferrer continues to be the share holder of the company and he remains liable for the unpaid amount if any.

The main advantage of blank transfer is, it helps in saving the trouble of complying with the formalities of transfer every time and also in saving the payment of stamp duty on every successive transfer.

The facility of blank transfer is often used for illegal purposes or to avoid taxes and for not revealing the identify of real owner. It is laid down that, every instrument of transfer shall be in a prescribed form, with the date of presentation stamped or otherwise endorsed and it should be delivered to the company for registration, within twelve months if shares are dealt in or quoted on a recognized stock exchange and in any other case within two months from the date of presentation.

5.3.2 Transmission of Shares

A company can register a transfer on the basis of duly executed instrument of transfer. But there is one exception. A company may register any person as a shareholder, to whom the right to any shares in the company has been transmitted by operation of law. Transmission of shares occurs on the death or bankruptcy or lunacy of a member or if the company is the member, on its liquidation. The person to whom the shares are transmitted should make an application to the company for transmission of shares in his name. If a company refuses to register transmission of the shares, the right of appeal arises in the same manner as in the case of transfer. For the purpose of transmission instrument of transfer is not required.

Transmission of Shares : When shares get transferred under operation of law in the event of death, insolvency or lunacy of a members, it is called Transmission.

Transmission of shares is different from Transfer of shares. On the death of shareholder his shares are transmitted to his legal heir or representative. In the case of insolvency of a shareholder, his shares are transmitted to the official assignee appointed by the court to dispose off his property and to pay off his debts. In case of insanity of a shareholder his shares are transmitted to his legal representative as decided by the court.

Transmission of shares is an involuntary assignment of shares from the owner to his legal representative without a formal Transfer Deed. Since there is no transfer deed, no stamp duty or registration fee is to be paid by the Legal representative for passing the title to him. The person who receives the shares by transmission becomes entitled to all the rights of a shareholder, like to attend the meeting and to vote at meeting.

Procedure For Transmission of Shares

(i) On becoming entitled to any shares on transmission, the legal representative enjoys all the rights and privileges of the original member in respect of these shares.

(ii) Such a legal representative may elect to be a member or may decide to transfer the shares to another person. If he elects to be a member, he has to submit documentary proof of his title (such as succession certificate, letter of Probate, etc.) along with a letter of request to the company for getting his name registered in place of the earlier member. He has to send the original share certificates to the company. After getting the approval in the Board Meeting, the secretary enters the name of the legal representative in the Register of Members and issues new share certificates to him.

(iii) If the legal representative wants to transfer the shares to another person, he has to attach the documents to the Instrument of Transfer and send it to the company so as to enable the secretary to follow the usual procedure of transfer.

Provisions For Transmission of Shares

(i) Survivor/Legal Representative to be Recognised :

On the death of a member, who was a joint holder, the survivor or survivors shall be the only persons recognised by the company as having any title to his interest in the shares. Where, however, he was a share holder, his legal representative shall likewise be recognised by the company.

(ii) Evidence by Person becoming Entitled :

A person becoming entitled to share in consequence of the death or insolvency of a member shall have to produce to the Board proof of his title. After that, he may select -

(a) to be registered himself as the holder of the share.

(b) to make such transfer of the share as the deceased or insolvent member could have made.

The Board shall have the right to decline or suspend registration as it would have had, if the deceased or insolvent member had transferred the shares before his death or insolvency.

(iii) Entitlement to Dividends

A person becoming entitled to a share by reason of the death or insolvency of the holder shall be entitled to the same dividends and other advantages to which he would be entitled to, if he were the registered holder of the share. But he shall not, before being registered as a member in respect of the share, be entitled in respect of it to exercise any right conferred by membership in relation to meetings of the company.

Secretarial Duties in Connection with the Transmission of Shares

The duties of a secretary in connection with the transmission of shares can be stated as under :

(1) Checking Letter of Request : The secretary has to check up whether the letter of request received by the company is a proper one.

(2) Ensuring Evidence of title : The secretary has to ensure the satisfactory evidence of the Letter of Request.

(3) Complying with the Provisions of Estate Duty Act: In the case of a deceased member, the secretary has to see that the successor has complied with the provisions of the Estate Duty Act and that the estate duty is paid.

(4) Furnishing the prescribed particulars under the Estate Duty Act: On coming to know of the death of a member, the secretary has to furnish the prescribed particulars under the rules framed under the Estate Duty Act, to the Controller of Estate Duty within 3 months of the knowledge of such death.

(5) Performing the duties regarding Transfer of Shares : The secretary has to perform all other duties regarding transfer of shares.

(6) Other duties : Finally, the secretary has to convene a Board meeting in which he should pass the necessary resolution and introduce necessary alteration in the same certificates and the Register of Members. The secretary has to enter the contents of the probate. Letters of Administration and Succession Certificates in the Register of Probates.

5.4 NOMINATION OF SHARES

Under this section it is provided that

(1) Every holder of shares or holder of debentures of a company may, at any time, nominate in the prescribed manner a person to whom his shares or debentures of the company shall vest in the event of his death. Where the shares and debentures of a company are held by more than one person jointly, the joint holders may together nominate, in the prescribed manner, a person to whom all the rights in the shares or debentures of the company shall vest in the event of death of all the joint holders. The nominee shall, on the death of the shareholder or holder of debentures of the company or on the death of the joint holders becomes entitled to all the rights with shares or debentures of the company, unless nomination is varied on cancelled in the prescribed manner.

Where the nominee is minor, it shall be lawful for the holder of shares on debentures to make the nomination to appoint any person to become entitled to shares or debentures, in the event of his death during the minority.

Nomination of shares/debentures Provisions in respect of nomination are as follow –
A share-holder or debenture holder can nominate a person in the prescribed manner. The shares/debentures will vest in the nominee in case of death of the nominator. Though the section uses the word 'person', it can be stated that singular includes plural, as per General Clauses Act. Form 2B makes provisions for appointing more than one nominee. Thus, they can be appointed as joint nominees'. Presumably, their names will appear in share/debenture certificates in the order in which they appear in nomination form.

* Of course, if shares are held in different folios, different nominations will be permissible.

* It shares/debentures are held jointly, all joint holders must sign the nomination form. In case of joint holding, the title passes to the nominee only if all joint holders die [if one of the joint holder dies, the shares are transferred in name of surviving joint holder/s].

* The nomination overrides any provision in respect of transmission by opcration of law or by will. Thus, if a person has been appointed as nominee, the shares will be transfered in his/her name, irrespective of any provision in will or succession certificate or probate.

* Nomination can be varied or cancelled in prescribed manner, but nomination prevails over any provision of law of succession, will etc.

* If nominee is minor, the holders of shares/debentures can appoint a person who will be entitled to hold shares/debentures in the event of death, during minority.

* If nominee becomes entitled to any shares/debentures by virtue of nomination, he will apply to company along with proof of death of holder/joint holders. He can either request Board to register himself as the share holder/debenture holder *or* he can transfer the shares/debentures of deceased share/debenture holder. Thus, the nominee can either register his name or directly transfer the debentures/shares in some other's name.

* If he elects to be registered holder of shares/debentures, he will have to send a written notice to the company stating that he elects to be the registered holder. Such notice should be accompanied by death certificate of share/ debenture holder.

* All limitations, restrictions and provisions of the Act relating to the right of transfer and registration of transfer will apply as if the application is for transfer of shares. In other words, transfer in name of nominee or other person to whom nominee intends to transfer shares/ debentures can be declined only on the grounds on which any transfer can be declined, and on no other grounds.

* The nominee is entitled to all rights of deceased member/debenture holder like dividend and bonus. However, he will not be eligible for voting rights, or other rights as a member, unless he makes application is writing and is registered as a member in respect of the shares/debenture.

* The nominee must either register himself as member or transfer the shares/debentures in some other's name. If he does neither, company can send him a notice to elect either to become a member or transfer the shares/ debentures. If the nominee does not comply within 90 days, Board can withhold payment of dividends, bonuses or other money payable, till the requirement of notice is complied with.

* As is clear from the provisions, facility of nomination is available only to natural persons (who can die). Nomination by non-individuals like trust, society, body corporate, partnership firm, Karta of HUF or a power of attorney holder is not permissible.

* Procedure for nomination - The nomination should be made in prescribed form No. 2B. The form should be signed by all joint holders and should be dated. It should be signed by two witnesses. If nominee is minor, name and address of guardian shall be given by holder. Nomination form should be submitted to company.

* Nomination form does not require specimen signature of nominee. However, it is advisable to ask for signature of nominee (or guardian, if nominee is minor) duly verified by the members who are nominating him.

* Nomination form should be sent in duplicate to company/registrar and share transfer agents of the company. They will return one copy of nomination to the holder of shares/debentures/deposit holders (presumabaly duly signed in token of accepting the nomination). This will serve as acknowledgment. This should serve as confirmation about noting of

nomination, though the form 2B (On which these instructions are given at Sr No. 6) does not specifically say so.

* Who cannot be nominee - A trust, society , body corporate, partnership Karta of HUF or a power of attorney holder can not be appointed as nominee. However, a NRI can be nominee on repatriable basis (Sr. No. 3 of form 2B).

* Nomination stands rescinded upon transfer of share/debenture or repayment/renewal of deposits made.

* Power to make nomination implies power to withdraw nomination. Thus, a person can always withdraw nomination and make fresh nomination. Normally, submission of fresh nominalion implies withdrawal of earlier nomination, however, it is highly advisable to withdraw earlier nomination in writing to avoid ambiguity and possible disputes.

* No stamp duty should be payable when name of nominee. is entered in register of company, as this would not amount to 'share transfer'.

* In case of demat shares, company has no record of nominations.The shareholder can submit his nomination to participant. This nomination is similar to nomination in case of a bank account. Participants permit only one nominee per account.

Difference between Transfer and Transmission of Shares :

Points	Transfer of Shares	Transmission of Shares
(1) Meaning	Transfer of shares means transfer of ownership from one person to another person on account of sale or gift of shares. insolvency or insanity of a person.	Transmission of shares means transfer of ownership from one person to another on account of operation of Law on death,
(2) Parties	There are two parties in the transfer of shares,one is the transferrer and the other is the transferee.	There is only one party in transmission of shares i. e. – legal representative (Legal heir).
(3) Stamp Duty	In this case, the stamp duty is payable.	In this case, the stamp duty is not payable.
(4) Nature of Action	It is a voluntary act.	It is by operation of law.
(5) Documents Required	Transfer form and share certificate are required.	Death certificate, Succession certificate, Court order etc.
(6) Consideration	There must be adequate consideration for the transfer of shares unless shares are transferred by way of gift.	The question of consideration does not arise in the case of transmission, as it is due to the operation of law.
(7) Right to Refuse	The company can refuse transfer of shares on grounds like nonpayment of call money.	The company can not refuse transmission of shares, as it is the result of operation of law.
(8) Nature of Act	It is a deliberate act done by a shareholder (i.e. the transferrer)	It is the result of operation of law.
(9) Authorised Party	Transfer is by the member himself and not by the legal heirs of the member.	Transmission is always by the legal heirs of the member.

QUESTIONS

A) Answer in 20 words.

1. Define 'share.'
2. What do you mean by for feiture of shares ?
3. What is transfer of share ?
4. What is Blank transfer ?
5. What is forged transfer ?
6. What is Trammission of shares?
7. What is surrender of share ?
8. What do you mean by 'allotment of shares ?
9. Define 'call'.
10. What do you mean by 'share' warrant?

B) Answer in 50 words.

1. Explain the procedure for issue of share at premium.
2. Explain in brief issue of shares for consideration other than cash.
3. What are the effects of transfer of shares?
4. What are the effects of forfeiture of shares ?
5. State the contents of share certificate
6. State the provision regarding transmission of share.
7. How duplicate share certificte may be issue.
8. What do you mean by lien on shares?
9. What are the effects of transfer of share?
10. State the procedure of re-issue of forfeited shares.

C) Answer in 150 words.

1. Define 'share'. Explain the procedure of issue of share.
2. What is allotment of shares. Explain its procedure.
3. Define 'Transfer and Transmission' of shares. Distinguish between them.
4. What is 'Forfeiture of shares'? Explain the procedure for forfeiture of shares.
5. Define 'share warrant', What is the difference between share certificate and share warrant?
6. Explain the procedure of issuing duplicate share certificate.
7. What are the different ways of issuing shares?
8. State the procedure of Transfer of shares under Depository system.

D) Answer in about 300/500 words.

1. Define 'Shares.' What are its differents types?
2. What do you mean by 'Shares'? Explain the procedure for issue of shares.
3. What is 'Transfer and Transmission of Shares' ? Explain the statutory provisions regarding forfeiture of shares in physical form .
4. What is 'Forfeiture of Shares' ? What are its effects?Explain the statutory provisions regarding forfeiture of shares.
5. What is the meaning of 'Share Certificate' ? Explain the statutory provision regarding issue of share certificates.
6. What are the different ways of issuing shares?
7. What do you mean by 'Call on Shares' ? What are its provisions ? Explain the procedure of making calls on shares.
8. Write the procedure of issuing duplicate share certificate. Distinguish between share certificate and share warrant.
9. What is 'Surrender of Shares' ? Distinguish between forteiture and surrender of shares.
10. What is lien on shares? Distinguish between lien and surrender of shares.

<table>
<tr><td>**Chapter 6**</td><td>**E-GOVERNANCE AND E-FILING**</td></tr>
</table>

CONTENTS

6.1 Introduction
6.2 Meaning of E-Governance
6.3 Objectives of E-Governance
6.4 E-filing
    6.4.1 MCA Portal
    6.4.2 Infrastructure for E-filing
    6.4.3 Facilities available
    6.4.4 Benefit of E-filing
    6.4.5 DIN

6.1 INTRODUCTION

The concept of e-gorvernance chosen by the council of Europe covers the use of electronic technologies in three areas of public actions:

i) relations between the public authorities and civil society

ii) functioning of the public authorities at all stages of the democratic process (electronic democracy)

iii) the provision of public services

This is a broad definition covering the different aspects of relations between the state and civil society. The European Union is supporting the development of electronic governarance which is the modernisation of public administration bringing it close to civil society and business through the use of information and communication technologies.

Democracies in the world share a vision of the day when electronic governance will become reality. E-governance is about the use of information technology to raise the qualtiy of the services governments deliver to citizens and businesses.

The term E-government has different connotations :

1) E-administration : The use of ICIs to modernize the state; the creation of data repositories for MIS, computerisation of records.

2) E-services : The emphasis here is to bring the state closer to the citizens e.g. provision of online services. E-administration and E-services together constitute E-Government.

3) E-Governance : The use of IT to improve the ability of government to address the needs of society. It includes the publishing of policy and programme related information to transact with citizens.

4) E-democracy : The use of IT to facilitate the ability of all services of society to participate in the governance of the state.

Origin In India :

E-governance originated in India during the seventies with a focus on in-house Government, application in the areas of defence, electronic monitoring, planning Development of ICI to manage data intensive functions related to election, census, tax administration etc. From the early nineties E-governance has seen the use of IT for wider sectoral application with emphasis on reaching out to the rural areas and taking in greater inputs from NGO's and private sector as well. There has been an increasing involvement of international donor agencies such as the DFID, G-8, UNDP, WB under the frame work and e-governance for development.

6.2 MEANING OF E-GOVERNANCE

Before presenting an overall definition of E-governance, it is better to explain E-democracy, E-government. **E-democracy** refers to the process and structures that encompass all forms of electronic interaction between the Government and the citizens.

E-government is a form of e-business in government and referes to the process and structures needed to deliver electronic services to the public (citizens and businesses), collaborate with business patterns and to conduct the electronic transactions within an organisational entity.

E-governance : It is defined as "the application of electronic means in (1) the interaction between government and citizens and government and businesses as well as (2) in internal government operations to simplify and improve democratic, government and business aspects of Governance."

The term interaction stands for the delivery of Government products and services, exchange of information - communication, transaction and system integration. **Government consists** of levels and branches. Government levels include central, national regional, provincial, departmental and local Government institutions. Example of Government branches are Administration, Civil Service, Parliament and Judiciary functions.

Government operations are all back-office process and inter-governmental interaction within the total government body. Example of electronic means are Internet and other ICT applications.

6.3 OBJECTIVES OF E-GOVERNANCE

1) To support and simplify governance for all parties- Government, citizens and Businesses. The use of ICTs can connect all three parties and support processes and activities. In other words, E-governance uses electronic means to support and stimulate good governance.

2) To provide citizens access to information and knowledge about the political processes, about services and about choices available.

3) To make possible the transition from passive information access to active citizen participation by :

i) Informing the citizen

ii) Representing the citizen

iii) Encouraging the citizen to vote

iv) Consulting the citizen

v) Involving the citizen

The external objective of e-government is to satisfactorily fulfil the people's needs and expectations on the **front office** side, by simplifying their interaction with various online services. The use of ICT's in government operations facilitates speedy, transperent, accountable, efficient and effective interaction with the public, citizens, businesses and other agencies.

In the back-office, the objective of e-government in government operations is to facilitate a speedy, transparent accountable, efficient and effective process for performing government administration activities. Significant cost saving (per transaction) in government operations can be the result.

It can be concluded that e-governance is more than just a Government on website on the internet. Political, social, eonomic and technological aspects determine **e-governance**.

6.4 E-FILING

E-filing or electronic filing is a system of filing tax returns via the internet.

E-filing - major changes in company law (regarding e-filing) procedure -

6.4.1 MCA Portal and E-filing

The Ministry of Company Affairs (MCA) has launched a major e-governance initiative

'MCAZI.' On its implemantion all documents need to be filed electronically with the ROC through the MCA Portal. Hence, the old forms have become redundant. New forms have been designed for each event and the same needs to be filed currently with the ROC.

The e-filing is mandatory w.e.f. 15th Sept. 2006. The basis of e-filing would depend upon the following three factors -

1) Every company needs to have CIN Company Incorporation Number.

2) Every Director needs to have a DIN -Director Identification Number.

3) Every document needs to be attested by using digital signature.

1) CIN - CIN is the 21 digit registration number that is being issued to companies that have been formed say in the past 4 year. However, companies registered prior to issue of CIN would now be required to obtain CIN. The earlier registration numbers were of the type - 08-12450.

The new CIN is of the format U74140 KA 2005-PTCO 36795. The new CIN can be obtained from the MCA portal. Companies need to manually request the ROC to provide them their CIN.

2) DIN : Director Identification Number (DIN) is a unique identification number for an existing director or a person intending to become the director of a compnay. All the persons who are already directors of a company / companies or propose to be director are required to have a DIN compulsory. In the present scenario of e-filing DIN will be a pre-requisite for filing of certain company related documents. No fee is required to be paid for the same. To get DIN an online application is to be filed. A provisional DIN will be issued after online filling. Thereafter, the printed detail of the fields entered has to be generated. A photo has to be attached on the form with proof of residence duly attested by Notary / Gazetted Officer / Certified professional (CA/CS/ICWA). The same will then be submitted in the RD Office (Regional Director). The RD Office will issue the DIN. While filing forms, the CIN also needs to be mentioned. It has been clarified by MCA that on registration of the Director from a company the DIN obtained does not have to be cancelled. The DIN will remain with the individual only. This is intended to be a lifetime number.

3) Digital Certificate : A Digital Certificate is an electronic signature duly attested by a certifying authority that shows the authenticity of the person signing the same - For MCAZI the following category of persons are identified as users of Digital Signature Certificates (DSC's)

a) MCA (Government) employees

b) Professionals (CA, Cost Accountants, Company Secretaries and Lawyers who interact with MCA)

c) Authorised signatories and Directors of Companies

d) Representatives of Banks and Financial Institutions.

Other features of e-filing

Certification of e-forms :

Certification of company documents by practicing professionals as is presently required, has not only been confirmed by MCA-21 in its e-forms but the same has also been extended to serveral other form comprising of form Nos. 2, 3, 5, 8, 10, 17, 18, 23, 24, AB 32. This pre-certification can be carried out by CA, a whole time practitioner. Besides form 1 of the companies (Declaration of Dividend out of Reserves Rules,1975 and form No. 1 of Investor Edcucation and Protection Fund (Awaress and Protection of Investor Rules 2001) are also to be certified.

6.4.2 Infrastructure for e-filing

The prerequisite for using the portal of MCA -21 will be :
1) P-4 computer with printer
2) Internet Explorer 6.0 version
3) Adobe Acrobat Reader 7.05 version and
4) Digital Signature Certificate

6.4.3 Facilities

The following facilities will be available as e-filing.
1) Pre-filing (based on information already provided)
2) Pre-Scrutiny (validation of various entries made)
3) Attachment of documents
4) Payment calculated by system
5) Payment may be 'Challan' based or online through payment Gateway.

Payment Gateway

The traditional 'Challan' based system may be used. MCA has tied up with 200 branches of SEBI, PNB, Indian Bank, ICICI and HDFC Bank for this purpose. For online payment the payment Gateway of ICICI Bank has been implemented.

Same Clarifications

MCA has clarified on the following issues :
1) The filing will be done only through the portal of MCA of and not through E-mail.
2) The transaction will be deemed as completed only after clearance of the payment by the Bank.
3) The systems will hold the applications for five days till the payment is made.
4) Stamp Duty will be paper based. It is proposed that, payment of stamp duties will also be made online in phases through banks in near future. 15 states have already authorised the central government in this regard and authorisation from the remaining states is expected.

All the information relating to MCA-21 is made available on the new portal www. mca. gov.in. In the above context, it is necessary to have all the necessary pre-requisites in place before the MCA portal becomes live to interact efficiently and in timely manner with the Registrar of Companies and for filing of documents in time.

6.4.4 Benefit of e-filing

1) No paperwork : This is one of the main benefit of e-filing. When you e-file there is no need to work with pieces and pieces of forms. These forms usually arrive in the mail. But becaues they are delivered by mail, they may arrive late, or they may get lost. This will hinder the filing process and may even cause you to file late. When you e-file, you avoid all those problems, hence saving yourself lots of time.

2) Minimal error : Another great benefit for e-filing is that there is very little room for error. We shall look at calculating earned income credit (EIC) later as an example. But for now, its good enough to be reminded about human introduce errors when filing taxes.

When you use an online system for e-filing the system will have built in handling that will prevent errors from being introduced accidentally. For example, there are some required fields that are missing. the system will prompt you immediately and will not allow the submission to go through.

3) Greater Convenience : Compared to traditional paper filing, it is much more convinient to e-file. You can e-file any time you like when you woke up or in the middle of the night. You can even save the draft, and continue the e-filing process at a later date if you are using same number.

4) Calculating earned credit income (EIC) : When filing for tax, you may be unaware of some tax-policies. This is where the system can help. For example, EIC is for the people who are working but earning low wages. It reduces the amount of tax that an individual owes. The amount is also dependent on various conditions. For instance if you do not have any children, the ceiling comes down.

The problem with such policies is that they may change. And when you paper file, you have to find out what those changes are and make normal calculations before submission. This, again, may result in errors. If you visit the IRS website, you will find that there are penalties for submitting errors formation even though you are not aware of it. For instance if the mistake was due to recklessness, you could be denied EIC for upto 2 years. Therefore, it is always better to e-file.

When you e-file, the system automatically informs you about the policies, and even calculate the number automatically for you. In other words, the system will let you know, whether you qualify for EIC or not, based on the numbers that you have provided. That way you never have to worry about errors and you can find out whether you qualify for a tax credit or not.

6.4.5 Director Indentification Number (DIN)

The concept of DIN has been introduced for the first time with the insertion of sections 266A to 266 G of Companies (Amendment) Act, 2006. As such, all the existing and intending Directors have to obtain DIN within the prescribed time frame as notified.

Steps

Step by step process to be followed by the Applicant is as follows :-

Step I - Obtain provisional DIN

The applicant is required to fill-up and submit form DIN-1 online for obtaining provisional DIN. Form DIN-1 is available under 'Apply for DIN' tab on the left hand side panel under DIN' link on the homepage of MCA Portal.

If the name of a person does not have last name then his/her father's first name should be filled in the mandatory 'Last Name' filed in form DIN-1. In such a case, an affidavit duly notarized by a Notary Public should also be submitted along with DIN application.

Step II - Pay Din application fee

The applicant is required to login to the MCA portal and click on 'Pay miscellaneous fee' link available under the 'services' tab. Select 'DIN application fee' option and enter the provisional DIN. Applicant can make the payment of fee by using any three markers of payment available on MCA portals. Form DIN-1 will be prossessed only after the DIN Application fee is paid.

Step III : Dispatch DIN application to MCA DIN cell

The applicant is required to take out a print out of Form DIN-1 (containing provisional DIN generated online). Fill the Service Request Number (SRN) of the fee paid, sign the DIN application form manually and paste a good resolution photograph in the space earmarked. Attach the photocopies of the 'Proof of Identity' (Attach additional proof, if father's name and Date of Birth is not includes in the 'Proof of Identity') and the 'proof of residence' with DIN application form and tick the relevent checkbox against the document name. Get the photogrph and the attached supporting documents attested from an approved authority as specified in form DIN-1. The certifying authority must mention its particulars such as Name, COP No. etc. and affix its seal /stamp.

Complete set of documents is required to be sent to MCA DIN cell, by post, courier or hand delivery, as per convenience, within 60 days from the date of generation of provisional DIN online.

Processing of DIN Application

DIN application is received by MCA DIN cell. DIN application form and attached supporting docurments are scrutinised and if found in order the provisional DIN is approved and activated in the system. If there is any defect in the DIN application, the provisional DIN is rejected. It takes about a week's time to complete this process. DIN approval/ rejection letter is generated and sent by post to the applicant. The status of application can also be tracked from the 'DIN Approval Status" tab in the DIN corner.

Steps after approval of DIN : (Applicable only for existing director appointed upto 30th June 2007).

1) Intimate approved DIN to your companies

On approval of DIN, intimate your DIN to all the company files (within a period of 30 days from the date of approval) in which you are a Director in form DIN-2. Form DIN-2 can be downloaded and printed from the 'DIN' link on the homepage of MCA portal.

2) Company to intimate your DIN to ROC

After the Director has intimated the DIN alloted to the company (ies) is /are then required to intimate the DINs of its directors to the ROC in form DIN-3 within a period of seven days of receiving form DIN-2.

Post Approval changes in particulars of DIN-1.

If there is any change in the particulars submitted in form DIN-1, File form DIN-4 for intimating the change in the particulars within 30 days. For instance, in the event of change of address of a director, he/she is required to intimate this change by submitting form DIN-4 along with the required attached documents with MCA DIN cell.

QUESTIONS

A) Answer in 20 words

1) What is E-governance?
2) What do you mean by E-files?
3) What do you mean by E-government?
4) What is E-service?
5) What is E-administration?

B) Answer in 50 words

1) What is E-governance? State its objectives.
2) What is E-filing ? Explain CIN
3) What is MCA Portal? Explain.
4) What do you mean by DIN ?
5) Which infrastructure facilities are needed for E-filing?

C) Answer in 150 words.

1) Define E-governance. What are its objectives?
2) What is E-filing? Explain changes in company law rejecting e-filing through MCA portal.
3) Explain the process of geting DIN.
4) Define E-filing. What are the benefits of E-filing?

D) Answer in 300 words.

1) Explain the concept of E-governance and E-filing.
2) What do you mean by E-filing? What are the major changes in copmany law filing procedure.
3) What is DIN ? Explain the steps in achieving DIN.
4) What is E-filing ? Explain its benefits.

Chapter 7

MANAGEMENT OF COMPANY

CONTENTS

7.1 Organisational set-up of a Company / Administrative Hierarchy

7.2 Board of Directors : Definitions, Powers and Functions.

7.3 Director : Meaning, Types

    7.3.1   Legal Position of Directors

    7.3.2   Who may be appointed as a Director

    7.3.3   Qualifications of Directors

    7.3.4   Disqualifications of a Director

    7.3.5   Appointment of Directors

    7.3.6   Assignment of Office by Director (Sec. 312)

    7.3.7   Number of Directors

    7.3.8   Number of Directorship

    7.3.9   Vacation of office of a Director

    7.3.10 Removal of a Director

    7.3.11 Resignation by a Director

    7.3.12 Compensation for loss of office

    7.3.13 Office or place of profit

    7.3.14 Interested Director

    7.3.15 Duties of Directors

    7.3.16 Liability of Directors

    7.3.17 Loans to Directors

    7.3.18 Remuneration of Directors (Managerial Remuneration)

INTRODUCTION

A company is a legal or artificial person. It has neither a mind nor a body of its own. Hence, it has to act through some human agency. The persons by whom the business of a company is carried on are called as directors. The institution of the company has two main organs, the general body of shareholders and the Board of directors. The Board is a managerial body which is constituted by a general body. Constituting the Board means appointment of directors. The directors are the brain of a company.

7.1 ORGANISATIONAL SET-UP OF A COMPANY / ADMINISTRATIVE HIERARCHY

Administrative hierarchy or structure of Company Management

The fundamental authority in the management and control of company affairs vests with the shareholders. The shareholders delegate their authority to a Board of Director and the directors act as an agents of the company and the general body of shareholders.

The directors are given wide powers of management, particularly all executive and administrative powers for conducting the business in a very efficient manner. The Board of Directors in turn delegate their authority to the chief executive of the company. It is because the directors cannot look after the complications of management and the technical aspect of the business. The Chief executive is responsible for exclusion of the policies laid down by the Board of Directors. The Chief executive is assisted by the department of functional managers who are responsible for the affairs of various departments under them.

Agencies of management / organisation chart

The actual conduct of the company's forms of organisation may be in the hands of the following managerial personnel :

1. **Board of Directors :** This is the principal authority in all forms of company organisation. The board of directors exercises powers of the company, conducts its business and controls its property and funds. They are acting as agents, trustees and managing partners of the company.

2. **Managing Director or Manager :** Managing Director or Manager is the highest paid Chief Executive Officer as the head of the entire enterprise and incharge of the routine management and day-to-day affairs.

3. **Secretary :** A secretary is an agent of the board, who is responsible for all company secretarial work and he is incharge of office administration.

4. **Chief Accountant :** Chief Accountant is incharge of accounts and finance department.

5. **Treasurer or Cashier :** Treasurer or cashier is incharge of cash department or treasury.

6. **Heads of Departments :** This category includes managers or various executives and administrative departments working under the Managing Director or General Manager.

7. Auditors : Auditors are statutory representatives of members who are meant for the statutory audit of accounts of company.

Thus, from the given below chart it is clear that there are number of H.O.D. known as functional heads and many manager, subordinate manager and supervisors etc. The flow of authority is downwards i.e. from top to bottom. The flow of responsibility is upwards i.e. from the bottom to the top in the managers pyramid.

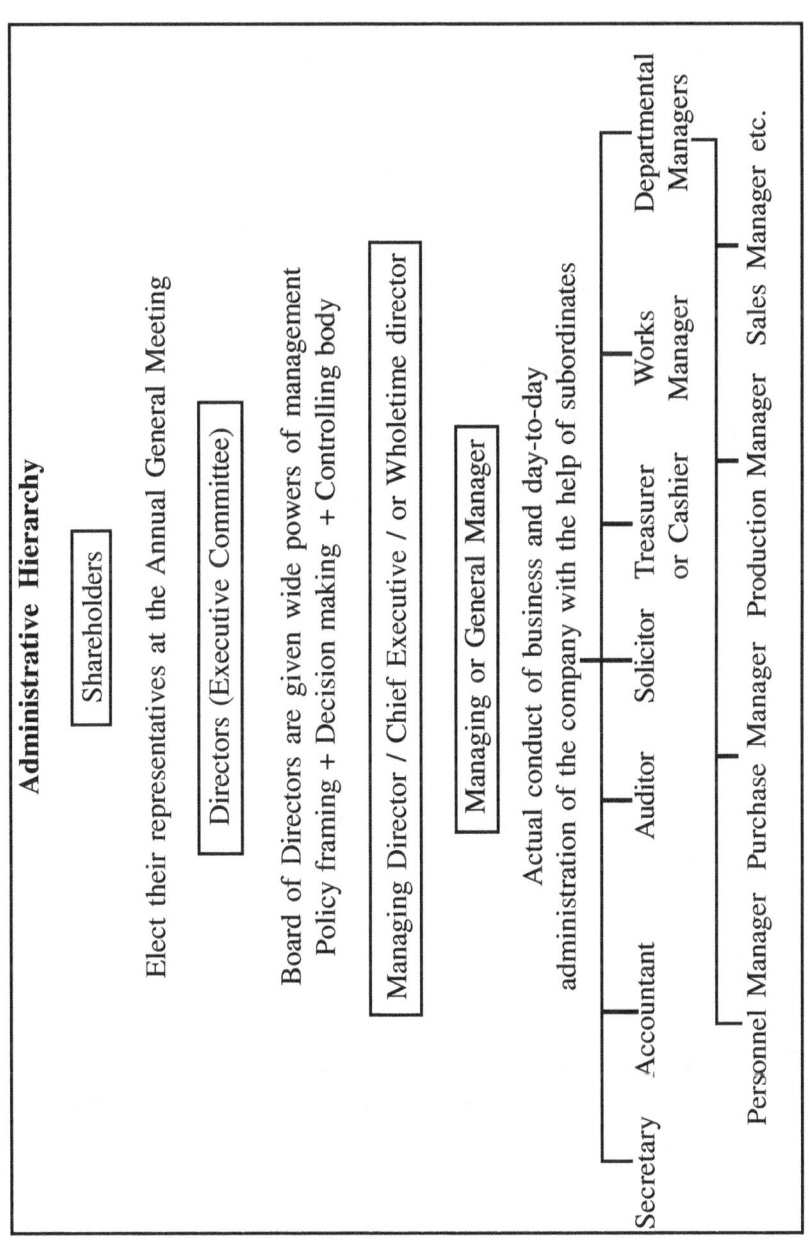

Thus, from the above chart it is clear that there are number of H.O.D. known as functional heads and many manager, subordinate manager and supervisors etc. The flow of authority is downwards i.e. from top to bottom. The flow of responsibility is upwards i.e. from the bottom to the top in the managers pyramid.

7.2 BOARD OF DIRECTORS

Meaning - Sec. 2(10): "Board of Directors or Board, in relation to a company, means the collective body of the directors of the Company."

The shareholders of a Company are real owners. The owners of a Company cannot manage the business of a company because they are widely scattered and large in number. Also there is lack of continuity in membership as shares of a company are freely transferable. Thus, to remove this difficulty they appoint directors of company and collectively they are known as Board of Directors. The act makes it clear that the Board of Directors of a company shall be entitled to exercise all such powers, and to do all such acts and things, as the company is authorised to do. The act authorises Board to do every thing in the name of the Company. Decision of the Board are taken collectively at the meeting. The decisions are minute in the form of 'Resolutions'.

Powers and Functions of Board of Directors (Sec. 179) :

A company is an artificial person. It acts through its directors. The directors represent the mind and will of the company. They manage and control all the activities of the company. The Board of Directors derives powers from

i) The companies Act

ii) Memorandum and Articles of Association

iii) Board Resolutions

iv) Resolutions in General Meetings

v) Agreements or contracts with the company

The powers of the Board may be classified into three categories as follows.

I) Powers which can be exercised in accordance with Articles.

II) Powers which can be exercised only at Board meetings.

III) Powers which can be exercised with the consent of share holders at general meetings.

General powers

Sec. 179 lays down the general powers of the Board of Directors. It empowers the Board to exercise all such powers and do all such acts and things as the company is authorised to do unless there is express restriction on their powers, in the articles of the company. However,

(a) The Board shall not exercise those powers which under the companies Act or memorandum of association or otherwise are required to be exercised by the company in general meeting.

(b) In exercising all such powers or doing of any such act, the Board will be subject to provisions of this or any other Act, the memorandum or the articles.

(II) Powers exercisable at Board meetings only.

The Board can only exercise power by means of resolutions passed at meetings of the Board.

i)   The power to make calls on shareholders in respect of money unpaid on their shares.
ii) The power to authorise the buy back.
iii) The power to issue debentures.
iv) The power to borrow moneys otherwise than on debentures.
v)   The power to invest the funds of the company, and
vi) The power to make loans.
vii) The power to fill up casual vacancies in the Board
viii) The power to appoint alternate directors
ix) The power to appoint additional directors
x)   The power to appoint first auditors
xi) The power to grant consent to contracts in which any dirctor, or his relative or his partner etc. are interested.
xii) The power to appoint a person as 'Managing director' or 'manager', who is already holding such office in another comapny.
xiii) The power to invest in companies in the same group beyond a certain limit and
xiv) The power to receive notice of disclosure of shareholding by director.

Delegation of Board's Powers

Directors cannot delegate their powers unless the power to delegate is granted to them. However, the Board may, by a resolution passed at a meeting, delegate to any committee of directors, the managing director the manager or any other principal officer of the company or a principal officer of the branch office, the power to borrow money otherwise than debentures, to invest the funds of the company and to make loans, to the extent and on such conditions as the Board may prescribe. The power to make calls and to issue debentures cannot be delegated by the directors and must be exercised by the directors only at a Board Meeting.

The power of the Board of directors may be delegated only by resolutions passed is Board Meetings and not by circulars, resolutions or in any other manner.

Restrictions on powers of the Board (sec. 180)

The Board of Directors of a public company or of a private company which is subsidiary to a public company shall not exercise the following powers except with the consent of the company in General meeting.

i) Power to sell, lease or otherwise dispose off the whole or substantially whole of the undertaking of the company in case of improper sale or lease by director, the title of the purchaser will not be affected, if he buys it in good faith, with due care and caution.

ii) Power to remit or give time for the payment of any debt due by a director to the company. However, such a consent is not required in case of renewal or continuance of an advance made by a banking company to its director in the ordinary course of business.

iii) Power to invest, otherwise than in trust securities, the amount of compensation received by the company in respect of the compulsory acquisition of any undertaking or property of the company.

iv) Power to borrow money, where the money to be borrowed together with the money already borrowed by the company will exceed the aggregate of the paid up capital of the company and its free reserves. This will not include temporary loans obtained from the company's bankers in the ordinary course of business.

v) Power to contribute to charitable and other funds not directly relating to the business of the company or the welfare of the employees, any amounts the aggregate of which will, in any financial year, exceed Rs. 50000/- or five percent of its average net profits during the three financial years, immediately preceding, which ever is greater.

Political Contributions

a) No Government company and

b) no other company which has been in existence for less than three financial years shall contribute any amount or amounts directly or indirectly (i) to a political party or (ii) for any political purpose to any person.

Contribution to the National Defence Fund

The Board of directors of any company or any person or authority exercising the powers of the Board of directors of a company or of the company in general meeting may contribute such amount as it thinks fit to the National Defence Fund or any other Fund approved by the Central Government for the purpose of national defence.

Validity of Acts of Directors (sec. 176)

Under Sec. 176 it is provided that, acts done by a person as a director shall be valid, notwithstanding that it may afterwards be discovered that his appointment was invalid by reason of any defect or disqualification or had terminated by virtue of any provision contained in this Act or in the articles.

The main object of this provision is to protect people dealing with the company by providing that, the acts of a person acting as a director shall be held valid although later on his appointment as a director turns out as invalid or he is terminated.

7.3 DIRECTOR

Meaning

Sec. 2 (34) of the Companies Act, defines director as " any person occupying the position of director, by whatever name called". Thus, the Act does not define their position. According to Sir George Jessel, "Directors have sometimes been called trustees, or commercial trustees, and sometimes they have been called managing partners, it does not matter what you call them so long as you understand what their true position is, which is that they are really commercial men managing a trading concern for the benefit of themselves and of all other shareholders in it". Thus, the important factor determining a person as a manager is to refer to the nature of the office and its duties. Thus, function is everything, name matters nothing.

The director may be defined as the individual who directs, controls, manages or superintends the affairs of the company. As a body they frame the general policy of the company, direct its affairs, appoint the company's officers, ensure that they carry out their duties and recommend to the shareholders regarding distribution of dividend. The directors of a company collectively are called as the Board of Directors or the Board.

According to explanation act, "Any person in accordance with whose directions or instructions, the Board of directors of a company is accustomed to act shall be deemed to be a director of the company, except when the Board of Directors so acts on advice given by him in a professional capacity.

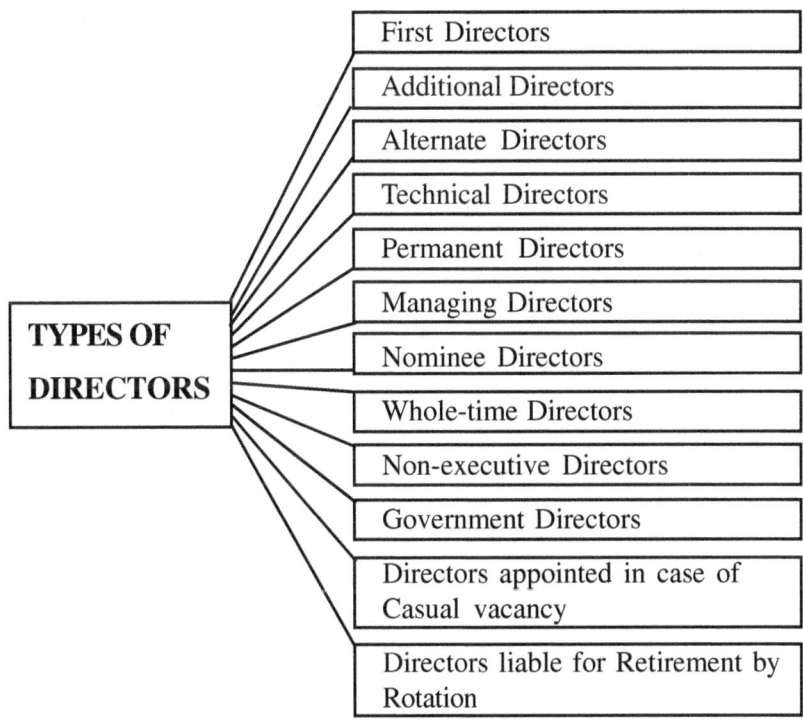

Directors liable for Retirement by Rotation

1. First directors

The first directors are the persons whose names appear in Articles of Association of the Company, at the time of Incorporation of the Company as Directors. In the case of default and subject to any regulations in the Articles of the company, subscribers of the Memorandum who are individuals, shall be deemed to be the Directors of the Company, until the Directors are duly appointed in accordance. In the First Annual General Meeting of the Company. The First Directors can be appointed as permanent Directors by making necessary provision in the Articles of Association of the Company.

2. Additional directors (sec. 161)

The act recognises the powers of articles to empower directors to appoint additional directors and states that the Board of Directors of a company, is empowered by the articles, may appoint additional directors without consulting the company in general meeting and a general meeting has no power to do so. If, however, the directors cannot agree, or are unable to appoint, the company may exercise its power in general meeting to appoint new directors. Such additional directors and the number of directors constituting- the Board together should not exceed the maximum number fixed by the articles, and they are entitled to hold office only upto the date of the next annual general meeting of the company.

3. Alternative directors (sec. 161)

Alternative Director, in a place of director absent from the State in which Board Meetings are held, for not less than three months, may be appointed by the Board if so authorised by the Articles or by a resolution passed by the company in general meeting, The alternate director shall not hold office for a period longer than that permissible to the original director and shall vacate office when the original director returns to the said state. Also if the term of office of the original director is determined before he so returns, any provision for the automatic re-appointment of retiring directors, in default of another appointment shall apply to the original director and not to the alternative director. Where an alternate director is appointed by a resolution of the Board of Directors, the absence of the original director from the meetings of the Board, will not entail vacation of his office, as it is presumed in such a case that leave of absence has been granted to him by the Board of Directors.

4. Technical Directors

The directors who are entrusted with the technical nature of work are known as 'Technical Directors'. These directors are expert in performing their work due to their qualification, expertise, experience etc. Technical Directors are entitled to get professional fees for providing professional services to the company.

5. Permanent directors

The directors who are not liable to retire by rotation are Permanent Directors. They may be appointed for life or for a specific period, say 20 years subject to other provisions of the Act, Permanent directors will continue to act as directors until they resign or are removed or vacate office or become disqualified to act as director. In the case of a Public Company or a Private Company which is a subsidiary of a public company, except stated otherwise, all directors are liable to retire by rotation.

At least one third directors of the total number of Directors of a public company should be those who are liable to retire by rotation. All directors of private company can be permanent Directors. However, even a permanent director can be removed from his office. A company may, by ordinary resolution, remove a director before the expiry of the term. A special notice shall be required of any resolution to remove a director or to appoint somebody instead of a director so removed at the meeting at which he is removed.

6. Managing directors

Every Public Company, or a private company which is a subsidiary of a Public Company having a paid-up share capital of Rs. 5 Crores, shall have to appoint a Managing or Whole time director or manager. Managing Director is the director to take care of the day to day operations of the Company. Managing director may be appointed by way of making provision in the Articles of Association or by way of entering into an agreement entered into it, or by passing resolution passed by the Company in general meeting- or by its Board of Directors. The Company has to comply with the appointment of Managing Director. Managing Director works under the control and supervision of the Board of Directors. Managing Director has substantial powers of management.

For detailed discussion, please refer to chapter on 'Managing Director'.

7. Nominee directors (Sec. 161)

By virtue of an agreement or appropriate provision in the Articles to Financial Institutions, or other creditors some time acquire the right to appoint one or more directors as Nominee Directors. Such directors will have to be appointed out of the remaining one-third of the total number of directors. Nominee directors are not liable to retire by rotation; They are not required to hold qualification shares and cannot be removed; They will continue to act as a directors, until any change in the appointment is made by the institution/ creditors. The financial institution, has right to appoint nominee directors until the full repayment of their loans. The Articles of Association must contain provisions regarding the appointment of Nominee Directors, otherwise an alteration must be made in the Articles if the financial Institution is incorporated under the Companies Act, 2013. In case of the financial institution which provides financial assistance to the company constituted under separate Acts, providing for the right to appoint Nominee Director, notwithstanding anything contained in the Articles or the Companies Act, such financial institution can appoint Nominee Director.

8. Whole-time directors - sec. 2(94)

The directors who devote their whole time and attention to conduct the affairs of Company are known as wholetime directors. A Public company or a private Company which is a subsidiary of a Public company having a paid up share capital of Rs. 5 Crores or more has to appoint one or more whole-time directors. Whole time director may be appointed by the company in general meeting or by the Board. For the appointment of whole time director, the company has to comply with the provisions of Sec. 203 of the Companies Act, 2013. Any appointment and re-appointment of whole time directors requires the approval of the Central Government, unless the company complies with the provisions specified in Schedule XIII of the Companies Act 2013.

9. Non-executive directors

Non-executive directors are Professional directors or part-time directors. Non executive directors are experts in their own field. They are directors of one or more companies and provide their expert guidance to various companies. They help companies to solve their problems and to increase their effectiveness and achieve efficiency in the operations. Non-executive directors get sittings fees and professional fees for providing professional services to the Company. They have broad outlook and vision to look into matters of the company. Non-executive directors are not involved in routine operations of the company.

10. Government directors

The Central Government may on the application of the Company Law Board or on the application of not less than one hundred member of the company or on application by the members of the company holding not less than one-tenth of the total voting power therein order to prevent oppression or mis-management, or to protect public interest, appoint such number of persons to act as directors for a period not exceeding three years on any one occasion. The provisions regarding holding qualification shares, or retirement by rotation are not applicable in case of Government Directors. The Central Government may require the persons appointed as directors or additional directors to report to the Central Government from time to time with regards to the affairs of the Company.

11. Directors appointed in case of casual vacancy

The Board of Directors are empowered to fill the casual vacancy in the Board under the provisions of act of the Companies Act, 2013. In the case of a public company or a private company which is a subsidiary of a Public company, if the office of any director appointed by the company in general meeting is vacated before his term of office expires in the normal course, the resulting casual vacancy may, in default of and subject to any regulations in the articles of the company, be filled by the Board of directors at a meeting of the Board.

Any person so appointed shall hold office only upto the date upto which director in whose place he is appointed would have held office if it had not been vacated as aforesaid.

12. Directors liable for retirement by rotation

In the case of Public Company or a private company which is a subsidiary of a Public Company, unless the articles provide for the retirement of all directors at every annual general meeting, not less than two-thirds of the total number of directors whose period of office is liable to be determined by retirement of directors by rotation. The directors to retire by rotation at every annual general meeting shall be those, who have been longest in the office since their last appointment, but as between persons who became directors on the same day, those are to retire shall, in default of and subject to any agreement among themselves, be determined by lot.

At the annual general meeting at which a director retires as aforesaid, the company may fill up the vacancy by appointing the retiring director or some other person thereto.

7.3.1 Legal Position of Directors

Directors are described as trustees, agents, governors or managing partners. According to Lord Selborne "The directors are the mere trustees or agents of the company-trustees of the company's money and property-agents in the transactions which they enter into on behalf of the company." Thus, the directors are neither the servants nor the employees of the company.

1) Directors As Agents

Directors in the eyes of law are agents of the company for which they act. As Lord Cairns observed, "Directors are merely agents of the company. The company itself cannot act in its own person for it has no person; it can only act through directors and the cases as regards directors merely the ordinary case of principal and agent. Whenever an agent is liable, those directors would be liable; where the liability would attach to the principal and principal only, the liability is the liability of the company."

Where the directors make contract on behalf of the company, they incur no personal liability, provided they act only within the scope of their authority. In such a case, the company alone would be liable. Where the directors contract in their own names but really on behalf of the company, the other party on discovering the real principal, can sue the company as undisclosed principal in the contract where the directors act in the excess of their authority in entering into a contract. The company can by subsequent resolution ratify the act; but if the directors do something which is ultravires the company, such an act cannot be ratified.

2) Directors As Managing Partners

As the directors manage the affairs of the company like a partner of a firm they are called as managing partners. But the partners act on the principal of mutual agency which is not the case with the directors. A director has no authority to bind other directors and shareholders. The directors are also subject to retirement by rotation whereas the partners of the firm do not retire by rotation. Hence, the directors are not managing partners in real sense of the term.

3) Directors As Employees

Directors are agents of the company but not the employees or servants of the company. They cannot claim their remuneration as a preferential creditor, in the event of winding up of a company under Sec. 327 of the Companies Act. However, where any director, besides being a director, is also in the service of the company such as secretary, manager, accountant, etc. he will be treated as an employee. So he will be entitled to the remuneration and other benefits as an employee of the company in addition to his rights of director such as sitting fee etc.

4) Director As Officers

The act, are liable to certain penalties if the provisions of the Companies Act are not complied with.

5) Directors As Trustees

Directors are considered as trustees of the company. A trustee is a person who is the owner of the property, deals with it as principal, as owner and a master, subject only to an equitable obligation to account to some person to whom he stands in relation as trustees. The directors are trustees (1) of the company's money or property as they must account for all the money and property over which they exercise control (2) of the powers entrusted to them as they have to exercise their powers honestly and in the interest of the company and the shareholders and not in their own interest. Directors are the trustees for the company and not for the individual shareholders. They are not trustees for third persons who have made contracts with the company.

6) Directors in Fiduciary Relationship to the Company

Although directors are called as trustees of the company, they are not trustees in real sense of the term. The correct position of directors is that, they stand in fiduciary relationship with the company or they are quasi trustees, because
  (i) The company's money and property is vested in the company and not in them.
  (ii) The functions of directors are not exactly the same as trustees.
  (iii) Their duties of care are not as onerous as those of trustees.

According to Jessel, the directors are really commercial men managing a trading concern for the benefit of themselves and of all the shareholders in it. They stand in a fiduciary position towards the company in respect of their powers and capital under their control.

7.3.2 Who may be appointed as a Director ?

Under Sec. 149, no body corporate, association or firm shall be appointed director of a company and only an individual shall be so appointed. " If a director is an association or the body corporate then it becomes difficult to fix the responsibility to carry out obligations of such office. (Oriental Metal Processing Works Pvt. Ltd. Vs. B. K. Thakoor)

7.3.3 Qualifications of Directors - (Sec. 163)

The Companies Act has not prescribed any academic or professional qualifications for directors. Also, the Act imposes no share qualification on the directors. So, unless the company's Articles contain a provision to that effect, a director need not be a shareholder unless he wishes to be one voluntarily. But the Articles usually provide for a minimum share qualification. As per Reg. 66 of Table A, a Director must hold at least one share in a company. Where a share qualification is fixed by the Articles of a company, The act provides that -

   (i) it must be disclosed in the prospectus;

  (ii) each director must take his qualification shares within 2 months after his appointment;

 (iii) the notional value of the qualification shares must not exceed Rs. 5,000 or the nominal value of one share where it exceeds Rs. 5,000.

 (iv) share warrants will not count for purposes of share qualification.

If a director fails to obtain his qualification shares within 2 months, he vacates office automatically on the expiry of 2 months from the date of his appointment and if he acts as director after the expiry of said two months without taking qualification shares, he shall be liable to fine up to Rs. 500 for every day until he stops acting as such.

However, the Articles of a company cannot compel a person to hold qualification shares before he is elected a director nor can they require him to obtain qualification shares within a shorter period than two months after his appointment; and if any provision to this effect is made in the Articles, it shall be void.

The effect of this provision is that, if the company is wound up during this period of two months, the director cannot be placed in the list of contributories, in as much as there is no express or implied contract under which he would be bound to take the qualification shares, since his name cannot be put on the register of members unless he has applied for shares and those are allotted to him [Zamir Ahmed Raz. vs. D.R, Banaji (1957) 27 Comp. cas. 634].

It may be noted that

(a) Unless Articles provide otherwise, shareholding in joint names entitles any of the joint holders to be appointed as a director [Grundy vs. Briggs (1910)]. But, not more than one joint holder can be appointed.

(b) Mortgaging of shares shall not disqualify a person to be appointed as a director, unless Articles provide otherwise.

(c) On insolvency of a director, his shares are vested in Official Receiver/Assignee and the director cannot be said to hold the share qualification [Sutton vs. English & Colonial Produce Co. (1902)]. However, in India, an insolvent is otherwise also disqualified under act.

(d) A person who holds requisite qualification shares at the time of appointment, subsequent raising of the share qualification is not binding on such person [International Cable Co. ex. p. Official Liquidator (1892)].

Qualification Shares vis-a-vis Private Company, Provisions of act do not apply to a private company. Thus, a private company may or may not provide in its Articles any requirement of share qualification.

Thus, a provision in the Articles of a private company requiring its directors to obtain qualification shares is not repugnant to the provisions of act [Mrs. Aruna Suresh Mehra vs. Jifcon Tools (P.) Ltd. (1998) 18 SCL 79 (CLB, New Delhi.)].

7.3.4 Disqualification of a Director (Sec. 164)

Sec. 164 of the Companies Act, 2013 provides that the following persons shall not be capable of being appointed as directors of any company :
- (a) a person found by the competent Court to be of unsound mind;
- (b) an undischarged insolvent;
- (c) a person who has applied to be adjudged an insolvent;
- (d) a person who has been convicted by a Court of an offence involving moral turpitude and sentenced in respect thereof to imprisonment for not less than six months and a period of five years has not elapsed from the date of the expiry of the sentence;
- (e) a person whose calls in respect of shares of the company held by him, whether alone or jointly with others have been in arrears for more than 6 months; and
- (f) a person who has been disqualified by a Court in pursuance of Sec. 203, which empowers the Court to restrain fraudulent persons from managing companies, unless the leave of the Court has been obtained for his appointment,
- (g) such person is already a director of a public company which -
- (i) has not filed the annual accounts and annual returns for any continuous three financial years commencing on and after the first day of April, 1999; or
- (ii) has failed to repay its deposit or interest thereon on due date or redeem its debentures on due date or pay dividend and such failure continues for one year or more. The disqualification of act is not applicable to :

1. Special directors appointed under SICA,

2. Nominee directors directors appointed by public financial institutions and companies established under the Act of parliament having non-obstante provisions over the Companies Act, 2013, like IDBI, LIC, UTI, IIBI, etc. in their respective statutes shall not be liable to be disqualified under the act. Again, nominee directors of public financial institutions within the meaning of the Companies Act, 2013; Central or State Government; and Banking Companies shall not be disqualified.

However, such person shall not be eligible to be appointed as a director of any other public company for a period of five years from the date on which such public company, in which he is a director, failed to file annual accounts and annual returns under sub-clause (A) or has failed to repay its deposit or interest or redeem its debentures on due date or pay dividend referred to in sub-clause (B). The [Disqualification of Directors under the Companies Act, 2013 [Notification No. GSR 830(E), dated 21.10.2003 issued by Department of Company Affairs.

The Central Government vide powers conferred by clause (b) of Sec. 642 (1) has made certain rules to carry out. These Rules, inter alia, provide as follows :

1. Whenever a company fails to file the annual accounts and annual returns, persons who are directors on the last due date for filing the annual returns for any continuous three financial years commencing on and after the first day of April, 1999, shall be disqualified.

2. If a company has failed to repay any deposit, irrespective of the enactment, rules or regulations under which the deposits have been accepted by the companies, or interest thereon, or redeem its debentures, or pay any dividend declared on the respective due dates, and if such failure continues for one year, then the directors of that company shall stand disqualified immediately on expiry of that one year from the respective due dates, provided that all the directors who have been directors in the relevant year, from the due date to the expiry of one year after the due date, will be disqualified.

Provided further that disqualification on account of the reasons cited under this Rule shall also apply to the re-appointment as a director.

3.Duty of Statutory Auditor to report on disqualification

(a) It shall be the duty of statutory auditor of the appointing company as well as disqualifying company, as required under the act to report to the members of the company whether any director is disqualified from being appointed as director under the prorision of act and to furnish a certificate each year as to whether on the basis of his examination of the books and records of the company, any director of the company is disqualified for appointment as a director or not.

(b) It shall be the duty of statutory auditors of the 'disqualifying company' as required in to-report to the members of the company whether any director in the company has been disqualified during the year from being reappointed as director, or being appointed as director in another company.

4. Duty of company to intimate disqualification

Whenever a company fails to file the annual accounts and returns, or fails to repay any deposit, interest, dividend, or fails to redeem its debentures, as described the company shall immediately file a return in duplicate in Form 'DD-B', prescribed under these rules for this purpose, to the Registrar of Companies, furnishing therein the names and addresses of all the Directors of the company during the relevant financial years.

Provided that names of such directors who have been exempted from application by the Central Government, from time to time, shall be excluded.

Provided further that no unusual abbreviations or short forms shall be used in filling up the Form 'DD-B', which shall give such details as may be necessary to distinguish and identify each director without any ambiguity.

5. Failure to intimate disqualification shall render director as officer in default

When a company fails to file the Form 'DD-B' as above within 30 days of the failure that would attract disqualification, officers of the company listed in Sec. 5 of the Companies Act, 2013 shall be officers in default.

6. Registrar to register

(a) Upon receipt of the Form 'DD-B' in duplicate under Rule 5, the Registrar of Companies shall immediately register the document and place one copy of it in the document file for public inspection.

(b) The Registrar of Companies shall forward the other copy to the Central Government.

7. Names of the disqualified directors on the website, etc.

(a) The Central Government shall place on the website of the Department of Company Affairs the names and addresses and such other details including names and details of the companies concerned, as may be necessary, in respect of all the disqualified directors.

(b) The Central Government may also publicise the names of disqualified directors in such manner as it may consider appropriate.

(c) The Central Government shall take such steps as may be required to update its website to ensure that name of the person, in whose respect disqualification period has expired after 5 years, is deleted from the website.

8. Duty of every Director

Every director in a public company registered under the Companies Act, 2013 shall file Form 'DD-A', prescribed under these Rules, before his appointment or reapointment.

9. Punishment for contravention of the rules

If a company or any other person contravenes any provision of these rules for which no punishment is provided in the Companies Act, 2013, the company and every officer of the company who is in default or such other person shall be punishable with fine which may extend to five thousand rupees and where the contravention is a continuing one with a further fine which may extend to five hundred rupees for every day after the first, during which the contravention continues.

The disqualifications may be removed by the Central Government by a notification in the Official Gazette.

On the other hand, a private company which is not a subsidiary of a public company may add to the above list of disqualifications.

In other words, a public company or a private company which is a subsidiary of a public company cannot provide for any other disqualification. Thus, such a company cannot provide for any qualifications either, say, directors must at least be graduates, in as much as it will mean that those who do not possess those qualifications shall be disqualified. In view of the above observation, Sec. 164. The contradiction should, therefore, be set right.

A director who has been removed from office by the Central Government shall not be a director of a company, for a period of 5 years from the date of order of removal.

7.3.5 Appointment of Directors (Sec. 52)

The success of the company depends upon the experience, competence and honesty of its directors. So, the administration of the company should be carried out by efficient directors. The appointment of directors is regulated by the Act. Directors may be appointed as follows-

1) By the articles as regards first directors (Sec. 152)
2) By the company in general meeting (Sec. 151)
3) By the directors (Sec. 152)
4) By third parties
5) By the principle of proportional representation
6) By the Central Government

(1) First Directors (Sec. 152)

The Articles of a company usually contain names of the first directors. The articles may also provide that the number and the names of the first directors shall be determined in writing by the subscribers to the memorandum, or a majority of them.

If the directors are not named in the articles, the subscribers to the memorandum, who are individuals, shall be deemed to be the directors of the company, until the directors are duly appointed in the first annual general meeting.

(2) Appointment by company (Sec. 151)

Sec.151 provides that unless the articles provide for the retirement of all directors at every annual general meeting, not less than two thirds of the total number of directors of a public company or of a private company which is a subsidiary of a public company, must be appointed by the company in general meeting. These directors must be subject to retirement by rotation. The remaining directors of such a company and the directors of a private company which is not a subsidiary of a public company, must also be appointed by the company in a general meeting. It implies that not more than one third of the total number of directors can act as non retiring directors. For example, if a company has six directors, then it can appoint only two directors, which is one third of the total number of directors, as permanent directors if it wants to do so. The remaining four directors are subject to retire by rotation.

At every subsequent annual meeting one third of the directors of a public company or a private company which is not a subsidiary of a public company are liable to retire by rotation.

The directors to retire by rotation at every annual general meeting shall be those who have been longest in the office, since their last appointment, but as between persons who became directors on the same day, those who are to retire shall, in default of and subject to any agreement among themselves, be determined by a lot.

Rotational director means a director retiring by rotation and does not include additional, alternate, debenture holder's or Central Government's nominee directors.

At the annual general meeting at which a director retires, as aforesaid, the company may fill up the vacancy by appointing the retiring director or some other person thereto.

Appointment of a Director other than Retiring Director

A person who is not a retiring director shall be eligible for the appointment to the office of director subject to his necessary qualifications. A notice in writing under his hand signifying his candidature for the office of the director, must be left at the office of the company at least fourteen days before the date of meeting alongwith a deposit of five thousand rupees, which shall be refunded to a person if he succeeds in getting elected as a director.

The company shall inform its members of the candidature of a person, by serving individual notices on themselves at least seven days before the meeting.

A person who is being proposed as a candidate for the office of a director must sign and file with the company his consent in writing to act as a director if appointed.

Such a person shall not act as a director unless he has within 30 days of his election signed and filed with the Registrar his consent in writing to act as a director. This requirement does not apply to a director retiring by rotation.

Appointment of Directors to be voted Individually

At a general meeting of a public company or of a private company which is a subsidiary of public company, appointment of directors must be voted individually by separate ordinary resolution, unless, the company has in its general meeting unanimously so resolved. Thus, each director shall be appointed by a separate resolution unless it is unanimously decided in the general meeting that more than one director may be appointed by a single resolution. A resolution moved in contravention of this provision shall be void even if no objection was raised at the time of its being moved.

3) Appointment by Directors

The directors are empowered to appoint (i) additional directors (ii) alternate directors and (iii) directors filling casual vacancy

a) Additional Directors

The Board of directors may appoint additional directors if so authorised by articles of the company. Such additional directors shall hold office only up to the date of the next annual general meeting of the company, and the number of the directors and additional directors together shall not exceed the maximum strength fixed for the Board by the articles. This provision enables the Board to appoint competent persons who may find it difficult to come in by way of elections.

If annual general meeting of the company is not held or cannot be held, then the person appointed as a additional director vacates his office on the last day on which the annual general meeting should have been held.

b) Alternate Directors

The Board of directors may appoint an alternative director if authorised by the articles or by a resolution of the company in the general meeting. An alternate director acts in the place of a original director who is absent for more than three months from the state in which the Board meetings are held. He shall not hold office for a period longer than that permissible to the original director in whose place he has been appointed. He shall vacate office if and when the original director returns to the state.

Where articles prescribe a share qualification for the office of the director, the alternate director must possess or acquire the qualification.

c) Director filling Casual Vacancy

In case of a public company, if the office of any director appointed by the company in general meeting is vacated before his term of office expires in the normal course, the resultant casual vacancy may be filled by the Board of directors at a meeting of the Board. Such vacancy may occur by reason of death, resignation, bankruptcy, disqualification or failure of an elected director to accept the office. The director so appointed shall hold office only up to the date up to which the director was to hold the office. The term casual vacancy does not include vacancy caused by retirement by rotation of a director.

4) Appointment by Third Parties

One third of the total number of directors of a public company and of a private company which is a subsidiary of a public company, may be appointed by parties other than shareholders on non rotational basis.

The articles may provide for giving right to debentureholders, financial institutions or banking companies who have advanced loans to the company to nominate directors on the Board of the company.

5) Appointment by Proportional Representation

In case of a public company, directors of company are appointed by the majority of shareholders and hence a minority is not in position to elect even a single director on the Board. The act aims at protecting interests of minority shareholders by giving them opportunity to elect their nominee on the Board.

The articles of a company may provide for appointment of not less than two thirds of the total number of the directors of a public company or of a private company which is a subsidiary of a public company, according to the principle of proportional representation, whether by the single transferable vote or by a system of cumulative voting or otherwise; such appointments shall be made once in every three years and interim casual vacancies may be filled up.

6) Appointment by the Central Government

The Central Government has powers to appoint director on an order passed by the Tribunal to effectively safeguard the interests of the company or its shareholders or the public interests, to prevent mismanagement or oppression. Such directors shall hold office for a period not exceeding three years on any one occasion.

The power can be exercised by the Tribunal either on reference made by the Central Government or on an application (1) of not less than one hundred members of the company or (2) of the members of the company not holding less than one tenth of the total voting power therein.

The directors appointed by the Central Government, according to the provisions of the act shall not be required to hold any qualification shares nor his period of office shall be liable to determination by retirement of directors by rotation. Such a director may be removed by the Central Government from his office at any time and another person may be appointed by that Government in his place to hold office as a director.

Restrictions on Appointment as Directors

A person shall not be capable of being appointed as director of a company by the articles and shall not be named as a director or proposed director of a company in a prospectus issued or statement in lieu of prospectus, unless he or his agent authorised in writing has

a) signed and filed with the Registrar his consent in writing to act as such director and
b) either
(i) signed the memorandum for his qualification shares.
(ii) taken his qualification shares from the company and paid or agreed to pay for them or
(iii) signed and filed with the Registrar, an undertaking in writing to take from the company his qualification shares if any and pay for them.
(iv) made and filed with the Registrar an affidavit to the effect that his qualification shares, if any, are registered in his name.

These provisions do not apply to,

a) a company not having share capital
b) a private company
c) a company which was a private company before becoming a public company or
d) a prospectus issued by or on behalf of a company after the expiry of one year from the date on which the company was entitled to commence business.

7.3.6 Assignment of office by a Director

The act prohibits assignment of his office by director. The section applies to all companies. Section reads.

"An assignment of his office made after the commencement of this Act by any director of a company shall be void".

The supreme court has made a distinction between 'assignment' and 'appointment' and has held that where in the case of a private company a managing director who was holding his office for life and was empowered by the articles to appoint a successor, appointed by will to succeed him as managing director after his death, the appointment of the succssor did not come within the prohibition of the section. 'The Court observed "The section talks of assignment of his office by a director". The word 'his' would indicate that the office contemplated was one held by the director at the time of assignment.

7.3.7 Number of Directors (Sec. 165)

Sec. 165 provides that every public company (other than a public company which has become such by virtue of Sec. 43 A) shall have at least three directors, provide that a public company having (a) a paid up capital of five crore rupees or more (b) one thousand or more small shareholders, may have a director elected by such small shareholders in the manner as may be prescribed. A small shareholder means a shareholder holding shares of nominal value of twenty thousand rupees or less in a public company. Every other company (e.g. a private company or a deemed public company) shall have at least two directors. This is statutory limit, and subject to it the articles of a company may prescribe the maximum and minimum number of directors for its Board of directors. A company in a general meeting may by ordinary resolution change the number of its directors within the limits fixed by its articles. Beyond such limits, a variation can be made by passing a special resolution. Any increase beyond the limit fixed by articles must be approved by the central government except where the increase in the number of directors does not exceed more than twelve. This provision is not applicable to a government company and to a private company which is not a subsidiary of a public company.

7.3.8 Number of Directorship (attatchment)

The Companies Act, a person cannot hold office at the same time as a director in more than 15 companies. However, Sec. 278 provides that in computing this number of 15 directorships, the directorships of--

  (i) private companies (other than subsidaries or holding of public company (ies);
  (ii) unlimited companies;
  (iii) associations not carrying on business for profit or which prohibit the payment of dividend,
  (iv) alternate directorships,
        will be omitted.

In case any company ceases to fall in the categories (i), (ii) or (iii), above the directorships shall continue to remain excluded upto of 3 months from such cessation.

If a person, who is already a director of 15 companies or less in appointed, after the commencement of the Companies (Amendment) Act, 2000, as a director of other companies making the total number of his Directorships more than 15, the appointment will not be effective unless within 15 days thereafter, the director has vacated his office in any of the companies in which he was already a director so as to keep the number within the maximum allowed. None of the new appointments of a director shall take effect until such choice is made; and all the new appointments of a director shall take effect until such choice is made; and all the new appointments will become void if the choice is not made within 15 days as aforsaid.

Where a person is already holding the office of director in 14 companies or less and is appointed as a director of other companies taking the total number of directorships to more than 15, he must, out of new and old directorship, choose 15 companies within 15 days of the day on which the last appointment was made or else all his new appointments shall become void.

* As per the Companies (Amendment), Act, 2000.

Any person who holds office of, or acts as a director of more than 15 companies in contravention of the foregoing provisions shall be liable to be find up to Rs. 50,000 in respect of each of those companies after the first 15 companies.

Query, If a person is director of 15 public limited companies and if a private company of which he is a director becomes a public company, will be cease to be the director of that company, if he does not resign his directorship in any other public company?

Answer, If a person is already a director of 15 public companies and if a private company of which he is a director has become a public company, then the Department of Company Law Administration has poined, he will have to give up the directorship of one of those companies.

7.3.9 Vacation of Office of a Director (Sec. 167)

Sec. 167 provides for the office of the director becoming vacant on the happening of certain contingencies. It provides that the office of a director shall become vacant if -

(i) he is found to be of unsound mind by a competent Court;
(ii) he is adjudged insolvent;
(iii) he fails to obtain within 2 months of his appointment, or ceases to hold at any time thereafter his share qualification, if any;
(iv) he is convicted of an offence involving moral turpitude and sentenced to imprisonment for not less than 6 months;
(v) he fails to pay any call within 6 months from the last date fixed for the payment.
(vi) he absents himself from three consecutive meetings of the Board of Directors or from all meetings of the Board for a continuous period of three months, whichever is longer, without obtaining leave of absence from the Board; Where there was no proof that notices of Board meetings were served on directors, directors could not be removed on the ground that they abstained from attending meetings [Vijay Krishan jaidka vs. Jaidka Motor Co. Ltd. (1996) 10SCL244(CLB)J.

Again, where the director had been deliberately kept out of the affairs of the company and eventually was not allowed to continue in office as director of the company and there was no definite evidence as to the service of notices of Board meetings, he could not be removed from his position of a director by reason of non-attendance of three Board Meetings [Bagri Cereals (P). Ltd., In re: (1997) 5 Comp. L. J. 145(Cal.)].

(vii) he becomes disqualified by an order of the Court under Sec. 203 which restrains fraudulent persons from managing companies;

(viii) he is removed in pursuance of Sec. 284 by an ordinary resolution of which special notice was given;

(ix) he accepts a loan from the company in contravention.

(x) he falls to disclose to the Board his interest in any contract entered into by the company as required by Sec. 299; and

(xi) if he became the director by virtue of an office, on coming to an end of that office. A private company may provide additional grounds in its Articles for vacation of office of a director.

When shall Vacation of Office Takes Effect ?

Sec. 167, in this regard, provides that the disqualifications referred under (ii), (iv) and (v) above shall not take effect for 30 days from the date of the adjudication, sentence or order. Where any appeal or petition is preferred within 30 days, as aforesaid, against the adjudication, sentence or conviction, the disqualification shall not take effect until the expiry of 7 days from the date on which such appeal or petition is disposed off. However, where within 7 days, as aforesaid, any further appeal or petition is preferred and the appeal or petition, if allowed, would result in the removal of the disqualification, then the disqualification will not take effect until such further appeal or petition is disposed off.

Penalty. If a person functions as a director after his office has become vacant on account of any of the disqualifications specified under Sec. 167, he shall be punishable with fine up to Rs. 5,000 for every day during the period he so functions.

7.3.10 Removal of a Director (Sec. 169)

The discussion on removal of a director may be grouped under the following three heads:

1. Removal by shareholders,
2. Removal by Central Government, and
3. Removal by Company Law Board.

1) Removal by Shareholders

Sec. 169 provides that a company may, by ordinary resolution passed in general meeting after giving special notice of such resolution, remove a director before the expiry of his term of office.

On receipt of the special notice for removal of a director, the company must forthwith send a copy thereof to the director concerned to enable him to make a representation. If he makes a representation in writing and requests the company to notify it to the members, the company must, unless it is received by it too late for it to send to the members, state the fact of the representation to every member of the company to whom notice of the meeting is sent. If the representation is not sent as aforesaid, the company must at the instance of the director read it out at the meeting. The director is also entitled to be heard on the resolution at the meeting.

In Queen Kuries and Loans (P) Ltd. vs. Sheena, Jose [(1993) 76 Comp. Cas. Ker, 821] the Kerala High Court observed as follows : "Under Sec. 285 of the Companies Act, for removal of a director, special notice has to be given of a resolution seeking to remove a director. The notice must disclose the ground on which the director is proposed to be removed. The disclosure of the ground for removal is a matter of substance and not of form because the directors concerned are entitled to make a representation in writing against their removal at the meeting. The company is bound to send a copy of the representation to every member of the company to whom the notice of the meeting has been sent. It is only after these steps are taken that the resolution can be passed. So, where special notice of the resolution was not given; it amounted to a serious lapse depriving the directors of their statutory right to make a representation. The resolution removing the directors was, therefore, held to be invalid.

Please note that it is not necessary that there should be proof of mismanagement, breach of trust, misfeasance or other misconduct on the part of the directors sought to be removed. Where the shareholders feel that the policies pursued by the directors or any of them are not to their liking, they have the option to remove the directors by passing an ordinary resolution as per Sec. 284.

The following directors, however, cannot be removed by the company in general meeting :
   (i) a director appointed by the Central Government.
  (ii) a director of a private company holding office for life on April 1,1952;
 (iii) director elected by the principle of proportional representation.
 (iv) director appointed by Central Government under Industries (Development & Regulation) Act, 1951;
  (v) director appointed under SICA, 1985;
 (vi) director appointed by financial institutions under statutory powers;
(vii) nominee director;
(viii) director appointed by Company Law Board.

2) Removal by Central Government

The Central Government has the power to make a reference to the Company Law Board against any managerial personnel. The power can be exercised where, in the opinion of the Central Government, there are circumstances suggesting :

(a) that any person concerned in the conduct and management of the affairs of a company is or has been guilty of fraud, misfeasance, persistent negligence or default in carrying out his obligations and functions under the law, or breach of trust in connection therewith; or

(b) that the business of the company is not or has not been conducted and managed by such person in accordance with sound business principles or prudent commercial practices; or

(c) that the business of the company is or has been conducted or managed by such person in a manner which is likely to cause or has in fact caused, serious injury or damage to the interest of trade, industry or business to which such company pertains; or

(d) that the business of the company is or has been conducted and managed by such person with an intent to defraud its creditors, members, or any other person or otherwise for a fraudulent or unlawful purpose in a manner prejudicial to public interest.

The reference may be made by stating a case against the person aforesaid with a request that the Company Law Board may inquire into the case, record findings as to whether or not such person is fit and proper person to hold the office of director or any other office connected with the conduct and management of any company.

At the conclusion of the hearing of the case, the Company Law Board shall record its findings, stating therein specifically as to whether or not the director is a fit and proper person to hold the office of director or any other office connected with the conduct and management of any company.

On the basis of the aforesaid findings, the Central Government may, by order, notwithstanding any other provisions contained in the Act, remove the delinquent respondent from his office. The said order must not, however, be passed against any person unless he has been given a reasonable opportunity to show cause against the order.

After the delinquent person has been, by order, removed, he shall not hold any office for a period of 5 years from the date of the order of removal, nor will he be paid any compensation for loss of office as a result of removal. The time limit may, however, be relaxed by the Central Government with the previous concurrence of the Company Law Board.

In Marutti Udyog Ltd. v. R. C. Bhargava [1998] 17SCL269, the CLB, Principal Bench New Delhi dismissed a petition under Sec. 388 B as the reference was made by the Central Government after 5 to 13 years of occurrences of matters alleged on ground of gross and inordinate delay which remained unexplained by the Central Government which was in full knowledge of the matters as possessing substantial control over the company. However, the Bench held that no period of limitation exists for making a reference to CLB but gross and inordinate delay in the absence of justifiable ground to make the reference renders it liable to be dismissed.

3) Removal by Company Law Board

Where an application has been made to the Company Law Board under Sec. 241 against oppression and mismanagement of a company's affairs, the Company Law Board may order for the termination or setting aside of an agreement which the company might have made with its directors. Such a director shall not be entitled to serve as a manager, managing director or director of the company without leave of the Company Law Board for a period of 5 years from the date of Company Law Board's order terminating or setting aside his contract with the company. He shall also not be entitled to claim any compensation from the company for the loss of office.

7.3.11 Resignation by a Director (sec. 168)

A director can resign from his office in the manner laid down in the Articles of the company. Where Articles do not contain any provision in this regard, a director may still resign at any time by giving a reasonable notice to the company.

In S. S. Lakshaman Pillai vs. Registrar of Companies (1977) 47 Comp. Cas. 652 Mad., the Madras High Court held that if there is a provision in the Articles, resignation will take effect in accordance with such provision and, if there is no provision, resignation will take effect in accordance with its terms. Notice may be written or oral.

In the aforesaid case, the Madras High Court also held that the resignation shall be effective even when no other director was in office. In this case, of the two directors of a company, one died and the other wanted to resign.

A verbal resignation accepted at a meeting is sufficient, even if the Articles provide for resignation in writing (Latchford Premier Cinema vs. Ennion). Once made, resignation is irrevocable (Glossop vs. Glossop). A managing or wholetime director cannot resign merely by giving a notice. In his case, a formal acceptance of the resignation by the company is essential. This is because of the fact that such a director, besides being an ordinary director, is also in the wholetime employment of the company. He has to be relieved of the duties and responsibilities attaching to his office. Notice that, if a director holding office both of a wholetime and ordinary director resigns, his resignation shall apply to both the offices (Mosley vs. Koffyfontein Mines Ltd).

7.3.12 Compensation for loss of Office (Sec. 169)

Sec. 169 provides that removal of a director would not deprive the person of any compensation or damage for the termination of appointment as a director or for an appointment terminating with that as director. The act does not provide for payment of compensation for loss of office or any other payment for loss of office or place of profit except the loss of office held by the director in the capacity of managing director, wholetime director or manager. Further, the managing or wholetime director or manager would not be entitled to any compensation :

(a) where the director resigns his office in view of the reconstruction of the company, or of its amalgamation with any other body corporate or bodies corporate, and is appointed as the managing director, manager or other officer of the reconstructed company or of the body corporate resulting from the amalgamation;

(b) where the director resigns his office otherwise than on the reconstruction of the company or its amalgamation as aforesaid;

(c) where the office of the director is vacated by virtue;

(d) where the company is being wound up, whether by or subject to the supervision of the court or voluntarily, provided the winding up was due to the negligence or default of the director;

(e) if it can be shown that he had been guilty of fraud or breach of trust in relation to, or gross negligence in or, gross mismanagement, in the conduct of the affairs of the company or any subsidiary or holding company thereof;

(f) if it can be shown that while he was a director he had instigated or taken part directly or indirectly in bringing about the termination of his office;

(g) if the winding up commences, within 12 months of his removal.

Amount of Compensation. A ceiling on the amount of compensation payable to a director eligible for compensation for loss of office. The sub-section provides that any payment made to a managing or other director in pursuance shall not exceed the remuneration which he would have earned if he had been in office for the unexpired residue of his term or for three years, whichever is shorter.

The amount payable shall be calculated on the basis of the average remuneration actually earned by him during the period of three years immediately preceding the date on which he ceased to hold the office. But, where he held the office for a lesser period than three years, the amount shall be calculated with reference to the period he actually worked.

Payment to director, for loss of office in connection with transfer of undertaking or property.

In case of transfer of the whole or any part of any undertaking or property of the company the act prohibits every director of a company to receive any payment by way of compensation for loss of office or as consideration for retirement from office. The compensation/consideration cannot be received -

(a) from such company; or

(b) from the transferee of such undertaking or property or from any other person. However, the aforesaid payment may be received if -

(a) the same had been disclosed to the members of the company; and

(b) the proposal has been approved by the company in general meeting. Any amount received by a director in contravention of the aforesaid provisions shall be deemed to have been received by him in trust for the company.

Payment to director for loss of office in connection with transfer of shares.

The acquisition of a company may take place either through purchase of an undertaking or through purchase of shares. The act prohibits receipts, by any director, of any compensation for loss of office or consideration for retirement from office in connection with the transfer to any person of all or any shares in a company. The compensation/consideration cannot be received either from the company or the transferees of shares or from any other person without disclosure of the same to the shareholders.

The aforesaid transfer of shares may result from -

   (i) an offer made to the general body of shareholders;

  (ii) an offer made by or on behalf of some other body corporate with a view to the company becoming a subsidiary of such body corporate or a subsidiary of its holding company;

 (iii) an offer made by or on behalf of an individual with a view of obtaining the right to exercise, or control the exercise of, not less than one-third of the total voting power at any general meeting of the company; or

 (iv) any other offer which is conditional on acceptance to a given extent.

A director who fails to disclose the particulars, with respect to the aforesaid payment, to the shareholders shall be punishable with fine which may extend in Rs. 2,500/-. Besides, any sum received by such director shall be deemed to have been received by him in trust for any persons who have sold their shares as a result of the offer made. The expenses incurred by him in distributing that sum amongst those persons shall be borne by him and not retained out of that sum.

However, if at a meeting called for the purpose of approving any payment, as aforesaid, a quorum is not present and, after the meeting has been adjourned to a later date, a quorum is again not present, the payment shall, for the purposes of that sub-section, be deemed to have been approved.

7.3.13 Office or Place of Profit

(a) Meaning of 'Office or Place of Profit' held by a Director

As per Sec. 188 (a) of the Companies Act, 2013, any office or place shall be deemed to be an office or place of profit held by a director under the company, if the director holding it obtains from the company anything by way of remuneration over and above the remuneration to which he is entitled as such director. Such remuneration may be by way of salary, fees, commission, perquisites, the right to occupy free of rent any premises as a place of residence or otherwise.

The word 'office' means any employment directly under the company, 'Place' means a position which may not be directly under the employment of the company but the remuneration comes from the company. Any regular payment received by a director so long as he holds the post will be an 'office or place of profit' [Astley vs. New Tivoli Co. (1899)]. The office of legal or technical advisor is an office of profit. Also, the appointment of a managing director or director of a company or his relative as sole selling agent shall be regarded as office or place of profit under the company within the meaning of Sec. 188 of the Act.

Posts not 'Office or Place of Profit'. The posts of managing director, manager, banker, trustee for debenture-holders are not office or place of profit for the purposed of this Section.

(b) Restriction on a Director for Holding an Office or Place of Profit

Sec. 314 (1) provides that a director may be appointed to hold an office or place of profit in a company or its subsidiary provided a special resolution is passed to that effect. However, it shall be sufficient if the special resolution according to the consent of the company is passed at the general meeting of the company held for the first time after holding of such office or place of profit.

Previous consent is thus not necessary. Consent shall be necessary for each appointment and for each increase in salary (except on a time-scale) but not for renewal of appointment at the same or lower remuneration.

(c) Restriction on an Associate of a Director for Holding an Office or Place of Profit. (Sec. 188)

Sec. 188 while disallowing the appointment of a relative of a director to any office or place of profit carrying monthly remuneration of the prescribed sum (presently, Rs. 10,000/- p.m.) without approval of the shareholders by way of a special resolution makes certain exceptions including appointment as managing director. Accordingly, the appointment in question shall not require any approval by way of special resolution.

It may further be noted that the appointment of certain persons to an office or place of profit carrying a total monthly remuneration of, presently, Rs. 50,000/- or more (w.e.f. 5.2.2003) cannot be made unless the prior consent of the company by passing a special resolution and the approval of the Central Government is obtained. These persons include :

(i)   partner or relative of a director or manager;
(ii) firm in which such director or manager or relative of either is a partner;
(iii) a private company of which such a director or manager or relative of either is a director or member.

It may be noted that the exemption available with respect to appointment as managing director, manager, banker or debenture-trustee is not available to appointments made.

7.3.14 Interested Director (Sec. 184)

Sec. 184 of the Companies Act, 2013 provides that except with the consent of the Board of directors of a company, a director shall not enter into any contract with the company :

(a) for the sale, purchase or supply of any goods, materials, or services; or - (b) for underwriting the subscription of any shares in, or debentures of, the company. Where the paid-up share capital of a company is Rs. 1 crore or more, the aforesaid contracts shall also require the approval of the Central Government.

Exceptions : The aforesaid approvals shall not apply to or affect:(a) the purchase of goods and materials from the company or the sale of goods and materials to the company for cash at prevailing market prices ; or

(b) any contract or contracts between the company on one side and any such director on the other for sale, purchase or supply of any goods, materials and services in which either the company or the director regularly trades or does business provided the value of goods in any year does not exceed Rs. 5,000/- ; or

(c) any 'transaction of a banking or insurance company in the ordinary course of business.

However, in circumstances of urgent necessity, a director may enter into any contract for the sale, purchase, or supply of goods, materials or services without obtaining the consent of the Board. The consent of the Board, in such cases, may be obtained within 3 months of the date on which the contract was entered into.

The consent of the Board, as aforesaid, shall be given by way of a resolution passed at a meeting of the Board. In case the Board does not give consent to any contract, anything done in pursuance of the contract shall be voidable at the option of the Board.

Disclosure of Interest by Director :

In respect of contracts with a director, Sec. 184 casts an obligation on the director to disclose the nature of his concern or interest (direct or indirect), if any, at a meeting of the Board of Directors. The said Section provides that in case of a proposed contract or arrangement, the required disclosure shall be made at the meeting of the Board at which the question of entering into the contract or agreement is first taken into consideration. In the case of any other contract or an arrangement, the disclosure shall be made at the first meeting of the Board held after the director becomes interested in the contract or an arrangement.

For the aforesaid purpose, a general notice given to the Board by a director, to the effect that he is a director or a member of a specified body corporate or is a member of a specified firm and is to be regarded as concerned or interested in any contract or arrangement which may, after the date of the notice, be entered into with that body corporate or firm, shall be deemed to be a sufficient disclosure of concern or interest in relation to any contract or arrangement so made.

Any such general notice shall, however, expire at the end of the financial year in which it is given, but may be renewed for further period of one financial year at a time, by a fresh notice given in the last month of the financial year in which it would otherwise expire.

No such general notice, and no renewal thereof, shall be of effect unless either it is given at a meeting of the Board, or the director concerned takes reasonable steps to ensure that it is brought up and read at the first meeting of the Board after it is given.

Effect of Failure to Disclose Interest

1. Fine. As per sub-Sec. 184 every director who fails to comply with the aforesaid requirements as to disclosure of concern or interest shall be punishable with fine which may extend to Rs. 50,000/-.

2. Interested Director not to Participate or Vote in Board's Proceedings. provides that no director of a company shall, as a director, take part in the discussion of, or vote on, any contract or arrangement entered into, or to be entered into, by or on; behalf of the company, if he is in any way, whether directly or indirectly, concerned or interested in the contract or arrangement.

Besides, his presence shall not count for the purposes of forming a quorum at : the time of any such discussion or vote. In case he does vote, his vote shall be void.

The aforesaid bar on an interested director to participate or vote at a meeting shall not apply to :

(a) a private company which is neither a subsidiary nor a holding company of a public company;

(b) a private company which is a subsidiary of a public company, in respect of any contract or arrangement entered into or to be entered into, by the private company with the holding company thereof;

(c) any contract of indemnity against any loss which the director, or any one or more of them, may suffer by reason of becoming or being sureties or a surety for the company;

(d) any contract or arrangement entered into or to be entered into with a public company, or a private company which is a subsidiary of a public company in which the interest of the director aforesaid consists solely -

(i) in his being a director of such company and the holder of not more than shares of such number or value therein as is requisite to qualify him for appointment as a director thereof, he having been nominated as such director by the company referred to in sub-Sec. (1), or

(ii) in his being a member holding not more than 2 per cent of its paid-up share capital; and

(e) a public company, or a private company which is a subsidiary of a public company in respect of which a notification is issued under sub-Sec. (3) to the extent specified in the notification.

3. Cessation of Office of Directorship. An office of a director shall fall vacant in case he acts in contravention.

Allotment of Shares to close relatives of Directors without disclosure of interest — Whether violation of the act.

The question was addressed to the Kerala High Court in Mukkattukara Catholic Ltd. v. M. V. Thomas (1995) 4 Comp. L. J. The learned judge observed that Sec. 300 does not cover a case of registration of transfer of shares where the company only performs a statutory function. The operation of Sec. 300 is made limited to contracts or arrangements made by or on behalf of the company. The court further observed that under Sec. 110 of the Companies Act, an application for registration of transfer of shares or other interest of a member of a company may be made. The company, by virtue of Sec. 111, may refuse to register the transfer or transmission. However, in exercising power under Sec. 111 no element of contract or arrangement within the meaning of Sec. 300 is involved with respect to which there can be an interested director, in the sense in which the expression could be understood under the Act.

7.3.15 Duties of Directors (Sec. 166)

As the directors occupy key position in the management of a company, they possess immense powers. Their duties are usually regulated by the Articles of the Company Law also imposes certain duties on them in the interest of the company, shareholders and the public. Although the duties of the directors vary from company to company, certain common duties may be discussed under various heads as follows-

1) Fiduciary duties
2) Duty of care, skill and diligence
3) Duty to attend Board meetings
4) Duty not to Delegate
5) Duty to disclose own interest
6) Statutory duties

Let us discuss these duties briefly.

1) Fiduciary Duties

As the directors occupy fiduciary position in the organization, they must exercise their powers honestly, in good faith and in the interest of the company. The directors must not enter into engagements in which there is a possibility that the personal interests of the director could conflict with those of the company, which they are bound to protect. The directors owe a fiduciary duty to the company, they hence should not misuse their position to make a secret profit. If they do so, they have to account for it to the company. The fiduciary is owed to the company as a whole and not to an individual shareholder of it.

2) Duty of Care, Skill and Diligence

A director should carry out his duties with such care, skill and diligence as is reasonably expected from persons of their knowledge and skill. If he fails to do so, then he is guilty of negligence. However, the duty of care, skill and diligence will depend upon the nature, usages and customs of the business and the division of power between directors and other officers. However, he must act honestly and should exercise his skill and diligence that would amount to a reasonable care which is expected to take on his own behalf. He is not expected to show performance of his duties a greater degree than what is reasonably expected from him. He is also not bound to give continuous attention to the affairs of the company as his duties are of intermittent in nature, to be performed at periodical board meetings. "In respect of all duties that having regard to the exigencies of business and the Articles of Association, may properly be left to some other official, a director is, in the absence of grounds for suspicion, justified in trusting that official to perform such duties honestly". (Re City Equitable Fire Insurance Co. Ltd.)

3) Duty to Attend Board Meetings

A director should attend the Board meetings whenever he is able to do so, although he is not bound to attend all the meetings. If he fails to attend meetings continuously, it may make him liable for the acts of his co-directors. If he absents himself from three consecutive meetings of the Board or from all meetings of the Board for a continuous period of three months, whichever is longer, without obtaining leave of absence from the Board, then the office of the director becomes vacant.

4) Duty Not To Delegate

As a rule, directors must perform their duties personally and they should not delegate their office. However, they can delegate their duties if the Act or the Articles specifically authorise them for it. Secondly taking into consideration the exigencies of business, the directors may distribute the work among themselves and with other officials of the company.

5) Duty To Disclose Interest

"For the proper exercise of the functions of a director, it is essential that he be disinterested, that is to say, he should be free from any conflicting interest." It implies that a company can avoid a contract in which the director has an interest unless the prior sanction of the Board has been taken.

Any director who is interested in any transaction of the company, is bound to disclose his interest to the Board. The act provides that an interested director cannot take part in the discussion or vote on any contract in which he is directly or indirectly interested.

6) Statutory Duties

The directors have certain statutory duties laid down by the Act. Some of the important duties are listed below.

1) Duty not to allot shares until minimum subscription is raised
2) Duty to sign annual returns and the certificate attached there to
3) Duty to forward statutory report to every member of the company
4) Duty to call an annual general meeting every year within the proper time
5) Duty to call an extraordinary general meeting on a valid requisition
6) Duty to prepare Profit and Loss Account and Balance Sheet and lay before the company with the director's report as to the state of company's affairs
7) Duty to take share qualification
8) Duty to disclose shareholding
9) Duty to submit a statement of affairs on winding up etc.

7.3.16 Liabilities of Directors

The liabilities of directors may be classified in civil liability and criminal liability. Let us discuss them

    (A) Civil Liability

Civil liability of directors include
a) Liability towards the company and
b) Liability to the Third Parties

a) Liability towards the company

Directors are the trustees and agents of the company, hence they owe certain duties to the company. Breach of these duties or negligence in the performance of these duties may make them liable to the company and its members. They may be liable for 1) negligence 2) misfeasance 3) breach of trust and 4) ultravires acts.

(1) Negligence- Fidelity or faithfulness alone is not sufficient and a director has to perform his functions with reasonable care. He has to attend with due diligence and caution the work assigned to him. A director is not liable for mere errors of judgment resulting in a loss to the company, provided he acted bonafide in the interest and for the benefit of the company.

According to Sec. 201 of the Act, any provisions in the articles of the company or in any agreement with the company, exempting any offer of the company from any liability arising from any negligence, default or misfeasance shall be void.

(2) Misfeasance- Misfeasance is defined as any breach of duty in the conduct of the company's affairs which causes loss to the company. It is something more than negligence. Any fraud or underhand dealing by the director will render him liable to the company for any loss suffered by the company as a result of it. In order to take action against a director on the ground of misfeasance, two conditions must be satisfied.

(i) There must be misconduct or negligence on the part of a director and
(ii) Such act must be willful.

(3) Breach of Trust- As the directors are the trustees of the company, they must exercise their powers bonafide and in the interest of the company as a whole. The assets of the company are entrusted to the directors to be applied for achieving certain defined objects and if they are applied for other objects, then the directors are liable for a breach of trust. Thus, any misapplication of funds of the company amounts to a breach of trust.

(4) UltraVires Act- Any acts of directors which are in excess of their powers or ultra vires, as a result of which the company suffers a loss then the directors shall be personally liable to the company to make good the loss. For example, where the directors pay dividend out of their capital, they would be compelled to pay back the amount to the company.

(b) Liability to Third Parties

(i) As to Contracts - Directors as agents of a company are not personally liable on contracts entered into as agents on behalf of the company. As Lord Cairns pointed out in the case of Fergusson V Wilson, "wherever an agent is liable, those directors will be liable, where the liability would attach to the principal and the principal only, the liability is the liability of the company".

(ii) As to Frauds and Torts - A director who is a party to a fraud or to the commission of any tort is personally liable to the injured party. For example, if by the order of directors the patent is infringed or any other wrongful act is committed, the directors who are parties to it are personally liable. But a director is not liable for the fraud of his co-directors unless he has participated or has been authorised by him.

(iii) Liability Under the Provisions of the Act - The directors are personally liable to third parties under the provisions of the Companies Act.

(a) Misstatements in the prospectus

Directors are liable for any fraudulent statement in the prospectus which has induced a person to subscribe for shares in the company.

(b) Failure to repay the application money for shares

Where the minimum subscription as stated in prospectus has not been subscribed, then the allotment of shares cannot be made by the company. If the allotment of shares is not made within 120 days after the first issue of the prospectus, all money received from the applicants has to be repaid without interest. Where such money is not repaid, within further ten days, the directors of the company are jointly and severally liable to repay the money with interest at a rate of six percent per annum.

(c) Irregular Allotment

Where the directors knowingly contravene the provisions of the act regarding the allotment of shares, they are liable to compensate the company and the allottee for any loss or damage suffered thereby. The proceedings against the directors must be commenced within two years of the allotment.

(d) Failure to repay application money

Where no application has been made or where permission has not been granted by the stock exchange, the company has to repay all money received from the applicants within eight days after the company becomes liable to pay. If the application money is not repaid within eight days, the directors are jointly and severally liable to repay the money with interest at the rate of 15% per annum from the expiry of the 8th day.

(e) Fraudulent Trading by the Company

In case of a fraudulent trading by the company, the directors may be held personally liable by an order of the court.

(B) Criminal Liability

Under the Companies Act 2013 there are certain duties of the Directors appointed in accordance with the principle of proportional representation.

Special Notice

The special notice shall be required of any resolution to remove a director or to appoint somebody instead of a director so removed at the meeting at which he was removed.

On receipt of notice of a resolutions to remove a director, the company shall send a copy thereof to the director concerned and the director (whether or not he is a member of the company) shall be entitled to be heard on the resolution at the meeting.

Director's Right to Make Representation

The director concerned may make a representation in writing to the company (not exceeding a reasonable length) and request their notification to members of the company. The company shall -

I) In any notice of the resolution given to members of the company, state the fact of the representation having been made and

II) Send the copy of the representation to every member of the company to whom the notice of the meeting is sent. If a copy of the representations is not sent, because of the company's default the director may require that, the representations shall be read out at the meeting.

Copies of the representations need not be sent out and representations need not be read out at the meeting if-

(I) On the application either of the company or of any other person who claims to be aggrieved, the Central Government is satisfied that the rights conferred by this subsection are being abused to secure needless publicity for defamatory matter and

(II) The Central Government may order the company's costs on the application, to be paid in whole or in part by the director, notwithstanding that he is not a party to it.

Compensation-A director so removed shall not be deprived of any compensation or damages payable to him in respect of termination of his appointment as a director.

7.3.17 Loans to Directors (Sec. 185)

Sec. 185 provides that, without obtaining prior approval of the Central Government, a company cannot give any loan to or give any security or guarantee for any loan taken or given by -

(a) any director of the lending company or of a company which is its holding company or any partner or relative of such director;

(b) any firm in which any such director or relative is a partner;

(c) any private company of which any such director is a member or director;

(d) any company where such director or two or more such directors may exercise or control not less than 25 per cent of the total voting power; and

(e) any company, the Board of directors, managing director or manager of which is accustomed to act in accordance with the directions of the Board, or any director or directors of the lending company.

The further prohibits a company from :
(i) giving any guarantee for a loan taken by a director from any other person and providing of any security for any such loan, and
(ii) providing of any guarantee or security for a loan given by a director to any other person.

Exemptions : The aforesaid restrictions, however, do not apply to any loan made, guarantee given or security provided by :
(i) a private company (unless it is a subsidiary of a public company);
(ii) a banking company;
(iii) a holding company in respect of any loan given by it to its subsidiary company or any security or guarantee provided by it for any loan given to its subsidiary company.
(iv) There is also no prohibition against a banking company lending money to concerns of which a director of the bank is also a director [Re. Bank of Commerce Ltd. (1947) C.W.N. 662].
(v) any facility given by the company to its directors for payment of a flat/ accommodation in instalments;
Thus, in Dr. Fredie Ardeshir Mehta v. Union of India (1991), it was held that where a director was given official accommodation by the company in the matter of payment of the debt, such official accommodation was not and did not amount to a loan. When act refers to an indirect loan to a director, what it means is that, the company shall not give a loan to a director through the agency of one or more intermediaries. The word 'indirectly' in the Section cannot be read as converting what is not a loan into a loan. Thus, there was no contravention.
(vi) any salary advance given to the relative of a director who is also an employee. Thus, in the absence of any evidence that there has been circumvention of the Section by disguising the loan to the wife of a director, who is also an employee, as salary advance, the Court refused to accept the case of prosecution - M. R. Electronic Components Ltd. v. Assistant Registrar of Companies [1987] 61 Comp.Cas.8(Mad.).

Penalty : Every person, including the director or any person to whom the loan is made, who is a party to any contravention of act shall be punishable with fine which may extend to Rs. 50,000/- or with simple imprisonment which may extend to 6 months. However, where any such loan, or any, loan in connection with which any such guarantee or security has been given or provided by the lending company, has been repaid in full, no punishment by way of imprisonment shall be imposed. Further, where the loan has been repaid in part, the maximum punishment which may be imposed under the act by way of imprisonment shall be proportionately reduced. Again, all persons who are knowingly parties to any contravention of the act shall be jointly and severally liable to make good the amount which the company has paid on account of the loan, guarantee or security.

The aforesaid restrictions of Sec. 185 also apply to any transaction represented by a book debt which was from its inception in the nature of a loan or an advance.

7.3.18 Managerial Remuneration (Sec. 197)

Directors are not servants of the company, hence they have no right for payment unless it is provided in the articles.

Sec. 197 provides that remuneration payable to directors shall be determined either by the articles of the company or by a resolution of the company in general meeting. The resolution may be ordinary or special as the articles require. Unless there is a clear provision to that effect in the articles, the remuneration cannot be determined at a meeting of the directors themselves.

Sec. 197 lays down the overall maximum managerial remuneration which can be paid by a public company or a subsidiary of a public company. The total managerial remuneration payable to directors on manager for a financial year shall not exceed eleven percent of the net profits of the company. If in any financial year, a company has no profits or its profits are inadequate, the company shall not pay to its directors, including any managing or wholetime director or manager by way of remuneration, any sum exclusive of any fees payable to directors, except with the previous permission of the Central Government. However, where the appointment and remuneration of the managerial personnel is subject to the provisions of Sec. 197 read with schedule XIII of the Act, the company can pay minimum remuneration inspite of losses or inadequacy of profits, without the approval of the Central Government.

Remuneration - Meaning

In order to make this limit meaningful and to protect the interests of the company, the explanation to Sec. 198 provides that the term remuneration includes -

i) any expenditure incurred by the company in providing any rent free accomodation or any other benefit or amenity in respect of accomodation free of charge.

ii) any expenditure incurred by the company in providing any other benefit or amenity free of charge or at a concessional rate.

iii) any expenditure incurred by the company in respect of any obligation or service which otherwise would have been incurred by the directors or manager.

iv) any expenditure incurred by the company to effect any insurance on the life of the person or his spouse or in providing any pension, annuity or gratuity.

Rules Regarding Director's Remuneration

The remuneration payable to the directors including managing or wholetime directors, shall be determined according to the provisions of Sec.s 197

(i) articles of the company or

(ii) a resolution passed in general meeting, or

(iii) a special resolution passed by the Company in general meeting.

The remuneration payable to any director shall include the remuneration payable to director for all services rendered by them in any other capacity except where

i) the services rendered are of a professional nature and

ii) in the opinion of the Central Government, the director possessd the requisite qualifications for the practice of the profession.

A director may receive remuneration by way of a fee for each meeting of the Board or a committee thereof, attended by him.

Mode of Payment

Sec. 197 lays down that, a director who is neither in the wholetime employment of the compnay nor a managing director may be paid remuneration either

a) by way of monthly, quarterly or annual payment with the approval of the Central government.

b) by way of commission if the company by special resolution authorises such payment.

Maximum Remuneration

The remuneration paid to such director or where there is more than one such director, to all of them together shall not exceed.

i) one percent by the net profits of the company, if the company has a managing or wholetime director or a manager.

ii) three percent of the net profits of the company in any other case.

However, the company in general meeting may, with the approval of the Central Government increase these rates of remuneration.

The sepcial resolution shall not remain in force for a period of more than five years, but may be renewed, from time to time, by special resolution for further periods of not more than five years at a time. But no renewal shall be effected earlier than one year from the date on which it is to come into force.

Excess Payment

If any director draws or receives, directly or indirectly, by way of remuneration any such sums in excess of the limit prescribed by this section or without the prior sanction of the Central Government, where it is required, he shall refund such sums to the company and until such sum is refunded, hold it in trust for the company.

The Compay shall not wave the recovery of any sum refundable to it, unless permitted by the Central Government.

Payment of Remuneration to Managing or wholetime Director

Mode of Payment - A director who is either in wholetime employment of the company or a managing director may be paid remuneration either by way of a monthly payment or at a specified percentage of the net profits of the company or partly by one way and partly by the other.

Maximum Remuneration

(I) The remuneration shall not exceed five percent of the net profits for the such director and

(II) If there is more than one such director ten percent for all of them together.

Increase in Remuneration of Managing or whole time Director.

With the approval of the Central Government, remuneration may be paid in excess of 5% or 10% as the case may be.

Increase in Remuneration

In the case of a public company or a private company which is a subsidiary of public company, any increase in remuneration of director, wholetime and managing director, shall not have any effect.

I) In case where Schedule XIII is applicable, unless such increase is in accordance with the conditions specified in that Schedule and

II) in any other case, unless it is approved by the Central Government.

But no such approval is needed to increase fees payable to directors for attending meetings of the Board or a Committee there of, provided the amount of such fee after the increase, does not exceed such sum as may be prescribed.

A private company which converts itself into a public company or becomes a public company under the provisions of Sec. 43A, cannot pay without approval of the Central Government more than the prescribed amount as sitting fees to its directors.

———————————

QUESTIONS

A) Answer in 20 words.

1) Define 'Director'.
2) State the Number of Directors necessary in Private Ltd. Co. & Public Ltd. Co.
3) Explain the positions of director as a trustee.
4) What do you mean by retirement of directors by rotation?
5) What is overall limit of managerial remuneration when there is profit and when there is no profit?
6) Explain the position of director as a representative of shareholders.
7) How first director is appointed?

8) How casual vacancy of director is filled up?

9) What do you mean by 'Alternate Director'?

B) Answer the following in 50 words.

1) What are the provisions regarding appointment of directors?

2) What are the restrictions on appointment of directors?

3) Define 'Director' and explain its position.

4) What are the provision and regarding removal of director?

5) State the provisions under companies Act 1956 regarding Managerial Remuneration.

6) State the liabilities of directors.

C) Answer the following in 150 words.

1) Define the term 'Director'.How Directors are appointed?

2) Define 'Director'. What are the restrictions on appointment of directors?

3) What are the rules regarding payment of remuneration to directors.

4) Define 'Director.' What are the powers of the Board of Directors?

5) State the duties and liabilities of directors.

6) Define the term 'Director'. Explain the positions of directors.

7) Define 'Director'. What are the provisions regarding removal of directors?

8) Explain the activites specified in schedule VII relatives to corporote social responsibility.

D) Answer in details (about 300/500 words)

1) Explain the term 'Director'. What are the duties and liabilities of director?

2) Define 'Director'. How first and subsequent Directors are appointed?

3) What is 'Director'. Explain the provisions regarding removal and retirement of directors.

4) Explain the powers of the Board of Directors.

5) Define 'Director'. Explain the position of company director.

6) Explain the term 'Director'. What are the different provision regarding managerial remuneration.

7) Explain the procedure of removal of director.

8) What are the rights, duties and liabilities of company directors.

Chapter 8 | KEY MANAGERIAL PERSONNEL (KMP)

CONTENTS

8.1 Managerial Personnel
    8.1.1   Manging Director
    8.1.2   Manager
    8.1.3   Whole time Director

8.2 Role of Board of Director

8.3 Corporate Social Responsibility

8.4 Prerention of Oppression and Mismangement

8.1 MANAGERIAL PERSONNEL

8.1.1 Managing Director [Sec. 2(54)]

A) Meaning

Managing Director means a directors, who, by virtue of an agreement with the company or of a resolutions passed by the company in general meeting or by a Board of Directors or by virtue of its memorandum or articles of association, is entrusted with substantial powers of management, which would not otherwise be exercisable by him and includes a direction occupying the position of a managing director, by whatever name called. A managing director of a company shall exercise his powers subject to the superintendence, control and direction of its Board of Directors.

A whole time director is a person who is in the wholetime employment of the company. Thus, he is also an employee of the company. Like a managing director he occupies dual capacity, namely that of a director and of an employee. A whole time director is actually a managing director. Even a director in charge is also in the same position as a managing director. A managing director is a part of the Company's Board of Directors and not subordinate to it. He is not a servant of the company. But he is an agent of the Company with capacity to bind the company within the sphere of powers authorised to him. He can be regarded as principal employer.

B) Appointment of managing Director (Sec. 196)

A managing director may be appointed by following ways.

i) by memorandum of association
ii) by articles of association
iii) by a resolution passed by the company in general meeting.
iv) by a resolution passed by the Board of directors.
v) by an agreement with the company.

Under Sec. 196 every public company or a private company which is subsidiary of a public company, having a paid up share capital of rupees five crores or more, shall have a managing or wholetime time director or a manager in a public company or a private company which is subsidiary of a public company, shall be made except with the approval of the central Government.

Every application seeking approval to the appointment of a managing on wholetime director or a manager shall be made to the Central Government within a period of ninety days from the date of such appointment.

The central Government shall not accord its approval to an application, if it is satisfied that,

i) the managing or wholetime director or manager appointed is, in its opinion, not a fit and proper person to be appointed as such or such appointment is not in the public interest. or

ii) the terms and conditions of the appointment of managing or wholetime director or the manager, are not fair and reasonable. It shall be competent for the Central Government while according approval to an appointment, to accord approval for a period lesser than the period to be made. If the appointment of a person as a managing or wholetime director or a manager is not approved by the central Government, the person so appointed shall vacate his office as managing or wholetime director or manager, on the date on which the decision of the Central Government is communicated to the company and he omits or fails to do so, he shall be punishable with fine which may extend to rupees five thousand for every day during which he omits or fails to vacate such office.

Whether the central government suo-moto or of any information received by it is, primafacie of the opinion that any appointment made without the approval of the central government has been made in contravention of the requirements of schedule XIII, it shall be competent for the central government to refer the matter to the Tribunal for decision.

The Tribunal shall, if after giving a reasonable opportunity to the company, the managing on wholetime director or the manager or the officer who is default, as the case may be, comes to the conclusion that the appointment has been made in contravention of the requirements of schedule XIII, make an order declaring that a contravention of the requirements of the schedule XIII has taken place.

On making of an order by the Tribunal -

a) The company shall be liable to a fine which may extend to fifty thousand rupees.

b) every officer of the company who is in default shall be liable to a fine of one lakh rupees.

c) The appointment of the managing or whole time director or manager, as the case may be, shall be deemed to have to come to an end and the person so appointed shall, in addition to being liable to pay fine of rupees one lakh, refund to the company the entire amount of salaries, commissions and prequisites received or enjoyed by him between the date of his appointment and the passing of such order.

If a company contralens the above provisions or any direction given by the Tribunal, every officer of the company, who is in default and the managing or wholetime director or the manager, as the case may be, shall be punishable with imprisonment for a term which may extend to three years and shall also be liable to a fine which may extend to five hundred rupees for every day of default.

C) Disqualification of a Managing Director

No company shall appoint or employ or continue the appointment or employment of, any person as its managing on wholetime director who--

i) is an undischarged insolvent or has any time been adjudged an insolvent.

ii) suspends or has at time suspended, payment to his creditors or makes or has at any time made, a composition with them or,

iii) is or has at any time been, convicted by a court of an offence involving moral turpitude.

Moral turpitude means anything done contrary to justice honesty, modesty or good morals.

These provisions of disqualification also apply to a wholetime director. These provisions are mandatory and absolute. The Central Government may remove disqualification in the case of manager but it cannot do so in the case of managing or wholetime director.

Number of Companies in which one person may be appointed as managing director.

A person can be the managing director or manager of only one public company or a private company which is subsidary of a public company. A person who is already the managing director or manager of any other company, including private company which is not a subsidiary of a public company, is not eligible for such appointment.

A person can be appointed as a managing director or manager of one more company under following conditions.

i) Such appointment or employment is made or approved by a resolution passed at a meeting of the Board with the consent of all the directors present at the meeting.

ii) Specific notice of a meeting and resolution to be moved there at, regarding the appointment of a managing director of more than one company has been given to all the directors then in India.

The Central Government may, by order permit any person to be appointed as a managing director of more than two companies, if the Central Government is satisfied that it is necessary that the companies should, for their proper working, function as a single unit and have a common managing director.

These provisions do not apply to a private company which is not a subsidiary of a public company.

D) Tenure of Appointment

All acts done by a managing or whole time director or a manager, as the case may be, purporting to act in such capacity and whose appointment has been found to be in contravention to schedule XIII, shall if the acts so done are valid otherwise, be valid, notwithstanding any order made by the Tribunal provides that --

i) No company shall appoint or employ any individual as its managing director for a term exceeding five years at a time

ii) Any individual holding the office of managing director in a company shall unless his term expired earlier, be deemed to have vacated his office immediately on the expiry of five years.

iii) He may be reappointed, reemployed or of the term of office may be extended by further period not exceeding five years on each occasion. However, any such reappointment re-employment or extension shall not be sanctioned earlier than two years from the date on which it is to come into force.

These provisions shall not apply to a private company unless it is subsidiary of a public company.

When the term of a managing director expires, he cannot continue as a managing director without being reappointed.

E) Remuneration (Sec. 197-198)

A managing director may be remunerated either by way of a monthly payment or as a spacified percentage of the net profits of the company or partly by one way and pattly by the other. However, such remuneration should not exceed 5% of the net profits without the sanction of the Central Government. Where there are more than one managing director, the total remuneration payable to all of them must not exceed 10% of the net profits without the sanction of the Central Government.

8.1.2 Manager - Sec. 2(53)

A) Meaning

According to Sec. 2(53) "manager means an individual who, subject to superintendence, control and direction of the Board of Directors, has the management of the whole, or substantially the whole, of the affairs of the company, and includes a director or any other person occupying the position of a manager, by whatever name called and whether under a contract of service or not."

B) Features of a Manager

i) According to act no company shall appoint or employ any firm, body corporate or association as its manager. Thus, only an individual can be appointed as a manager of the Company.

ii) A managers shall have the management of the whole or substantially the whole of the affairs of a company.

iii) A manager is not an agent who is to do a particular thing or a servant to obey orders only, but he is a person entrusted with power to look after whole of the affairs of the company.

iv) Manager includes a director or any other person occupying the position of a manager.

v) A manager is subject to the superintendence, control and discretion of the Board of Directors.

vi) A manager may be appointed under a contract of service or otherwise.

vii) If a director is also a manager, then for any reason his office of director is vacated the office of manager held by him is not affected. but it is not so in case of a managing director.

C) Disqualification of the office of Manager

i) Manager

A person will not be appinted as a manager of a company if he

i) is an undischarged insolvent or has at any time within the preceeding five years been adjudged an insolvent, or

ii) suspends or has at any time within the preceding five years suspended, payment of his creditors or makes or has at any time within the preceding five years made, a composition with them, or

iii) is, or has at any time within the preceding five years been, convicted by a court in India of an offence involving moral turpitude.

The Central Government may, by notification in the official gazette, remove the disqualification incurred by any person, as stated above, either generally or in relation to any company or companies specified in the notification.

ii) Appointment of a Manager

Provisions that are applicable to the managing director regarding appointment, reappointment, term of office and number of companies that can be managed also apply to a manager the appointment or reappointment of a manager can be made by the company without approval of the Central Government if the same is made in accordance with the conditions specified in schedule XIII.

iii) Term of office

No company shall appoint or employ any individual as its manager for a term exceeding five years at a time. He may be reappointed or the term of office may be extended by successive periods of five years each. The appointments or extersion shall not be sanctioned earlier than two years each.

iv) Number of Managerships

No public company shall appoint or employ any person as a manager if he is either a manager or managing director of any other company. A person already holding such an office can be appointed provided the appointment is made or approved by a resolution passed at the meeting of the Board with the consent of all the director present at the meeting and in respect of which a specific notice has been given to all the directors in India.

The Central Government may permit any person to be appointed as a manager of more than two companies if it is satisfied that, it is necessary that, the Companies should, for proper working, function as a single unit and have a common manager.

D) Remuneration (sec. 197-198)

The manager of a company may receive remuneration either by way of a monthly payment or by way of specified percentage of the net profits of the company. The remuneration payable to a manager shall not exceed five percent of the net profits of the company. However, this limit can be exceeded with the approval of the Central Government.

Compensation for loss of office (Sec. 202)

Under Sec. 318 a company may pay compensation for loss of office or as consideration for retirement from office of a director holding the office of a manager.

Office of Manager cannot be assigned

Any assignment of office made by a manager of a company shall be void.

Age limit for appointment of a manager

The age group for the appointment of a managing or wholetime director or manager without approval of the Central Government has been 25 to 70 years.

E) Distinction between Manager and Managing Director

MANAGER	MANAGING DIRECTOR (MD)
1) A manager may not be a director.	1) MD must be a director of the Company.
2) There cannot be more than one manager in a company	2) There may be more than one MD in a company.
3) A manager may be appointed under a contract of service or otherwise.	3) MD may be appointed by virtue of an agreement with the Company or by board of directors or memorandum.
4) Disqualification grounds remain effective only for five years.	4) Disqualification grounds remain effective for the whole life.
5) Conviction for moral turpitude by a foreign court is not a disqualification	5) Conviction for moral turpitude by a foreign court or any court in India is a disqualification.
6) The Central Government may remove the disqualifications either generally or in relation to any company or companies by notification in the official gazette (sec. 385)	6) The Central Govt. has no such power to remove the disqualification under Sec. 267.
7) A manager has management over whole or substantially the whole of the affairs of the company i.e. His powers are relatively wider.	7) MD has substantial power of management which would not otherwise be exercised by him.
8) The maximum remuneration payable to a manager cannot exceed 5% of net profit.	8) Where more than one managing directors are working on the same company the maximum limit has been fixed at 10% of the net profits

8.1.3 Whole Time Director (Sec. 196)

A) Meaning - Sec 2 (94)

The company Act does not define the term 'whole time director'. The term whole time director is used in the Companies Act to denote such a director who is in the whole time employment of a company and is not entrusted with substantial power of management. Thus, if a director is appointed as the 'Controller of finance and Accounts' of the Company, he becomes a whole time director. He is also called 'executive director.'

Appointment of a whole time Director : In the case of a public or private company there are some restrictions on the appointment of a wholetime director such as :-

1) No person can be appointed as a whole-time director in a company without the approval of the Central Govt.
2) No change can be made in the terms of appointment or re-appointment of a wholetime director without the approval of the Central Govt.
3) There is no restriction regarding the tern of appointment of a wholetime director.
4) A wholetime director, being a wholetime employee of the company, cannot obviously act in more than one company at a time.
5) No person can be appointed whole time director who :
   i) is an undischarged insolvent or has at any time been adjudged an insolvent or
   ii) Suspended or has at any time suspended payment to his creditors, or make or has made a 'composition' with them, or
   iii) is or has been convicted by a court of an offence involving moral tarpitude
   Thus, as per Act, the whole-time director should be a man of charcter and integrity.

B) Remuneration : Under Sec. 197-198 of the Companies Act, 2013, the remuneration payable to a whole-time director cannot be more than 5% of the net profits of the financial year. If there are more than one managing director or wholetime director in a company, the maximum limit is fixed at 10% of the annual net profits of the company subject to overall managerial remuneration of 11% of the net profits of the company.

C) Distinction between Managing Direcor and Wholetime Director

Managing Director (MD)	Wholetime Director
1) Appointment of MD may be made without consent of the members.	1) Appointment of wholetime Director requires sanction of the shareholders by a special resolution.
2) He can be appointed for a maximum period of 5 years at a time.	2) There is no such restriction for the term of appointment of a wholetime director.
3) A person can be MD of two companies. The Central Govt. may permit a person to be appointed as a MD of more than 2 companies if is satisfied that, it is necessary to have a common MD for their proper functioning as a single unit.	3) A wholetime Director is a wholetime employee of the company so he cannot be wholetime director of more than one company.
4) A MD is provided with substantial powers of management. He has a discretionary power to take policy decisions like pricing of products, buying and selling policy, etc.	4) A wholetime Director is an ordinary employee who has only those powers as per terms of employment.
5) MD and manager cannot exist simultaneously (sec. 197A)	5) A Wholetime Director can be appointed together with the managing Director or manager.

8.2 ROLE OF BOARD OF DIRECTORS

The Role of Board of Directors are as follows:

i) **Hiring of Executive Director**

    The Board of Directions hires, evaluates, supports and fires the executive director. The Board of Directors is responsible for hiring the executive director and assuring that she or he has the skills, experience, and leadership qualities necessary to manage the agency on a day-to-day basis, The board should be prepared to support the executive director as she/he requests, and to see that the executive director is adequately compensated and that her authority over staff is assured. The board should evaluate the executive director's performance on an annual basis and provide her with measurable performance goals for the next evaluation period. When an executive director's job performance is judged inadequate and interventions to improve it have not worked, the board is responsible for terminating her.

ii) **Developing Agency Policies**

    The Board of Directors develops agency policies governing human resource management and facilitate staff and client grievance issues : Only the board of directors can establish policies for the company. A policy is a rule that follows a standard process by which to measure whether or not the rule has been followed. Policies govern the day-to-day operation of the company. It is the executive Director's function to carry out the board's policy decisions.

iii) **Fiduciary Responsibility**

    The Board of Directors accepts fiduciary responsibility for the agency and assure the integrity of its financial records and reports. The board of directors has to see how honestly, accurately, and adequately the company handles the money it receives from any source. If there is anything wrong about the agency's financial reports, about how it spends its money, or about how it protects its money, it is the board's fault and it is the board's problem to fix. The board is also responsible for assuring theat the company has enough money to carry out any plans the board has agreed to complete.

iv) **Developing Strategic Plain**

    The Board of Directors develops a strategic plan for the agency and monitor compliance with the goals and objectives of the plan. When the company is just starting up, and usually at five-year intervals, it develops a strategic plan that predicts, reasonably estimates, and anticipates what the company will "look-like" financially, programmatically, institutionally, and so on, by the end of the five year period. Strategic plans also include descriptions of what "steps" are necessary to assure successful attainment of the plan, who will be responsible for completing a particular step and by what date the step will be completed. Board of directors most often include the executive director, staff and community members in its strategic planning process and assign responsibility for attaining step success to staff. Consultants are often hired to help boards develop strategic plans and strategic plans are used to educate funders, clients and other constituencies about what the agency will need from them, and why. Boards of Directors often use the strategic plan as one measurable tool in evaluating the performance of the executive director.

v) Periodical Review

The Board of Directors should periodically evaluate what the company is doing against the criteria expressed in its mission statement and values statements. In short, directors should ask, "is this program, activity, idea, deal, etc., consistent with what we say we do in our mission statement?" and "are the methods we're using to accomplish this program, activity, idea, deal, etc., consistent with our philosophical, cultural, moral, or religious values?" Companies that practice periodic review of compliance with its mission and values stay out of trouble. They rarely cause hard feeling among their non-profit colleagues and they rarely fall into the trap of "chasing money" to provide a service they may not be genuinely capable of fulfilling. They earn the trust of funders and they develop competencies over the long haul. These are companies that are viewed as genuine community resources with wise and effective leadership.

vi) Maintenance of Records

The Board of Directors maintains records (minutes) of the boards activities and decisions. The Board of Directors has to keep a written record of its meetings and decisions and storing those records in a "Minute Book". The Company's auditor will certainly review the minutes book during the annual audit and the executive director will use the minutes to carry out the decisions of the board. In short, the minutes book is a legal document that must be maintained by law.

vii) Representation of Company

The Board of Directors represents the company to its constituents-with the advice and consent of the executive director. Board members should take every opportunity to publicise the successes of the company and its availability for service. "Problems" within the company should not be discussed outside of board meetings. Only "positive" information about the company should be discussed in public. Board members may elicit opinions and comments from constituents such as "How do you think my company is doing?" in order to develop quality improvement plans or to reshape public relations efforts, but they should never agree that the company has done something wrong until that agreement has been discussed and reached by the board of directors as a whole. From time to time the executive director may ask a board member to represent the company at a meeting or community event. Board members should view these requests as reasonable and accept as possible.

viii) To Attend Meetings :

The Board of Directors serves on company sub-committees and attend meetings as scheduled. Boards of Directors should meet on a regularly scheduled basis. However, Boards of Directors have no authority unless a quorum is present. A quorum is a set number of directors-established in the bylaws-who must be present for a decision to be legally binding. If that set number is not available then no decisions can be made. Any board member can chair a meeting in the absence of a board officer if a quorum is present.

As a way to facilitate quick decision-making and streamline meetings and effort, Board will frequently establish sub committees to complete necessary research of ideas and to make recommendations to the Board as a whole. Committees are usually of two types : Standing (permanent) Committees and Special or Ad Hoc (temporary) Committees. Membership in these committees is usually comprised of board members and sometimes staffs who have special expertise in the area addressed by the committee.

8.3 CORPORATE SOCIAL RESPONSIBILITY (U/S- 135)

The Ministry of Corporate Affairs (MCA) had introduced the Corporate Social Responsibility Voluntary Guidelines have now been incorporated within the 2013 Act and have obtained legal sanctity. Sec. 135 of the 2013 Act, seeks to provide that every company having having a net worth of 500 crore INR, or more or a nurnover of 1000 crore INR or more, or a net profit of five crore INR or more, during any financial year shall constitute the corporate social responsibility committee of the board.

This committee needs to comprise of three or more directions, out of which, at least one director should be an independent director. The composition of the committee shall be included in the board's report. The Board's Report under sub Sec. (3) of the Sec. 134 shall disclose the composition of the Corporate Social Responsibility Committee (CSRC).

A) The Committee shall-

a. Formulate and recommend the policy, including activities specified in Schedule VII, which are as follows :

1) Eradicating extreme hunger and poverty
2) Promotion of education.
3) Promoting gender equality and empowering women
4) Reducing child mortality and improving maternal health
5) Combating human immunodeficiency virus, acquired immune deficiency syndrome, malaria and other diseases.

6) Ensuring evironmental sustainability.

7) Employment enhancing vocational skills

8) Social business projects

9) Contribution to the Prime Minister's National Relief Fund or any other fund set-up by the central government or the state governments for socio-economic development and relief, and funds for the welfare of the scheduled castes and Tribes, other backward classes, minorities and women.

10) Such other matters as may be prescribed.

b) Recommend the amount of expenditure to be incurred on the activities referred to in clasuse (a); and

c) Monitor the Corporate Social Responsibility Policy of the company from time to time.

B) The board of every company reffered to in sub-Sec. (1) shall-

a) after taking in to account the recommendation made by CSRC, approve the policy for the company and disclose contents of such policy in its reports and also place it on the company's website, if any, in such manner, may be prescribed, and

b) Ensure that the activities as are included in policy of the company anre undertaken by the company.

C) The Board of every compnay referred to in sub-Sec. (1), shall ensure that the company spends, in every financial year at least 2% of the average net profit of the company made during the 3 immediately preceding financial years, in pursuance of its CSRP.

Provided further that if the company fails to spend such amount, the Board shall, in its report made under clause (O) of sub-Sec. (3) of Sec. 134, specify the reasons for not spending the amount.

There have beeen mixed reactions to the introduction of the 'spend or explain' approach taken by the MCA with respect to CSR. It may take a while before all of Corporate India imbibes CSR as a culture.

However, activities specified in the Schedule are not elaborate or detailed enough to indicate the king of projects that could be undertaken, for example, environment sustainability or social business projects could encompass a wide range of activities.

The committee will aslo need to recommend the amount of expenditure to be incurred and monitor the policy from a time-to-time. The board shall disclose the contents of the policy in its report, and place it on the website, if any, of the company. The 2013 Act mandates that these companies wold be requied to spend at least 2% of the average net-profits of the immediately preceding three years on CSR activities, and if not spent, explanation for the reasons threof would need to be given in the director's report.

8.4 PREVENTION OF OPPRESSION AND MISMANAGEMENT

The management of the company is based on the principles of majority rule. Ordinarily, decision of majority is the rule for minority. This sound principle has occasionally been abused by the majority shareholders and decision taken for the benefits of majority shareholders.

8.4.1 Oppression (Sec. 241)

Oppression means,

"The company's affairs are being conducted in a manner prejudicial to public interest or in a manner oppressive to any member or members".

The Act does not define what is oppression. Normally oppression means violation of condition of fair play. It involves lack of fair dealing to a member in the matter of his rights as a shareholder. The oppression should be in the capacity of shareholder and not in any other capacity. A continuous and persisting course of unjust conduct must be shown. It should be of continuing nature and be continue upto the date of petition.

8.4.2 Mismanagement (Sec.-244)

The term 'Mismanagement' has not defined in the Companies Act, 2013. The mismanagement means "that affairs of the company are being conducted in a manner prejudicial to public interest or in manner prejudicial to the interests of the company." or

"That a material change not being a change brought about by, or in the interest of, any creditors (including debenture holders) or any class of shareholders, of the company has taken place in the management or control of the company, whether by an alteration in its Board of Directors or Manager of in the ownership of the company's shares, or if its has no share capital, in its membership, or in any other manner whatsoever, and that by reason of such change, it is likely that the affairs of the company will be conducted in a manner prejudicial to public interest or in a manner prejudicial to the interests of the company."

Normally mismanagement means gross mismanagement of the affairs of the company. It may include, drawing of funds for personal expenses or gross negligence in managing the affairs.

8.4.3 Who can apply (Sec. 244)

Following members of a company shall have the right to apply in case of oppression and mismanagement :

a) In case of company having share capital, not less than 100 members or not less than 10% of the total number of members, whichever is less or any member or members holding not less than 1/10 of the issued capital of the company.

b) In case of company not having share capital, not less than 5% of the total number of its members.

c) The Central Government may authorise any member or members to apply to the company, if these members have applied to the Central Government for relief.

d) The Central Government may, on his own, apply to the Company Law Board against oppression and mismanagement.

8.4.4. Powers of Central Government

The powers of the Central Government to prevent oppression and mismanagement may be summerised as follows:

1) To appoint directors

Action under Sec. 408 can be taken by the Central Government on its own motion or on the application of not less than 100 members or of members holding not less than 1/10th of the total voting power. The Central Government shall hold an enquiry under this section. But in such enquiry the company should be given an opportunity to be heard though it is not necessary to give notice to individual shareholders-

i) either in a manner oppressive to any member, or

ii) in a manner prejudicial to the interest of the company or the public interest.

It may appoint such number of persons, as the Central Government may think fit, as directions of the company for a period not exceeding 2 years on any one occasion. In the alternative, the Central Government may direct the company to adopt the method of proportional representation and to amend the articles for that purpose. In the meanwhile, until new directors are appointed after alteration of articles the Central Government may appoint additional directors.

When such an order is made, for the purpose of reckoning two-thirds or any other proportion of the total number of directors the directors appointed by the Central Government shall not be taken into account.

Such directors or additional directors shall not be required to hold any qualification shares.

They shall not be liable to retire by rotation but they may be removed by the Central Government at any time and another persons may be appointed in their place to hold office as directors or as additional directors as the case may be.

After the Central Government has appointed one or more directors or additional directions under this section and so long as they remain in office, no change in the Board of Directors shall have effect unless confirmed by the Central Government. This means, no new candidate can be elected as director in the annual meeting unless such appointment is confirmed by the Central Government.

The Central Government may issue directions to the company which it may consider necessary or appropriate in regard to its affairs.

The Central Government may also require the persons appointed as directors or additional directors to report to the Central Government from time to time with regard to the affairs of the company.

When the power is to be exercised under Sec. 408, there is no limit on the number of persons that the Central Government may appoint as directors.

If the Government directors are in management and the Government is of the opinion that allowing them to manage the affairs of the company would be prejudicial to the interest of the company or the general public, then the Government directors can be reappointed by the Government even if at the time when the order of reappointment is passed the company is being managed properly."

2) To prevent change in the Board of Directors likely to affect company prejudicially :

If the managing Director or any other Director or the Manager of a company complains that as a result of a change which has taken place or is likely to take place in the ownership of any shares held in the company there would be a change in the Board of Directors which is likely to affect the company prejudicially, the Central Government shall make such enquiries as it thinks fit. After that enquiry, the Central Government may make an order directing that no resolution passed or that may be passed or no action taken to change in the Board of Director shall have effect unless confirmed by the Central Government. The Central Government may also make interim order pending enquiry. However, this is not applicable to a private company unless it is a subsidiary of the public company.

3) To remove managerial personnel

The Central Government has power to remove managerial personnel from office on the recommendation of the Company Law Board. Where in the opinion of the Central Government there are circumstances suggesting -

a) that any person concerned in the conduct and management of the affairs of a company is or has been in connection therewith guilty of fraud, misfeasance, persistent negligence or default in carrying out his obligations and functions under the law or breach of trust; or

b) that the business of a company is not or has not been conducted and managed by such person in accordance with sound business principles or prudent commercial practices;

c) that a company is or has been conducted and managed by such person in a manner which is likely to cause or has caused serious injury or damage to the interest of the trade, industry or business to which such company pertains; or

d) that the business of a company is or has been conducted and managed by such person with intent to defraud its creditors, members or any other person or otherwise for a fraudulent or unlawful purpose or in a manner prejudicial to public interest. The Central Government may state case against the person aforesaid and refer the same to the Company Law Board with a request that the Company Law Board may inquire into the case and record decision as to whether or not such person is a fit and proper person to hold the office of director or any other office connected with the conduct and management of any company. In the case of Alok Prakash Jain vs Union of India (1973) 43 Comp. Cases 68 the court has held that the Central Government is under duty to make a reference to the Company Law Board and remove a person from office if the Company Law Board found him guilty. Every case shall be stated in the form of an application which shall be presented to the High Court or such officer thereof as it may appoint in this behalf. Every such application shall contain a concise statement of such circumstances and materials as the Central Government may consider necessary for the purpose of the inquiry and shall be signed and verified in the manner laid down in the code of civil procedure for the signature and verification of a plaint in a suit by the Central Government.

The Central Government shall by order remove from office any director or any other person concerned in the conduct and management of the affairs of a company against whom there is a decision of the Company Law Board on such reference.

The person against whom such order of removal from office is made shall not hold the office of a director or any other office connected with the conduct and management of the affairs of any company during a period of five years from the date of the order of removal.

However, the Central Government may, with the previous concurrence of the Company Law Board, permit such person to hold any office before the expiry of the said period of five years.

On the removal of a person from office of a director or any other office connected with the conduct and management of the affairs of the company that person shall not be entitled to or be paid any compensation for the loss or termination of office.

On the removal of a person from the office of a director or any other office connected with the conduct and management of the affairs of the company, the company may, with the previous approval of the Central Government, appoint another person to that office in accordance with the provisions of this Act.

8.4.5 Power of Company Law Board (CLB) (Sec. 242)

Under Sec. 242, the Company Law Board is authorised to pass an order in case of oppression and mismanagement, providing any of the following -

a) Regulation of conduct of the company's affairs in future.

b) To order the purchase of share or interest of any member or members of the companies by the other members thereof or by the company.

c) If Company Law Board orders purchase of shares by the company itself, Company Law Board can also order consequent reduction in share capital.

d) Termination, setting aside or modification of any agreement between the company and Managing Director or Directors.

e) To set aside any transfer, delivery of goods, payments, execution of other acts, relating to property made or done by or against the company within 3 months before the date of application.

f) To deal with any other matter for which, in the opinion of Company Law Board, it is just and equitable that provision should be made.

The Company Law Board may pass an interim order for regulating the conduct of company's affairs. It can also order to change in Memorandum and Articles of Association.

QUESTIONS

A) Answer in 20 words.

1) Explain the term 'Wholetime Director.'
2) What is oppression?
3) What is mismanagement?

B) Answer in 50 words.

1) Define 'Managing Director.' What are the provisions regarding appoint of M. D?
2) Explain the procedure of retirement of directors by rotation.
3) Distinguish between Director and Managing Director.
4) Distinguish between Managing Director and Whole-time director.
5) Define 'manager.' State its features.
6) State corporate social responsibility.

C) Answer in 150 words.

1) Define the term 'Managing Director'. What are the different ways of appointment of M. D?
2) What is 'Managing Director.' State the provision regarding managing director.
3) Define the term 'Wholetime Director'. Distinguish between managing director and wholetime director.
4) Define 'Manager.' What is the difference between Managing Director and Manager.
5) Explain the power of Company lawBoard to prevent oppression & mismangement.
6) Explain the activities specified in schedule VII relating to Corporate Social Respensibility.

D) Answer in details (about 300/500 words)

1) What is 'Managing Director'? State the provisions regarding Managing Director.
2) Explain the term 'Wholetime Director.' Distinguish between Managing Director and wholetime director.
3) Explain the Role of Board of Director.
4) Explain the Power of Centrol Govt. to prevent oppression & mismangement.

| Chapter 9 | COMPANY MEETING |

CONTENTS

9.1 Company Meetings I - General
  9.1.1   Meaning of a Meeting
  9.1.2   Kinds of Meeting
  9.1.3   Requisites of a Valid Meeting
  9.1.4   Methods of Voting
  9.1.5   Proxy - Meaning, Appointments - Rights etc.
  9.1.6   Motions, Amendments and Point of order
  9.1.7   Formal Motions
  9.1.8   Resolutions
  9.1.9   Minutes of the Meeting

9.2 Company Meetings II - General Body Meetings
  9.2.1   General Body Meetings
  9.2.2   Statutory Meetings
  9.2.3   Annual General Meetings
  9.2.4   Extraordinary General Meetings
  9.2.5   Class Meetings
  9.2.6   Meeting of Debentureholders and Creditors

9.3 Company Meetings III - Board Meetings
  9.3.1   Need for Board Meetings
  9.3.2   Frequency of Board Meetings
  9.3.3   Notice of the Meetings
  9.3.4   Agenda of Board Meetings
  9.3.5   Time and Place of Board Meetings
  9.3.6   Chairman of the Meetings
  9.3.7   Quorum of Board Meetings
  9.3.8   Resolution by Circualtion
  9.3.9   Meetings of Committee of the Directors

9.1 COMPANY MEETINGS I- GENERAL

9.1.1 Meaning

When two or more persons come together to discuss matters of common interest there is said to be a meeting. Meeting is the best medium for group discussion and group decisions in an organisation. A meeting means the act of coming together of two or more persons for discussion and transaction of some Lawful business.

In a democratic participating managerial set-up, meetings have unique place. They provide the best means of communication i.e. a bridge of understanding through interchange of thoughts. They provide opportunity for face to face contact of direct exchange of ideas and views. The collective decision arrived at a meeting, represent combined Judgement and such joint decisions are sound and matured. They can be applied with least resistance.

9.1.2 Kinds of Meetings

In a company various types of meetings are held, such as :
1) General meetings of shareholders
2) Board meetings committees i.e. meetings of directors
3) Committee meeting i.e. meeting of the committees constituted by the Board.
4) Class meeting i.e. meetings of creditors debendureholder etc. Chawla and others have classified meetings as follows :

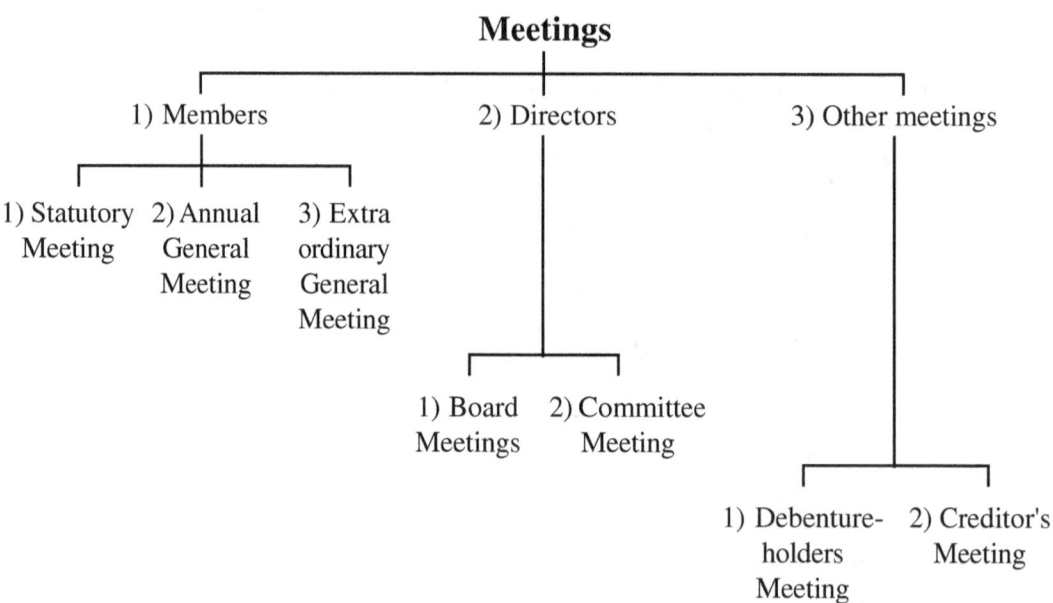

9.1.3 Requisites of a Valid Meeting

A meeting to be valid must be called and held in a manner provided by the Companies Act and the Articles. Any irregularities involved in the procedure followed in convening and conducting a meeting will invalidate the proceedings of that meeting. In order to have valid transactions of any business, the essential requirements stated below must be strictly followed.

(1) Proper Authority

The first essential requisite of a valid meeting is that it should be called by a proper authority. The proper authority is the Board of Directors. However, in case of default by the directors, the meeting may be called by the requisitionists or by the Tribunal. Any defects in the appointment or qualifications of the directors present at the meeting of the Board, will not make resolution passed at the meeting invalid, provided that the Board has acted bonafide. However, where certain directors held a meeting of the Board but they prevented some lawfully constituted directors from attending the meeting and a quorum was present. But, it was held that the meeting of the Board was unlawful, the notice convening the general meeting also becomes invalid. Directors have to fix the time and place or whether the meeting should be held at all. [N.V.R. Nagappa Chettiar V. Madras Race Club (1949) MLJ 662].

(2) Notice (Sec. 101)

The second requirement of valid meeting is that a proper notice of the meeting should be given to all the members. The notice should mention the date, time, place and business of the meeting. The notice should be in writing and must be given twenty one days before the date of meeting. While calculating the number of days, the date of posting and the date of meeting should be excluded. The gap should be 21 clear days. The private company's articles may contain its own special provisions regarding the duration of notice.

The meeting can, however, be called by giving short notice in the following cases.
I) By the consent of all the members entitled to attend and vote for annual general meeting.
II) By consent of the members holding not less than 95% paid up share capital of the company or holding not less than 95% of the total voting power of the company, if the company does not have any share capital, any other meeting may be called at a short notice.

The notice, must be given to,
I) every member of the company.
II) every person entitled to shares in consequence of the death or insolvency of a member.
III) The auditor or auditors of the company
IV) The public trustees.

In case a share is held jointly by more than one person, notice may be served on the joint holder named first in the register of the shares.

Deliberate omission to give notice of the meeting to the members or to a single member will make the meeting invalid. But an accidental omission to give notice or non receipt of the notice to any member shall not make the proceedings at the meeting invalid.

Notice in case of adjourned meeting (Sec. 102)

In case of adjourned meeting, a fresh notice of such a meeting is not required to be given to the members, unless Articles so provide. According to the regulation 53 of Table A, when the meeting is adjourned for thirty or more days, notice of adjourned meeting shall be given as in the case of original meeting.

The contents of the notice

Every notice of a company must specify the place, day and hour of the meeting and also shall contain a statement of business to be transacted at the meeting. If the necessary details as required under section 172 are not mentioned in the notice, the meeting shall be invalid and the resolutions passed in the meeting will have no effcet.

(3) Ordinary and Special Business

A notice of meeting must contain a statement of nature of the business to be transacted in meeting. According to act the business is classified into two categories.

(a) Ordinary Business - The following shall be ordinary business transcated in the Annual General Meeting.

   i) The consideration of accounts, balance sheet, and the report of the Board of Directors and auditors.

   ii) The declaration of dividend.

   iii) The appointment of directors in place of those retiring.

   iv) The appointment of and fixing of the remuneration of the auditors.

(b) Special Business - Any business other than ordinary business transacted at the Annual General Meeting and any business transacted in any other meeting shall be deemed to be special business.

(3) Explanatory Statement

If any special business is to be transacted at annual meeting, a statement to that effect must be annexed to the notice calling the meeting. The statement must set out all the material facts concerning each item of special business and should also disclose the interest of any director or other managerial personnel in the matter.

Where any item of special business transacted affects any other company, the extent of shareholding interest in that other company of every director and the manager, if any, of the first mentioned company shall also be set out in the statement, if the extent of such shareholding interest is not less than 20% of the paid up share capital of that other company. Where the item of such business relates to the approval to any document by the meeting, the statement annexed to the notice must specify the time and the place where the document can be inspected.

(4) Quorum - (sec. 103)

Quorum is the minimum number of members who must be present at a meeting in order that the business of the meeting could be transacted validly. Unless the articles of the company provides for a larger number, five members personally present in the case of a public company and two members present in the case of any other company shall be the quorum for a meeting of the company. The Articles may prescribe for a larger quorum but not for a smaller one.

Absence of Quorum

If within half an hour from the time appointed for holding a meeting of the company, a quorum is not present, the meeting, if called upon by the requisition of members shall stand dissolved. In any other case, the meeting shall stand adjourned to the same day in the next week, at the same time and place or to such other day and at such other time and place as the Board may determine. If at the adjourned meeting also, a quorum is not present, within half an hour from the time appointed for holding the meeting, the members present shall be a quorum.

5) Chairman of Meeting (Sec. 104)

Appointment of Chairman

A Chairman is necessary for the proper conduct of business at meeting. His appointment is generally regulated by the Articles of association Regulations 50-52 of Table A of schedule 1, provide for, as follows.

The Chairman, if any, of the Board shall preside as Chairman at every general meeting of the company (Regulation 50)

If there is no such chairman, or if he is not present within fifteen minutes after the time appointed for holding the meeting or is unwilling to act as chairman of the meeting, the directors present shall elect one of their members to be chairman of the meeting. (Regulation 51)

If at any meeting no director is willing to act as chairman or if no director is present within fifteen minutes after the time appointed for holding the meeting, the members present shall choose one of their members to be chairman of the meeting (Regulation 52).

Election of Chairman

If the articles of association of a company do not contain any provision for the appointment of a chairman, then the appointment of chairman shall be made as provided by the companies Act. -

I) Unless the articles of the company otherwise provide, the members personally present at the meeting shall elect one of themselves to be the chairman there of on the show of hands.

II) If the poll is demanded on the election of the chairman, it shall be taken forthwith in accordance with the provisions of this Act. The chairman elected on show of hands shall exercise all the powers of the chairman.

III) If some other person is elected as chairman as a result of the poll, he shall be the Chairman for the rest of the meeting.

Powers and Functions of Chairman

The chairman has to preside over the meetings of the company. His main duty is to keep order and conduct the meeting properly. He must give a reasonable chance to the members present to discuss proposed resolutions and keep discussion relating to the issues at hand. He must act at all times bonafide and in the interest of the company as a whole. He has to preserve order in the meeting. He must ascertain the sense of the meeting properly regarding any question before it. He must put motions in their proper form and declare the result of the voting. He cannot arbitrarily adjourn the meeting or dispose it at his own choice without the consent of the shareholders, unless the business for which the meeting was convened has been concluded. The power of adjournment rests with the majority and they can appoint another chairman and conduct business unfinished by the former chairman.

A chairman does not have a casting vote, unless Articles provide for it. When the articles provide for it, in the case of equality of votes he may have a casting or second vote.

Subject to the provision of the Act, the Chairman of the meeting shall have the power to regulate the manner in which a poll shall be taken. However, the way in which the meeting is to be conducted is to be decided by the Chairman with the consent of the meeting in the light of general law and the articles of association of the company.

9.1.4 Voting and Poll

The business of a meeting is carried out by way of passing resolutions. Shareholders have the right to discuss every proposed resolution and to move amendments. The shareholder's right to vote is a right to property which he is free to use in any way he likes. In case of a company which has no share capital, each member is entitled to only one vote, but in case of company having share capital, each member is entitled to one vote for each share, if Articles are silent.

A member entitled to more than one vote, need not, use all his votes in the same way. Thus, he may split his votes for voting for and against the resolution.

Restriction on Voting Rights

The articles of a company may provide that no member shall exercise any voting rights in respect of shares registered in his name on which (I) any calls or sums payable by him have not been paid or (II) the company has exercised any right of lien in respect of these shares. It implies that, where the articles of a company do not contain such provisions, a member cannot be prevented from voting, even if calls or sums are payable by him, are not paid.

A public company shall not prevent any member from exercising his voting right on the ground that he has not held his share or other interest in the company for any specified period preceding the date on which the vote is taken.

Methods of Voting

Voting may be by show of hands or by poll.

(1) Voting by show of hands in the first instance (Sec. 107)

At any general meeting, a resolution put to the vote of the meeting shall, unless a poll is demanded, be decided on a show of hands, chairman's declaration of result of voting by show of hands to be conclusive -

A declaration by the chairman that the resolution on a show of hands has or has not been carried either unanimously or by a particular majority and entry to that effect in the books containing the minutes of the proceedings of the company, shall be conclusive evidence of the fact.

(2) Voting through electronic means - (Sec. 108) -

The central Govt. may prescribed the classes of companies & manner in which a member may be exercise his right to vote by the electronic mean.

(3) Voting by Poll

Before or on the declaration of result of the voting on any resolution on a show of hands, a poll may be ordered to be taken by the chairman of the meeting on his own motion or on a demand by members specified below.

a) In the case of a public company having share capital, by any member or members present in person or by proxy and holding shares in the company -

i)   which confer a power to vote on the resolution not being less than one tenth of the total voting power in respect of resolution or

ii) on which an aggregate sum of not less than fifty thousand rupees has been paid up.

b) In case of private company having a share capital, by one members having a right to vote on the resolution and present in person or by proxy, if not more than seven such members are personally present, and by two such members present in person or by proxy, if more than seven such members are personally present.

c) In the case of any other company, by any member or members present in person or by proxy and having less than one tenth of the total voting power in respect of resolution. (sec. 179)

(4) Postal ballot (Sec. 110)

The central Govt. may prescribed the classes of companies & manner in which a member may be exercise his right to vote by the postal ballot.

Withdrawal of Demand for Poll

The demand for a poll may be withdrawn at any time by the person or persons who made the demand. Such withdrawal of demand must be before the result of the poll is declared.

Time of Taking Poll

When a poll is demanded on a question of adjournment and on the election of chairman, it must be taken forthwith.

A poll demanded on any other question, shall be taken at such time not being less than 48 hours from the time when the demand was made, as the chairman may direct. However, a poll may be taken immediately.

Manners of taking Poll

The chairman of the meeting shall have the power to regulate the manner in which a poll shall be taken

The chairman of the meeting shall appoint two scrutineers to scrutinise the votes given on the poll and to report thereon to him. The chairman shall have power, at any time before the result of the poll is declared, to remove a scrutineer from office and to fill vacancies in the office of scrutineer arising from such removal or from any other cause. Out of the two scrutineers, one shall always be a member (not being an officer or employee of the company) present at the meeting, provided such a member is available and willing to be appointed. The result of the poll shall be deemed to be the decision of the meeting on the resolution on which the poll was taken.

9.1.5 Proxies (Sec. 105)

"A proxy is a person representative of a shareholder at a meeting of the company, who may be described as his agent to carry out a course which the shareholder has himself decided upon". A proxy has to act according to the instructions of the shareholder in the matter. It is basically a relationship of principal and agent.

Appointment of a proxy

Any member of a company entitled to attend and vote at the meeting of the company shall be entitled to appoint another person (whether a member or not) as his proxy to attend and vote instead of himself. But a proxy so appointed shall not have any right to speak at the meeting. A member of a private company shall not be entitled to appoint more than one proxy to attend on the same occasion and a proxy shall not be entitled to vote except on a poll.

In every notice calling a meeting of a company which has a share capital or the articles of which provide for voting by proxy at the meeting, there shall appear with reasonable prominence a statement that a member entitled to attend and vote is entitled to appoint a proxy or where that is allowed one or more proxies to attend and vote instead of himself and that a proxy need not be a member. If default is made in complying these provisions regarding any meeting, every officer of the company who is in default shall be punishable, the punishment which may extend to five thousand rupees.

Instrument of proxy

The instrument appointing a proxy shall - (i) be in writing and (ii) be signed by the appointer or his attorney duly authorised in writing or if the appointee is a body corporate, be under its seal or be signed by an officer or an attorney duly authorised by it.

An instrument appointing a proxy, if in any of the forms set out in schedule IX, shall not be questioned on the ground that it fails to comply with any special requirements specified for such instrument by the articles.

Proxy is liable to stamp duty, which is at present Rs 21- and an unstamped proxy will be ignored. A proxy is to be used only for a particular meeting.

The instrument appointing a proxy must be deposited with the company 48 hours before the meeting of the company.

Where a company issues invitations at its expense to members giving names of persons to be appointed as proxies for the purpose of any meeting, then every officer of the company who knowingly issued the invitation or permitted the same, shall be punishable with fine which may extend to ten thousand rupees.

An officer shall not be punishable by reason only of the issue of to a member at his request in writing of a form of appointment naming the proxy or of a list of persons willing to act as proxies, if the form or list is available on request in writing to every member entitled to vote at the meeting by proxy.

Inspection of proxies

Every member entitled to vote at a meeting of the company or on any resolution to be moved there at, shall be entitled during the period beginning twenty four hours before the time fixed for the commencement of the meeting and ending with the conclusion of the meeting, to inspect the proxies lodged, at any time during the business hours of the company, provided not less than three days notice in writing of the intention to inspect is given to the company.

A Body Corporate and Proxy

A body corporate can be a member or creditor of another company, by resolution of its directors or other governing body, authorise a person to act as its representative at any meeting of the company and he shall be entitled to exercise the same right and powers (including the right to vote by proxy) on behalf of the body corporate which he represents.

9.1.6 Motions, Amendments and Point of Order (Sec. 114-117)

Motions and Resolutions

A 'motions' is a definite proposal put before a meeting for its consideration and adoption. The business of a meeting is transacted through motions or definite proposals and no discussion can take place unless there is a definite proposal or subject for discussion before the meeting.

Subject to rules, a motion should be in writing and signed by the mover. Excepting some formal motions, the wording of motions should be in the affirmative and the terms of a motion should be definite and unambiguous. Subject to the rules, previous notice of a motion is necessary before it is brought before the meeting except in the case of formal motions, motion for adjournment, motion for appointement of chairman, etc. The articles of a company usually provide for notice of a motion. If notice of a motion is received, it is usually included in the agenda. Ordinarily, a motion must be proposed by one and seconded by another. However, a motion proposed by the chairman needs no seconding.

A 'resoluton', on the other hand, is the formal expression of the decision of a meeting. When a 'motion' has been duly voted upon and passed by a majority with or without amendment, it is called a 'resolution.' A resolution once adopted and recorded in the minutes becomes the official decision of the meeting. It cannot then be rescinded or revoked except by the consent of two-thirds majority in a meeting specially called for the purpose. Usually, there are two types of resolutions–Ordinary and Special–passed in a general meeting.

Moving of Motion and its Disposal

A member wishing to move a motion first of all secures the permission of the Chair and then 'introduces' the motion, after making a speech in support of his motion. Any member may rise and second the motion with or without making any speech in support, after which the motion is said to be 'before the meeting'. If the motion is not seconded by any member, it is said to 'fall to the ground'. After a motion is formally put before the meeting, the chairman asks members to express their views on the same. No member can speak twice on the same motion except the mover, who is allowed a second speech before the motion is put to vote. When the motion has been thoroughly discussed, it is put to vote and the chairman declares the result. A main motion may be withdrawn by the mover before it is put to vote, provided the seconder agrees to it and the meeting gives its assent. But once passed by vote, a motion becomes an agreed decision of the meeting and cannot be withdrawn. However, the chairman may allow reconsideration of a motion after it is adopted, if it is clear that a majority of members have changed their views.

Amendments

An 'amendment' is any alteration proposed by a member in terms of the wording of the 'main motion' before it is voted upon and adopted. An amendment may be proposed by any member who has not already spoken on the main motion or has not previously moved an amendment thereto. Any motion, including a motion of amendment can be amended, but a formal motion cannot be amended. Like a main motion, an amendment should ordinarily be in writing, signed by the mover and seconded. The terms of the amendment should be definite and in the affirmative and it should not raise any question already decided upon at the same meeting. It should be relevant to and in keeping with the main motion which it seeks to amend, and must not merely be negative to the main motion or introduce entirely new considerations.

The procedure for moving an amendment is similar to that of a main motion but the chairman has the right to accept or reject a motion of amendment on various grounds, such as inconsistency, redundance, irrelevance with the main motion, etc. When a motion of amendment has been moved, admitted and seconded, discussion on the main motion ceases and discussion on the amendment starts. Any one may speak on the amendment even if he has already spoken on the main motion, but no one is allowed to speak twice on the same amendment. After the amendment has been thoroughly discussed it is put to vote. If the amendment is carried, it is incorporated in the body of main motion The altered motion, known as a 'substantive motion', is then put before the meeting. If the amendment is lost, discussion on the main motion is resumed but if the substantive motion is put to vote and lost, the original motion cannot be revived.

Theoretically, any number of amendments to the main motion can be moved. An amendment to alter another amendment can also be moved, but an amendment can be amended only once. When a large number of amendments to the main motion have been moved, the original motion may be withdrawn by common consent and a new motion incorporating the changes may be taken up. The chairman has the discretion to decide in what order the various amendments should be taken up for consideration.

Interruption of Debate

When a motion has been duly moved and seconded, it is put before the meeting. The chairman then calls upon intending speakers on the motion to speak. When discussion or debate on a motion is going on, it can be interrupted by members in various ways, viz. by moving an amendment or by raising a Point of Order or by moving any of the Formal Motions. The rules regarding moving of amendments have been discussed earlier. Any member can raise a point of order to interrupt the debate on a motion, at least for a short period. When a point of order has been raised, all discussion on the main motion will stop. The chairman has to give his ruling on the point of order which will be final. After the point of order has been disposed off, debate on the main motion is resumed. Formal Motions, viz., Closure, Previous Question, Next Business and Adjournment, can be moved by any member to interrupt the debate either for the time being or for a longer period. A formal motion takes precedence over all other motions and is always in order.

Point of Order

A point of order is a question regarding the procedure of a meeting. When debate on a particular motion is in progress, any member can raise a 'point of order' to draw the attention of the chairman to some irregularity in the procedure of the meeting. For instance, a member may draw attention to the fact that there is no quorum. He must do it immediately when he notices the irregularity. As soon as a point of order is raised, debate on the main motion will stop. The chairman will then settle the matter at once by giving his ruling which will be final. If he rules out the point of order, debate on the motion will be resumed.

9.1.7 Formal Motions

These are motions which relate to the procedure at a meeting and are moved for the purpose of interrupting or delaying or speeding up the discussion on a motion. That is why these are also known as 'procedural' or 'dilatory' motions. Formal motions take precedence over all other motions and are always in order. These need not be in writing, nor do these require any previous notice. The principal types of formal motions are: (i) The Closure, (ii) Previous Question, (iii) Next Business, and (iv) Adjournment.

(i) The Closure

This motion is moved when the object is to close prolonged and useless discussion on a motion. Any member may rise and move 'that the question be now put'. This motion is known as a 'Closure' or 'Gag'. After it has been seconded, it is put to vote. If the motion is carried, discussion on the main motion immediately stops and it is at once put to vote. If the closure motion is lost, discussion on the main motion is resumed. The chairman may refuse permission to move such a motion if he thinks that it is being used unfairly by the majority to impose their will on the minority.

(ii) Previous Question

The object of moving this motion is to prevent a vote being taken on the main motion under discussion. Any member who has not already spoken on the main motion may move this motion. The member rises and moves 'that the question be not now put'. This motion can be moved with regards to a main motion only and has to be properly seconded. The formal motion is then put to vote and, if it is carried, discussion on the main motion automatically ceases and it cannot be taken up again at the same meeting. If the formal motion is lost, the main motion is immediately put to vote without any further discussion. The chairman may not permit the moving of such a motion if he thinks that it is being used improperly.

(iii) Next Business

This motion is similar to the 'previous question'. The object of moving such a motion is to shelve discussion on the main motion before the meeting. Any member may rise and move 'that the meeting do proceed to the next business'. After it is seconded it is put to vote and, if it is carried, the main motion under discussion is dropped at once. If it is lost, discussion on the motion is resumed. This formal motion can be moved again after some time.

(iv) Adjournment

The motion of adjournment takes precedence over every other motion before the house. The object of moving this motion is to suspend the entire proceedings of the meeting either for a particular period or indefinitely (i.e., sine die). This motion may also be used to postpone discussion on a motion. Any member may rise and move that the meeting be now adjourned. After seconding, the motion is put to vote. If the motion is carried, the proceedings of the meeting cease forthwith. The motion may be for adjournment to a later date or sine die, i.e. indefinitely. The date, time and place, at which the adjourned meeting will be resumed are generally fixed at the same meeting unless it is adjourned sine die.

Subject to rules, the chairman is also empowered to adjourn a meeting under the following circumstances: (a) when the meeting becomes disorderly; (b) when a quorum is not present; (c) when the business of the meeting cannot be finished within the time available; and (d) when the members demand it.

Except in the above cases, the chairman cannot adjourn a meeting without the consent of the house. The chairman is, however, not bound to adjourn a meeting even when the meeting consents to it, if the rules so provide and if he does not think it is in the best interest of the members to do so. Sometimes, when the meeting is disorderly, the chairman may adjourn a meeting for a short time to enable members to calm down and settle their differences. After that the meeting is resumed.

Notice of an adjourned meeting is not necessary as it is a continuation of the original meeting. The adjourned meeting can transact only the business left unfinished at the original meeting. If the meeting is adjourned to a date ten days or more or is adjourned sine die, fresh notice has to be given.

Postponement

A meeing once it has been properly convened, cannot be postponed or cancelled by a subsequent notice unless the rules (Articles) specifically provide for it. If for some justifiable reason, it is found impossible to transact any business of the meeting on the scheduled date, the proper procedure would be to hold the meeting at the date, place and time stated in the notice and then adjourn the meeting without transacting any business. In that case the rules regarding adjournment will apply. If a meeting is not properly convened, then such a meeting cannot be held at all and it has to be cancelled. The procedure for adjournment or postponement will not apply in such a case. The members have to be informed in time about the cancellation and a fresh and proper notice of the meeting will have to be sent to them.

9.1.8 Resolutions

Resolution is a formal decision of a meeting on any motion before it. A proposal when passed and accepted by the members of a company, it becomes resolution. Decisions are made by the company through passing resolutions of its members in the meeting of its members.

The Companies Act recognises three kinds of resolutions; (i) Ordinary resolutions, (ii) Special resolutions and (iii) Resolutions requiring a special notice.

(1) Ordinary Resolution

A resolution shall be an ordinary resolution when at a general meeting of which the required notice has been duly given, the votes cast (wheher by show of hands or on a poll) in favour of the resolution (including casting vote, if any of chariman) by members being entitled so to do, vote in person or where proxies are allowed, by proxy, exceed the votes, if any, cast against the resolution by members so entitled and voting.

A resolution which is not special or which do not require a special notice is ordinary resolution. An ordinary resolution normally does not require filing with the Registrar of Companies but the usual notice of twenty one days is required for passing an ordinary resolution. Ordinary resolution is necessary for the following.

I) Rectification of name of the company with the previous approval of the Central Government

II) Issue of shares at discount subject to sanction of the Central Government

III) Alteration of share capital

IV) Reissue of redeemed debentures

V) Adoption of Statutory Audit Report

VI) Passing of annual accounts and balance sheet, along with reports of Board of directors and auditors

VII) Appointment of auditors and fixation of their remuneration

VIII) Appointment of first directors who are liable to retire by rotation

IX) Increase or reduction in the number of directors within the limit fixed by articles

X) Appointment of a managing / wholetime director

XI) Removal of a director and appointment of a director in his place

XII) Approval of appointment of sole selling agents

XIII) Winding up of a Company Voluntarily in certain events

XIV) Appointment and fixation of remuneration of liquidators in a members' voluntary winding up

XV) Nomination of a liquidator in a creditor's voluntary winding up

(2) Special Resolutions

A resolution shall be a special resolution when -

a) the intention to propose the resolution as a special resolution has been duly specified on the notice.

b) The notice required under the Act has been duly given and

c) the votes cast in favour of the resolution by members entitled to vote either in person or by proxy are not less than three times the number of votes, if any, cast against the resolution.

An explanatory statement setting out all material facts concerning the subject matter of the special resolution including the nature of the concern or interest if any therein, of every director and manager, if any, shall be annexed to the notice of the meeting.

A copy of every special resolution together with the copy of the explanatory statement shall, within thirty days of the passing of the resolution be filed with the register who shall record the same.

The articles may provide that certain types of business shall be approved by a special resolution. The Act provides that, a special resolution is required in the following cases.

i) To alter the provision of Memorandum for changing the place of registered office from one state to the other or objects of the company

ii) To change the name of the company

iii) To alter the Articles of the company

iv) To offer further issue of subscribed capital when shares are offered to outsiders

v) To create reserve capital

vi) To reduce share capital of the company

vii) To authorise payment of interest out of capital

viii) To request the Central Government to appoint inspectors for investigation of the affairs of the company.

ix) To authorise payment of remuneration to directors who are not in the whole time employment of the company

x) To make the liability of directors unlimited

xi) To have the company wound up by the court

xii) To wind up the company voluntarily

Thus, in case of special resolution, notice must specify the intention to propose the resolution at a special meeting and votes cast in favour of a resolution must have 3/4 majority. In order to be ordinary or special resolution to be valid, a notice convening the general meeting as required under the Act must be given.

(3) Resolution requiring special notice

Where by any provision contained in the Company Act or in the articles special notice is required of any resolution, notice of the intention to move the resolution shall be given to the company, not less than fourteen days before the meeting at which it is to be moved, exclusive of the day on which the notice is served or deemed to be served and the day of meeting. The object of giving special notice of a resolution is to invite special attention of the members to appreciate someting special in the proposed revolution. Thus, special notice is required in the following cases.

I) For appointment of an auditor other than the retiring auditor

II) For express resolution that the retiring auditor shall not be reappointed.

III) For removing a director before the expiry of his term.

IV) For appointing another person as director in place of the director removed.

The articles of a company may provide for additional matter for which special resolution may be required.

Circulation of Members Resolution

Section 188 provides that, a company shall on the requisition in writing of such number of members as hereafter specified and (unless the company resolves otherwise) at the expense of requisitionists-

a) give members of the company entitled to receive notice of the next annual general meeting, notice of any resolution which may be properly moved and is intended to be moved at that meeting.

b) circulate to members entitled to have notice of any general meeting sent to them, any statement not more than 1000 words, with respect to the matter referred to in any proposed resolution or any business to be dealt with at that meeting. The number of members for requisition shall be -

i) not less than 1/20th of the total voting power of all the members having at the date of requisition a right to vote on the resolution or business to which the requisition relates, or

ii) not less than one hundred member having the right as aforesaid and holding shares in the company on which there has been paid up an aggregate sum of not less than one lakh rupees in all.

On receipt of the requisition, the company shall give notice of the proposed resolution to all the members of the company entitled to have notice of the next general meeting. The company shall give a copy of the resolution or statement to each member. A company shall not be bound to give notice of any resolution if the Central Government is satisfied, on the application of the company or of any aggrieved person, the same to be defamatory or abuse of the provisions of this section. The cost of such applications may be recovered from the requisitionists.

If default is made in complying with the provisions of this section, every officer of the company who is in default shall be punishable with fine which may extend to fifty thousand ruppes.

For Registration of certain Resolutions and Agreements act provides that certain resolutions and agreements shall be registered with the Registrar, so that he can maintain complete record of the important transcations of the company.

The resolution and agreements are to be registered as follows.

i) special resolutions

ii) Resolution which have been aggreed to by all the members of a company on a subject which otherwise require a special resolution.

iii) Any resolution of the Board of directors of a company or agreement executed by a company, relating to the appointment, reappointment, or removal of the appointment of a managing director.

iv) Resolutions or agreements which have been agreed by all members of any class of shareholers on a subject which required to be passed by a resolution of a particular majority or in a particular manner.

v) All agreements and resolutions which effectively bind all the member of any class of shareholders though not agreed to by all those members.

vi) Resolutions authorising the directors of the company to-
  a) sell, lease or otherwise dispose off the whole or any part of the undertaking of the company.
  b) borrow money beyond the limits of the paid up capital and free reserves.
  c) contribute to charitable and other funds a sum exceeding Rs. 50,000/- or 5 percent of the average of the net profits of the last three years, which ever is greater.

vii) Resolutions approving the appointment of sole selling agents

viii) Resolutions requiring a company to be wound up voluntarily.

Resolutions and agreements to be printed or type written and certified by an officer of the company shall be filed within thirty days of the passing of the resolution or the making of the agreement.

In case of default made in complying these provisions the company and every officer of the company who is in default shall be punishable with fine which may extend to two hundred rupees per day during which the default continues.

9.1.9. Minutes of the Meeting

Minutes are the official record of the company meetings. These summarise the business transacted in the meeting and decisions taken and the resolutions passed at the meeting.

Every company shall cause,

(I) minutes of all proceedings of every general meeting and (II) of all proceedings of every meeting of its Board of directors or (III) of every committee of the Board, to be kept by making within thirty days of the conclusion of every such meeting concerned, entries thereof in books kept for that purpose with their pages consecutively numbered. Each page of every such book shall be initialled or signed and the last page of the record of proceedings of each meeting in such books shall be dated and signed,

(a) In case of minutes of proceedings of a meeting of the Board or of a committee thereof, by the chairman of the said meeting or the chairman of the next succeeding meeting.

(b) In case of minutes of proceedings of a general meeting by the chairman of the same meeting within the period of thirty days or in the event of the death or inability of that chairman within that period, by a director duly authorised by the Board for the purpose. In no case the minutes of proceedings of a meeting shall be attached to any such book as foresaid by pasting or otherwise.

Contents of Minutes

(I) The minutes of each meeting shall contain a fair and correct summary of the proceedings there at.

(II) all appointments of officers made at any of the meetings aforesaid,
In the case of a meeting of the Board of directors or of a committee of the Board, the minutes shall contain -

a) the names of the directors present at the meeting and

b) in the case of each resolution passed at the meeting, the names of the directors, if any, dissenting from or not concurring in, the resolution.

Matters to be excluded

The minutes must not contain any matter which, in the opinion of the chairman of the meeting -

a) is or could reasonably be regarded as defamatory of any person or

b) is irrelevant or immaterial to the proceedings or

c) is detrimental to the interests of the company.

The chairman shall exercise an absolute discretion in regard to the inclusion or noninclusion of any matter in the minutes on the grounds specified above.

Penalty

If default is made in complying with the foregoing provisions or of this section, in respect of any meeting, the company and every officer of the company who is in default, shall be punishable with fine which may extend to five hundred rupees.

Minutes to be Evidence

Minutes of meetings kept in accordance for the evidence of the proceedings recorded therein.

Presumptions to be drawn

Where minutes of the proceedings of any general meeting of the company or any meeting of the Board of directors or of a committee of the Board have been kept, in accordance with the provisions of act, then, until the contrary is proved, the meeting shall be deemed to have been duly called and held, and all proceedings there at to have duly taken place and in particular, all appointments of directors or liquidators made at the meeting shall be deemed to be valid.

Inspection of Minute Books of General Meeting

The books containing the minutes of the proceedings of any general meeting of a company shall-

a) be kept at the registered office of the company and

b) be open, during business hours, to the inspection by any member without charge.

Any member shall be entitled to be furnished, within seven days after he has made a request in that behalf to the company with a copy of any minutes on payment of such sum of Rs one for every one hundred words or fractional part thereof required to be copied.

If any inspection is refused or if any copy required is not furnished within time specified, the company and every officer of the company who is in default, shall be punishable with fine which may extend to five thousand rupees for each offence.

In case of any such refusal or default the Central Government may by order compel an immediate inspection of the minute books or direct that the copy required shall be sent to the person requisitioning it.

Publication of Reports

No document purporting to be a report of the proceedings of any general meeting of a company shall be circulated or advertised at the expense of the company, unless it includes the matters required by act to be contained in the minutes of the proceedings of such meeting. If any report is circulated or advertised in contravention, the company and every officer of the company who is in default, shall be punishable, for each offence, with fine which may extend to five thousand rupees.

9.2 COMPANY MEETINGS - II

9.2.1 General Body Meetings

General Body meetings are meetings of shareholders or members. The expression 'General Meeting' is not defined in the Company Act, but is employed to refer to those assemblies of a company which are attended by all the members who have a right to vote.

Following are the various type of general meetings -

9.2.2 Statutory Meetings

Every Company limited by shares, and every company limited by gurantee and having a share capital, shall, within a period of not less than one month nor more than six months from the date at which the company is entitled to commence business, hold a general meeting of the members of the company which shall be called 'The Statutory meeting'.

This is a special kind of meeting. It is held only once during the whole life time of a company. It is also the first meeting of the shareholders of a public company.

The main objects to hold this meeting are,

I) To discuss about the success of floatation

II) To approve any modification in the contracts included in the prospectus, if necessary.

A statutory meeting is not required for,

I) private company

II) an unlimited company

III) a company limited by gurantee, not having share capital.

Provisions of the Companies Act

The Companies Act makes the following provisions relating to statutory Meetings.

(i) Every company limited by shares and limited by guarantee and having a share capital must hold a general meeting of members, called 'Statutory Meeting' within a period of not less than one month and not more than six months from the date at which the company is entitled to commence business.

(ii) The Board of Directors must forward to every member of the company a report, known as 'Statutory Report.' along with the notice of the meeting at least 21 days before the day of the meeting. A statutory report forwarded to members later than the above period may also be regarded as valid if all members entitled to attend and vote at the meeting agree to that.

(iii) After the statutory report has been sent to members, the Board must also file a certified copy of the statutory report with the Registrar.

(iv) The Board must also produce at the commencement of the statutory meeting a list showing the names, addresses and occupations of members and the number of shares held by them. The list shall remain open for inspection of members during the continuance of the meeting.

(v) The members of company shall have the right to discuss at the meeting all matters relating to the formation of the company or arising out of the statutory report, whether previous notice of the same has been given or not. But the meeting cannot pass any resolution of which notice has not been given according to the Act.

(vi) If default is made in holding the meeting or submitting the report in accordance with law, every director and other officer in default shall be punishable with fine up to Rs. 5000 and the Court, on application of the Registrar, or a contributory, may order the winding up of the company, or may direct that the meeting be held.

Notice and Agenda of the Statutory Meetings

The Companies Act requires that the directors must send a notice of the meeting to all members of the company at least 21 days before the date of the meeting. The notice must expressly state that the meeting is the Statutory Meeting of the company held in accordance with the provisions of the Act. A copy of the Statutory Report required under the Act must also be sent along with each notice of the meeting. The notice must also state that a member entitled to attend and vote at the meeting is entitled to appoint one or more proxies and that the proxy need not be a member. The proper authority for convening the statutory meeting is a duly constituted Board meeting. However, the notice is actually issued by the Secretary under the instructions of the Board meeting.

The main purpose of the Statuatory Meeting is to consider and adopt the statutory report and matters arising from it. No other business can be taken up at this meeting unless previous notice has been given. So the notice of the statutory meeting usually refers to the agenda briefly as "To consider and adopt the Statutory Report and any other matter that may be considered at such meeting." A more detailed agenda may also be given referring to the order in which the different items of business are to be taken up, including therein any other business (e.g. approval of modifications of any contract stated in the statutory report) for which previous notice is given. Where the notice gives the agenda briefly, the secretary usually prepares a separate Agenda Paper giving the detailed agenda for the use of the chairman and himself.

Statutory Report

The Board of Directors shall at least 21 days before the day on which the statutory meeting is to be held, forward a report called 'Statutory Report' to all the members of the company. This report shall contain the following information.

(I) Share allotted - The total number of shares fully or partly paid up and in case of partly paid up, the extent to which they are so paid up and in either case the consideration for which they have been allotted.

(II) Cash Received - The total amount of cash received by the company in respect of all the shares allotted, distinguished as aforesaid.

(III) An abstract of Receipts - An abstract of the receipts of the Company and of the payments made there out, upto a date within seven days of the date of the report, exhibiting under distinctive headings the receipts of the company from shares and debentures and other sources and the payment made thereout and the particular concerning the balance remaining in hand and an account or estimate of the preliminary expenses of the company, showing separately any commission or discount paid or to be paid on the issue of shares and debentures.

(IV) Names of directors, auditors manager etc. - The names, addresses and occupations of the directors of the company and of its auditors and also manager if any and secretary and the changes which have occured since the date of incorporation.

(V) Contracts - The particulars of any contract and modifications or the proposed modification of any contract which is to be submitted to the meeting for its approval of the members of the meeting.

(VI) Understanding Contract - The extent to which each underwriting contract, if any, not been carried out and the reasons therefor.

(VII) Arrears of calls - The arrears, if any, due on calls from every director and from the manager.

(VIII) Commission and brokerage - The particulars of any commission or brokerage paid or to be paid in connection with the issue or sale of shares or debentures to any director or to the manager.

Certification of Report

The statutory report shall be certified as correct by not less than two directors of the company, one of whom shall be a managing director, if any. After the statutory report has been certified, the auditors of the company shall, in so far as report relates to the shares allotted by the company, the cash received in respect of such shares and the receipts and payments of the company, certify as correct. The Board shall cause a copy of the statutory report certified as stated, to be delivered to the Registrar for registration forthwith, after copies thereof have been sent to the members of the company.

Procedure at the Meeting

At the commencement of the meeting the Board shall place a list showing the name, addresses and occupations of the members of the company and the number of shares held by them respectively. The list shall be open and accessible to any member of the company during the continuance of the meeting.

The member of the company, present at the meeting shall be at liberty to discuss any matter relating to the formation of the company, or arising out of statutory report whether previous notice has been given or not, but no resolution may be passed of which notice has not been given in accordance with the provisions of this Act.

The meeting may adjorn from time to time and a resolution may be passed at any such adjourned meeting if due notice thereof has been given in the meantime. The adjourned meeting shall have the same powers as an original meeting for the purpose of transaction of business.

Effect of Non-Compliance

If default is made in complying with provisions of the act, every director or the officer of the company who is in default shall be punishable with fine which may extend to five thousand rupees.

It default is made in delivering the statutory report to the Registrar or in holding statutory meeting, the company may be wound up by the court.

The court may, however give directors for the statutory report to be filed or a meeting to be held, as the case may be, and refuse to order the winding up of the company

Rights of Members Regarding Statutory Meeting

The Statutory Meeting is the first official meeting of the shareholders of a company where they get an opportunity to exercise their rights as members for the first time. It also gives them an opportunity to check up the performance of the promoters and first directors since incorporation. Because of the importance of this meeting the Companies Act allows some statutory rights to members relating to the statutory meeting.

(1) Right to Discuss the Statutory Report

Members present at the meeting have the liberty to discuss any matter relating to the formation of the company or arising out of the statutory report, whether previous notice of the meeting has been given or not. They have also the right to discuss other matters not set out in the report by giving previous notice of the same as per the Act.

(2) Right to Adjourn the Meeting

Members present at the statutory meeting have also the right to adjourn the meeting from time to time, to enable them to discuss at the adjourned meetings any resolution of which previous notice has been given either before or after the original meeting. At the adjourned meetings, the members shall have the same powers and privileges as in the original meeting.

(3) Right to Inspect List of Members

The Act requires the directors of the company to prepare a list showing the names, addresses, occupations of members and number of shares held by each of them and keep it ready for production at the statutory meeting for inspection of members. The members have a right to inspect the list of members any time during the continuance of the meeting.

(4) Right of Appeal to the Court

Members have the right to file petition to the Court for compulsory winding up of the company, if the company makes default in holding the statutory meeting or in issuing and filing the statutory report as per the act.

Secretarial Duties

The duties of the secretary relating to the holding of the statutory meeting are enumerated below :

A) Before the Meeting

(i) To draft the Statutory Report in Form No. 22 and the notice of the meeting in consultation with the directors.

(ii) To arrange for convening a Board meeting and get the notice and Report approved by the Board.

(iii) To get the notice and Report certified as correct by two directors including the Managing Director, and also by the auditor of the company.

(iv) To get the statutory report and notice printed and send them to the members at least 21 days before the date of the meeting. Also to file a certified copy of the report with the Registrar.

(v) To prepare a detailed agenda of the meeting in consultation with the chairman and also a list showing names, addresses, etc., of members which is to be produced at the meeting.

(vi) To make other arrangements for holding the meeting.

B) At the Meeting

(i) To ascertain the quorum of the meeting and to read the notice of the meeting, if required to do so by the chairman.

(ii) To read the statutory report, if required.

(iii) To produce the list of members at the commencement of the meeting and keep accessible to members for their inspection.

(iv) If directed by the chairman, to supply necessary information and explanations before the meeting.

(v) To take notes of the proceedings from which minutes are to be prepared.

C) After the Meeting

(i) To prepare the minutes of the meeting from the notes taken by him during the meeting and to get it approved and signed by the chairman at the next Board meeting.

(ii) To carry out the decisions arrived at in the meeting.

SPECIMEN OF NOTICE AND AGENDA OF STATUTORY MEETING

(1) Specimen Notice of Statutory Meeting

............Co. Ltd.

Address ....
Date......................

NOTICE is hereby given that pursuant to Section .... of the Indian Companies Act. 2013. the Statutory Meeting of the........Co. Ltd. will be held at the Registered Office at.......on......2014 at...... P. M. for the purpose of considering the Statutory Report and any other matter that may be considered at such Statutory meeting.

A copy of the Statutory Report required to be submitted to the meeting under Section .... of the Companies Act. 2013 is sent herewith.

By order of the Board

....
Secretary

(2) Specimen Agenda of Statutory Meeting ....Co. Ltd.

Agenda for the statutory meeting to be held at the Registered Office at.........on........2014 at .... P. M.

1. Chairman to read the Notice Convening the meeting.

2. Consideration and adoption of the Statutory Report.

3. Any other matter with the permission of the Chairman.

4. Vote of thanks to the Chair.

SPECIMEN OF STATUTORY REPORT

No. of Company,.......   Form No. 22

THE COMPANIES ACT. 1956
Statutory Report
Pursuant to Section ....

Name of Company

Statutory Report of the

Certified and filed pursuant to Section ....

Date of notice for holding statutory meeting.................

Date of meeting........

Place where meeting is to be held........

Presented by........

The Board of Directors submits this statutory report to the members, in pursuance of Section ....

1. Shares allotted and cash received up to...............(a)

Particulars	No. of shares	Nominal value of each share	Cash received up to (a)
(a) Allotted subject to payment thereof in cash: (i) Equity (ii) Redeemable Preference Shares (iii) Preference Shares other than Redeemable Preference Shares			
(b) Allotted as fully paid up otherwise than in cash and the consideration for which they have been allotted: (i) Equity (ii) Redeemable Preference Shares (iii) Preference Shares other than Redeemable Preference Shares			
(c) Alloted as partly paid up to the extent of Rs..... per share, and the consideration for which they have been so allotted : (i) Equity (ii) Redeemable Preference Shares (iii) Preference Shares other than Redeemable Preference Shares			

(a) The date should be a date within 7 days of the Report.

2. Abstract of receipts and payments up to.....(a)

Receipts	Rs.	Payments	Rs

Shares
(i) Equity
(ii) Redeemabale
    Preference Shares
(iii) Preference Shares
    other than Redeemable
    Preference Shares
 	
(b) Advance payment for
    shares and debentures
    Deposits
    Other Sources
[to be specified]
		Preliminary Expenses
		Commission on issue or
		sale of shares
		Discount on issue or
		sale of shares
		Capiial Expenditure
		Land
		Building
		Plant
		Machinery
		Other items to be specified
		In hand
		[to be specified]
		At Banks
		At Post Office
		Savings Bank	

Total.....		Total.....	

(a) The date should be a date within 7 days of the Report.

3. Preliminary Expenses as estimated in the Prospectus or Statement in lieu of Prospectus.

Particulars	Preliminary expenses actually incurred up to the aforesaid date Rs.	Preliminary expenses estimated to be incurred after the aforesaid date Rs.
Law Charges, Other charges in connection with the preparation of the Memorandum and Articles of Association Printing expenses Registration charges Advertisement charges Commission on issue or sale of shares , Discount on issue or sale of shares, Other initial expenses (To be specified as far as possible.)		
Total Rs.		

4. Names, addresses and occupations of the Company's Directors, Auditors, Manager and Secretary

Name (s)	Address(es)	Occup-ation(s)	Particuar (s) of if any, in entries in columns (1), (2).(3), since the date of the change date of incorporation	Date of the change
(1)	(2)	(3)	(4)	(5)

    A.   Directors
    B.   Auditors,
    C.   Manager
    D.   Secretary
These particulars must include dates of changes.

5. Particulars of any contract which is to be submitted to the statutory meeting for approval.

(If any modification or proposed modification of a contract is to be submitted for such approval, brief particulars of contract and particulars of modification or proposed modification should be given.)

6. Underwriting contracts.

Brief description of each contract.

If contract not carried out fully, extent to which it has not been carried out and reasons therefor.

7. The arrears. If any. due on calls from Directors and Manager

Names   Amount due
                                                          Rs.

Directors

1.

2. Manager

8. Particulars of any commission or brokerage paid or to be paid in connection with the issue or sale of shares to any director or manager.

Names	Commission or Brokerage paid or to be paid	
	On. Shares	On Debentures
Directors		
1.		
2. Manager		

this............day of.......2014

  We hereby certify that the given report is correct.

Signature of two or more Directors*

    We hereby certify as correct so much of the report as relates to the shares allotted by the company and to the cash received in respect of such shares and to receipts and payments.

Auditors

this............day of.......2014
(*Where there is managing director, he shall be one of the signatories.)

9.2.3 Annual General Meetings (Sec. 96)

    Under the Companies Act, every company, public or private, must hold an Annual General Meeting of shareholders once every calendar year. Such a meeting is to be held in addition to any other general meeting of shareholders that may become necessary during the same year. It is held to enable the members to discuss the affairs of the company on the basis of the annual report of directors and audited accounts submitted at the meeting, as well as to exercise their rights and privileges of membership. Unlike the statutory meeting which is held only once in the lifetime of the company, the annual general meeting is a yearly and recurrent affair. It is in this meeting that the performance of the company for the past year is reviewed annual accounts and balance sheet are adopted, dividends are declared and directors and auditors are appointed or re-appointed.

    The first annual general meeting must be held within 18 months of the Incorporation of the company and thereafter it must be held every year within six months of the expiry of the financial year of the company. The authority for convening the annual general meeting is the Board of Directors. The resolution for convening the annual general meeting must be passed in a properly convened and duly constituted meeting of the Board, otherwise it will become invalid. The secretary can issue the notice only when authorised by such a Board meeting.

Importance of Annual General Meeting

The Annual General Meeting is very important to the shareholders because it is only at this meeting of a company, the shareholders get an opportunity to discuss affairs and the review the working of the company. They also get an apportunity to take steps to protect their interests. Several important decisions such as appointment of auditors, declaration of dividends etc. are taken in annual general meeting. The shareholders may take up issues relating to the affairs of the company for discussion and get clear view about the financial health of the company.

Provisions of the Companies Act

The Companies Act makes the following provisions relating to Annual General Meeting :

(i) The first annual general meeting must be held within a period of not more than eighteen months from the date of incorporation of the company. If it is so held, then it shall not be necessary to hold any such meeting in the year of incorporation and in the next year. Thereafter, it must be held every year and not more than fifteen months must elapse between the date of one annual general meeting and the next. Except in the case of the first annual general meeting, the Registrar may, for any special reason, grant an extension of up to three months for holding the annual general meeting of any company.

(ii) A notice, specifying the meeting as such and giving the date, time and place of the meeting, must be sent to every member at least 21 days before the date of the meeting.

(iii) The meeting must he held at the registered office of the company or at some other place within the city, town or village in which the registered office is situated and must be held within the business hours. The Central Government may exempt any class of companies from this provision.

(iv) The notice of the annual general meeting must be accompanied by a copy of audited balance sheet and profit and loss account for the previous financial year and also the Annual Report of Directors.

Time and Place of Holding AGM

As stated earlier, every annual general meeting of a company must be held— (a) during business hours; (b) on a day which is not a public holiday; and (c) either at the registered office of the company or at some other place within the same city, town or village in which the registered office is situated. The Central Government, may exempt a company from these restrictions, subject to such conditions as it may impose.

Length of notice. Moreover, every annual general meeting of a company must be called by giving not less than 21 clear days' notice in writing. It may be called with a shorter notice if it is agreed to by all the members entitled to vote at the meeting.

Extension of Time

The Registrar of Companies may, for any special reason, extend the time for holding an annual general meeting (except the first AGM) for a period not exceeding three months (Proviso to Sec. 166(1)). Thus, there can be no extension of time for the first AGM (Dalmia

Cement (Bharat) Co. Ltd vs. Registrar of Companies, A.I.R. (1954) Mad. 276). It has been clarified by the Department of Company Affairs that a delay in completing the audit of annual accounts of a company does not constitute a "special reason" to justify extension of time for holding annual general meeting.

Statutory Requirement

The holding of the annual general meeting is a statutory requirement which must be complied with. The annual general meeting of a company must be called and held whether or not the annual accounts are ready for consideration at the meeting. The meeting is to be called even where the company did not function or transact any business during the year.

Consequences of Default

The Companies Act lays down stringent penalties for failure of a company to hold the annual general meeting as per the Act. If a company makes a default in holding the annual general meeting in accordance with the provisions of the Act, the Company Law Board may, on the application of any member of the company, call the meeting or direct the company to call the meeting. The Company Law Board may also give any other direction as it thinks fit, which may even include a direction that one person present in person or proxy shall constitute the annual general meeting.

If a company fails to hold the annual general meeting as per the Act or fails to comply with the directions given by the Company Law Board under the act, then the company and every officer of the company in default shall be liable to be fined up to Rs. 50,000 and also to a further daily fine of Rs. 2,500 for a continuing default.

Business Transacted at Annual General Meeting

The Companies Act makes a distinction between 'ordinary business' and 'special business' to be transacted at a general meeting. In the case of annual general meeting, Sec. 96 of the Act specifies the business which will be considered as ordinary business, all other business transacted at the meeting will be deemed to be 'special' business. In the case of other general meetings, all businesses are deemed 'special'. Thus, the annual general meeting can transact both ordinary and special business. However, in the usual course, the annual general meeting transacts only ordinary business. That is why it is sometimes called the Ordinary General Meeting.

Ordinary Business

Under Sec. 96 of the Act, the following are considered to be ordinary business :
(1) Consideration and approval of the annual accounts and balance sheet and the Auditor's Report thereon.
(2) Consideration and approval of the Annual Report of Directors.
(3) Declaration of dividends, if any.
(4) Appointment of directors in place of those: retiring by rotation.
(5) Appointment of the auditors and fixing their remuneration.

Special Business

Any other business scheduled to be transacted at the meeting will be deemed to be special business.

Where any items of business to be transacted at the meeting are deemed to be special as aforesaid, there shall be annexed to the notice of the meeting a statement setting out all material facts concerning each such item of business, including in particular, the nature of the concern or interest, if any, therein, of every director, and the manager, If any.

However, where any item of special business as aforesaid, to be transacted at a meeting of the company relates to, or affects, any other company, the extent of shareholding interest in that other company of every director, and the manager, if any, of the first mentioned company shall also be set out in the statement, if the extent of such shareholding interest is not less than 20 per cent of the paid-up share capital of that other company.

Further, where any item of business consists of according approval to any document by the meeting, the time and place where the document can be inspected shall be specified in the statement aforesaid.

Special business may be passed by an ordinary resolution or special resolution as required by the Act. For instance, increase of authorised capital of the company is deemed a special business, but it can be passed by an ordinary resolution. On the other hand, alteration of the Articles of the company is also a special business but it requires a special resolution to pass it. A special resolution is one of which due notice as per the Act has been given specifying the intention to propose it as a special resolution, and which is passed by a three-fourths majority.

Annual Accounts and Balance Sheet

The purpose of the annual general meeting is to enable the members to discuss the affairs of the company and exercise their rights and privileges on the basis of the audited annual accounts and the director's report. Consideration and approval of the annual accounts and balance sheet is one of the most important items of business transacted at this meeting.

The Companies Act requires that the Board of Directors of a company must place before every annual general meeting an audited balance sheet and profit and loss account of the company for the relevant financial year. 'Financial year' refers to the period for which the profit and loss account is prepared and may be less or more than a calendar year, but it must not exceed 15 months. The Registrar may, by special permission, extend the period to 18 months.

For the first annual general meeting, the accounts must relate to a period beginning from incorporalion and ending on a date not more than nine months prior to the meeting. For the second and subsequent annual general meetings, it must relate to a period beginning with the day just after the period for which the accounts were last submitted and ending on a date not earlier than six months of the date of the meeting.

The balance sheet and profit and loss account must give a true and fair view of the state of affairs and profit and loss of the company. The profit and loss account and the auditor's report must be attached to the balance sheet.

Under the Companies Act (as amended by the Amendment Act of 1988). a copy of the balance sheet along with profit and loss account, auditors' report, and other documents must be sent to every member of the company, every trustee for debenture-holders and to all other persons entitled to receive notice of the meeting, at least 21 days before the meeting. Copies of the above documents need not be sent : (i) to members, debenture-holders, Joint holders of shares or debentures etc. who are not entitled to receive such notice and whose address is not known : and (ii) in the case of a company, whose shares are listed on a recognised stock exchange, if the copies of such documents are kept open for inspection at the registered office during working hours for 21 days before the meeting, and a statement containing salient features of these documents is sent to the persons entitled to receive notice, at least 21 lays before the meeting.

Any member or debenture-holder of a company, or any person from whom the company has accepted money by way of deposit, shall be entitled to be furnished, on demand, with a copy of the last balance sheet and other documents required to be annexed thereto.

After the annual general meeting is over, three copies of the Balance Sheet and profit and loss account along with other documents annexed thereto must be filed with the Registrar within 30 days of the date of the meeting. These must be signed by the managing director, manager or secretary or one director, before filing.

Under the Companies Act, it is obligatory for companies to file balance sheet and profit and loss account with the Registrar, even where the annual general meeting of the company has not been held for any year. The sub-section provides that, where the annual general meeting has not been held, three copies of the balance sheet and profit and loss account along with other annexed documents must be filed with the Registrar within 30 days of the latest day on or before which the meeting should have been held under the provisions of the Companies Act.

Authentication

The Act also requires that the balance sheet and profil and loss account must be signed on behalf of the Board by two directors including the managing director if there is any or the secretary, if authorised by the Board. The balance sheet and the profit and loss account must also be approved by the Board of Directors before they are signed on behalf of the Board and submitted to the auditors for their report.

Form and contents of Balance Sheet and Profit and Loss Account

The Companies Act lays down that every balance sheet of a company must give a true and fair view of the state of affairs of the company as at the end of the financial year. The balance sheet must be drawn in the form set out in Part I of Schedule VI, or in such other form approved by the Central Government, and it must be prepared according to the instructions given under the heading 'Notes' at the end of that Part. It also provides that every profit and loss account of a company must give a true and fair view of the profit or loss of the company for the financial year. The profit and loss account must be drawn and prepared according to the requirements of Part II of Schedule VI.

However, the above provisions will not apply to insurance, banking, electricity and other companies governed by separate Acts applicable to such companies. The Central Government may also, by notification in the official gazette exempt any class of companies from the provisions of this section.

For any default in complying with the requirements of this section, any person charged by the managing director, manager or the Board with the duty of complying with the provisions of this section will be punishable with imprisonment for a term upto six months or with fine of up to Rs. 1,000 or with both.

Further Amendment to Schedule VI

The Central Government has again amended Schedule VI requiring companies to show in their balance sheet 'Balance of unutilised moneys raised by issue' separately. Besides the form in which such unutilised funds have been invested must also be given.

The balance sheet will be prepare only in the vertical form.

Uniform Financial Year

From the financial year beginning on 1st April 1989, all companies are required to prepare their annual accounts and balance sheet for the financial year ending on 31st March of every year. It means that companies would have to hold their annual general meeting before 30th September of every year.

Previously, for preparing annual accounts and balance sheet a company could adopt a financial year ending on any date of the calendar year (say, 31st March, 30th June, and so on). But under Section 3 of the Direct Tax Laws (Amendment) Act, 1987, all assessees to Income-tax, including companies, are now required to prepare their accounts for Income-tax purposes for a uniform financial year ending on 31st March.

Annual Report of Directors

The Companies Act requires that the Annual Report of Directors must be attached to every Balance sheet laid before a company in general meeting. The Report must be dated and signed by the Chairman of the company, if he is authorised to do so, or by such number of directors as are required to sign the balance sheet and profit and loss account of the company (i.e., by not less than two directors, one of whom shall be the managing director, if there is one). The Report must contain the following information :

(a) Disposal of profits. A statement regarding the total profits of the company and the manner of its disposal, i.e., the amount proposed to be carried to reserves, the balance available for distribution and the recommendations of the directors regarding dividends, etc.

(b) State of affairs. A statement on the trading results of the past year and the state of affairs of the company.

(c) Changes in business. Changes that may have occurred in the nature of business of the company or of its subsidiaries.

(d) Material changes. Material changes affecting the financial position of the company, if any.

(e) Future prospects. Prospects of the company for the next year.

(f) Directorate and Auditorate. Changes in the directorate and auditorate of the company, i.e., retirement and re-election of old directors or election of new ones, and retirement and re-appointment of the auditors and changes in their remuneration, if any.

(g) Special business. Any other special business to be transacted in general meeting.

(h) Conservation of energy, etc. Particulars regarding conservation of energy, technology absorption, foreign exchange earnings and outgo.

(i) Highly paid employees. A statement showing the name of every employee of the company—(i) employed throughout the financial year or part of the financial year, and drawing such sum as annual or monthly remuneration as may be prescribed, or (ii) was in receipt of remuneration in that year which, in the aggregate, is in excess of the remuneration drawn by the managing/whole-time director or manager, and was holding himself or along with his spouse and dependent children not less than 2 per cent of the equity shares of the company. The statement must also indicate whether any such employee is a relative of any director or manager of the company and, if so, the name of such director.

Chairman's Speech

After the Annual Report of Directors is placed before the annual general meeting, it is customary for the chairman of the company to make a speech or address the shareholders. It is not required by law, but it has become a custom or practice with most companies. Since the Directors' Report merely supplies the information as required by law. it may not be sufficient in itself to explain to the members the background of the state of affairs of the company and its future prospects. The chairman's speech is a complementary document which supplies to the members the detailed information about the trading results and financial position of the company, which is missing from the directors' report.

In his speech, the chairman elaborates the information given in the directors' report, reviews the company's working and progress during the year, explains the reasons for the favourable or adverse trading results, and refers to the plans for development and future prospects of the company. While doing this, he may also point out the various economic and political problems, as well as the policies of the Government, which may help or hamper the activities of the industry in general and the company in particular. In short, he may give a general review of the country's economic and political situation which is likely to affect the prosperity of the company.

The secretary is usually entrusted with the work of drafting the chairman's speech. When it is approved, printed copies of the speech are kept ready for circulation among members at the meeting. After his speech has been delivered, it is usual for the chairman to move for the adoption of the audited statement of accounts and the directors' report.

Notice and Agenda of the Annual General Meeting

The proper authority for convening an annual general meeting is a duly constituted Board meeting. The Board usually authorises the secretary to prepare and issue the notice. The notice must specify that the meeting is an annual general meeting to be held pursuant to the Companies Act. It must state the date, time and place of the meeting. The time of the meeting must be within the business hours and place must be either the registered office of the company or some other place within the same city, town or village. The notice must also specify the period during which the Transfer Books will remain closed and the fact that members are entitled to appoint proxies to attend and vote on their behalf.

The notice must be sent to each member, debentureholder, trustees for debentureholders and others entitled to receive notice at least 21 days before the date of the meeting. The notice must be accompanied by all relevant ocuments, viz., annual accounts and balance sheet with auditors' report, directors' report, explanatory statement (if any), proxy form, admission card and A public notice of the annual general meeting is also published in the newspapers to notify the fact to members who have not given their addresses in India and also to the general public.

The Agenda of the annual general meeting is fixed by the Board meeting which authorises the convening of the meeting. The secretary prepares the agenda as per instructions of the Board and in consultation with the chairman. Usually the ordinary business to be transacted at the meeting is given first and special business, if any, given later. The agenda is annexed to every copy of the notice as part of it or in a separate sheet. The secretary also prepares a detailed agenda in consultation with the chairman for use during the meeting. This includes. besides the usual items, the names of proposer and seconder of each motion to be moved at the meeting.

Closing of Transfer Books

If the Board of Directors decide to recommend declaration of dividend, it will be necessary to close the transfer books so that the share register can be balanced and dividend lists and warrants can be prepared. The Board meeting held just before the annual general meeting fixes up the period during which the transfer books are to be closed and passes a resolution authorising the closing of the books. Usually the transfer books are closed for a period of fourteen days ending a week before the day of the notice. As no transfer can be registered during this period, it helps in determining the names of members who are entitled to attend the annual general meeting and receive dividends. The notice convening the annual general meeting includes notification to members that the transfer books will remain closed for the specified period. In case of listed shares a notice is also sent to the stock exchange. On the first day of the closed period, the secretary will complete the registration of the pending transfers and the proceed to balance the share ledger so that the names of those who are entitled to receive notice of the meeting and receive dividends can be ascertained. He then proceeds to prepare the divedend lists and warrants.

Proxies

The Companies Act allows every member of a company to appoint another person, whether a member or not, as his proxy to attend a general meeting and vote, if need be. Unless provided in the Articles, members of companies not having a share capital cannot appoint proxies. The appointment of proxy is to be made through an instrument, also known as Proxy, which must be deposited with the company not less than 48 hours before the time for the meeting. Any provision in the Articles requiring members to deposit the proxies more than 48 hours before the meeting will be void ab initio. In a public company a member can appoint more than one proxy for the same meeting, whereas a member of a private company cannot appoint, more than one proxy unless provided for in the Articles. The law also requires that, every notice of the meeting must incorporate a statement that a member entitled to attend and vote is also entitled to appoint one or more proxies.

On receipt of the proxies, the secretary should scrutinize them to see that they are in proper form and properly signed. Proxies found incorrect in any respect must be returned to the members with a note for necessary correction. Proxies lodged after the prescribed time must be returned to the members with a note that they cannot be accepted. The proxies received in time and found in order are then to be countersigned by the secretary, recorded in the register of proxies and returned to the members with an admission card made out in the name of the proxy. If a proxy is revoked by the member granting it or by his death, the secretary should record the fact in the register of proxies. On the day before the meeting, he should prepare a list of valid proxies in force for the purpose of regulating admission to the meeting and to facilitate counting of votes if a poll is taken.

Preparations for Polling

The Companies Act provides for voting by 'poll' it demanded by the chairman or a prescribed number of members after being dissatisfied with the result of voting by show of hands. If a poll is demanded, the chairman must arrange to take it. If it is a question of adjournment or election of chairman it must be taken forthwith, otherwise it may be taken at any time within 48 hours of the time when the demand was made.

If it is expected that a poll may be demanded, advance preparations should be made for taking the poll. There are various ways of conducting a poll, and the chairman has the power to regulate the manner in which the poll shall be taken. However, usually printed 'polling papers' are used having spaces for indicating the shares held, votes cast for and against, signature of the member or proxy, etc. At the time of taking the poll, blank polling papers are distributed among members and proxies entitled to vote after checking their names with the list of voters (voting list) and list of valid proxies. After the voting is complete. the polling papers are collected by the scrutineers, the papers are scrutinised and votes counted.

Procedure Relating to Annual General Meeting

The procedure relating to the holding of Annual General Meeting of a public company may be discussed in three stages — (1) Before the meeting i.e., preparatory stage; (2) During the meeting; and (3) After the meeting.

(I) Before the Meeting

Several important steps have to be taken at this stage to comply with statutory requirements and prepare for the annual general meeting.

(i) Annual accounts and balance sheet

At the end of the financial year, the balance sheet and profit and loss account are prepared and placed before a Board meeting for approval. After that these are signed and submitted to the company's auditors for audit. In due course the Auditors' Report on the annual accounts is obtained.

(ii) Directors' Report

The secretary then prepares the draft annual report of directors and a provisional statement of disposal of profit in consultation with the chairman.

(iii) Board Meeting

A Board meeting is convened sufficiently before the annual general meeting to transact the following business :

(a) to consider the disposal of profit and determine the rate of dividend;

(b) to consider and approve the auditors' report and the annual report of directors, and to authorise the managing director and one other director to sign the same;

(c) to fix the date, time, place and agenda of the meeting;

(d) to authorise the secretary to arrange for the printing of the notice and relevant documents and to issue the notice;

(e) to authorise the secretary to close the Register of Members and transfer books, balance the share register and prepare the dividend lists and warrants.

(f) to decide the names of directors who are to retire by rotation as per Articles and to consider the names of directors who are to seek election or re-election in their place, and

(g) to consider any change in the auditorate and remuneration of auditors.

(iv) Printing of Documents and Notice

The secretary then arranges for the printing of the notice, annual accounts and Balance sheet, reports of auditors and directors, explanatory statement (if any), proxy forms, admission cards for the meeting, etc. (An Explanatory Statement. Explaining all material facts relating to any 'special business', to be transacted at the meeting, has to be attached to the notice as per the Act).

(v) Issue of Notice

The notice of the annual general meeting along with the relevant documents (viz., balance sheet and profit and loss account, with auditors' report, directors report, explanatory statement, blank proxy form, admission card, etc.) are sent by registered post to members and others entitled to receive the notice.

(vi) Public notice of Annual General Meeting

At the same time as the notice of the meeting is issued, arrangements are made to publish a public notice of the meeting in newspapers. Copies of the notice and directors' report are sent to the Stock Exchange for their information and copies of the notice and annual accounts are also hung up on the notice board at the registered office of the company.

(vii) Preparation of Agenda, etc.

Next the secretary prepares in consultation with the chairman a detailed agenda of the meeting, the chairman's speech and the annual return.

(viii) Work regarding : dividend distribution

The secretary then completes the preliminary arrangement for dividend distribution, viz., making the Register of Members up to date, preparation of the dividend list and writing up of the dividend warrants. This will enable him to start sending the dividend warrants to members as soon as the formal declaration of dividend is made at the meeting.

(ix) Scrutiny of Proxies

The secretary also scrutinises the proxy forms received up to two days before the meeting, registers them and prepares a list of proxies for use during the meeting.

(x) Arrangements for the meeting

Arrangements are made for the seating of members and recording their attendance, for stenographers to take down the proceedings and for reporting the proceedings in the Press, etc.

(2) During the Meeting

The steps to be taken and procedure to be followed during the meeting consist of the following :

(i) Admission and Attendance

Before the start of the meeting, the secretary has to see that the admission cards of members are collected at the gate and their attendance recorded in the attendance register. (Admission cards are sent to members along with the notice. This is done to ensure that no unauthorised person gains entry into the meeting hall).

(ii) Chairman

The chairman then takes the chair. Usually, the chairman of the Board of Directors is authorised by the Articles to act as chairman in general meetings.

(iii) Quorum

At the instance of the chairman, the secretary ascertains whether a quorum is present or not. If quorum is present, the chairman declares the fact and the meeting starts. In the absence of any provision in the Articles, the quorum for a general meeting is five present in person for public companies and two present in person for private companies. If quorum is not present within half an hour of the scheduled time, the meeting is adjourned.

(iv) Reading of Notice, etc.

The secretary reads out the notice of the meeting and presents the register of directors' shareholdings for inspection of members. He may also be required to read the directors' report, if necessary.

(v) Auditors' Report

The auditors' report on the balance sheet and accounts is read by the auditors or by the secretary, if they are absent.

(vi) Business as per agenda

The business of the meeting is then taken up in the order set out in the agenda, viz., adoption of the minutes of the last meeting:, consideration and approval of the annual accounts, auditors' report and directors' report, chairman's speech, appointment of directors and auditors, etc.

(vii) Declaration of dividend

The chairman then moves that the dividends recommended by the directors be declared.

(viii) Vote of thanks

The meeting ends with a vote of thanks to the chair.

(3) After the Meeting

After the annual general meeting is over, the following steps have to be taken:

(i) Minutes

The secretary prepares the minutes from the notes taken during the meeting, records them in the Minute Book and keeps it ready for signature of the chairman at the next Board meeting.

(ii) Execution of instructions

The secretary has to carry out the directions and instructions of the annual General meeting, viz.. arranging issue of notices to directors and auditors appointed or re-appointed at the meeting, making necessary changes in the register of directors, sending dividend warrants to members, arranging payment of dividends, etc.

(iii) Filing of documents

The secretary has to arrange for the filing of the annual accounts and balance sheet, annual return, etc., with the Registrar within the prescribed time.

9.2.4 Extraordinary General Meetings (Sec. 100)

All general meetings of a company other than the Statutory Meeting and Annual general Meeting are called 'Extraordinary General Meeting'. An Extraordinary general Meeting is required for transacting business of special or extraordinary nature that is, business which do not fall within the scope of the annual general meeting. It is also held for transacting special business which are so urgent that these cannot be deferred till the next annual general meeting.

Business Transacted of Extraordinary General Meeting

Extra-Ordinary General Meeting may be called at any time when it is formal necessary to transact - urgent and important matters (Special Business) such as

1) Issue of debentures
2) Increase is or decrease of share capital
3) Issue of loans shares
4) Capitalisation of profits
5) Alterations in the Memorandum of Association and Articles of Association.
6) Re-organisation of share capital.
7) Removal of a director before the expiry of his term.

Authority for Convening Extraordinary General Meeting

An Extraordinary General Meeting may be called or convened by : (a) the Board of Directors, (b) the Board of Directors on the requisition of members, (c) the requisition inists themselves, and (d) the Company Law Board.

(a) By the Board

The Articles usually empower the Board of Directors to call an extraordinary general meeting, whenever it thinks fit, by passing a resolution to that effect at Board meeting. In calling and holding such a meeting it has to abide by the provisions of the Companies Act relating to holding of a general meetings.

(b) By the Board on Requisition of Members : The Companies Act also empowers the members to requisite or demand the convening of an extraordinary general meeting. The letter of requisition must be duly signed by the required number of members and must set out the object for which the meeting is to be called. The requisition must be signed by (i) members holding at least one-tenth of the paid-up capital carrying voting power (if the company has a share capital); or (ii) members enjoying one-tenth the total voting power of all members entitled to vote on the matter in view (if the company has no share capital). The letter of requisition must be deposited at the registered office of the company.

On receipt of the requisition, the Board of Directors must call, witin 21 days of the deposit of the requisition, an extraordinary general meeting as per requisition to be held at a date not later than 45 days of the deposit of the requisition. That is, the notice convening the meeting must be issued by the Board within 21 days and the meeting itself must be held within 45 days of the deposit of the requisition.

(c) By the Requisitionists

If the Board fails to call the meeting within 21 days and the meeting is not held within 45 days of the requisition, the requisitionists themselves may call the meeting within 3 months of the date of requisition. The meeting may be called by all the members who signed the letter of requisition as per Act or a majority of them. Such a meeting called by the requisitionists must be held in the same manner, or as nearly thereto as possible, in which the meeting would have been held by the company, e.g., with 21 day's notice and so on. The expenses incurred by the requisitionists for holding such a meeting can be recovered by them from the company. The company in its turn can recover such sum from the directors in default out of sums due or likely to be due to them.

(d) By the Company Law Board (Power of the Tribunal)

Under the Companies Act, the Company Law Board can also order an extraordinary general meeting to be called, held or conducted, if for any reason it is not practicable to call or hold such a meeting. The Company Law Board may pass order for calling such a meeting on its own initiative or on the application of any director or any member entitled to vote at the meeting. In its order, the Company Law Board may give such direction for calling, holding or conducting the meeting as it thinks fit, including a direction that even one member present in person or proxy may constitute the meeting. An extraordinary general meeting can be held even on holiday.

Notice of Extraordinary General Meeting

Like any other general meeting, the notice of the Extraordinary General Meeting must also be issued at least 21 days before the meeting specifying the date, time and place of the meeting. It must also specify the special business to be transacted at the meeting. Under the Act, any business transacted at the extraordinary general meeting is deemed to be 'special business'. The notice must also give the term of the resolutions to be adopted at the meeting and the intention to move the resolution as 'ordinary' or 'special' resolution. The notice convening the meeting must also be accompanied by an 'Explanatory Statement" setting out the material facts relating to the special business to be transacted at the meeting.

The notice of the extraordinary meeting must be sent to all members and others entitled to receive the notice of the meeting, along with the explanatory statement in the form of a circular letter. At the same time a public notice is also published in the newspapers giving the date, time and place of the meeting and the nature of the business to be transacted. However, the text of the resolution to be moved may not be included in such public notice.

It must be noted that unlike an annual general meeting, extraordinary general meeting may be held on any day including a public holiday. Moreover, the meeting may be held at a place other than the registered office of the company or even outside the city in which the registered office is situated.

Explanatory Statement

The Companies Act provides that where any item of business to be transacted at a general meeting is deemed to be 'special business', there must be annexed to every notice convening the meeting a statement setting out all the material facts relating to such item of business, particularly including the nature of concern or interest therein of every director, manager, etc. This statement is called Explanatory Statement. Where any item of special business transacted at a meeting affects any other company, the extent of shareholding Interest of any director or manager of the company in that other company, exceeding 20 per cent of the paid-up share capital of that other company, must also be mentioned in the explanatory statement. The statement must also state the time and place where the document, if any, proposed for approval at the meeting can be inspected by members.

It also provides that all business transacted at any meeting, other than the annual general meeting, shall be deemed to be 'special' business. The business transacted an Extraordinary General Meeting being special business, every notice of such meeting must be accompanied by an Explanatory Statement. The object of such a statement is to explain to the members the reasons and importance of passing such a resolution so as to ensure its smooth adoption.

Procedure for holding the Meeting

When the directors decide to hold the Extraordinary General Meeting on their own initiative, a Board meeting has to be convened to decide the date, time and place of the meeting, as well as the resolution to be passed at the meeting. The notice and explanatory statement to be sent to shareholders are then drafted. The notice must contain the text of the resolution to be proposed at the meeting and must state that the resolution is to be passed as an ordinary or a special resolution. The notice is then sent to the shareholders along with the explanatory statement at least 21 days before the meeting. At the same time the notice is also published in the newspapers giving the date, time and place of the meeting as well as the nature of the resolution to be passed. The secretary then prepares a detailed agenda in consultation with the directors.

If the directors decide to convene the Extraordinary General Meeting on the requisition of members, they must first ascertain that the requisition letter is in order, is signed by shareholders holding in the aggregate not less than 1/10th of the paid-up capital carrying voting power (if the company has a share capital) or members enjoying at least 1/10th of the total voting power (if the company has no share capital) and the letter is deposited at the registered office of the company. The directors must then issue the notice of the meeting within 21 days of the deposit of the resolution.

At the meeting, the chairman of the Board will act as the chairman. The chairman must first ascertain that the meeting is duly convened and constituted, is attended by members who are entitled to attend and that quorum is present. After the notice has been read by the secretary, the chairman will proceed with the business as per agenda. Before moving the resolution, the chairman usually addresses the meeting and explains the need and importance of passing the resolution. After that he moves the resolution and invites the members to take part in the discussion. After thorough discussion it is put to vote and adopted. If the members demand a poll, he must arrange to take it with the help of the secretary. If the resolution is a 'special' resolution. It must be passed by a 3/4th majority. The meeting terminates with a vote of thanks to the chair.

After the meeting, a duly certified copy of the special resolution must be filed with the Registrar within 30 days. Also a printed copy of the special resolution must be embodied or annexed to every copy of the Articles issued by the company after the passing of the resolution. The secretary must also prepare the minutes of the meeting and keep it ready for signature of the chairman at the next Board meeting.

Secretarial Duties

The duties of the Secretary before, at and after an Extraordinary General Meeting may be enumerated as follows :

A) Before the Meeting

1. If the requisition is received from members, to scrutinise the same to ascertain whether it is in order. Also to arrange for the convening of a Board meeting in consultation with the chairman for fixing the date and time of the Extraordinary meeting.
2. If the extraordinary meeting is convened on the Board's initiative, to arrange for holding a Board meeting to fix the date, time, place and special business of the extraordinary meeting.
3. To prepare the draft resolution and explanatory statement and get it approved by the Board meeting.
4. To arrange for the printing of the notice, explanatory statement and other documents.
5. To issue the notice to members along with the explanatory statement, proxy forms, admission cards, etc.
6. To send intimation of the meeting to stock exchange and arrange for the publication of the notice in newspapers.
7. To scrutinise the proxies received and register them.
8. To arrange for the seating of members, recording of attendance, reporting of proceedings to the Press, etc.

B) At the Meeting

1. To see that admission cards are checked at the entrance and attendance of members is recorded in the attendance register, if required.
2. To ascertain whether a quorum is present or not and inform the chairman accordingly.
3. To read the notice of the extraordinary general meeting, if required to do so.
4. To assist the chairman in conducting the meeting, including taking of poll, counting of votes, etc.

5. To supply necessary information and documents as required by the meeting.
6. To take notes of the proceedings of the meeting.

C) After the Meeting

1. To carry out the instructions of the meeting and execute the resolutions adopted therein.
2. To file with the Registrar, within 30 days, certified copies of the Special Resolutions passed by the meeting along with relevant documents. Also to obtain approval of the Company Law Board, if necessary.
3. To incorporate changes or alterations in the Memorandum and Articles, if any, adopted at the meeting and to file revised copies of the same with the Registrar within three months.
4. To draft the minutes of the extraordinary meeting and get them approved by the chairman at the next Board meeting.
5. To send copies of the minutes to the concerned stock exchanges with which the shares are listed.

9.2.5 Class Meetings

These are meetings held by a particular class of shareholders (i.e., Preference Shareholders) for the purpose of making changes in the Articles of the company as regards their rights and privileges or for the purpose of conversion of one class of shares into another. These meetings can be attended by the shareholders of that class only. The Articles usually provide for the holding of class meetings and lay down the rules and procedure for convening and holding of such meetings. A class meeting for changing the rights and privileges of that class of shares can be held subject to the provisions of the Memorandum and Articles and in so far as such is not prohibited by the terms of issue of such shares. Where the variation is permissible, it must be sanctioned by a special resolution in that class meeting, i.e., by a three-fourth majority or with the written consent of holder of 3/4 th of the issued shares of that class.

9.2.6 Meeting of Debenure-Holders and Creditors

These meetings are required for the purpose of : (i) compromising a disputed matter with creditors or compounding of debts : or (ii) securing the consent of the creditors to any scheme of reorganisation, reconstruction or amalgamation : or (iii) securing the consent of creditors and debenture-holders at the time of winding up. In each case, the purpose is to secure the support and approval of the creditors and debenture holders to any scheme of rearrangement or for saving the company from financial difficulty.

As regards Creditors' Meeting for effecting a compromise in a dispute, or to obtain their approval to a scheme of reorganisation, the procedure laid down in the act is as follows :

Under the Act. the Court may order the holding of a meeting of creditors or of a class of creditors on the application by the company or any creditor or member or liquidator of the company. The company must send a notice of the meeting to the creditors concerned along with a statement setting forth the terms of the proposed compromise or reorganisation. The statement should particularly explain the effect of the proposal on the interest of the company's directors, managing director, and the manager. If the proposal affects the rights of debentureholders also, a similar statement should be sent giving similar information and explanation in respect of the trustees for debentureholders. If the notice is advertised, the statement should form part, of such advertisement or must indicate the place where copies of such statement will be available.

After the proposal has been approved by a majority of the creditors whose claims amount to at least three-fourth of the total amount of such claims, the Court sanctions the proposed compromise or scheme of reorganisation and issues an order accordingly. A certified copy of the order must be filed with the Registrar and a copy of the same must also be annexed to every copy of the Memorandum of Association.

Meetings of debentureholders are called by the company with the purpose of (i) varying the terms of the security, or (ii) modifying the rights of debentureholders. These meetings are usually held by a company to enable it to issue fresh debentures or to vary the rate of interest payable lo existing debenture-holders. The rules and procedure of holding such meetings are usually laid down in the Debenture Trust Deed or endorsed on the back of the Debenture Bond.

SPECIMEN NOTICE AND AGENDA OF
ANNUAL GENERAL MEETING

(1) Specimen of Notice (with Agenda) of Annual General Meeting of a company.

WESTERN TRADING COMPANY LIMITED

NOTICE

NOTICE is hereby given that the Eighth Annual General Meeting of the shareholders of Western Trading Co. Ltd. will be held at the Registered Office of the Company at Kolkatta on the 25th June, 2014 at 2 pm. to transact the following business :

AGENDA
1. To read out the notice of the meeting,
2. To receive and adopt the Directors' Annual Report and the Annual Accounts.
3. To receive and adopt the Auditors' Report on the Accounts and Balance Sheet.
4. Chairman to deliver his address.
5. To declare dividends as recommended by the directors.
6. To elect two directors in place of those retiring by rotation.

7. To appoint the Company's Auditor for the current year.
8. Vote of Thanks.
9. Chairman to declare meeting closed.

A member entitled to attend and vote at the meeting is entitled to appoint one or more proxies to attend and vote instead of himself and that the proxy need not be a member of the Company.

The Transfer Books of the Company will be closed on 30th of May. 2014 and will re-open on 15th of June, 2014.

By order of the Board

A. Gokhale
Secretary

9.3 COMPANY MEETING – III BOARD MEETINGS (Sec. 173)

9.3.1 Need for Board Meetings

The directors are the representatives of the shareholders and are responsible for the management of the affairs of the company. They are required to meet frequently to discuss and decide upon policy matters, to take decision on matters relating to the management of the company and to review its progress. Normally, all powers of management are granted to the directors by the Act and the Articles of a company can be exercised only by passing resolutions at duly constituted meetings of directors. These meetings are also called Board Meetings. The Board of Directors is also usually empowered by the Articles to appoint committees of directors for specific purposes and to help the Board in its decision-making process. Meetings of such committees can also be held as and when required.

9.3.2 Frequency of Board Meetings

The decision of a Board Meeting will not be considered valid unless it is properly convened and duly constituted. That means it must be convened by the proper authority by a proper notice, the proper person must be in chair, and the requisite quorum must be present. The rules regarding the holding and conduct of Board Meetings are laid down by the Act and the Articles. The Companies Act also allows the Board to frame its own rules and regulations (known as Standing Orders) for the conduct of Board meetings where the Act and the Articles are silent.

According to the provisions of the Companies Act, a Board meeting must be held at least once in every three calendar months, and at least four such meetings must be held in every year. However, Board meetings may be held more frequently, if the circumstances so demand. The requirements of the Act in this respect may be waived or modified by the Central Government in the case of companies which do not have sufficient work to justify quarterly meetings.

9.3.3 Notice of the Meetings

The Companies Act requires that notice of every Board meeting must be given in writing to every director who is present in India at his usual address. Failure to give notice will make every officer responsible for giving such notice liable to fine. If, however, the Articles provide for holding of Board meetings on fixed days of each month or at regular intervals, notice of the meetings need not be sent. But even in such cases, a notice is usually sent to the directors as a reminder. Usually, it is the duty of the secretary to send notices of Board meetings as per Articles or as directed by the Board or on the requisition of a director. The notice must state the date, time and place of the meeting, as well as the business to be transacted thereat. Usually a copy of the agenda is sent as part of the notice. The notice must be of a length prescribed by the Articles. If the Articles do not prescribe the length, it must be of reasonable length which will enable the directors to attend the meeting. Usually a week's notice is considered sufficient.

9.3.4 Agenda of Board Meetings

Although it is not obligatory in law, it is customary to send a copy of the agenda. i.e. the business to be transacted at the meeting, along with the notice of every Board/Meeting. It is usually the duty of the secretary to prepare the agenda of a Board meeting in consultation with the Chairman of the Board of Directors, and the Managing Director, if any. Although Board meetings are held frequently and many of the items of business transacted at these meetings are of routine nature the agenda should be prepared carefully and the relevant reports, statements, accounts, etc., should be kept ready for each item of the agenda. The agenda should be complete and sufficiently explicit to enable the directors to form opinions on them and come prepared to give their views at the meeting.

Copies of the agenda are also prepared on large sheets of paper, known as Agenda Paper, on which the items of business are typed on the left-hand side keeping sufficient blank space on the right to enable the Chairman and Secretary to keep agenda notes. The Secretary makes agenda notes in his copy of the agenda paper carefully as it enables him to prepare the minutes later on. Sometimes, an Agenda Book is used instead of agenda paper for the same purpose. This helps to maintain a permanent record of the agenda and agenda notes.

While setting out the items of business in the agenda, the usual order followed is to place routine items first and special or controversial items later. The agenda of the First Board Meeting, held just after the incorporation, contains many important items as this meeting has to deal with many matters arising out of incorporation and vital steps necessary for setting up and conduct of the company's business. The agenda of subsequent Board meetings usually include some routine items of recurring nature (e.g., approval of minutes, finance and accounts, transfer and transmission of shares, reports of committees, etc.) as well as some special items which vary from meeting to meeting (e.g., calls and forfeiture of shares, staff matters, appointment of committees, approval of agreements and contracts, convening of general meetings, dividends, investment of company's funds, borrowings, etc.).

First Board Meeting

The first Meeting of Directors or the First Board Meeting is held Just after the incorporation of the company. This meeting has much importance and needs special attention as many matters consequent upon the incorporation and necessary for carrying on the business of the company have to be decided upon at this stage. For instance, the Chairman of the Board and of the company has to be elected and the managing director, secretary and other officers of the company have to be appointed at this meeting, so that management and administration of the company's affairs is not hampered. Similarly, the bankers, auditors and solicitors of the company are appointed at this meeting. If it is a public company, this meeting has to finalise and approve the draft of Prospectus and fix the date of its release to the public. The other important matters required to be dealt with in this meeting are adoption of preliminary contracts, adoption of the company's seal, fixing of quorum of Board meetings, etc.

Preparations for Board Meetings

As required by law, meetings of directors must be held at least once in every three months. But it may be held more frequently as and when necessity arises or at fixed intervals. The secretary must make preparations for such meetings-well in advance so that important matters to be placed before the Board for its decision may not be left out.

During the period between two Board meetings, the Secretary should make notes of the matters that are to be placed before the next Board meeting, statements of reports to be prepared therefor and documents to be kept ready for the reference of the directors. On the basis of these notes, he should prepare the agenda of the meeting in consultation with the Chairman. Any motion or resolution for which notice has been given by any director should be included in the agenda. He should then prepare the notice of the meeting, unless the meetings are held on fixed days and notice has been dispensed with by the standing orders and send them to all directors at reasonable time before the date of the meeeting.

After the notice of the meeting has been issued, the secretary should start making ready the books, registers, documents, etc., required at the meeting. He should write up the minutes of the last Board meeting in the Minute Book of the Board Meeting and keep it ready. The other things to be kept ready are an indexed copy of the Memorandum and Articles, the seal of the company, financial, statements, bank pass book, transfer Instruments and books, share certificates, contracts, agreements, correspondence to be considered, etc.

Minutes of Board Meetings

Under the Companies Act, every company is required to have the minutes of proceeding of all Board meetings and meetings of committees of the Board entered in a separate Minute Book kept for the purpose. This is to be done within 30 days of the conclusion of the meeting. The pages of the Minute Book must be consecutively numbered and each page of the book must be initialled or signed, and the last page of the book must be dated and signed by the chairman of that meeting or the chairman of the next succeeding meeting. Failure to comply with these provisions will make the company and its officers liable to line of Rs. 500/-.

The minutes of the Board meetings and meetings of committees of the Board must contain a fair and correct summary of the proceedings of the meeting. It must include: (a) all appointments of officers made at the meeting; (b) the names of the directors present at the meeting; and (c) the names of the directors dissenting in each resolution passed at the meeting. However, the chairman of the meeting has the discretion to exclude any matter from the minutes if it is considered to be defamatory or irrelevant or immaterial or detrimental to the interest of the company. If the minutes of a meeting of the Board or its committee are kept in accordance with the provisions of the Act, then the meeting will be deemed to have been duly called and held and the decisions of the meeting will be deemed to be valid. Such minutes when signed by the chairman become evidence of the proceedings of the meeting.

It is the duty of the Secretary to prepare the minutes from the notes of the proceedings taken by him and the Chairman during the meeting. He should ensure that the exact wordings of the resolutions adopted at the meeting are recorded properly so that the minutes may be a fair and accurate summary of the proceedings. The secretary should see that the provisions of the Act and the articles are complied with in regard to writing of minutes and maintenance of the Minute Book.

Secretarial Duties

The secretary plays an important role in the holding of Board meetings. As the principal officer of the company, he must ensure that, every Board meeting is properly convened and duly constituted and that the provisions of the Act, Articles and standing orders are compiled within the conduct of these meetings. The principal duties of the Secretary relating to Board meetings may be outlined as follows :

A) Before the Meeting

(1) If the date. time and place of the Board meeting has not been fixed by the preceding meeting, to fix the same in consultation with the Chairman of the Board.
(2) To prepare the agenda in consultation with the chairman or as directed by the Board.
(3) To ascertain from the Articles the proper authority for convening Board meetings. In the absence of such provision, to prepare and issue notice of the meeting as per directions of the chairman of the Board. Also to ensure that the length of the notice is as per Articles.
(4) To send notice of the meeting along with the agenda to all directors in India and to the usual address in India of all directors not in India.
(5) To receive resolutions from directors proposed to be discussed at the meeting and circulate them among other directors.
(6) To issue invitation letters to solicitors, auditors, etc.. who are required to attend the meeting by special invitation.

(7) To prepare and keep in readiness statements and reports regarding the company's trading activities, documents including cheques, contracts, transfer instruments, etc., for sealing and signatures, and other materials likely to be required at the meeting.

(8) To keep ready the Bank pass book and certificate of cash balances, the Minute Book of Board Meetings, indexed copies of Memorandum and Articles, the company's seal. etc.

(9) To arrange for the seating arrangement, stationery and other equipment necessary for holding the meeting.

B) At the Meeting

(1) To obtain signatures of the directors present in the Directors' Attendance Book.

(2) To help the chairman by ascertaining whether quorum is present or not as per Articles.

(3) To read the notice of the meeting if required or if requested by the chairman.

(4) To read the Minutes of the last Board meeting if requested by the chairman and to obtain the signature of the chairman to the minutes when it is approved by the meeting.

(5) To assist the chairman in conducting the meeting including taking of votes.

(6) To supply necessary information and explanations to the directors when required.

(7) To take notes of the proceedings on the agenda paper including exact terms of the resolutions passed.

C) After the Meeting

(1) To prepare the minutes from his own and chairman's agenda notes and enter the same in the Minute Book within a reasonable period.

(2) To carry out the instructions issued to him by the Board meeting and to carry out the statutory duties specifically imposed on him.

(3) To start collecting and preparing materials for the next Board meeting.

9.3.5 Time and Place of Board Meetings

Unlike annual general meeting, there is no provision in the Companies Act regarding time, day and place of Board meetings. A Board meeting can be held at any place outside the registered office of the company, outside business hours and even on a public holiday. The Act an adjourned Board meeting cannot be held on a public holiday.

Authority for Convening Board Meeting

The companies Act does not prescribe the authority competent to convene a Board meeting. The Articles of a company usually provide for the procedure and competent authority for convening Board meetings. Under Regulation 73(2) of Table 'A', a director may and the manager or secretary on the requisition of a director must, summon a meeting of the Board. The usual procedure is that, the directors at a meeting held decide on a date for holding the next Board meeting and the secretary is authorised to issue notice of the meeting at the appropriate time.

9.3.6 Chairman of Board Meetings

Every Board meeting must have a Chairman to preside over the meeting. There is no specific provision in the Act in this regard. The Articles of a company usually provide who shall preside over Board meetings. If the Articles do not name the chairman, the directors themselves may elect the chairman and fix his term of office at the first Board meeting or in any subsequent Board meeting as necessary. Usually the Chairman named in the Articles or elected by the directors at the first Board meeting after incorporation presides over all Board meetings. He may also be empowered to preside over general meetings of members. If the Chairman named in the Articles or elected by directors is not present within five minutes of the time fixed for the meeting, the directors may elect one of their members as temporary chairman for that meeting.

Voting by Directors

Each director has one vote which he can exercise on any motion except where he is debarred from voting as an interested director. If the Articles so provide, the Chairman of the Board meeting can exercise his casting vote in case of a tie, in addition to his vote as a director. Voting in Board meeting is done by show of hands and all motions are passed by a simple majority, unless the law requires a motion to be passed unanimously. The Companies Act requires that motions or approval of the prospectus, appointment of a person as manager or managing director in a second company, inter-company investments, etc., must be passed by the Board unanimously.

9.3.7 Quorum of Board Meetings (Sec. 174)

As per the provisions of Section 174 of the Companies Act, the quorum for a Board meeting shall be one-third of the total strength of the Board or two directors whichever is higher. Any fraction contained in that one-third is to be rounded off as one. The total strength of the Board is to be calculated by excluding the number of directors whose seats are vacant at that time and also the number of interested directors. Interested directors are those who have any interest in any contract being considered by the Board meeting and whose presence cannot be counted for the purpose of quorum at the time of discussion or voting on that contract. If at any time number of interested directors exceeds or is equal to two-thirds of the total strength of the Board, the number of the remaining disinterested directors (being not less than two) shall be the quorum during that time. The minimum number of members forming the quorum of a Board meeting can also be fixed by the Articles or the Board at a higher figure than that required by the Act. The provisions of the Act will apply if there is no Board resolution or provision in the Articles.

The quorum fixed by the Act, Articles or Board resolution must be present at the beginning as well as throughout the meeting. The proceedings of the meeting will be invalid, if the quorum is not maintained throughout the meeting, unless the Articles specifically provide for exceptions to this rule. Unless otherwise provided in the Articles, if a quorum is not present at a Board meeting, it will automatically stand adjourned to the same day in the next week and at the same time and place. If that day is a public holiday, then it shall be adjourned to the next succeeding day.

9.3.8 Resolutions by Circulation (Sec. 175)

Normally all decisions are taken by the Board by passing resolutions at the board meeting. But if it is not possible to hold a Board meeting for some reason, the Articles usually empower the Board to pass resolutions by circulation among directors. However, according to the Act, no such resolution will be deemed to have been passed by the Board unless (a) the resolution has been circulated in draft, together with all necessary papers, to all directors present in India at their usual address; (b) the number of directors among whom it is circulated is not less than the quorum fixed for Board meetings; and (c) the resolution has been approved by a majority of the directors entitled to vote on the resolution (i.e., majority of the disinterested directors).

POWERS OF BOARD (Sec. 179)

A) General Powers of the Board

Subject to the provisions of the Companies Act, the Board of Directors of a Company is entitled to exercise all such powers and to perform all such acts as the company is authorised to exercise or do by its Memorandum and Articles.

However, the Board is not empowered to exercise any power or do any act which is required to be exercised and done by a company in general meeting under the Act, Memorandum or Articles of the company. Moreover, while exercising these powers the Board shall be subject to the provisions of the Act, Memorandum and articles, as well as any regulations framed thereunder or by the company in general meeting.

Thus, the usual powers which can be exercised by the Board by passing resolutions at Board meetings include :
  (a) Determination of management policy, trading policy, etc.
  (b) Appointment, promotion and dismissal of staff.
  (c) Issue of shares and debentures.
  (d) Allotment of shares.
  (e) Calls on shares.
  (f) Forfeiture and re-issue of shares.
  (g) Transfer and transmission of shares.
  (h) Convening meetings of shareholders.
  (i) Disposal of profits and determination of rates of dividend, as also declaration of interim dividend.
  (j) Entering into contracts with third parties on behalf of the company,
  (k) Investment of company's funds.

(l) Exercising borrowing powers on behalf of the company.

(m) Filing of statutory returns and statements,

(n) Maintenance of statutory and other books of the company, etc.

B) Powers to be Exercised only at Board Meetings

The Companies Act provides that the Board of Directors shall exercise the following powers only by means of resolutions passed at a meeting of the Board :

(a) the power to make calls on shares;

(b) the power to issue debentures of the company;

(c) the power to borrow money otherwise than on debentures;

(d) the power to invest the funds of the company; and

(e) the power to make loans.

The right to exercise power under (a) and (b) above cannot be delegated by the Board to any committee or executive of the company. However, the right to exercise the other three powers mentioned above can be delegated by the Board to any committee of directors or the managing director or any other principal officer by a resolution passed at a Board meeting on such conditions as the Board may deem fit.

C) Restrictions on Powers of Board (Sec. 180)

Ordinarily, the Board is entitled to exercise all powers and perform all acts on behalf of the company, subject to the provisions of the Act, Memorandum and Articles. Some of these powers can be exercised only by passing resolutions at Board meetings, some others by passing resolutions by circulation. The Companies Act, 2013 has imposed certain restrictions on the exercise of certain powers by the Board. It prohibits the Board of a public limited company or a subsidiary private company from exercising any of the following powers, except with the consent of members in general meeting :

(1) powers to sell, lease or otherwise dispose off the company's undertaking;

(2) power to invest, otherwise than in trust securities, the sale proceeds of the company's undertaking;

(3) power to remit or give time for repayment of a debt due by a director;

(4) power to borrow money exceeding the aggregate of paid-up capital and free reserves of the company; and

(5) power to appoint a sole selling agent.

Consent of the general meeting to exercise any of the above powers may be obtained through an ordinary resolution, a copy of which must be filed with the registrar within 30 days of their passing.

D) Other powers to be exercised at Board Meetings : In addition to powers to be exercised at Board meeting under Section 179, certain other powers of the Board, under several other Sections of the Act, are also to be exercised by passing resolutions at Board

meetings. These powers and relevant sections are noted below :

(1) The power to appoint additional directors, if authorised by the Articles.
(2) The power to fill up casual vacancy in the office of director.
(3) The power to accord sanction to a director or his relative to enter into certain specified contracts with the company.
(4) The power to appoint or employ a person as managing director who is the managing director or manager of not more than one other company.
(5) The power to invest in any shares of any other body corporate, subject to the limits prescribed by sub-section (2) as amended in 1988.
(6) The power to appoint or employ a person as manager who is the manager or managing director of not more than one other company.
(7) The power to make declaration of solvency in the case of members' voluntary winding up.

N. B.: Among the above-mentioned powers, the powers under clauses (4), (5) and (6) are to be exercised by the Board by a resolution passed at the Board meeting with the consent of all the directors present, i.e., unanimously.

Director's Attendance Book

In order that the names of directors attending a Board meeting may be properly recorded and to fix responsibility for acts done at a meeting, it is necessary to maintain a 'Directors' Attendance Book'. Signatures of all directors as well as of those in attendance are taken by the secretary in this book before the Board meeting begins.

9.3.9 Meetings of Committees of Directors

It is not always possible for the Board of Directors as such to devote time and energy to carry on investigations on different matters connected with the conduct of the company's affairs. It is the usual practice with the Board to appoint small committees consisting of a few directors with expert knowledge to investigate and report on various matters and thus facilitate decision-making work of the Board. The Articles of a company usually empower the directors to appoint such committees and delegate some of their powers to these Committees of Directors. Unless the Articles otherwise provide, a committee of one may also be appointed. These committees have to meet at regular intervals to carry on their work. These are known as Meetings of Committees of Directors.

Sec. 179 of the Companies Act empowers the Board of directors to delegate, by a resolution passed at a meeting, powers to any committee of directors, the Managing Director or manager or any other principal officer of the company,

(a) to borrow money otherwise than on debentures;
(b) to invest the funds of the company; and

Abstituted for Rs. 50 by the Companies (Amendment) Act, 2000.

(c) to make loans to the extent specified in this section and on such conditions as the Board may prescribe.

Some of these committees are entrusted with work of routine nature, viz. of transfer of shares, raising of finance, etc. These are usually of permanent nature and are called Standing Committees. Committees may also be appointed from time to time to deal with special matters of temporary duration, such as allotment of shares. These committees are known as Ad Hoc Committees and these wound up as soon as their task is finished and they have submitted their reports to the Board of Directors.

After completing the investigations entrusted to them, these committees submit their reports to the Board for their consideration and final decision. The committees are entitled to adopt resolutions by circulation subject to the same conditions as are applicable to the Board. The rules and procedure for convening and conducting committee meetings are usually laid down by the Board or framed by the committees themselves.

SPECIMENS OF NOTICE AND AGENDA

(1) Specimen Notice of the First Board Meeting.

ROYAL MANUFACTURING CORPORATION LIMITED

19, Royal Buildings,
Circular Road.
Chennai, the 12th June, 2014

To

_____
_____
_____
(Director)

Dear Sir/Madam,

I have to inform you that the first meeting of the Board of Directors will be held at the Registered Office of the Company on 4th July, 2014, at 3 P.M. to transact the following business.

You are requested to please attend the meeting.

Yours faithfully.
....
Secretary

(2) Specimen Agenda of the First Board Meeting

AGENDA

1. Election of the Chairman of the meeting.
2. To produce the Certificate of Incorporation, the Memorandum and the Articles of Association.
3. Appointment of the first Directors.
4. Election of the Chairman of the Company.
5. Appointment of Managing Director, Secretary, Solicitors, Auditors and Bankers.
6. Adoption of the Company's Seal.
7. Fixing a quorum for the Board meetings.
8. Consideration and adoption of the Preliminary Contracts and Underwriting contract.
9. Consideration and approval of the draft of Prospectus.
10. Consideration of the application to the Stock Exchange for the listing of shares.
11. Any other business.
12. Fixing the date of the next Board meeting.

(3) Specimen of Notice and Agenda of Subsequent Board Meeting

IDEAL MANUFACTURERS LIMITED

Ideal Buildings,
New Delhi-2,
The 17th May, 2014

To,
N. Batra Esq.,
56, Daryaganj,
New Delhi - 2.

Dear Sir,

This is to inform you that the next meeting of the Board of Directors will be held at the Registered Office of the Company on 8th June, 2014, at 4 P.M. to transact the following business.

You are requested to be present.

AGENDA

1. To read and approve the minutes of the last Board meeting.
2. To consider application for transfer of shares.
3. To consider letter of resignation of the Manager of Agra Branch.
4. To consider trading returns for the quarter ended....2014.
5. List of accounts for payment to be produced and passed.
6. Any other business with the permission of the chair.
7. Fixing the date of the next Board meeting.

Yours faithfully,
Secretary

SECRETARIAL DUTIES IN COMPANY MEETINGS
I. Before the Meeting

Board Meeting	Statutory Meeting	Annual General Meeting	Extraordinary General Meeting
1. Prepare and issue Notice and agenda letters to special invitees.	1. Draft Statutory Report.	1. Get annual accounts and B/Sheet prepared, audited and certified.	1. Scrutinise requisition from members, if any.
2. Receive and circulate resolutions received from directors.	2. Call Board meeting to aprove Report.	2. Draft Directors Report. Notice and agenda.	2. Draft resolution and Explanatory Statement.
3. Keep ready Minutes Book, Seal, M/A, A/A and other documents.	3. Get report certified by two directors and auditors.	3. Call Board meeting to approve annual accounts. Balance Sheet, Directors Report, etc., and to fix date of meeting.	3. Call Board meeting to fix date and approve resolution and Explanatory statement.
	4. Print and issue notice and statutory report.	4. Print and issue notice with necessary documents.	4. Print and issue notice with necessary documents.
	5. Prepare detailed agenda.	5. Draft detailed agenda, Chairman's speech. Annual Return, etc.	5. Draft detailed Agenda.
	6. Close Transfer Books etc.	6. Close transfer books, balance share register and prepare Dividend List and Warrants.	6. Scrutinise and register proxies.
	7. Scrutinise proxies and register them.	7. Keep all documents, registers, seal etc., ready for meeting.	7. Keep documents ready for meeting.
	8. Keep documents ready for meeting.	8. Make arrangements for holding meeting.	8. Make arrangements for holding meeting.
	9. Make arrangements for holding meeting.		

II. At the Meeting

Board Meeting	Statutor Meeting	Annual General Meeting	Extraordinary General Meeting
1. Obtain signature of directors in Attendance Book.	1. Check attendance and collect admission cards.	1. Check attendance and collect admission cards.	1. Check attendance and collect admission cards.
2. Help chairman to ascertain quorum.	2. Help chairman to ascertain quorum.	2. Help chairman to ascertain quorum.	2. Help chairman to ascertain quorum.
3. Read notice and minutes, if required.	3. Read notice and statutory report if required.	3. Read notice, directors report, etc., if required.	3. Read notice, if required.
4. Obtain signature of chairman to the minutes.	4. Produce list of members and keep it ready for inspection.	4. Assist chairman in conducting meeting and taking of poll, counting of votes etc.	4. Assist chairman in conducting meeting and taking of poll, counting of votes etc.
5. Assist chairman in conducting meeting and taking of votes.	5. Assist chairman in conducting meeting and taking of poll, counting of votes etc.	5. Supply necessary information and explanations if required.	5. Supply necessary information and explanations.
6. Supply necessary information and explanations.	6. Supply necessary information and explanations.	6. Take notes of the proceedings.	6. Take notes of the proceedings.
7. Take notes of the proceedings.	7. Take note of the proceedings.	-	-

III. After the Meeting

Board Meeting	Statutory Meeting	Annual General Meeting	Extraordinary General Meeting
1. Prepare minutes and get it approved and signed by chairman at the next Board meeting.	1. Prepare minutes and get it approved and signed by chairman at next Board meeting.	1. Prepare minutes and get it approved and signed by chairman or authorised director within 30 days.	1. Prepare minutes and get it approved and signed by chairman at the next Board meeting.
2. Carry out decisions and instructions of the meeting.	2. Carry out decisions and instructions of the meeting.	2. Send intimation of appointment/re-oppointment to directors and auditors.	2. Carry out all other decisions and instructions of meeting.
		3. Issue Div. warrants and arrange payment.	3. Incorporate the changes, if any, in M/A and A/A.
		4. File Directors, Report, Annual accounts, Annual Return, Special Resolution, etc. with Registrar.	4. File certified copies of special resolution, if any, with the Registrar.
		5. Carry out all other decisions and instructions of meeting.	

COMPANY MEETINGS–COMPARED

	Board Meeting	Satutory Meeting	Annual General Meeting	Extraordinary General Meeting
1. Purpose	Sec. 285 and A/A* To enable directors to determine policy, make decisions and exercise control, direction and supervision over management.	Sec. 165 To acquaint members, as soon as possible after incorporation, with matters reformation of the Co. and its financial position and prospects.	Sec. 166 To enable members to review at the end of each year, the performance of the Co. on the basis of report and annual accunts, to elect directors and auditors and in general to exercise the rights.	Sec. 169 and A/A To transact business outside the scope of Annual General Meeting and other business of urgent nature.
2. When to be held	Once in every 3 monts–at least four meetings during the year.	Once in Co.'s life time. Within not less than 1 month and not more than 6 months of the date of commencement certificate	Once in every year–within 15 monts of last Annual General Meeting and 6 Months of end of financial year.	As and when Board thinks necessary or when requisitioned by members.
3. Proper Convening Authority	As per A/A and Standing Order.	Duly constituted Board meeting/Court.	Duly constituted Board meeting/Central Government.	Duly constituted Board meeting/Requisitionists/Company Law Board.
4. Notice	To every director– as per A/A or reasonable length.	To all members and Auditors–21 day's clear notice.	Same as Statutory Meeting	Same as Annual General Meeting

5. Documents with Notice	Proposed resolution of any director.	Statutory Report, Proxy Form, Admission Card.	Audited Accounts and Balnce Sheet, Auditors' Report, Directors' Report, Proxy form, Admission Card, Explanatory statement (if special business).	Explanatory Statement, Proxy Form, Admission Card.
6. Quorurm	1/3rd of total (disinterested directors or 2 whichever is higher) -A/A may provide larger number.	Public Co.-5, Private Co.-2	Public Co.–5 Private Co–2 (A/A may provide larger quorum).	Same as Annual General Meeting.
7. Usual Agenda	Approval of minutes consideration of financial and trading reports, passing accounts for payment, transfers, staff matters, convening of general meetings, etc.	Adoption of Statutory Report, approval of any modification of any contract.	Adoption of Directors' Report, Audited Accounts, B/Sheet, etc., declaration of dividend, election of directors and auditors and any special business.	Any special business.
8. In chair	As per A/A and Standing Order–usually Chairman of the Board.	As per A/A–usually Chairman of the Board.	Same as Statutory Meeting.	Same as Annual General Meeting.

9. Proxies	Proxy cannot be appointed.	Member entitled to attend and vote can appoint proxy / proxies. Members of Co. without share capital can not appoint proxy unless provided by A/A. Members of Private Co. can appoint one proxy.	Same as Statutory Meeting.	Same as Annual General Meeting.
10. Resolutions	Only Ordinary Resolution—passed at meeting or by Circulation.	Special business—ordinary resolution.	Ordy. Business—ordinary resolution. Special business—ordinary or special resolution.	Special business—Ordy. or Special Resolution.
11. Voting	Each director has one vote, chairman has casting vote if allowed by A/A. Voting usually by show of hands. Decisions by simple majority.	Each member has one vote; by show of hands—voting right proportional to share-holding only in poll. Voting by show of hands unless poll demanded.	Same as Statutory Meeting.	Same as Annual General Meeting.
12. Penalty for default	Fine up to Rs. 100 for every officer for default in issuing notice.	For default in holding meeting, fine up to Rs. 500 for company and every officer in default.	For default in holding meeting, fine up to Rs. 5,000 and Rs. 50 per day for continuing default for company and every officer in default.	

QUESTIONS

A) Answer in 20 words.

1) Define 'Meeting'.
2) What do you mean by Proper Authority?
3) What is Notice?
4) What is Explanatory statement?
5) What is Quorum?
6) What do you mean by Poll?
7) What do you mean by 'Proxy'?
8) What is 'Resolution?'
9) What is 'Minutes'?
10) What is 'Statutory meeting'?

B) Answer in 50 words.

1) Give contents of Notice.
2) Explain the provision regarding quorum.
3) Explain the method of voting - Poll.
4) How minutes are recorded?
5) What are the provision regarding 'Special resolution'?
6) What is 'Resolution by Circulation'?
7) What are the purposes of holding A.G.M.?
8) What is class meeting?
9) Give the names of special business activities.
10) Explain the powers of a chairman of the meeting.

C) Answer in 150 words.

1) What is Poll? Why and how it is demanded?
2) What do you understand by the term 'Proper Notice'?
3) What are the normal power and duties of a chairman during a Meeting?
4) What types of company rasolution have to be filed with the registrar?
5) What is 'Quorum'? Explain the provision regarding quorum.
6) Distinguish between 'Ordinary resolution' and 'special resolution'.
7) What are the precautions of Minutes? What important points should be borne in mind by the secretary while writing the minutes?
8) What is 'Statutory Meeting'? Why and when it is held?
9) What is statutory report? What are its contents?
10) What is an Annual General Meeting of a company? State its objects.

D) Answer in 300/500 words.

1) What are the reguisities of a valid meeting?

2) Explain in detail the two principal methods of ascertaining the reuse of a meeting of a company. Mention advantage of each.

3) What is 'Poll'? Why and how is it demanded? Discuss the procedure of conducting poll when it has been granted by the chairman of a meeting.

4) Distinguish between 'Motion' and 'Resolutions'. State the rules regarding the moving of motion at meetings.

5) What is 'agenda' and 'minutes'? What points would you take into consideration while drafting the agenda and the minutes?

6) What is a 'Statutory meeting'? Mention the duties of a company secretary in connection with this meeting.

7) What is an Annual General Meeting? Explain its legal provisions and state the secretarial duties is relation to this meeting.

8) Who can call an extra-ordinary general meeting? Describe the duties of a company secretary with regard to the extra-ordinary general meeting.

9) What are the requisites of a valid Board Meeting? Point out special powers to be exercised by the Board of Directors. Also state routine secretarial work in conection with a Board Meeting.

Chapter 10

COMPROMISES, ARRANGEMENTS, RECONSTRUCTIONS, AMALGAMATIONS AND WINDINGUP OF COMPANY

CONTENTS

10.1 Revival and Rehabilitation of sick companies
    10.1.1 Determination of Sickness
    10.1.2 Overview of the Process

10.2 Compromises and Arrangements
    10.2.1 Meaning of 'Compromises' and 'Arrangements'
    10.2.2 Statutory Provisions regarding Compromises and Arrangements
    10.2.3 Power of High-Court to approve and implement compromises and Arrangements
    10.2.4 Procedure to be followed for compromises and arrangements

10.3 Reconstruction and Amalgamation
    10.3.1 Meaning of 'Reconstruction'
    10.3.2 Purpose of 'Reconstruction'
    10.3.3 Meaning of 'Amalgamation'
    10.3.4 Purpose of 'Amalgamation'
    10.3.5 Difference between reconstruction and amalgamation

10.4 Winding Up of a Joint Stock Company
    10.4.1 Meaning of winding up
    10.4.2 Types of winding up
    10.4.3 Voluntary winding up

10.1 REVIVAL AND RE-HABILITATION OF SICK COMPANIES: (U/S 253-269)

10.1.1 Determination of Sickness

Where on a demand by the secured creditors of a company representing 50% or more of its outstand amount of debt, the company has failed to pay the debt within a period of 30 days of the service of the notice of demand or to secure or compound it to the reasonable satisfaction of the creditors, any secured creditors may file an application to the Tribunal in the prescribed manner along with the relevant evidence for uch default, non-repayment or failure to offer security or compound it, for a determination that the company be declared as a sick company.

Chapter XIX of the 2013 Act lays down the provisions for the revival and rehabilitation of sick companies. The chapter describes the circumstances which dternmine the declaration of a company as sick compay, and also includes the rehabilitation process of the same. Although it aims to provide comprehensive provisions for the revival and rehabilitation of sick companies, the fact that several provisions such as particulars, documents as well as content of the draft scheme in respect of application for revival and rehabilitation, etc. have been left to substantive enactment, leaves scope for interpretation.

The coverage of this chapter is no longer restricted to industrial companies, and the determination of the net worth would not be relevant for assessing whether a company is a sick company.

The coverage of Sick Industrial Companies Act, 1985 (SICA) is limited to only industrial companies, while the 2013 Act covers the revival and rehabilitation of all companies, irrespective of their sector.

The determination of whether a company is sick, would no longer be based on a situation where accumulated losses exceed the net worth. Rather it would be determined on the basis whether the company is able to pay its debts. In other words, the determining factor of a sick company has now been shifted to the secured creditors or banks and financial institutions with regard to the assessment of a company as a sick company.

The 2013 Act does not recognise the role of all stakeholders in the revival and rehabilitation of a sick company, and provisions predominantly revolve around secured creditors. The fact that the 2013 Act recognises the preence of unsecured creditors, is felt only at the time of the approval of the scheme of revival and rehabilitation. In accordance with the requirement of Sec. 253 of the 2013 Act, a company is assessed to be sick on a demand by the secured creditors of a company representing 50% or more of its outstanding amount of debt under the following circumstance:

The company has failed to pay the debt within a period of 30 days of the service of the notice of demand.

The company has failed to secure or compound the dept to the reasonable satisfaction of the creditors.

The speed up the revival and rehabilitation process, the 2013 Act provides a one year time period for the finalisation of the rehabilitation plan.

10.1.2 Overview of the process

*   In response to the application made by either the secured creditor or by the company itself, if the Tribunal is satisfied that a company has become a sick company, it shall give time to the company to settle its outstanding debts if Tribunal believes that it is practical for the company to make the repayment of its debts within a reasonable period of time.

*   Once a company is assessed to be a sick company, an application could be made to the Tribunal under Sec. 254 of the 2013 Act for the determination of the measures that may be adopted with respect to the revival and rehabilitation of the identified sick company either by a secured creditor of that company or by the company itself. The application thus made must be accompanied by audited financial statement of the company relating to the immediately preceding financial year, a draft scheme of revival and rehabilitation of the company, and with such other document as may be prescribed.

*   Subsequent to the receipt of the application, for the purpose of revival and rehabilitation, the Tribunal, not later than seven would be required to fix a date for hearing and would be appointing an interim administrator under Sec. 256 of 2013 Act to convene a meeting of creditors of the company in accordance with the provisions of Sec. 257 of the 2013 Act. In certain circumstances, the Tribunal may appoint an interim administrator as the companyadministrator to perform such functions as the Tribunal may direct.

The administrator thus appointed would be required to prepare a report specifying the measures for revival and rehabilitation of the identifed sick industry. The measures that have been identified under the Sec. 261 of the 2013 Act for the purpose of revival and rehabilitation of a sick company provides for the following options:

-Financial reconstruction

-Change in or takeover of the management

-Amalgamation of the sick company with any other company, or another company's amalgamation with the sick company.

*   The scheme thus prepared, will need to be approved by the secured and unsecued creditors representing three-fourth and one-fourth of the total representation in amounts outstanding respectively, before submission to the Tribunal for sanctioning the scheme pursuant to the requirement of sectin 262 of the 2013 Act. The Tribunal, after examining the scheme will give its approval with or without any modification. The scheme, thus approved will be communicated to the sick company and the company administrator, and in the case of amalgamation, also to any other ocompany concerned.

*   The sanction accorded by the Tribunal will be construed as conclusive evidence that all the requirements of the scheme relating to the reconstruction or amalgamatioin or any other measure specified therein have been complied with. A copy of the sanctioned scheme will be filed with the ROC by the sick company within a period of 30 days from the date of its receipt.

* However, if the scheme is not approved by the creditors, the company adminstrator shall submit a report to the Tribunal within 15 days, and the Tribunal shall order for the winding up of the sick company. On passing of an order, the Tribunal shall conduct the proceeding for winding up of the sick company in accordance with the provisions of Chapter XX,.

10.2 COMPROMISES AND ARRANGEMENTS

10.2.1 Meaning of Compromise

'Compromise' means an amicable settlement of differences by mutual concessions by the parties to dispute or difference by agreeing not to try it out. In *Sneath Vs. Valley Gold Ltd.* [1983]1 Ch. 447, 'Compromise', was described as an agreement terminating a dispute between parties as to the rights of one or more of them, or modifying the undoubted rights of a party which he has difficulty in enforcing.

The result of this case and others is that there can be no compromise unless there is some dispute, e.g., as to the power to enforce rights or as to what those rights are.

Meaning of Arrangement

An 'Arrangement', as the expression is used in the Companies Act, 2013, embraces a far wider class of agreements than a 'Compromise'. It includes agreements which modify rights about which there is no dispute. Thus, 'Arrangement' includes a reorganisation of the share capital of the company by the consolidation of shares of different classes, or by division of shares into shares of different classes or by both these methods. An arrangement may also involve : (i) Debentureholders being given an extension of time for equity shares in a new company; (ii) the creditors agreeing to receive cash in part payment of the claims and the balance in shares or debentures of the company; (iii) the preference shareholders giving up their rights to arrears of dividends, further agreeing to accept a reduced rate of dividend in the future, and so on.

Thus, when a company has a dispute with a member or a class of members or with creditor or a class of them, a scheme of compromise may be drawn up. But, where there is no dispute but there is need for readjusting the rights or liabilities of a member or a class of them or of a creditor or a class of them, the company may resort to a scheme of arrangement with them. The act provides that "the expression 'arrangement' includes a reorgnisation of the share capital of the company by the consolidation of shares of different classes, or by the divisions share of into shares of different classes, or by both these methods."

It is not, however, appropriate to use the expression 'Arrangement' where membership rights are proposed to be surrendered or otherwise terminated or confiscated without compensation.

Implied Power to Compromise / Arrangement (Sec. 230)

Companies may need to enter into agreements compromising claims or modifying rights which other persons have against them, or which they have against other persons. A company has an implied power to compromise disputes in which it is involved with outsiders or with its own members - *Re Norwich Provident Insurance Society, Bath's* case [1878] 8 Ch. D 384, and it probably also has implied power to enter into arrangements with such persons modifying the undoubted rights which they or the company has. In any case, the express power to do these things is usually inserted in objects clause of its Memorandum of Association as one of the standard provisions. The reason why the subject of compromises and arrangements is deserving a separate treatment is that, rights enforceable against companies are often vested in large classes of persons with whom it would be practically impossible to negotiate individually, and in such cases a machinery is required by which the claims of the classes collectively may be compromised or their rights modified with the assent of a majority of their number given at meetings called for the purpose.

This machinery may be provided by the original agreements between the company and the classes of persons entitled to the rights, but whether such machinery is provided by agreement or not, it is provided by the Companies Act. 2013.

10.2.2 Statutory Provisions (Procedure) :

The Companies Act, 2013 empowers a company to make compromise or arrangement with its creditors (or any class of them) or members (or any class of them) and makes suitable provisions under Sec. 230.

Sec. 230 makes the following provision :

1. Where a compromise or arrangement is proposed.

(*a*) between a company and its creditors or any class of them; or (*b*) between a company and its members or any class of them;

The Court may, on the application of the company or any creditor or member or of the class involved, or liquidator, order that a meeting of the creditors or members (or any class of them) be called and held in the manner directed by the Court [Sub-Sec. (1)].

The application to the Court under Sec. 230 may be made in the case of company in liquidation, not only by the liquidator but also by a creditor or a member. This right of a creditor or member is not taken away by reason of the company being wound up -- *Rajendra Prasad Aggarwal* Vs. *Official Liquidator* [1978] 48 Com. cas. 476.

Application by Transfer of Shares and Financiers. Transferees of shares and financiers may apply with the leave of the court-- A. K. Mishra Vs. Wearwell Cycle Co. (India) Ltd. [1993] 87 Comp. Cas. 252 (Delhi). In this case, two persons (one of whom was the Managing Director) proposed to provide funds to the company for its revival. The court directed the Official Liquidator to register them as members in pursuance of who were to be paid with then money. They, thus, became competent to file a petition for leave of the court for confirmation of the scheme.

2. If at the meeting, a majority of the number representing in value 3/4 th of the conditors or members (or any class of them) present in person or by proxy agree to the compromise or arrangement, then the compromise or arrangement will be binding on :

(a) all the creditors or creditors of the class or all the members or members of the class, and

(b) the company or, if the company is being wound up, on the liquidator or contributories of the company.

Scope of Sec. 231. The aid of the section may be invoked when it is not otherwise possible to made some arrangement or compromise which would be in the interests of the company and the other party or parties to the arrangement. It can be used whether the company is a going concern or is in the course of winding up.

Exericse of the Court's discretion

Before the Court sanctions a scheme, it will normally need to be satisfied on the following matters :

1. The Statutory Provisions must have been complied with. The court must see that the resolutions are passed by the statutory majority in value and number in accordance with the legislation at a meeting or meetings duly convened and held. In this regard, it may be noted that the act contemplates a scheme between a company and its creditors or any class of them or between the company and its members or any class of them. Thus, where a scheme was agreed to by the company and its ordinary shareholders only, without interfering with the rights of the preference shareholders, the scheme was held to be valid even though a meeting of the preference shareholders was not called to ascertain their views --*Mcleod & Co.* Vs. *S. K. Ganguly* [1975] 45 Comp. Cas. 563.

The Court shall not make any order sanctioning the compromise or arrangement unless it is satisfied that the company or any other party making the application has disclosed to the Court, by affidavit or otherwise, all material fact relating to the company, such as:

(a) the latest financial position of the company;

(b) the latest auditor's report on the accounts of the company;

(c) whether any investigation or proceedings

Further, an order made by the Court sanctioning the compromise or arrangement shall have no effect until a certified copy of the same is filed with the Registrar. Moreover a copy of every such order must be annexed to every copy of the Memorandum, issued after the filing of the certified copy of the order or, if the company has no Memorandum, to every copy of the instrument constituting or defining its constitution.

Stay of Any Suit or Proceedings After application for compromise or arrangement is made, the Court may at any time stay the commencement or continuation of any suit or proceedings against the company on such terms as it thinks fit, until the application is disposed of.

2. The Class must have been Fairly Represented. The Court must be satisfied that those who attended the meeting are fairly represntatives of the class and that the statutory majority did not coerce, the minority in order to promote interest adverse to those of the class whom they purport to represent.

This requirement is, in part, an off-shoot of the first. As regards the majority, there are two requirements. The majority who vote in favour of the scheme must be first a majority in number of those members of the class (whether of creditors or shareholders) who are present and voting, and second, it must be 3/4th in value of the holding of such persons.

Thus, if there are 100 members voting, of whom (to take an extreme example) one member holds 901 shares and the remaining hold one each, the 99 shareholder holding one share each cannot force a scheme against the vote of the holder of the 901 shares, because they do not muster 3/4 th in value. Conversely, that shareholder and 49 of the others cannot force a scheme against the votes of the remaining fifty because there would not be a majority in number. The same principle applies to creditors.

It may be noted that the majorities are of those voting and not of those entitled to vote nor of those who are present -- *Re Bessemer Steel & Ordnance Co.* [1875] 1 Ch. D 251 Thus, shareholders who are not present in person or by proxy, or who, although present, do not vote, may be ignored.

However, this is not the whole requirement because, in addition, the company requires to be satisfied that the class is fairly represented. If, for instance, there were altogether one thousand shareholders holding ten thousand shares in all, the Court is unlikely to be satisfied by the statutory majority at a meeting at which members holding hundred shares in all were present and voted [*Palmer's Company Law*, 24th Edition, page 1146].

Petition of Majority in Guarantee Companies. Problems in computing this percentage are likely to arise in case of guarantee companies and others not having share capital. In such cases, it will be assumed that each shareholder holds one share in the company and the percentage is calculated accordingly.

3. The Scheme should be Fair and Reasonable. Even on the face of the fact that a scheme of compromise or arrangement was approved by the requisite majority and without coercion on minority, the Court is not bound to confirm the scheme.

There is no doubt that the Court will be strongly influenced by a big majority vote, provided the scheme is fair and equitable. The Court will not itself judge the commercial merits of the compromise or arrangement, which is the function of the class itself. But, the

Court should not be taken to be a mere rubber stamp. The Madras High Court in *Calicut Bank Ltd. Vs. Devani Ammal AIR* 1940 Mad. 621 observed "that the Court does not sit merely to see that the requirements of law have been complied with, nor does it simply register a resolution passed by the majority of shareholders or creditors. Court is bound to consider the proposal and decide whether they are fair and reasonable taking everything into consideration."

Thus, if the Court concludes that there is "such an objection to it as that any reasonable man might say that he could not approve it," then the Court may refuse to confirm the scheme. In a case where income tax or sales tax or similar other tax ability has arisen and has crystallised, the Court will not interfere in such a case so far as the incidence of tax on the company is concerned.

The Scheme Should be Bona Fide to Save the Company From Liquidation. It should not be directed to set up a part or whole of the principal and interest of a particular class of its creditors.

10.2.3 Powers of the Court [Now NCLT] (Sec. 231)

The Court has very wide powers in sanctioning or rejecting a scheme of compromise arrangement. The Court shall have, *inter alia,* the following powers :

1. Power to Stay any Suit / Proceeding. It may, at any time, after an application has been made to it under Sec. 231, stay the commencement or continuation of any suit or proceeding against the company on such terms as it thinks fit, until the application finally disposed of.

2. Power to Supervise of Modify Compromise or Arrangement. Where an order sanctioning a compromise or an arrangement has been made by the Court, it;
  (i) shall have power to supervise the carrying out the compromise or arrangement; and
  (ii) may at the time of making such order or at any time thereafter, give such direction in regard to any matter or make such modification in the compromise or arrangement as it may consider necessary for the proper working of the compromise or arrangement.

3. Power to Make on Order for Winding Up. If the Court is satisfied that a compromise or arrangement sanctioned under Sec. 231 cannot be worked satisfactorily with or without modification, it may make an order for winding up of the company on its own or on the application of any interested persons.

10.2.4 Procedure for Compromise and Arrangement

The act lays down the following rules regarding providing of information to the affected persons under a scheme of compromise or arrangement :
  1. Where a meeting of the creditors (or any class of creditors), or of members (or any class of members) is called under Sec. 391, the notice calling the meeting must be accompanied by a statement setting forth the terms of compromise or arrangement

and explaining its effect. The statement must, in particular, state any material interest of the directors, Managing Director or Manager and every trustee of debenture holders of the company, whether in their capacity as such or as members or creditors of the company or otherwise.

2. In case notice calling the meeting is given by advertisement, there must be included either such a statement as aforesaid or a notification of the place to which and the manner in which creditors or members entitled to attend the meeting may obtain copies of such a statement as aforesaid. Such copies must be furnished by the company free of charge.

3. If default is made in complying with any of the above requirements, the company and every officer of the company who is in default, shall be punishable with fine, which may extend to Rs. 50,000. The Company and its officers can avoid liability if it can be proved that the default in sending the notice and the statement was caused by the refual of a person responsible to supply the necessary particulars as to his material interests.

10.3 RECONSTRUCTION AND AMALGAMATION (Sec. 232)

10.3.1 Meaning of 'Reconstruction'

The term 'reconstruction', *inter alia,* indicates the process which involves (i) the transfer of undertaking of an existing company to another company, usually incorporated for the purpose. The old company ceases to exist. However, all the assets might not pass to the new company; (ii) the carrying on of substantially the same business by the same persons; (iii) the rights of the shareholders in the old company are satisfied by their being allotted shares in the new company.

10.3.2 Purposes of 'Reconstruction'

The recontruction may be resorted to for the following purposes :

1) For the purpose of taking new powers and adopting new objects in the memorandum and widening the company's range of activities.

2) For the purpose of raising fresh capital by issuing partly paid shares in the new company in exchange of fully-paid shares in the old company and calling up the balance of such new shares as and when required. This would provide additional working capital for the company.

3) For reorganising or arranging the capital and the rights of members between themselves.

4) For writing off the lost or unrepresented assets and thus avoiding evils of over-capitalization.

5) For changing the domicile of the company.

6) For effecting or compromise with creditors or the allotment to them of shares or debentures in settlement of their claims.

10.3.3 Meaning of 'Amalgamation'

Amalgamations is the blending of two or more undertakings into one undertaking the shareholders of each blending company becoming substantially the shareholders of the other company which holds blended undertaking. Amalgamation takes many forms from the pooling of profits etc. to complete mergers. Amalgamation companies may dissolve and a new company may be formed to take over the existing business of the companies. Sometimes, an existing company may retain its separate entity but another company may acquire only a controlling interest in the share capital of that company i.e. it may become a holding or parent company having a number of such subsidiary companies. The process of amalgamation may be resorted for the following purposes :

10.3.4 Purposes of 'Amalgamation'

1) For securing a monopoly by eliminating competition
2) For safe guarding supplies of raw materials, technical operations or markets.
3) For effecting economies in the management etc. or otherwise for rationlisation of an industry.

When there is a simple amalgamation the amalgamating company goes into voluntary liquidation and its business in taken over by another company and the shareholders of the amalgamation or transferor company are given shares in the transfree company.

When the amalgamation involves any arrangement or compromise with the shareholders or the creditors of the transferor company, the scheme of amalgamation shall be carried. The companies Act empowers the Central Government to pass an order for amalgamation of companies in national interest.

10.3.5 Difference between Reconstruction and Amalgamation

Points of Distinction	Reconstruction	Amalgamation
1) Formation of a New Company	Reconstruction must lead to the formation of a new company, formed for the specific purpose of acquiring the assets and liabilities of the old company, which is to be reconstructed.	Amalgamation may not lead to the formation of a new company to acquire an existing business. An existing stronger company may absorb the business of another company or it may simply acquire a controlling interest in another company.

2) Sale of assets	Assets are not sold to an outside party but in the new company the membership and the business are substantially the same. The old concern is allowed to continue in the new form and with modified objects.	Under amalgamation one may come across blending of two or more companies into one big concern. The old companies lose their individuality in complete amalgamation.
3) Legal procedure	Reconstruction requires legal procedure and the schemes can be carried out either as per Sec. 494 or as per Sec. 394 and 395.	Amalgamation also requires legal procedure u/s Sec. 494, 394 and 395

10.4 WINDING UP OF A JOINT STOCK COMPANY

10.4.1 Meaning of Winding Up

Winding up or "Liquidation" of a company is the last stage of the life of a company. It means a procedure of dissolving a company. According to Prof. Gower, "Winding up of a company is the process whereby its life is ended and its property is administered for the benefit of its creditors and members. An administrator called a liquidator is appointed and he takes the control of the company, collects its assets, pays its debts and finally distributes any surplus among the members in accordance with their rights."

The company is not dissolved immediately at the commencement of winding up. Its corporate status and powers continue. Winding up preceds dissolution.

10.4.2 Types of winding up

The winding up of a company may be either,

a) by the Tribunal or
b) Voluntary.
Thus,

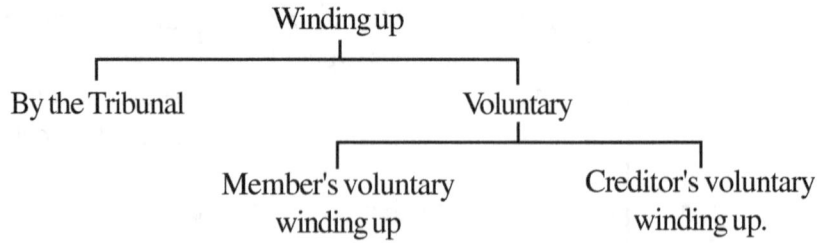

10.4.2.1 Winding up by Tribunal (Sec. 271)

A company may be wound up by the Tribunal under the following circumstances.

a) If the company has, by special resolution, resolved that the company be wound up by the Tribunal.

b) If default is made in delivering the statutory report to the Registrar or in holding the statutory meeting.

c) If the company does not commence its besiness within a year from its incorporation or suspends its business for a whole year.

d) If the number of members is reduced, in the case of a public company below seven and in the case of a private company below two.

e) If the company is unable to pay its debts.

f) If the Tribunal is of the opinion that it is just and equitable that the company should be wound up.

g) If the company has made a default in filing with the Registrar its Balance Sheets and Profit and Loss Account or Annual Return for any five consecutive financial years.

h) If the company has acted against the interests of the sovereignty and integrity of India, the security of the state, friendly relations with foreign states, public order, decency or morality.

i) If the Tribunal is of the opinion that the company should be wound up under the circumstances specified in Sec. 271.

Provided that the Tribunal shall make an order for winding up of a company under clause (h) on application made by the Central Government or a State Government.

A company may be wound up by the order of the Tribunal. This is called as compulsory winding up. A company may be wound up under the following conditions.

1) Special Resolution

If the company has, resolved by special resolution that it be wound up by the Tribunal, the Tribunal may order to do so. But the power of the Tribunal is discretionary and it may not be exercised if the winding up would be opposed to the interests of the public or the company.

2) Default in holding Statutory Meeting

If the company has made a default in delivering the statutory report to the Registrar or in holding a statutory meeting, it may be ordered to be wound up. The petition on this ground, for winding up, can be presented by the Registrar or by a contributory. In case, it is brought by some other person, say a creditor, then it must be filed before the expiration of fourteen days after the last day on which the statutory meeting ought to have been held. The power of the Tribunal is discretionary and instead of making order for winding up, the Tribunal may direct that the statutory report shall be delivered or that the meeting shall be held.

3) Failure to Commence Business

If a company fails to commence its business within a year of its incorporation or has suspended the business for a whole year, it may be ordered to wound up.

In this case also the power is discretionary and it is used only when there is fair indication of the absence of intention to carry out business. If the suspension is satisfactorily accounted and if it is due to certain temporary causes, then the order may be refused.

4) Reduction in membership

If the number of members is reduced to the statutory minimum in case of a public limited company below seven and in case of a private company below two, the company may be ordered to wound up.

This provision enables the member, to escape personal liability for the company's debts which he will incur under Sec. 45 of the Act.

5) Inability to pay Debts

If the company is unable to pay its debts, it may be ordered to be wound up. Under, the company shall be deemed to be unable to pay its debts in the three cases as follows

a) Statutory Notice - If a creditor to whom the company owes a sum of rupees exceeding one lakh, has served on company a demand for payment and the company has neglected for three weeks to pay or otherwise satisfy him.

b) Decreed Debt - A company shall be deemed to be unable to pay its debts if the execution or other process issued on a decree or order of any court or Tribunal in favour of a creditor of the company is returned unsatisfied in whole or in part.

c) Commercial Insolvency - If this is proved to the satisfaction of the Tribunal that the company is unable to pay its debts, taking into account the contingent and prospective liabilities of the company.

6) Just and Equitable

When the Tribunal is of the opinion that it is just and equitable that the company should be wound up. Thus, the Tribunal has been provided with wide discretionary powers for ordering winding up of whatever it appears to be desirable. The Tribunal may give due weight to the interest of the company, its employees, creditors, shareholders and general public interest.

The circumstances in which the courts have dissolved, in the past, companies on this ground may be stated as follows.

a) Deadlock - When there is a deadlock in the management of a company, it is held just and equitable to order winding up.

b) Loss of substratum - When main object of the company has failed to materialise or it has lost its substratum, it is held just and equitable to wind up a company.

c) Losses - When a company cannot carry on its business except at losses, then it was considered just and equitable to wind up a company.

d) Oppression of Minority - Where the principal shareholders have adopted an aggressive or oppressive or squeering policy towards minority, it was held just and equitable to wind up a company.

e) Fraudulent Purpose - If the company has been conceived and brought for the fraudulent or for illegal purposes, then it was held as just and equitable to wind up a company.

f) In corporated or Quasi partnership - Where a private company is in essence or substance a partnership, it may be ordered to be wound up under just and equitable clause.

g) Public Interest - When public interest demands it, widing up can be ordered. For example, company posed danger to the investing public and was also technically insolvent, it was ordered to be wound up in public interest.

(7) Default in filing Balance Sheet etc.

If the company has made a default in filing with the Registrar, its Balance Sheet and Profit and Loss Account or Annual Return for any five consecutive years, the company may be wound up by the Tribunal.

(8) Acts of the Company against Sovereignty and integrity of India.

A company may be wound up if it has acted against the interests of sovereignty and integrity of India, the security of the State, friendly relations with foreign states, public order, decency and morality.

For winding up a company on the grounds of its acts against sovereignty and integrity of India the application under this clause should be made by the Centre or State Government.

(9) Winding up under Circumstances of Sec. 272.

A company may be wound up by the order of the Tribunal, if it is of the opinion that the company should be wound up under the circumstances mentioned in the act as a sick industrial company.

It may be concluded that the remedy of winding up is the last remedy and hence it should not be allowed "where an equally effective remedy is available. Allegations of misuse of funds, fraudulent transactions, removal of a director under a forged resignation, failure to supply essential documents to shareholders, increase in remuneration of directors without general body approval, illegal allotments of shares, could have been taken care of by a petition against mismanagement of the company's affairs." A petition under such grounds for winding up may not be entertained.

Who can Apply (sec. 272)

An application to the Tribunal for the winding up of a company shall be by petition presented. A petition may be presented by any one of the following.

i) by the company or

ii) by any creditor or creditors including any contingent or prospective creditor or creditors or

iii) by any contributory or contributories i.e. on the commencement of the winding up of a company, its shareholders are called contributories.

iv) by the Registrar of Companies.

v) by Central Government, by any person authorised by the Central Government in that behalf.

vi) Central Government or State Government

Commencement of Winding Up

Winding up commences not from the date of the order, it shall be deemed to commence from the time of the presentation of the petition. But where, before the presentation of the petition, a resolution has been passed by the company for winding up, the winding up shall be deemed to have commerced at the time of the passing of the resolution. Where there were more than one petitions, winding up was deemed to have commenced from the date of the earliest of the creditor's petition. Any proceedings taken in voluntary winding up will be deemed to have been validly taken unless the Tribunal directs otherwise on profit of fraud or mistake.

In all other cases the winding up of a company by the Tribunal shall be deemed to commence at the time of the presentation of the petition for the winding up.

A voluntary winding up shall be deemed to commence at the time when the resolution for voluntary winding up is passed

Power of Tribunal on hearing Petition

On hearing a winding up petition, the Tribunal may -

i) dismiss it with or without costs or

ii) adjourn the hearing conditionally or

iii) make an interium order that it thinks fit or

iv) make an order for winding up the company with or without costs or any other that it thinks fit :

The Tribunal shall not refuse to make a winding up order on the grounds only, that the assets of the company have been mortgaged to an amount equal to or in excess of those assets or that the company has no assets.

Where the petition is presented on the ground that it is just and equitable that the company should be wound up, the Tribunal may refuse to make an order of winding up, if it is of the opinion that some other remedy is available to the petitioners and that they are acting unreasonably in seeking to have the company wound up instead of pursuing that other remedy.

Where the petition is presented on the ground of default in delivering the statutory report to the Registrar or in holding the statutory meeting the Tribunal may -

a) instead of making a winding up order direct that the statutory report shall be delivered or that a meeting shall be held and

b) order the costs to be paid by persons, who, in the opinion of the Tribunal, are responsible for default.

Consequences Of Winding Up Orders

The various consequences of the winding up order of the Tribunal may be stated as follows

I) Communication to Official Liquidator and Registrar

Where the Tribunal makes an order for the winding up of the company, the Tribunal, shall within a period not exceeding two weeks from the date of passing of the order, cause intimation thereof, to be sent to the official liquidator or the Registrar.

II) Copy of winding up order to be filed with Registrar

On the making of a winding up order, it shall be the duty of the petitioner in the winding up proceedings and of the company to file with the Registrar a certified copy of the order, within thirty days from the date of the making of the order. If default is made in complying with these provisions, the petitioner or the company and every officer of the company who is in default shall be punishable with fine which may extend to one thousand rupees for each day during which the default continues.

In computing the period of thirty days from the date of the making of a winding up order, the time required for obtaining a certified copy of the order shall be excluded.

On the filing of a certified copy of the winding up order, the Registrar shall make a minute thereof in his books relating to the company and shall notify in the Official Gazette that such an order has been made. Such order shall be deemed to be notice of discharge to the officers and employees of the company, except when the business of the company is continued.

(III) Suits stayed on winding up order

When winding up order has been made or the Official Liquidator has been appointed as provisional liquidator, no suit or other legal proceedings shall be commenced or if pending at the time of the winding up order, shall be proceeded with, against the company, except by leave of the Tribunal and subject to such terms as the Tribunal may impose.

(IV) Power of the Tribunal (Sec. 273)

The Tribubal shall have jurisdiction to entertain or dispose off-
a) any suit or proceeding by or against the company.
b) any claim made by or against the company.
c) any application made under Sec. 391 (regarding members) by or in respect of the company.
d) any question of priorities or any other question, whether of law or fact, which may relate to or arise in course of the winding up of the company.

Nothing in this subsection shall apply to any proceeding pending in appeal before the Supreme Court or High Court.

(V) Responsibility of Directors and Officers

The directors and other officers of every company shall ensure that books of account of the company are completed and audited up to date of winding up order made by the

Tribunal and submitted to it at the cost of the company, failing which, such directors and officers shall be liable for punishment for a term not exceeding one year and fine for an amount not exceeding one lakh rupees.

(VI) Effect of winding up

An order for winding up a company shall operate in favour of all the creditors and for all the contributors of the company as if it had been made out on the joint petition of a creditor and of a contributory.

10.4.2.2 Official Liquidators (Sec. 275)

The procedure of winding up by the Tribunal starts with an appointment of liquidator. As soon as the winding up order is passed an official liquidator is appointed, who may be -

a) appointed from a panel of professionals, firms of chartered accountants, advocates, company secretaries, costs and works accountants or firms having combination of these professions, which the Central Government shall constitute for the Tribunal or

b) a body corporate consisting of such professionals as may be approved by the Central Government from time to time or

c) a whole time or a part time officer appointed by the Central Government.

Before appointment of the Official Liquidator the Tribunal may give due regard to the views or opinion of the secured creditors and workmen. The terms and conditions for appointment of official liquidator and remuneration payable to him shall be approved by the Tribunal or the Central Government as the case may be. The amount of remuneration payable shall form part of the winding up order made by the Tribunal and be treated as first charge on the realisation of assets and paid to the official liquidator or to the Central Government as the case may be.

The official liquidator shall conduct proceedings in the winding up of the company and perform such duties as specified by the Tribunal Provisional Liquidator.

The Tribunal may also appoint the official liquidator to be liquidator provisionally, after the presentation of a winding up petition but before the making of a winding up order. Before appointment a provisional liquidator, the Tribunal shall give notice to the company and give reasonable opportunity to make its representation, if any, unless, for special reasons to be recorded in writing the Tribunal thinks fit to dispose off with such notice. The official liquidator shall cease to hold office as provisional liquidator and shall become the liquidator of the company on a winding up order being made.

The liquidators shall conduct the proceedings in winding up the company and perform the duties imposed by the Tribunal. The acts of the liquidator shall be valid even if any defect in discovered afterwards in his appointment or qualifications.

Statement of Affairs (sec. 274)

Where the Tribunal has appointed the Official Liquidator as provisional liquidator, a statement regarding affairs of the company in the prescribed form and verified by an affidavit and containing the following particulars, be submitted to the official liquidator.

a) the assets of the company, stating seperately the cash balance in hand and at the bank, if any and the negotiable securities, if any held by the company.
b) its debts and liabilities.
c) the names and addresses, occupations of its creditors indicating the amount of secured and unsecured debts.
d) the debts due to the company and the names addresses and occupations of the persons from whom they are due and the amount likely to be realised.
e) such other information as may be required.

Statement of Affairs to be filed.

Every company shall file with the Tribunal a statement of its affairs along with the petition for winding up. Where a company opposes a petition for its winding up, it shall file with the Tribunal a statement of its affairs. The statement of affairs referred to shall be accompanies by-

a) the last known addresses of all directors and company secretary of such company
b) the details of location of assets of the company and their value.
c) the details of all debtors and creditors with their complete addresses.
d) the details of workmen and other employees and any amount outstanding to them
e) such other details as the Tribunal may direct.

The statement shall be submitted within 21 days from the relevent date or within such extended time not exceeding three months from the date as the Official Liquidators or Tribunal may decide for special reasons.

The statement shall be submitted and verified by the director, manager, secretary or other chief officer of the company.

Any person, without reasonable excuse, makes default in complying with these requirements, shall be punishable with imprisonment for a term which may extend to two years or with fine which may extend to one thousand rupees for every day during which the default continues or with both.

Duties of Liquidator (Sec. 290)

(1) To conduct all the proceedings of winding up

The main duty of a liquidator is to conduct equitably and impartially and according to the provision of the Act, all the proceeding of the winding up of the company along with such other duties imposed by the Tribunal. Some of the other important duties of the liquidator are as discussed below.

(2) To submit preliminary Report

The official Liquidator, as soon as practicable after the receipt of the statement of affairs of the company, has to submit a preliminary report to the Tribunal, not later than six months from the date of the order or such extended period as may be allowed by the Tribunal.

The report shall contain the following information.

(a) The amount of capital issued, subscribed and paid up and the estimated amount of assets and liabilities. The details of assets according to (i) cash and negotiable securities (ii) debts due from contributories (iii) debts due to the company and securities, if any (iv) movable and immovable properties belonging to the company and (v) unpaid calls.

(b) If the company has failed, the cause of such failure.

(c) Whether in his opinion, further inquiry is desirable as to any matter relating to the promotion, formation or failure of the company, or the conduct of its business.

If the Official Liquidator states in any of his further report that, in his opinion a fraud has been committed, then the Tribunal shall have the further powers as provided by act.

(3) Custody of Company's Property

Where a winding up order has been made or where a provisional liquidator has been appointed, the liquidator shall take into his custody or under his control, all the property, effects and actionable claims to which the company is entitled to. All the property and effects of the company shall be deemed to be in the custody of the Tribunal from the date of the order for the winding up of the company.

(4) Exercise and Control of Powers

The liquidator shall, in the administration of the assets of the company and its distribution among the creditors, give regard to any directions which may be given by resolution of the creditors or contributories at any general meeting or by the committee of inspection. Any directions given by the Creditors or Contributories at any general meeting shall, in the case of conflict, be deemed to overside any directions given by the committee of inspection.

(5) Meetings of Creditors and Contributories.

(a) The liquidator may summon general meetings of creditors or contributories whenever he thinks fit, for the purpose of ascertaining their wishes, (b) He shall summon such meetings at such times as the creditors or contributories may, by resolution, direct or whenever requested in writing to do so by not less than one tenth in value of the creditors or contributories, as the case may be.

(6) Directions from the Tribunal.

The liquidator may apply to the Tribunal in the manner prescribed if any for directions in relation to any particular matter arising in the winding up.

(7) To use his own Discretion

Subject to the provisions of the Act, Liquidator shall use his own discretion in the administration of the assets of the company and their distribution among the creditors.

(8) Keeping Proper Books.

The Liquidator shall keep in the manner prescribed, proper books in which he shall cause entries or minutes to be made of proceedings of meeting and of such other matters as may be prescribed. Any creditor or contributory may, subject to the control of the Tribunal, inspect any such books personally or by his agent.

(9) Audit of Liquidator's Accounts

(I) The Liquidator shall, at such times as prescribed but not less than twice in each year during his tenure of office, present to the Tribunal an account of his receipts and payments as liquidator.

(II) The account shall be in the prescribed form, shall be made in duplicate and shall be verified by a declaration in the prescribed form.

(III) The Tribunal shall cause the account to be audited in such manner as it thinks fit. For the purpose of the audit, the liquidator shall furnish the Tribunal with such vouchers and information as the Tribunal may require and the Tribunal may, at any time, require the production of and inspect any books or accounts kept by the liquidator.

(IV) When the accounts have been audited, one copy of it shall be filed and kept by the Tribunal and the other copy shall be delivered to the Registrar for filing and each copy shall be open to the inspection of any creditors, contributory or person interested.

(V) Where the account relates to a Government Company in liquidation, the Liquidator shall forward a copy of it to the Central or State Government or both if both are members of the Government Company.

(VI) The Liquidators shall cause the accounts when audited or a summary of it to be printed and shall send a printed copy of the account or summary by post to every creditor and contributory. However, the Tribunal may dispense with the compliance of this subsection.

(10) Appointment of commitee of Inspection

(I) According to the direction given by the Tribunal, the Liquidator shall, within two months from the date of such direction, convene a meeting of the creditors of the company, for the purpose of determining who are to be members of the committee.

(II) The Liquidator shall within fourteen days from the date of the Creditor's meeting or such further time as granted by the Tribunal, convene a meeting of the contributories to consider the decision of the Creditors' meeting regarding the membership of the committee and it shall be open to the meeting of contributories to accept the decision of the creditor's meeting with or without modifications or to reject it.

(iii) Except as the case where the meeting of contributaries accept the decision of the creditors meeting is its entirity, it shall be the duty of the liquidator to apply to the Tribunal for directions as to what the composition of the committee shall be and who shall be members thereof.

(11) Information about Pending Liquidation

(I) If the winding up of a company is not concluded within one year after its commencement, the liquidator shall, unless he is exempted by the Central Government, within two months of the expiry of such year and thereafter, until the winding up is concluded, at intervals of not more than one year or at such shorter intervals, if any, as may be prescribed, file a statement in the prescribed form and containing prescribed particulars, duly audited, by a person qualified to act as an auditor of the company with respect to the proceedings in and position of the liquidation. The statement shall be filed with the Tribunal in case of a winding up by the Tribunal or with the Registrar in case of a voluntary winding up, provided that when the statement is filed in the Tribunal, a copy shall simultaneously be filed with the Registrar and shall be kept by him along with the other records of the company.

Where a statement is related to a Government Company in liquidation, the copy is to be forwarded to the Central or State government both, as the case may be.

If a liquidator fails to comply with any of the requirements of this section, he shall be punishable with fine which may extend to five thousand rupees for every day during which the failure continues.

If the liquidator makes wilful default in causing the statement to be audited by a person qualified to act as an auditor of the company, the liquidator shall be punishable with imprisonment for a term which may extend to six months or with fine which may extend to ten thousand rupees or with both.

(12) To make payments into the Public Accounts of India.

Every official Liquidator shall in such manner and at such times as may be prescribed, pay the moneys received by him as liquidator of any company into the public account of India in the Reserve Bank of India.

Every liquidator of a company who is voluntary liquidator shall in such manner and at such times as may be prescribed, pay the money received by him in his capacity as such, into a scheduled Bank to the credit of a special banking account opened by him, under the directions of the Tribunal No Liquidator of a company shall pay any money received by him into a private banking account.

Unpaid dividends and undistributed assets are to be paid by the Liquidator into the Companies Liquidation Account. Enforcement of duty of Liquidator.

(1) If any Liquidator who has made default in filing, delivering or making any return, account or other document, or giving any notice, which he is required by law to file, deliver, make or give, fails to make within fourteen days after the service on him of a notice requiring him to do so, the Tribunal may on an application made to the Tribunal by any contributory or creditor of the company, or by the Registrar, make an order directing the liquidator to make good the default within such time as may be specified in the order.

(2) Any such order may provide that all costs of and incidental to the application shall be borne by the liquidator.

Powers of the Liquidator (Sec. 290)

The powers of the Liquidator under the provisions of the Companies Act, may be discussed under two categories.

a) Those which can be exercised with the sanction of the Tribunal and

b) Those which do not require such sanction.

Let us discuss them.

(A) Powers to be exercised with the sanction of the Tribunal (sec. 273)

(1) The Liquidator in a winding up by the Tribunal shall have power with the sanction of the Tribunal -

a) to institute or defend any suit, prosecution or other legal proceeding, civil or criminal, in the name and on behalf of the company.

b) to carry on business of the company so far as may be necessary for the beneficial winding up of the company.

c) to sell the immovable and movable property and actionable claims of the company by public action or private contract with power to transfer the whole thereof to any person or body corporate, or to sell the same in parcels, and to sell whole of the undertaking of the company as a going concern.

d) to raise on security of the assets of the company any money required.

e) to do all such things as may be necessary for winding up the affairs of the company and distributing its assets.

f) to appoint an advocate, attorney or a pleader entitled to appear before the court to assist him in the performance of his duties.

The act also provides that the Tribunal may by order confer on the Liquidator the power to exercise his discretion in certain matters where prior sanction of the Tribunal is not necessary. However, the Tribunal has power to scrutinise the acts of the Liquidator.

(B) Powers to be exercised without the Sanction of the Tribunal

The following are the discretionary powers of the Liquidator for which saction of the Tribunal is not required.

I) To do all acts and to execute, in the name and on behalf of the company, all deeds, receipts and other documents and for that purpose to use, when necessary, company's seal.

II) to inspect the records and returns of the company on the files of the Registrar without payment of any fee.

III) to prove, rank and claim in the insolvency contributory, for any balance against his estate and to receive dividends in the insolvency in respect of that balance, as a separate debit due from the insolvent and rateably with the other separate creditors.

IV) to draw, accept, make and endorse any bill of exchange, hundi or promissory note in the name and on behalf of the company.

V) to take out, in his official name, letters of administration to any deceased contributory and to do all things necessary for obtaining any money from a contributory or his estate, which cannot be conveniently done in the name of the company.

VI) to appoint an agent to do any business which the liquidator is unable to do himself.

VII) to appoint security guards to protect the property of the company taken into his custody and to make out an inventory of the assets in consultation with secured creditors after giving them notice.

VIII) to appoint as the case may be valuer chartered surveyors or chartered accountant to assess the value of the company's assets, within fifteen days after taking into custody of property, assets and effects or actionable claims subject to such terms and conditions as may be specified by the Tribunal.

IX) to give an advertisment, inviting bids for the sale of the assets of the company, within fifteen days from the date of receiving valuation report from the valuer, chartered surveyors or chartered accountants, as the case may be.

The exercise by the liquidator in a winding up by the Tribunal, of powers conferred by this section shall be subject to the control of the Tribunal and any creditor or contributory may apply to the Tribunal with respect to the exercise of any of the powers conferred by this section.

Control of Liquidator's Powers

Subject to the provisions of the Companies Act, the administration and distribution of the assets of the company has to follow directions given to him.

(I) Control by Contributories and Creditors

The Liquidator has to give regard to any direction given by resolution of the creditors or contributories at any general meeting or by the committee of inspection. Any directions given by the creditors and contributories, in case of conflict, be deemed to override any directions given by the committee of inspection.

(II) Control by Tribunal

The Liquidator may apply to the Tribunal in the manner prescribed, if any, for directions in relation to any particular matter arising in the winding up.

The Liquidator shall not less than twice a year present to the Tribunal an account of his receipts and payments.

The Tribunal shall cause the account to be audited and Liquidator shall furnish vouchers and information as required by the Tribunal.

(III) Control of Central Government

The Central Government shall take congnizance of the conduct of liquidator of companies. If the liquidator does not faithfully perform his duties and duly observe all requirements imposed on him by the Act, or if any complaint is made to the Central Government by any creditor or contributory, the Central Government shall inquire into the matter and take such action thereon as it may think expedient.

The Central Government may at any time require any liquidator to answer any inquiry in relation to any winding up and may apply to the Tribunal to examine him or any other person on oath concerning the winding up.

The Central Government may also direct a local investigation to be made of the books and vouchers of the liquidators.

(IV) Supervision by the Committee of Inspection

The Committee of Inspection can inspect accounts of the liquidator at all reasonable times. The committee may give directions to the liquidator.

Committee of Inspection

The Tribunal may, at the time of making an order for the winding up of company or at any time thereafter, direct that there shall be appointed a committee of inspection to act with the liquidator.

Where a direction is given by the Tribunal, the liquidator shall, within two months from the date of such direction, convene a meeting of the creditors of the company for determining who are the members of the committee.

The liquidator shall within fourteen days from the date of the creditor's meeting, or further time as the Tribunal may grant, cenvene a meeting of contributories to consider the decision of the creditors' meeting about membership of the committee.

It shall be open to the meeting of the contributories to accept the decision of the creditors' meeting with or without modifications or to reject it. If the decision is rejected then the liquidator shall apply to the Tribunal for directions as to what the composition of the committee shall be and who shall be member thereof [sec. 464].

A committee shall consist not more than twelve members, who are members and contributories of the company or attorneys of them and their proportion shall be determined as agreed on by the meetings of creditors and contributories. In case of difference of opinion between meetings, it may be determined by the Tribunal.

I) The committee of Inspection shall have the right to inspect the accounts of the liquidator at all reasonable times.

II) The committee shall meet at appointed times and the liquidator or any member of the committee may also call a meeting of the committee as and when he thinks necessary.

III) The quorum of the meeting of the committee shall be one third of the total number of members or two which ever is higher.

IV) The committee may act by a majority of its members present at a meeting but shall not act unless the quorum is present.

V) A member of the committee may resign by notice in writing signed by him and delivered to the liquidator.

VI) If a member of the committee is adjudged as an insolvent or compounds with the creditors or is absent for five consecutive meetings of the committee without the leave of those members, who represent the creditors or contributories, together with himself, as the case may be, his office shall become vacant.

VII) A member of the committee may be removed at a meeting of creditors if he represents contributories, by an ordinary resolution of which seven day's notice has been given, stating object of the meeting.

VIII) On a vacancy occuring in a committee, the liquidator shall summon a meeting of creditors or contributories, as the case may be, to fill the vacancy, and the meeting may, by resolution, reappoint the same or appoint another creditor or contributory, to fill the vacancy.

If the liquidator is of the opinion that it is unnecessary for the vacancy to be filled, he may apply to the Tribunal who may make an order that the vacancy shall not be filled except in such circumstances as may be specified in the order.

IX) The continuing members of the committee, if not less than two, may act notwithstanding any vacancy in the committee.

10.4.2.3 Powers of the Tribunal (Sec. 289)

General powers of the Tribunal is case of winding up by Tribunal are as follows.

(1) Power to stay winding up

The Tribunal may at any time, after making a winding up order, on the application of either the official liquidator or any creditor or contributory and on proof to the satisfaction of the Tribunal, that all proceedings in relation to the winding up, ought to be stayed, make an order staying the proceedings, either altogether or for a limited time, on such terms and conditions as the Tribunal thinks fit. While exercising this power, the Tribunal will consider the interests of commercial morality and not merely the wishes of the creditors. Once the order of winding up has been made, the Tribunal has no power, to vacate the order but it can stay the winding up procedure under this section. A copy of every order made under this section shall be forwarded by the company to the Registrar, who shall make a minute of the order in his books relating to the company.

(2) Settlement of List of Contributories and Application of Assets

As soon as, after making a winding up order the Tribunal shall settle a list of contributories. The settlement of the list of contributories is based on the names of shareholder, listed in the register of members. The Tribunal may rectify the register of members wherever necessary. However, if it appears to the Tribunal that it will not be necessary to make calls on or adjust the rights of contributories, the Tribunal may dispense with the settlement of a list of contributories.

The Tribunal also shall cause the assets of the company to be collected and applied in discharge of its liabilities.

(3) Delivery of the Property to the Liquidator

The Tribunal may, at any time after making a winding up order, require any contributory on the present list of contributories and any trustee, receiver, banker, agent, officer or other employee of the company to pay, deliver, surrender or transfer, within such time as Tribunal directs, to the liquidator any money property or books and papers in his custody or under his control, to which the company is prima facie entitled to.

(4) Payment of debts due to Contributory

The Tribunal may, at any time after making a winding up order, make an order on any Contributory for the time being on the list of contributories to pay, in the manner directed by the order, any money due to the company from him or from the estate of the person whom he represents, exclusive of any money payable by him or the estate by virtue of any call in pursuance of this Act.

The Tribunal while making such order may

a) In case of an unlimited company, allow to the contributory, by way of set off any money due to him or to the estate which he represents, from the company on any independent dealing or contract with the company, but not any money due to him as a member of the company in respect of any dividend or profit, and

b) in case of a limited company, make to any director or manager whose liability is unlimited or to his estate, the like allowance.

In case of any company, when all the creditors have been paid in full, any money due on any account whatever to a contributory from the company, may be allowed to him by way of set off against any subsequent call.

(5) Power to Make Calls

The Tribunal may, at any time after making winding up order and either before or after, has ascertained the sufficiency of the assets of the company -

a) make calls on all or any of the contributories for the time being on the list of contributories, to the extent of their liability, for payment of any money which the Tribunal considers necessary to satisfy the debts and liabilities of the company and the costs, charges and expenses of winding up and for the adjustment of the rights of the contributories among themselves and

b) make an order for payment of any calls so made

In making a call, the Tribunal may take into consideration the probability that some of the contributories may, partly or wholly, fail to pay the call.

(6) Payment Into Bank of Money due to Company

The Tribunal may order any contributory, purchaser or other person from whom any money is due to the company to pay the money into the public account of India in the Reserve Bank of India instead of to the liquidator.

(7) Power to exclude Creditors not proving in time

The Tribunal may fix a time within which creditors are to prove their debts or claims, otherwise they will be excluded from the benefit of any distribution made before those debts or claims are proved.

(8) Adjustment of Rights of Contributories

The Tribunal shall adjust the rights of the contributories among themselves and distribute any surplus among the persons entitled to it.

(9) Power to Order Costs

In the event of the assets of the company are proved insufficient to satisfy liabilities, the Tribunal may make an order for the payment out of the assets of the costs, charges, and expenses incurred in the winding up, in such order of priority as the Tribunal thinks just.

(10) Power to summon persons suspected of having property of the company

The Tribunal may, at anytime after the appointment of a provisional liquidator or making of a winding up order summon before it -

I) any officer of the company or

II) person known or suspected to have in his possession any property or books or papers of the company or

III) known or suspected to be indebted to the company or

IV) any person whom the Tribunal deems capable of giving information concerning the promotion, formation, trade, dealings, property, books or papers or affairs of the company.

The Tribunal may examine an officer or person so summoned, on oath concerning the matters stated above, either by word of mouth or on written interrogatories. If it is oral, reduce his answers to writing and get signed by him.

The Tribunal has power to compel any such person to produce before it any books or papers which may be in his custody or power relating to the company. If he claims any lien on them, the production shall be without prejuduce to that lien and the Tribunal shall have jurisdiction in the winding up to determine all questions relating to that lien.

If any officer or person so summoned, ofter being paid or tendered a reasonable sum for his expenses, fails to appear before the Tribunal at the time appointed, not having a lawful impediment, the Tribunal may cause him to be apprehended and brought before the Tribunal for examination.

If on his examination, any officer or person so summoned admits that he is indebted to the company, the Tribunal may order him to pay to the provisional liquidator or the liquidator at such time and in such manner as the Tribunal may think just.

If on examination, any such officer or a person admits that he has in his possession any property belonging to the company, the Tribunal may order him to deliver to the provisional liquidator or the liquidator, that property or any part of it, at such time and in such manner and on such terms as to the Tribunal may seem just.

Any person, after making any payment or delivery according to the order of the Tribunal, shall be held as discharged from all liability in respect of such debt or property.

(11) Power to Order Public Examination of Promoters, Directors etc.

When an order has been made for winding up of a company by the Tribunal and an official liquidator has made a report to the Tribunal that in his opinion a fraud has been committed by any person in the promotion or formation of the company or by an officer of the company in relation to the company since its formation, the Tribunal may direct that, that person or officer shall attend before the Tribunal on a day appointed by it and be publicly examined as to the promotion or formation or the conduct of the business of the company or as to his conduct and dealings as an officer of the company.

The Official Liquidator shall take part in the examination and if necessary and authorised by the Tribunal, employ legal assistance as may be sanctioned by the Tribunal.

Any creditor or contributory may also take part in the examination either personally or by any Chartered Accountant, or Company Secretaries or Cost Accountants or Legal Practitioners entitled to appear before the Tribunal.

The Tribunal may put such questions to the person examined as it thinks fit.

The person examined shall be examined on oath and shall answer all such questions the Tribunal may put or allow to be put to him. A person, before his examination, shall be furnished at his own cost a copy of the official Liquidator's report.

Notes of the examination shall be taken down in writing and shall be read over to or by and signed by the person examined and later on may be used as evidence against him and shall be open to the inspection of any creditor or contributory at all reasonable times.

(12) Power to arrest absconding contributory

At any time either before or after making a winding up order, the Tribunal may, on the proof of probable cause for believing that a contributory is about to quit India or otherwise to abscond or is about to remove or conceal any of his property, for the purpose of evading payment of calls or of avoiding examination regarding the affairs of the company, cause -

I) the contributory to be arrested and safely kept until such time as the Tribunal may order

II) his books and papers and movable property to be seiged and safely kept until such time as the Tribunal may order.

(13) Saving of Existing Powers of Tribunal

Any powers conferred on the Tribunal by this Act shall be in addition to, any existing powers of instituting proceedings against any contributory or debtor of the company or the estate of any contributary or debtor, for the recovery of any call or other sums.

10.4.2.4 Dissolution of the Company

The dissolution of a company is similar to the death of a living person. On its dissolution the company ceases to exist.

The Tribunal shall order for dissolution of a company on the following grounds.

I) When the affairs of the company are completely wound up. or

II) When the Tribunal is of the opinion that the liquidator cannot proceed with the winding up of a company for want of funds and assets, or

III) for any other reason what so ever and

IV) It is just and reasonable in the circumstances of the case that an order of dissolution of the company should be made.

The Tribunal shall make an order that the company is dissolved from the date of the order and the company shall be dissolved accordingly.

A copy of the order shall, within thirty days from the date of it, be forwarded by the liquidator to the Registrar, who shall make in his books a minute of the dissolution of the company.

If the liquidator makes default in forwarding a copy, he shall be punishable with fine which may extend to five hundred rupees for every day during which the default continues.

Difference between Winding up and Dissolution

Winding-up	Dissolution
1) Winding up precedes dissolution It is the first step	1) Dissolution is the final step in dropping the curtain over a company.
2) Winding up involves the collection and realisation of the company's assets among the contributories.	2) Dissolution announces that all these formalities are over at the date of dissolution or end of the company.
3) The liquidator can represent the company in the process of winding up.	3) On the dissolution he can no longer represent the company as it ceases to exist.
4) Creditors can prove their debts in the winding up.	4) Creditors can not prove their debts on the dissolution of the company.

10.4.2.5 Contributory

The liability of a shareholder is up to the face value of the shares and he is liable to pay full value of the shares held by him. This liability continues even if the company goes into liquidation. Then the shareholder becomes a contributory and certain changes take place in his status, rights and liabilities.

Sec. 428 defines the term contributory which means, every person liable to contribute to the assets of a company in the event of winding up and includes the holder of any shares which are fully paid up.

A holder of fully paid up shares is a contributory but as he is not liable to make any further contribution to the assets of the company, he is normally put on the list of contributories unless he so wishes or unless there is a prospect of the return of surplus assets. A minor cannot be a contributory so as to be liable to contribute to the assets of the company. if a contributory dies either before or after he has been placed on the list of contributories, his legal representatives shall be liable to contribute to the assets of the company in discharge of his liability and shall be contributories accordingly. He is only liable to contribute to the extent of the assets, if any, which have come into his hands from the deceased member. He is not personally liable as he is liable in his representative capacity.

The official assignee or receiver of a contributory who is adjudged insolvent either before or after he has been placed on the list of contributories, represent insolvent for all the purposes of the winding up and is to be considered contributory.

If a body corporate which is a contributory is ordered to be wound up, either before or after it has been placed on the list of contributories, the liquidator of the body corporate shall represent it for all purposes of winding up of the company and shall be contributory accordingly.

Liability as Contributory

In the event of a company being wound up, every present and past member shall be liable to contribute to the assets of the company to an amount sufficient for payment of its debts and liabilities and the costs, charges and expenses of the winding up and for the adjustments of the rights of the contributories among themselves.

After making the winding up order, the Tribunal shall settle the list of contributories, into list A and list B.

The list of present members is list A that includes names of persons who are members at the commencement of the winding up. The list of past members or list B includes the names of person who ceased to be members within a period of twelve months of the commencement of winding up.

The liability of contributories or present member is primary liability and it is limited to the amount remaining unpaid on the shares held by him or to the gurantee given by him in case of a company limited by gurantee. In case of a company limited by gurantee and having a share capital, a member's liability may be to the extent that he has guranteed plus the amount remaining unpaid on the shares held by him.

The liability of the past members is a secondary liability, having no liability generally. But they are liable to contribute to the assets if money payble by the present members are not paid by them and the debts have remained unsatisfied. A past member is not liable to contribute under following conditions.

I) A past member, shall not be liable to contribute if he has ceased to be a member for one year or more before the commencement of the winding up.

II) A past member shall not be liable to contribute in respect of any debt or liability of the company contracted after he ceased to be a member.

III) A past member shall not be liable unless it appears to the Tribunal that the present member are unable to satisfy the contributions required to be made by them.

IV) In case of a company limited by shares, no contribution shall be required from any past or present member exceeding the amount, if any, unpaid on the shares in respect of which he is liable as such member.

V) In case of a company limited by gurantee, no contribution be required from any past or present member exceeding the amount undertaken to be contributed by him to the assets of the company in the event of its being wound up.

Contributory's Right of set off

The Tribunal, after making an order of winding up, makes an order to any contributary to pay in the manner directed in the order any money due from him to the company and the company also owes him something, the right of set off is allowed in the following cases.

I) In the case of unlimited company, the Tribunal may allow to the contributory by way of set off any money due to him from the company on any independent dealing or contract with the company but not in respect of any money due to him as dividend or profit.

II) In the case of a limited company, the Tribunal may give the above allowance to any director or manager whose liability is unlimited.

III) In the case of any company whether limited or unlimited, when all the creditors have been paid in full, then any money due to a contributory from the company may be allowed to set off against any subsequent call.

10.4.3 Voluntary Winding Up

Voluntary winding up of a company means winding up by members or creditors of a company without interference of the Tribunal. A company may be wound up voluntarily -

I) By Passing an ordinary Resolution - When the period, if any, fixed for the duration of the company by the articles is expired or the event, if any, has occurred, on the occurrence of which the articles provide that the company is to be dissolved and the company in general meeting passes a resolution requiring that the company to be wound up voluntarily.

II) By Passing a Special Resolution - If the company passes a special resolution that the company be wound up voluntarily.

Publication of Resolution (sec. 307)

When a company has passed a resolution for voluntary winding up, it shall, within fourteen days of the passing of the resolution, give notice of resolution by advertisement in the Official Gazette and also in some newspapers circulating in the district, where the registered office of the company is situated. If default is made in complying with this provision, the company and every officer of the company who is in default, shall be punishable with fine which may extend to five hundred rupees for every day during which the default continues. In this case officer includes even the liquidator of the company.

Commencement of voluntary winding up

A voluntary winding up shall be deemed to commence at the time when the resolution for voluntary winding up is passed.

10.4.3.1 Consequences of Voluntary Winding up.

The consequences of voluntary winding up may be stated as follows.

I) Effect on Status of a company

In the case of voluntary winding up the company ceases to carry on the business from the commencement of the winding up, except so far as may be required for the beneficial winding up of such business. However, the corporate status and the corporate powers of the company will continue until it is dissolved.

II) Board's Power to cease on appointment of a Liquidator

On the appointment of a liquidator, all the power of the Board of directors and of the managing or wholetime directors, and manager, shall cease except for the purpose of giving notice of such appointment to the Registrar. However, the company in general meeting or the liquidator or the committee of Inspection or if there is no such committee, the creditors (in a creditor's winding up) sanction their continuance.

III) Avoidance of Transfers etc.

In the case of a voluntary winding up, any transfer of shares in the company, not being a transfer made to or with the sanction of the liquidator and any alteration in the status of the members of the company made after the commencement of the winding up, shall be void.

10.4.3.2 Types of Voluntary Winding Up

A voluntary winding up may be -
a) A member's voluntary winding up
b) A creditor's voluntary winding up.
Let us discuss them briefly.

(A) A member's voluntary winding up - A member's voluntary winding up takes place when the company is solvent. The members take initiative and manage it. The members appoint a liquidator. There is neither the meeting of creditors nor the appointment of committee of inspection. A declaration of solvancy has to be filed, in order to take benefit of this type of winding up procedure.

Declaration of Solvency (sec. 305)

Where it is proposed to wind up a company voluntarily, its directors or the majority of the directors, may, at the meeting of the Board, make a declaration, verified by an affidavit, to the effect that they have made a full inquiry into the affairs of the company and that they have formed the opinion that the company has no debts or that it will be able to pay its debts in full within such period not exceeding three years from the commencement of the winding up as may be specified in the declaration. Such declaration shall be made within five weeks immediately preceding the date of the passing of the resolution for winding up of the company and shall be delivered to the Registrar for registration before that date. It shall be accompanied by a copy of the report of the auditors of the company, on the profit and loss account and a balance sheet of the company prepared up to the date of the declaration and also embody a statement of the company's assets and liabilities as at that time.

Where such a declaration is duly made and delivered and the winding up follows, then it is called members voluntary winding up. But if the same is not duly made then it shall be called as creditor's winding up.

Provisions applicable to Member's winding up are given in Sec. 490-498 as follows.

(1) Appointment of Liquidator (sec. 310)

The company in general meeting shall

a) appoint one or more liquidators for the purpose of winding up the affairs and distributing assets of the company and

b) fix the remuneration to be paid to the liquidator or liquidators.

Any remuneration so fixed shall not be increased in any circumstances. The liquidator shall not take charge of his office before his remuneration is fixed.

The liquidator may be appointed at the meeting at which the resolution for voluntary winding up is passed.

(2) Board's Powers to cease

On the appointment of a liquidator, all the powers of the Board of directors and of the managing and wholetime directors and manager shall cease except for the purpose of giving notice of such appointment to the Registrar. But the company in general meeting or the liquidator may sanction continuance of the powers.

(3) Power to fill vacancy in office of Liquidator

If a vacancy occurrs by death, resignation or otherwise in the office of any liquidator appointed by the company, the company in general meeting may, subject to any arrangement with its creditors, fill the vacancy. The general meeting for the purpose may be called by a contributory or by a liquidator.

(4) Notice of appointment of Liquidator

The company shall give notice to the Registrar of the appointment of a liquidator or liquidators made by it, of every vacancy occurring in the office of the liquidator and of the name of the liquidator or liquidators appointed to fill every such vacancy. The notice shall be given by the company within ten days of the event to which it relates.

(5) Duty of Liquidator to call meeting of creditors

Where the liquidator at any time is of the opinion that the company will not be able to pay its debts in full within the period stated in the declaration or that period has expired without the debts having been paid in full, he shall summon a meeting of the creditors and lay before the meeting a statement of assets and liabilities of the company.

Where a liquidator has called a creditor's meeting for winding up then can proceed as if it was creditor's voluntary winding up.

(6) General Meeting at the end of the year

In the event of the winding up continuing for more than one year, the liquidator shall -

a) call a general meeting of the company at the end of the first year from the commencement of the winding up and at the end of each succeeding year or within three months from the end of the year or such longer period as the Central Government may allow.

The liquidator should lay before the meeting the account of his acts and dealings and of the conduct of the winding up during the preceding year, and the position of the liquidation.

(7) Final Meeting and Dissolution.

(1) As soon as the affairs of the company are fully wound up, the liquidator shall -

a) make up an account of the winding up, showing how the winding up has been conducted and the property of the company has been disposed off, and

b) call a general meeting of the company for the purpose of laying the account before it and giving explanation of it.

(2) The meeting shall be called by an advertisment, as it is the final meeting I) specifying time, place and object of the meeting II) the advertisement shall be made, not less than one month before the meeting, in the official gazette and also in some of the local newspapers, where the registered office of the company is situated.

(3) Within one week after the meeting, the liquidator shall send to the Registrar and the official Liquidator, a copy each, of the account and shall make a return, to each of them, of the holding of the meeting and of the date of it. If the copy is not so sent or the return is not so made, the liquidator shall, be punishable with fine which may extend to five hundred reupees for every day during which the default continues.

The Registrar, on receiving the account and either of the returns shall register the same.

The Official Liquidator on receiving the account and the return, shall as soon as, make a scrutiny of the books and papers of the company. The liquidator of the company, its past and present officers, shall afford an opportunity to the official liquidator for this purpose. The official liquidator shall send a report of the scrutiny to the Tribunal. If the report shows that the affairs of the company have been conducted bonafide and not in a manner prejudicial to the interests of its members or public interest, then from the date of the submission of the report to the Tribunal, the company shall be deemed to be dissolved.

If the report of the official liquidator shows that the affairs of the company have been conducted in a manner prejudicial, the Tribunal shall by order direct the official liquidator to make a further investigation of the affairs of the company. For this purpose, the Tribunal shall invest him with all such powers as it may deem fit. On receipt of the report of the official liauidator on such further investigation, the Tribunal may either make an order that the company stands dissolved or make such other order as the circumstances of the case brought out in the report permit.

B. CREDITOR'S VOLUNTARY WINDING UP

Where company proposes to wind up voluntarily and the directors are not in position to make the statutory declaration of solvency, then the winding up is a a creditor's voluntary winding up. The provisions for creditor's voluntary winding up are similar to those of the member's voluntary winding up, except that in the former, the creditors appoint the liquidator for remuneration and generally conduct winding up. The provision of the creditor's voluntary winding up may be stated as follows.

1) Meeting of Creditors (sec. 306)

Where the declaration of solvency is not made by the directors, the company shall call a meeting of the creditors of the company, to be called for the day or the day next following the day, on which there is to be held the general meeting of the company at which the resolution for voluntary winding up is to be proposed and shall cause notice of the meeting of creditors to be sent by the post to the creditors simultaneously with the sending of notices of the meeting of the company. The notice of calling the meeting of the creditors shall be advertised once at least in the official gazette and once at least in two newspapers circulating in the district, where the registered office of the company is situated. The Board of directors shall lay before the meeting of creditors, a full statement of the position of the company's affairs together with the list of the creditors of the company and the estimated amount of their claims. One of the director shall precide the meeting.

2) Notice to the Registrar

Notice of any resolution passed at a creditor's meeting, shall be given by the company to the Registrar within ten days of the passing of it.

3) Appointment of Liquidator (Sec. 310)

The creditors and the company at their respective meetings may nominate a person to be a liquidator for the purpose of winding up the affairs and distributing the assets of company. If the creditors and the company nominate different persons, the person nominated by the creditors shall be liquidator. Any director, member or creditor of the the company may, within seven days after the date on which the nomination was made by the creditors, apply to the Tribunal for an order directing that the person nominated as liquidator by the company shall be liquidator instead of, or jointly with the person nominated by the creditors or appointing the Official Liquidater or some other person to be liquidator instead of the person as appointed by the creditors.

If no person is appointed by the creditors, the person, if any, nominated by the company shall be liquidator. If no person is nominated by the company, the person, if any, nominated by the creditors shall be liquidator.

4) Appointment of Committee of Inspection (sec. 315)

The creditors at their meeting may appoint, if they think fit, a committee of inspection consisting not more than five persons.

If such a committee is appointed, a company also may at the meeting appoint such number of persons, not exceeding five, as they think fit, to act as members of the committee. The creditors may, if they think fit, resolve that all or any one of the person so appointed by the company ought not to be member of the committee of inspection. Hence, the persons mentioned in the resolution shall not, unless the Tribunal otherwise directs, be qualified to act as members of the committee. On any application to the tribunal for direction, the Tribunal may appoint other persons to act as member of the committee of inspection in the place of the person mentioned in the creditor's resolution.

5) Liquidator's Remuneration

The committee of Inspection or the creditors may fix the remuneration to be paid to the liquidators. Otherwise, the Tribunal may fix it. Any remuneration fixed, shall not be increased under any circumstances.

6) Power of Board to cease

On the appointment of a liquidator, all the powers of the Board of directors shall cease, except, when the committee of inspection or the creditors in general meeting may sanction to continue the exercise of the powers of the Board.

7) Vacancy in the Office of the Liquidator

If a vacancy occurs by death, resignation or otherwise in the office of the liquidator (other than a liquidator appointed by the Tribunal or by its directions), the creditors in general meeting may fill up the vacancy.

8) Meeting at the end of each year

Where the winding up continues for more than one year, the liquidator shall call a general meeting of the company and a meeting of the creditors at the end of the first year from the commencement of the winding up and at the end of each succeeding year or within three months from the end of the year, or such longer period as the Central Government may allow. The liquidator shall lay before the meeting an account of his acts and dealings and of the conduct of the winding up during the preceeding year. If the liquidator fails to comply with these provisions, he shall be punishable in respect of each failure with fine which may extend to one thousand rupees.

9) Final Meeting and Dissolution

As soon as the affairs of the company are fully wound up, the liquidator shall -

a) make up an account of the winding up, showing how the winding up has been conducted and the property of the company has been disposed off, and

b) call a general meeting of the company and a meeting of the creditors for the purpose of laying the account before the meeting and giving any explanation thereof.

Each such meeting shall be called by advertisement, specifying the time, place and object of it and the advertisment shall be published not less than one month before the meeting, in Official Gazette and also in some newspapers circulating in the district where the registered office of the company is situated.

Within one week after the meeting, the liquidator shall send to the Registrar a copy of the account and a return which will be registered. There after the procedure is the same as followed in the case of member's voluntary winding up.

C. Distinction between Member's Voluntary winding up and Creditor's Voluntary winding up.

Member's Voluntary winding up	Creditors Voluntary winding up
1) Declaration of solvency is must.	1) Declaration of solvency is not necessary.
2) Creditors meeting is not necessary.	2) It is statutory duty of the company to call a meeting of creditors.
3) The liquidator is appointed by the members.	3) Both the creditors and members appoint a liquidator.
4) No committee of inspection as the members control the winding up.	4) There is a committee of inspection to control the winding up.
5) The members control the winding up and creditors do not play an active role as the company is solvent.	5) The creditors control the winding up as the company is considered to be insolvent.
6) The liquidator can exercise some of the powers with the sanction of a special resolution of the company.	6) The liquidator can exercise some powers with the sanction of the Tribunal or the committee of inspection or of meeting of creditors.

10.4.3.3 Consequence of Winding up

Winding up affects a number of parties. The consequence (Effects) of winding up may be discussed as follows.

(1) Consequences to shareholders - A shareholder is liable to pay the full value or the amount upto the face value of the total number of shares held by him. This liability continues even though the company goes into liquidation. He is then described as a contributory.

Contributory may be present or past. The liability of present contributory is limited to the amount remaining unpaid on his shares. A past contributory may be called upon to pay only when present contributory is not able to pay.

(2) Consequences to Creditors - The main object of winding up is to realise the assets and discharge the liabilities and in case if there is any surplus, it is to be paid to the shareholders. When a compnay is unable to pay its debts, it goes into compulsory winding up. But a company may be wound up on other grounds also, even though it is solvent. Where a solvent company is wound up, all claims of its creditors, when proved, are fully met. Where an insolvent company is wound up the insolvency rules are applicable and only such claims that are provable against an insolvent person.

Rights of secured creditors - The creditors may be secured or unsecured. A secured creditor has three alternatives open to him.

    i) He may rely on securities and ignore liquidation or
    ii) He may value or realise the security and pay for the deficit in the winding up.
    iii) He may surrender his security and pay for the whole amount of the debt.

    Where secured creditor proceeds to realise the security, he is liable to pay all the expenses incurred by liquidator for the preservation of the security before its realisation.

Right of unsecured creditors

    All debts due to unsecured creditors of an insolvent company, preferential payment are made first. After that all the debts are to be treated equally and paid pari passu.

    When the list of claims is settled, the liquidator has to start making payments. The total assets available to the liquidator are applied in the following order.

    i) secured creditors
    ii) cost of the liquidation
    iii) Preferential payments
    iv) Debenture holders secured by floating charge.
    v) unsecured creditors
    vi) Balance returned to the contributories.

Preferential Payment

    Some unsecured debts are paid with priority to all other debts. Such payments are called as preferential payments. These include the following items.

    I) All revenues, taxes, cesses and rates due from the company to the central, state and local governments. The amount should have become due and payable within twelve months before the winding up.

    II) All wages and salary of an employee in respect of services rendered to the company and due for a period not exceeding four months within the twelve months before liquidation.

    III) All accrued holiday remuneration becoming payable to any employee, or in case of his death to any other person in his right, on the termination of his employment before or by the effect of winding up order or resolution.

IV) All amounts due in respect of contributions payable during the twelve months before winding up order for the Employees' State Insurance Act.

V) All amounts due in respect of compensation or liability under the Workmen's Compensation Act 1923, in respect of death or disablement of any employee of the company.

VI) All sums due to any employee from a provident fund, a pension fund, a gratuity fund or any other fund for the welfare of the employees maintained by the company.

VII) The expenses of any investigation are payable by the company.

Overriding Preference Payment

The provision under this section aims at protecting the interest of workmen in case of winding up. A company shall on its winding up pay in priority to all other debts (a) workmen's dues and debts to secured creditors.

These debts shall be paid in full. If the assets are insufficient to meet them, they shall abate in equal proportions

(3) Consequences to Servants and Officers

A winding up order is deemed to be a notice of discharge to the employees and officers of the company, except when the business of the company is continued. Such a discharge relieves them from all obligations under their contract of service. A voluntary winding up also operates as a notice of discharge to the company's servants. Where there is a contract of service for a particular period, an order of winding up will amount to wrongful discharge and damages will be allowed as for breach of contract of service.

(4) Consequences of Proceedings against the company

When a winding up order is made or an official Liquidater is appointed as a provisional liquidator, no suit or legal proceedings against the company can be commenced except by the leave of the Tribunal. If a suit is pending against the company at the date of winding up order, it cannot be proceeded with against the company except by leave of the Tribunal and subject to such terms as the Tribunal may impose. In case of a voluntary winding up the Tribunal may restrain proceedings against the company if it thinks fit.

(5) Consequences to Costs

Where the assets of the company are insufficient to satisfy liabilities, the Tribunal may make an order for the payment out of the assets, of costs, charges and expenses incured in the winding up. The payment must be made in such an order of priority as the Tribunal thinks just.

Similarly, all costs, charges, and expenses properly incurred in the voluntary winding up, including the remuneration of liquidator, shall, subject to the rights of secured creditors, if any, be payable out of assets of the company in priority to all other claims.

(6) Consequences to Documents

Where a company is being wound up, whether by the Tribunal or voluntary, every invoice, order for goods, or business letter issued by or on behalf of the company or a liquidator of the company or a receiver or manager of the property of the company, being a document in which the name of the company appears, shall contain a statement that the company is being wound up.

Where a company is being wound up, all books and papers of the company and of the liquidators shall, as between contributories of the company, be prima facie evidence of the truth of all matters purporting to be there is recorded.

When the affairs of the company have been completely wound up and it is about to be dissolved, its books and papers and those of the liquidator may be disposed off in such manner as the Tribunal directs.

In the case of a member's voluntary winding up, in such manner as the company by special resolution directs and in case of a creditor's winding up, in such manner as the committee of inspection or, if there is no such committee, as the creditors of the company may direct.

QUESTIONS

A) Answer in 20 words

1) What is the meaning of 'Compromise'?
2) What is the meaning of 'Arrangement'?
3) What do you mean by 'Reconstruction'?
4) What is 'amalgamation'?
5) What is the meaning of winding up ?
6) What do you mean by compulsory winding up?
7) Explain the term 'Voluntary winding up'.
8) What do you mean by 'Statement of Affairs'?
9) What is the meaning of the term 'Contributories'?
10) What is 'Declaration of solvency?
11) Explain the term 'Member's voluntary winding up'.
12) Explain the term 'Creditor's voluntary winding up'.

B) Answer in 50 words

1) Explain the term 'Compromise' and 'Arrangement'.
2) Explain the term 'Reconstrcution.'
3) What is the meaning of 'Amalgamation.' State its objects.
4) Distingush between 'Reconstruction and Amalgamation.'
5) Explain the term 'contributory.'

6) Explain the term 'Declaration of ?'
7) Write a note on committee of Inspection.
8) What is statement of Affairs ?
9) What do you mean by surplus of Assets?
10) Distinguish between winding up and Direction.
11) What is preferential payment ?
12) Explain the term Direction of the company.
13) What is Sick Company?

C) Answer in 150 words.

1) What are the statutory provisions regarding 'compromise' and 'Arrangement?'
2) Explain the procedure for compromise and Arrangement.
3) Define the term 'Reconstruction.' State its purpose.
4) Define the term 'Amalgamtion'. State its purpose.
5) What are the provision of the Act regarding compulsory winding up of public limited companies?
6) How and in what order are the claims of different classes of creditors and shareholders settled in case of compulsory liquidation ?
7) What are the effects of winding up ?
8) What are the powers of liquidator ?
9) Explain the order of payment of liabilities 415530.
10) Explain the procedure of member's voluntary winding up.
11) Explain the procedure of creditor's voluntary winding up.
12) Distinguish between member's voluntary winding up and creditor's voluntary winding up.
13) What is the difference between winding up and dissolution?
14) Explain the Reviral & Rehabilitation of Sick Company?

D) Answer in 300 words

1) Summorise the steps involved in carrying out an arrangement with member and / or creditors
2) Define the term Reconstruction What are its purposes?
3) Define the term 'Amalgamation'. What are its purposes?
4) Explain the procedure involved in compromise and arrangement.
5) Define the term 'Compromise' and 'Arrangement'. State the statutory provisions regarding compromise and arrangements.
6) What is winding up ? What are the provisions of the Act regarding compulsory winding up?
7) What is the meaning of winding up ? Explain the types of winding up.
8) What do you mean by 'Voluntary winding up'? Explain the different types of voluntary winding up.

9) Describe carefully member's voluntary winding up of a company and explain how it differs from creditor's voluntary winding up.

10) Who appoints an official liquidator ? Explain the powers and duties of an official liquidator.

11) Explain the term 'contributory'. How and in what order are the claims of different classes of creditors and shareholders settled in case of compulsory liquidation ?

12) What is 'Members voluntary winding up'? Explain the procedure for member's voluntary winding up.

13) What is 'Creditor's voluntary winding up'? Explain the procedure for creditor's voluntary winding up.

14) Explain the term 'winding up'. What are the effects of winding up.

15) What is winding up ? Explain the general power of the Tribunal in case of winding up.

REFERENCES

1) Ravi Puliani, 2013 with comments, Bharat's - Companies Act, 19th Edition, 2013. Advocate Mahesh Puliani, Bharat Law House Pvt.Ltd., New Delhi.

2) Karm Gupta, 2013- Introduction to Company Law, Publication : LexisNexis, Gurgaon, Haryana, India.

3) With notes to Legislative Clauses. Corporate Professionals where excellence is Law, CCH - a Wolters Kluwer business. Wolters Kluwer business. The Companies Act, 2013, 2014 Edition, Wolters Kluwer (India) Pvt. Ltd., DLF Cyber City, Gurgaon, Haryana (India).

4) Prachi Manekar, 2013- Insights into the New Company Law, LexixNexis, Gurgaon, Haryana, India.

5) V. S. Datey, 13th September, 2013- Taxman's, Company Law Ready Reckoner Printed at - Tan Prints (India) Pvt. Ltd. Jhajjar, Haryana, India.

6) Corporate Professionals - where excellence is Law., CCH - a Wolterskluwer business, Corporate Professionals India Pvt., New Delhi, India., 2013, Analysis of Companies Act, Published by - Wolters Kluwer (India) Pvt. Ltd.